Couples Threesor 1

Copyright © 2020 by Connie Cuckquean
This is a work of fiction. All characters appearing in this work are fictitious. Any resemblance to real persons, living or dead, is purely coincidental. All characters 18+.
Get **7 FREE EROTICA STORIES** and **WEEKLY DEALS** you join my Mailing List[1] - http://eepurl.com/b0ma0X
Adult Reading Material

*****

About This Book

Dirty bisexual wives are the order of the day here, granting their alpha husbands permission to take on feisty beauties that can give their man the pleasures that they sometimes can't. Read how mistresses get down and dirty as the wives in these bundles watch on, joining in and helping their husband's to the ultimate pleasure of two women at once.

Contains books 1 to 24 of the *'Couple's Threesomes'* series, featuring : 'Something For The Weekend,' 'Elevator Threesome With The Girl Nextdoor,' 'Joining My Husband With The Hot Female Chauffeur,' 'Helping My Husband With The Hotel Maid,' 'A Salsa Dancer Claimed My Husband While I Watched,' 'The Nurse Took Care Of My Husband,' 'Arousal Airways,' 'Treating My Husband To My Ex-Girlfriend,' 'A French Maid For Me And My Husband,' 'Surprising My Husband In The Tub,' Watching My Husband Fuck

1. http://eepurl.com/b0ma0X

'The Waitress,' 'My Husband's Salon Treatment,' 'My Husband Fucked A Hot Hitchhiker,' 'Hotel Sex,' 'The Marriage Counsellor Fucked My Husband,' 'Searching For Anal,' 'My Husband Likes Them Bigger,' 'The New Gardener Is Our Slut,' 'The Magical Bouquet,' 'The BJ Fairy,' 'Air B'n'J,' 'Club Sex,' 'All In,' and 'Making Rent.'

Read An Excerpt

"They look lovely," Rose said.

I offered them to her and the first thing she did was take a deep sniff. My eyes bulged with excitement as she did so and I looked back to my husband and gave him a wink.

He was still confused but gradually it started to dawn on him. For the past few years we'd been working with several flowering plants that had known aphrodisiacal properties. Our goal was to create a 'Viagra bouquet,' the likes of which you could keep in your home and smell whenever you needed a pep before sex. Rose was our trial subject.

"It smells"—she shifted her eyes to Monty and her pupils fattened—"*incredible.*"

"Ooh, can I smell?" I asked.

Monty watched in horror as I took the bouquet from her and took an equally large breath in through my nose.

I felt my pulse rise instantly and my cheeks turned hot. My pussy started to swell and my clit stiffened. I looked straight to Monty too, drinking in his dreamy physique. He looked so fuckable, stood there in his shorts and t-shirt.

"Now, now, girls," he said, backing off as the pair of us walked towards him like zombies.

"You're so sexy, honey," I uttered.

"I want to fuck you so bad, Monty," Rose said.

"Let's do it, Rose."

"Wait!" Monty cried holding up a hand.

Rose and I stopped in our tracks.

"Hand me that bouquet, would you?"

I smirked and gave him the flowers. Monty inhaled and now the three of us were under its powerful spell.

He set the flowers down in the corner and stood up straight to face us, no longer coy. He had an incredible swelling in his pants that seemed to arrive from nowhere.

"No chance of disappointing you now," he joked.

"There was no chance of that anyway," Rose said, and I watched in amazement as she made her advances on him.

I let her make the first move and so did Monty. He watched her with this commanding gaze in his eye, as though he was daring her to do things to him that she shouldn't.

"Open your shorts," Rose said.

Monty looked over her at me and I gave him a nod. I leaned back against the building and looked along the wall through the gap between the dressing of our stall and the front of the bank. The market was still fairly busy and around us people chattered and shouted between stalls, all of them oblivious to what was occurring at the back of the quaint little market-garden stall.

Monty opened his khaki shorts slowly, teasing Rose who by the looks of it didn't want to be teased. Rather than wait for him she dropped to her knees and started to undress him herself.

Her hands moved quickly and my husband and I watched in amazement. She tore open his pants frantically like she was unwrapping a present, then suddenly she tugged downwards and took shorts and underwear in one.

Monty's hard cock popped up out of his pants, looking stiffer than I'd ever seen it. It looked swollen beyond measure. The veins that normally ran under the skin of his shaft were now pronounced on the outside, to such an extent that his entire cock looked bigger.

Something For The Weekend : Couples Threesomes 1

"I just wish I could please you," I pleaded, looking across at my husband as he lay breathless beside me.

"You do," he urged.

"Well, I never see it," I scoffed, looking at his spent cock that had failed to come for the umpteenth time in recent months.

"It doesn't mean I don't love you."

I hung my head. "I know," I said softly.

He reached over and put an arm around me. "I must be going through some stuff," he said, kissing my cheek.

"Or maybe I am."

"What do you mean?"

I huffed. "I don't think you find me attractive anymore."

"Are you kidding?" he said, sitting up on his knees animatedly.

He looked me up and down, running his eyes up my legs and over my pussy and hips. He moved his hands forward to cup my breasts and then finally stared deep into my eyes.

"How could I not like that?"

I smiled warmly and he planted a tender kiss on my mouth.

"I'm not the woman I was," I shrugged.

"You think I'm the man I was?" he laughed. "Do you remember this when you first saw me?"

He took a grip of flesh around his stomach and squeezed it between his finger and thumb. I laughed and shook my head.

To me, Jake hadn't changed. He was still that feisty, athletic twenty-three year old that I'd met all those years ago. His sex-drive seemed higher than ever and many nights I refused his advances, but that didn't mean I didn't want to please him.

"I'll think of something," I said.

"Huh?

"I'll think of something," I said, thinking it a challenge now instead. "I'll think of a way of getting that cum out of you."

His eyes flashed with excitement and I leaned in to kiss him again. When my hands ventured down his body and touched his cock I noticed it was hard all over again.

Not wanting to waste the moment I kissed my way down his body until I was face-to-face with his thickness.

I looked down the long barrel and then pressed it into my mouth, winding my lips around him and using a hand on the inches that escaped me.

He let out a groan of arousal and in the excitement I plunged him deeper, sending as much of him inside me as I could until he was pressing at the back of my throat.

His breaths quickened and he held the back of my head against him, but then I felt the tickle on my tonsils and I convulsed in a gag, spitting out his cock with a splutter.

I looked up embarrassed and he laughed. His chuckle was infectious and I laughed too, but I was still a reminder of how limited my skills were. The moment felt ruined and I collapsed into the sheets.

He lay beside me and wrapped his big arms around me as I took another deep breath.

"Maybe I should let you see other people," I huffed.

"Where's this come from?"

"You deserve better."

"But I love *you*, honey."

"That doesn't mean you can't fuck other people."

There was a brief silence before he spoke again.

"What are you suggesting?"

I rolled over to look him in the eyes. "I'm suggesting that maybe you should seek that kind of satisfaction elsewhere."

His mouth twisted and he looked almost hurt.

"Look, I love you, Jake," I said, holding his face. "You know that. But it feels like I can't give you everything I want to. Maybe it's time to ... *outsource.*"

He stared forwards blankly.

"Look," I said, thinking aloud. "There are plenty of girls at the salon who—"

"I'm not gonna fuck *Jacqui.*"

"Not Jacqui," I said. "We've got a new starter. Teri. She's fiery. I like her."

"What so I just go and meet her and fuck her?" Jake asked, highlighting the flaw in the plan.

"No," I said calmly. "I talk to her first."

His expression flattened. "You're serious about this, aren't you?"

"You will be too when you see Teri."

He was in a state of disbelief.

"Listen," I said calmly. "I'll talk to her."

"You want this?" he asked, still in shock.

"I want you to be satisfied," I said. "I want Teri to satisfy you."

"And what about you?"

"I'll be satisfied if I see you satisfied."

"*See?*" he said. "You're going to be there?"

"I want to be there. I want to see the pleasure in those smoldering eyes of yours all over again."

Jake smiled warmly but didn't seem convinced.

"Trust me on this, honey," I said, kissing him. "I think it'll be good for us."

We said no more about it that night and Jake was quiet on the subject in the coming days. I was busy beavering away at the idea in the background.

I'd spoken to Teri the very next day and she seemed immediately struck by the idea. As I was explaining it I could see her getting excited.

"We should do it here," she said, looking around the salon.

"Here?"

"Why not?" she said and I joined her in assessing the scene. I tried to imagine the two of them here, sat on the wide barber's chair and doing something unspeakable.

"That might work," I said slowly. I was more inclined to go with whatever Teri wanted. I was asking a lot of her, after all, although from her enthusiasm you wouldn't think so.

"Is he hot?" she asked. "Your husband?"

"I think so."

"Of course you do," she said. "But is he?"

I took my phone out and scrolled to a photo of him, holding the screen up to her.

"Damn!" was all she said, looking from me to the photo as if the two didn't match.

"He's your husband?"

"Is that so hard to believe?"

"No," she said, struggling to find the words. "It's just ... he's ... *hot.*"

I smiled as though she'd given me the compliment instead of Jake. "I'm glad you think so."

"You want me to fuck him?" Teri said, leaning over the barber's chair so that I could see right down her cleavage.

"If you want to," I said.

She shrugged, chewing her gum. "Sure. Why not?"

I smirked and looked her up and down with quiet admiration. Teri had a body to die for, accentuated by the tight, high-waisted jeans that hugged her ass perfectly. She had a classic hour-glass figure with a big pair of tits and a full ass to go with it. I just knew Jake would be in heaven immediately when he saw the blonde bimbo.

"One more thing," I said.

Teri blew a pink bubble with her gum and it popped on her full lips. "What's that?"

"I want to watch," I said.

She chewed plainly as though she hadn't heard the words.

"Didn't figure you'd be into that," she said eventually. "But okay. You can watch."

I let out a deep breath. I'd been nervous about bringing it up but the whole thing went way better than I anticipated.

"You want me to do anything else?" she asked.

"Like what?"

"I don't know. Talk dirty? Spank him?"

"No, nothing like that," I said, but I couldn't help but let my mind explore the notion. *I might never get a chance like this again*, I thought.

"Well, if you think of anything—"

"Treat *me* dirty," I said. The words came out of my mouth without a filter.

"Say that again, Mrs. Parker."

I cleared my throat and tried my hardest not to turn red with embarrassment. "I want you to treat me dirty. Show my husband a good time and treat me dirty in the process. I'll be here. I'll be—uhm—watching."

"You want to watch? Damn, Mrs. Parker, you're more of a freak than I thought."

I laughed to ease the tension. I guess Teri was right.

"This Friday," I said. "Take your last haircut at around five o'clock and I'll be by at six with my husband for his special treatment."

"Right you are," Teri said, snapping her fingers.

I walked out of the shop with a smile, realizing I'd hired a good woman in Teri. I just had no idea how well she'd follow those instructions on the actual day.

I kept the whole thing secret from Jake. I didn't want it to be on his mind and hoped it would be a welcome surprise when I finally revealed it to him.

On Friday I dropped him off and work and told him I'd pick him up too. I think it was then that he realized something wasn't quite right. When he got back in the car later that day I decided to drop it on him finally.

"I thought we'd go and get you a haircut," I said, pulling out of the car-park and making my way to the salon.

I was staring straight ahead but I could feel his eyes on me.

"I'm not sure I need one," he said, checking himself in the mirror beneath the sun-visor.

"Oh, you do," I said, and I couldn't help but let a smile flourish across my face.

Jake was silent but just as excited. It seemed as though he didn't want to vocalize his assumption for fear he might be wrong, but at this point I'd say it wasn't much of a surprise any more.

We pulled up in the small parking-lot that was thankfully empty apart from Teri's car. As I moved to the front door of the shop Teri unlocked it and let me in. Jake followed behind and she held the door for him, chewing her bubble-gum and giving him the 'fuck-me' eyes that I'd seen her wear when she first saw the picture of him.

"You must be Jake," she said with a smirk.

"I am indeed," he said shuffling past her before looking back. Teri was definitely a woman you needed a double-take at. "And you are?"

Teri popped a bubble and pushed the door closer, twisting the lock. "Teri."

Jake looked to me and then back at Teri. I was trying desperately to hide my laughter as the penny dropped for him completely.

"So what'll it be, Mr. Parker," she said, walking over to him and circling him like a predator.

"I—uhhm—what do you think?"

"Let's get you in the chair," she said, taking his hand and guiding him over to the mirror.

She pushed out her hips as she walked, bouncing her big, round ass in her jeans and twisting a finger around her blonde hair.

She offered the seat to him with a hand, swiveling it on its podium so that it faced away from the mirror towards me.

"What do you think we should do to him, Mrs. Parker?" Teri asked.

Jake took off his jacket and Teri let out a gleeful chirp as she a little more of him.

"Something for the weekend, I think," I said, trying to be coy.

Teri was less subtle. "My mouth on his cock?"

I stared unblinking. "That's a start," I said, sitting back on the chair.

"You just watch, Mrs. Parker," she said, putting a hand on my husband's shoulder. "I'll show you how to fuck a man like Jake here properly."

I felt a pang of humiliation. Jake stared at me in shock and we shared a private moment. I nodded simply and he looked up to Teri who was moving around him.

"Your wife wants me to treat you, Mr. Parker," she said, opening the top two buttons of her plaid shirt and pulling it open wide. "Do you like treats?"

"Who doesn't," he said nervously.

"Your wife," Teri said, looking over at me, "she likes to treat other people. People like you, Mr. Parker. Would you like that?"

He nodded quickly, captivated by her intoxicating presence. The speed of his surrender to her was humiliating in itself.

"Let's give her a good view," Teri said, lining up the seat so that I could see the front of my husband.

He looked over at me and I stared, waiting. Teri crouched to her knees and went straight for his belt.

I saw him tense up, looking over cautiously for the slightest change in my demeanor. I watched her hands finger at the belt and slide it open. She tackled the button of his fly next and I watched close.

Jake swallowed and looked down at Teri who was eager to release him. She was immediately smitten by him and looked as though she was desperate for his cock.

"Let's see what we've got here," she giggled, pulling his pants open and rubbing her hand over the bulge. She looked back to me. "He's big, isn't he?"

I nodded. Jake was a good size bigger than average and I was keen to see how Teri would work him.

"I like them big," she said, smiling up at Jake.

She dragged down the waist of his jeans and boxer-shorts in one and I watched as his cock sprang up out of his underwear, already stiff and looking as delicious as I remembered it.

"Fuck," Teri cried as she caught eyes on it.

Jake seemed proud of the reaction, smiling over at me. For the moment I couldn't react. Instead I was rapt by the view. I felt my stomach flutter as she took that big cock of his in her hand.

"No wonder you need my help," she said, looking down. "I bet a woman like you doesn't know what to do with this, do you?"

She stared at me, waiting for my answer.

I shook my head and looked down. "No," I said.

"Teri will look after you," she said, smiling up at Jake as she got comfortable on her knees.

She moved her hands over his cock as though she was mapping it with her touch. She squeezed it and caressed it gently, stroking the back of her nails down the length and relishing the reaction it elicited from Jake.

He was breathing irregularly, his hands gripping the arms rests.

"Let me have a taste of your husband's cock," Teri said, holding the tip with her hand and starting with her tongue at the base.

She licked all the way up to the tip. When she arrived at the bulbous, soft-pink crown she turned her head down and slid her lips over him.

Jake let out a long breath and my eyes widened as the pair of us marveled at her skills. As though it was nothing she sank on it and we both watched her throat bulge as she pressed on, magically making his entire length disappear inside her.

With the entirety of his cock in her mouth she looked sideways at me and bounced her eyebrows. Then slowly she pulled back, revealing his wet inches again.

"I bet your wife can't do that, can she?" Teri said, looking back up to Jake now.

He was dumbfounded. He stared down and laughed, then he looked over to me to make sure he wasn't imagining what had just happened.

Teri pumped her hand over him slowly, looking straight at me as she did so. Jake was staring down in disbelief as she jerked him slowly. I could see the white on his knuckles as he clenched the chair.

Without a word she moved back to him, planting her lips over him and showing us both her party-trick.

"Fuck," Jake breathed, looking more excited than I'd ever seen him. "It's in her throat."

She moved her hair behind her head and Jake held it so the pair of us could see her go to work.

I watched as her tongue crept out and tickled the base of his shaft. Again she dragged him out of her, gasping as he vacated her throat. His dick was strewn in thick spit that she smothered over him as she slurped a breath over her teeth.

"This cock is gonna feel so good in my tight pussy," she said aloud, putting her mouth back over Jake and planting him back in her throat.

I watched her neck bulge and wondered how the hell she managed to do that without gagging. Teri clacked her neck over him fast and Jake moaned like never before. I saw a pleasure and delight in his eyes that I knew I couldn't give him and I felt the pang of jealousy in my stomach again.

My mouth turned dry as I watched her satisfy him. I started to feel more worthless the more Jake's pleasure grew, but I couldn't turn away. I was rapt by her prowess and it felt as though I needed to be humbled and humiliated like this, for Jake's sake.

"Does it feel good, honey?" I asked, desperate to know.

His eyes opened and he had a look of ecstasy etched across his face. "It feels *incredible*," he said, having never experienced a tightness like it.

Teri slipped her neck off him and pumped him in her hand. "I think you'll like my pussy better."

"Let's find out," Jake said, more comfortable in the scenario than I ever imagined him.

He started to touch Teri now as she stood in front of him, gripping his hand inside her thigh pulling him close to her.

Teri straddled one of his legs, rubbing her crotch along his thigh as I watched her ass work from behind.

"Let's have your wife undress me," she said, holding Jake's head against her tits and looking back at me. "Come here," she said.

I stood up as instructed, walking over to Teri who seemed to enjoy being the boss of me for a change.

"Unbutton my shirt," she said, turning the front of it to me and waiting.

Jake's hand rubbed over her ass as she turned to sit on his knee.

I moved my fingers to her buttons and popped each one of them open until there were none left. I pushed the shirt open and stared at those perfect tits of hers that sat bound in a bra that I'd long thought had padding. As it turns out Teri's tits were just as real as the rest of her.

"Bra too," she said, and Jake took the shirt back off her shoulders.

I reached behind her and she took a bite at my ear playfully as I popped open the clasp behind her.

When it as unfastened Jake pushed it off her shoulders and his hands came under her arms to grip at her charms.

I watched him squeeze her tits gleefully. They were a good size bigger than mine and twice as perky. Jake seemed to enjoy how they felt in his grasp.

"Get those pants off him, will you," she said now, nodding down at the floor.

I crouched at their feet like a servant, struggling Jake's boots off and then pulling the jeans and boxer-shorts off his legs.

When I stood back up the pair of them were kissing passionately and Teri was jerking his cock slowly. I watched their embrace quietly, stood only a foot from the action.

It was as though I didn't exist. I could hear the passion of their kisses as their lips smacked and their tongues wound around each other. I watched the sinful flesh of my husband move through her hand too and I felt like a dirty voyeur. I was helpless and incapable all at once.

Teri stopped kissing Jake and noticed I was still there.

"That's all for now," she said, wafting me away with a hand.

I returned to my chair and looked across as they enjoyed each other. Jake's legs were wide open and his cock looked gloriously big and delicious as it stood proud between his legs. Teri kept a hand around him at all times, gently stroking him as they got familiar.

"I bet your wife isn't this good," she teased, looking over at me. Her shoulders bunched together as she giggled and I watched those perfect tits of hers bounce.

"No, she isn't," Jake agreed, and the humiliation struck me harder than ever.

I felt like a spare wheel as the chemistry between the pair of them grew. By now Teri had straddled him and I was watching that perfect ass of hers grind over his cock as they kissed. At intervals she'd raise herself up on her knees and I'd listen as Jake wound his lips around those soft, pink nipples of hers.

She leant her head back and grunted joyously, holding his head on her tits and pumping his cock against his stomach.

"Okay," she said after several minutes. "I fucking want it now. I want that cock inside me. Get over here, Mrs. Parker. Help me out of these jeans."

I did her bidding, venturing over towards them and looking at my husband. His pupils were fat as though he'd been drugged and he had a reddish hue to his cheeks that I'd seen only a few times before in our earlier years together. It was a sign of extreme arousal in him.

"Take her pants off, honey," he said, breathless and eager. He was as focused on fucking her now as Teri was on being fucked. I'd happily play slave if it meant he'd be satisfied.

Teri turned to me and waited, with those delicious tits of hers sat on her chest.

"You like these?" she asked, noticing me enjoying them.

"You look good," I said.

"Come here."

She put a hand at the back of my head and pulled me towards her. At first I lay my cheek against the soft skin of her tits, but gradually I started to turn my head against her.

"Watch this, Jake," she said. "You're gonna want to watch this."

Jake did as suggested as I turned my mouth onto her, latching over one of her nipples and sucking it into my mouth. As I did so I unfastened her jeans and unzipped her fly.

Teri took my hand and pushed it down the front of her pants. I could feel her kempt fur against my skin and then she guided me to her clit and moved my finger over it.

"Fuck," Jake whispered, jerking his cock slowly as I played lesbian in front of him.

"That's it," Teri said, pushing my hand further inside her pants. I hadn't planned on this happening at all.

She pushed me in forcefully and her pants dropped a little, then I felt the warm, wet spot of her pussy and she guided me up into her.

My fingers broke inside and I felt her warmth on them. It was the first time I'd ever been near another woman's pussy. To feel another woman's wetness on my skin was electrifying, and Jake seemed to enjoy the view too.

He watched my hand move beneath the fabric of her jeans as Teri's breath fluttered.

"Take them down, honey," he said, eager to see the union of our flesh.

I pulled with one hand and kept the other in place as Teri started to moan. The tight fabric slid over her soft skin, hugging her hips before giving way and sliding down quickly.

Jake beat his cock quicker and gave a grunt of appreciation as he finally caught sight of it. Teri's hand was over my own and two of my fingers were plunged inside her. I massaged her core and felt the wetness of her sex drape over my fingers.

After a while she pulled me out of her, then she gave me an appreciative kiss on the lips. I was about to walk away but Teri pulled me back, bending my arm upwards and feeding my fingers into my mouth.

She said nothing but I could see the satisfaction in her eyes as she watched me lick her juices off my hand.

"Now let's see about that cock of your husbands," she said, turning back to address Jake and taking her pants off her ankles.

She unfastened his shirt and pushed it back as she stood naked in front of him. Her body was unblemished, as though an artist had drawn it. She had nothing to be ashamed of in the slightest. I watched her naked ass bounce as reached forward to rub her hands over my husband's powerful chest.

She put a knee up on the chair and then another until she was straddling my husband's legs. He looked up into her eyes as she stalked over him and I stared forwards into her sex, looking at that impossibly perfect asshole of hers that sat above the pink slit that was already drooling with desire.

She kissed his lips and then straightened her back, taking his cock underneath her. I don't know what possessed me but I fell forwards off the chair and knelt on the floor for a better look.

Teri looked back at the commotion and then smirked dirtily. "You wanna see, huh?" she said.

I nodded and looked back to the tip of my husband's cock that was now dangerously close to being inside another woman.

I watched as she slid the crown back and forth over her wetness, giving Jake a taste of what he was about to get.

He moaned softly and she began to kiss him, still sliding that big dick of his back and forth over her. I watched the tip of his cock catch her wetness and a string of her cum bridged a brief divide between them.

She smothered the tip of his dick with her pussy and then finally sank on him. I watched him go inside. Her pussy opened over him and she moaned along with Jake.

She dropped on him and his inches disappeared up inside her. I watched as she sat all the way down on him effortlessly. I could see the soft pinkish hue of her lips. Below hung Jake's heavy balls, surely more full of spunk now than ever before. Above that sat her winking asshole. Jake grabbed her butt in his hand and I watched his finger skirt dangerously close to her knot.

She started to bounce on him as though she was riding a rodeo bull. It was a sight to behold. Her hair flailed and her ass cheeks clenched. Each time she pulled up off him her tight buns would squeeze his pole and then relax, as though she was jerking him with her pussy and her ass together. It was a skill I'd never possess.

Jake was immediately breathless. I listened to him make the most erotic of groans—groans that I'd never heard him utter before with me.

I sat on the floor like a pet, looking up as my masters fucked each other. Teri bounced on him and Jake groped her tits, squeezing them before returning back to her ass to grip that too.

"His cock feels so good," she groaned. "Tell her how tight I am."

"She's fucking *tight*, honey," Jake growled, clearly struggling to hold himself back.

"I want your fucking cum," Teri said, and I felt another fierce jolt of jealousy.

Jake didn't seem to protest. He fucked her harder, thrusting up off the chair and meeting her bounces.

I watched her cum slide over his cock, pooling in a white ring around the hilt that got messier and messier with each of her bounces.

Jake's adventurous finger was at her ass now, jostling the knot playfully as Teri moaned. She didn't seem one bit concerned.

"Get in here," she said to me now. "Let's make her lick my ass."

Jake nodded quickly in agreement.

"Lick her ass, honey," he said, treating me just as nasty as Teri.

I crawled forwards towards her impeccable muscle, staring into it. She slowed her bounces and looked back.

"Get your fucking face in there," she ordered, looking down excitedly.

I pressed between her cheeks and licked at her asshole, feeling a depravity like no other.

"That's it," she snarled, putting a hand on my head and gripping my hair.

She held me on her ass as my tongue tickled over her flesh.

"She's tonguing my fucking ass, Mr. Parker," she announced. "Your wife is a real dirty, slut, you know that?"

I pushed the tip as far into her as I could, then I pulled back and looked at her wet knot. Beneath it sat my husband's cock, slotted inside her and with that powerful muscle of his running up the underside.

I licked downwards until I was tasting her cum on the base of his shaft.

"That's it," she grunted. "You clean my cum off him. Good girl."

She pulled up and Jake's dick slapped back wetly against his stomach. She looked underneath herself as I took it in my hand and slurped my tongue up the side of his length.

"That's it," she nodded, and the pair of them watched close as I cleaned their love off his cock.

"Clean it all up, honey," Jake said slowly.

Teri kissed his face as he watched. Her pussy sat above me, waiting to be planted back over him.

"Now put him back in," she said. "I'm gonna take his cum inside me now."

Jake smiled excitedly. He seemed in little doubt that she'd coax the climax from him, which was something I hadn't given him in too long.

I held his cock steady and marveled as that perfect pussy of hers slipped back over him.

"That's is," she said, dropping on him.

Jake's cock tensed up inside her as he revisited her honey-pot.

"I want it now," she said, talking to Jake, her face close to his. She kissed him on the lips. "I want your cum, okay?"

Jake nodded.

"I want that fucking cum inside me. I want all of it. More than you give your wife, okay?"

Teri had no idea that that had been cause for concern between us in recent months.

"You're gonna get it," Jake said, and it sounded like he really meant it.

I was as eager for it as the pair of them. To see him finally explode with bliss was a gift to myself as well as him.

"Fucking give it me," Teri snarled, holding his chin and kissing his lips roughly.

She started to bounce on his cock, looking back to me one last time.

"You," she said. "Watch this. Closely."

I did as commanded, sat on the floor fully clothed as the two naked lovers went at it. I watched that twenty-year-old pussy of hers massage my husband's mature length, sucking close to his shaft and gripping him tight as she bounced over and over.

She had a boundless energy to her that I doubt Jake could have matched. Thankfully all he had to do was sit there and Teri would do the rest. I sat there too. Watching.

Their breaths increased together until they were both a panting mess of ecstasy. Teri was sweating but looking no less sultry. The light of the salon hit her perspiration so that I looked as though she was glowing.

She writhed on him, calling out for his release as though she needed it more than anything else.

"Come inside me!" she growled, bouncing faster. "I'm ready."

Jake started to moan. It came from the depths of his stomach, wailing upwards with glorious delight.

"That's it," she goaded, rubbing his chest and squeezing her ass up his shaft. "Come in this tight pussy. Show your wife what you can do to me."

She bounced over and over and his groans increased. Suddenly he pulled his hands off her and gripped again at the arms of the chair.

The sound from his mouth stopped, but the slapping of Teri's ass on his legs continued.

"Yes!" she cried, urgently.

Jake let out a deep, long groan and I leant forward on my knees, staring at his cock and seeing the unmistakable throbbing of it inside her as he emptied himself. I let out a whimper of quiet joy.

"Ohh, yes!" Teri cried, looking back to me finally. "He's coming inside me."

She seemed as overjoyed as I was. Jake continued to moan and I watched his cock pulse, throwing out his delicious, plentiful seed.

"There's so much," she giggled, and I could believe that.

It started to slide out of her and I stared, infatuated by it. I hadn't seen his pearlescent seed in so long that I had to stop myself from reaching out for it.

"Fuck," I whispered, seeing it slide down his shaft before Teri dropped down on him.

It stuck against her pussy and webbed across their skin messily. There was so much of his spunk about her sex that I wondered if any of it was left inside.

"Damn!" Teri said, pulling herself up off him.

I watched her pussy slip off him and then a marble of cum arrived at her core. She moved a hand to smother it into her as she kicked a leg off Jake and admired her work.

"So much cum," she whispered, teasing his slickness around her pussy.

I stared forward in a trance as I watched it slide down his cock. Teri seemed to notice my catatonic state.

"Don't just look at it," she said. "Come and have a taste."

I crawled forward and lunged for it, savoring the taste of his seed on my tongue. It was bitter and silk like, but I didn't care. All that mattered was that it had happened, and I had witnessed it. I slurped up him and devoured all of the cum that I could find.

"Damn, Mrs. Parker," Teri said, shocked at how hungry I was for his seed.

As she admired my work another sinful idea seemed to strike her.

"Watch this now, Jake," she said, sitting on the barber chair that was beside his.

She opened her legs and fingered at his cum.

"Come and get it," she said to me.

I looked up at Jake who couldn't believe what was about to happen. I stalked over ravenously and Jake stood up to get a better look, keen not to miss this once-in-a-lifetime moment.

I thrust my face between her legs without a care, tonguing out my husband's love from her pussy and sliding it down my neck to join the rest of his seed in my stomach.

Jake moved my hair over so he could watch me. Teri sat back in the chair and her eyes rolled back in her skull.

"We should do this more often," she said, then a moan overcame her.

I licked up her groove and tickled at that swollen clit of hers, then my tongue returned to her honey-pot, pressing inside as though I was desperate to find more of his cum.

When I could taste no more of him I pulled back, breathing heavily and wiping a hand down my mouth and off my chin.

"You *really* love cum, huh?" Teri said, smiling.

I nodded and wiped at my mouth again. "It's been a while," I said.

I stood up finally and Jake hugged me close to him as Teri sat in the chair, spinning it left and right with a toe that she pressed against the floor.

"You two love-birds enjoy yourself?" she said, looking at both of us.

Jake looked down at me and kissed my forehead, pulling me close to him. "I think we did."

I smiled warmly. "You?" I asked her.

"Shit," she said, gleefully, then she leaned forward and gave Jake's spent cock another suck.

He pulled me tight to his body and let out another groan of pleasure.

"We should do this every week."

The three of us laughed. It was strange how an act like that can make you more comfortable with a person.

Jake and I moved into the backroom as Teri cleaned up and I watched him dress.

"So ... that was fun?" I said, half asking the question.

"Did you ... like it?"

"I did," I confessed. "It was a strange ... but I definitely liked it."

He smiled and kissed my head again as he pulled up his jeans. "Thank you, honey," he said.

I knew what he was thanking me for. The strangest thing is, it seemed to open the flood gates for him. From then on neither of us had a problem. Whether I'd learned something from Teri or he had, I couldn't say, but the results were obvious. I never had to worry about him coming again.

THE END

Elevator Threesome With The Girl Next Door : Couples Threesomes 2

"I don't know, I just think we could spice things up some more," I said, looking back to my husband John as he held the door of our apartment building open.

"How?" he asked. "More spontaneity?"

"Yes, that," I said, swinging my handbag and turning to him as I walked backwards across the foyer. "But also I think we should try something *new*. Something exciting."

"I'm all ears."

"Something like ..."

Just then we heard the clicks of heavy heels across the marble as our new neighbor Molly entered the complex.

"Can you hold the door," she called over casually as she fidgeted in her handbag.

"Something like *that*," I said, slapping John's ass.

He batted my arm away as I grinned. I knew for a fact he had the hots for her. I'd have been more concerned if he didn't. This cutesy, twenty-year-old fuck-machine would have gotten any man weak at the knees.

"Thanks," she smiled, stepping inside.

She stood in front of and I elbowed John playfully, nodding again at the temptress before him. He was embarrassed by me but I reveled in it. The idea of John with another woman was always something I'd have been willing to try, as long as it meant coming back to me.

I knew that now we were both in our late thirties that it was natural for him to fantasize about other younger, prettier women. Molly was just that. She had a bob of light blonde hair and a slender neck that led down to her square shoulders. Beneath that a pair of modest, tasty tits that sat all perky on her chest as though they demanded attention.

Today she wore a short, flowery summer dress and a pair of boots that almost looked at odds against the rest of her outfit. She had a confidence and figure that could pull it off though. John was in jeans and plaid shirt, and I wore a pair of yoga pants and a light sweater.

"So what do you say?" I said, continuing the conversation vaguely behind Molly. "Would you be interested in something like that?"

"I'd have to think about," John said, keen to change the subject.

"Make sure you do. I want to hear every last, *naughty* thought about it." I nudged him as I spoke and giggled.

Molly cleared her throat and stared forwards, looking up at the floors as they pinged by on the display.

"What's your opinion, Molly?" I said, and John looked instantly mortified.

She turned around, surprised.

"Sorry, forgive me. I saw your name on your mail. I'm Gail and this is John."

"Nice to meet you," John nodded, already blushing.

"A pleasure," Molly said, regaining her composure. "My thoughts on what?"

"It's noth—" John began.

"My husband and I were looking to spice things up, you know, in the bedroom. Have any ideas?"

Molly shrugged, unfazed by the topic. "Threesome," she said simply, and right after the words left her mouth the elevator stalled to a halt.

"Shit," I cursed.

"What is it?" Molly asked.

"Threesome?" John repeated.

"Broken down," I said. "This happened last year to a guy. Poor bastard was on his own for two hours before they got him out."

"Two hours?" Molly said, pulling out her phone to check the time.

"Two hours," I repeated.

"Like, a guy and two girls? Or two guys and a girl?" John continued.

"I've got a hair appointment at five," Molly said.

"You like fine," I said. "You got signal?"

Molly peered at her phone and sighed. "Nope."

John and I both looked at our cells and confirmed the worse.

"Must be the metal," John said, looking around our new home.

"There must be something—" Molly began, becoming flustered.

I hit the emergency button. "Relax," I said.

In a few seconds time a voice filled the elevator, coming through all tinny on the small speakers.

"Is there a problem?" it asked, with way too much sass.

"Our elevator's broken down," I cried, putting my face close to the sound.

"Building?" the voice said.

"Park Street apartments. On the corner of twenty-fifth and George."

"Someone will be with you in a few hours."

"A few hours!" I cried.

"Yes," it said back simply. "Hold tight."

"Excuse me, Ma'am," Molly asked, all sweet into the receiver.

No reply came.

"Ma'am?"

Nothing.

"Well I guess that's that," John said, throwing his hands up and then sliding his back down the wall. He sat on the floor and pulled out his cell.

I looked down at him and then at Molly. The three of us were trapped together for a while. *'Maybe this could be an opportunity,'* I thought.

Molly put her bag down and leaned back against the wall.

"I can't even get the internet," John said, cursing his cell. He threw it into the corner and then looked ahead, straight at Molly's long, smooth legs.

She was busy studying the room, looking up at the ceiling and peering at the hatch.

"Hey, we could—" she began.

"Too dangerous," I asserted. "It's safer to just wait it out."

Molly took a deep breath. "I guess then we just ... wait."

Several minutes of silence ticked by in which the three of us adjusted to our temporary fate, entombed in the small elevator and with hours to kill.

Before long we were all sat on the floor, our legs stretched towards the middle of the room and with a wall behind us each.

"This is cozy," I said, trying to lighten the mood.

Molly smiled.

"Tell me, Molly: do you have a boyfriend?" I asked, looking to John and then her.

"Not currently," she answered. "I'm in between relationships, you could say."

"Good place to look," John said. "In the city, I mean. Plenty of folks."

"All the good ones are already taken," Molly said, looking to me.

I looked over at her and bit my lip curiously. It was clear she found John attractive. Women can just kind of sense these things.

"So," I began, clearing my throat. "A threesome, you said?"

"Huh?" Molly asked, and John shuffled his feet and kicked mine.

"To spice up our sex life?"

Molly brought her knees up and smoothed her skirt over them. John sat opposite and peered underneath. I don't think she realized that the both of us could see her panties.

"If you both wanted to, of course," she said. "I didn't want to intrude or presume but—you know—you asked." She shrugged.

"Hey, we're all ears, aren't we, John?"

The both of us looked at him and he raised his eyes upwards. Molly seemed clueless as to where his gaze had been, but I knew how naughty he was.

"We are," he said.

Molly bit the inside of her lip.

"Have you ever ..." I hinted, looking to her.

"I'd like to," she answered quickly. "Umm, but I never have."

"That's interesting," I said slowly, leading the charge. "Here we are: a couple who'd very much like to try a threesome and here you are: a single woman who'd very much like to be in one."

There was a silence as I allowed the both of them to fill in the blanks. Molly pulled her ankles in an opened her knees slightly and I watched John's gaze flutter quickly down to her crotch. I could see it too. Beneath her red, lacy panties you could see a slight groove at the centre of the mound of flesh.

"That is interesting," she said, biting her lip.

I looked to John. His and Molly's eyes were locked now and I could feel the growing tension between them. I felt almost like a by-stander, but I didn't mind in the slightest. I wanted John to enjoy other women and I was already excited as I watched their feelings blossom right there and then.

"Well, would you look at that?" I said, and suddenly both their eyes were on me.

I was staring at the growing lump announcing itself beneath John's jeans and soon all three of us were looking at it.

John moved his leg to hide it. "Sorry," he said.

"Oh, no, honey," I said, pushing off the wall and moving over to him on my knees. "He doesn't have to apologize, does he Molly?"

I gently moved John's leg back down and watched as Molly's eyes found the bulge again.

"He doesn't," she said, mesmerized by the sight of him growing.

"We're grateful for it, aren't we Molly?" I said, unfastening the buckle of his belt now.

John was quiet. He was right to leave things to me.

"I am," she said, swallowing and taking a breath as I revealed John's underwear to her.

"Shall we see what he's got for us?" I asked, reaching inside before she answered and finding his stiff cock.

"Show me," Molly said, excited now.

She sat forward cross-legged as I moved his underwear down and brought his cock through the gap in his fly.

"Damn," she cooed, letting out a whistle.

I laughed and jerked back and forth along him. John let out a short chuckle too.

"That's big," she said.

"Would you like a taste?"

She looked at me as I held him and I bounced my eyebrows and tried to look as friendly as possible. I wanted her to understand that this wasn't a trick. I wanted her to take my husband, and I wanted to watch.

"You don't mind?" she said, rightly timid.

"I want you to suck him," I said clearly.

Molly stared forwards and I could see the trepidation in her. She watched my hand stroke slowly over his thick cock and she seemed to decide something.

"Hold him steady," she said finally.

I could feel my heart quicken as Molly started to move off the wall and crawl across to John. John too took an excited breath, preparing himself for a situation that most men can only dream of.

She curled her hair behind her ear and dropped quickly to it, wasting no time in putting those soft, pink lips over the crown of his cock.

John let out a groan and I watched on as the tip of his cock disappeared in her mouth. I held her hair aside so John could watch too. She closed her eyes and plunged over him, as though she was giving a real porn-star's performance. Molly seemed to enjoy the both of us watching.

Finally her eyes opened and she caught our mesmerized gaze. She started to giggle and I shook my head in disbelief.

"Enjoying yourself, John?" I asked.

"We need to get stuck in the elevator more often."

Molly laughed. It was a cutesy titter that endeared the both of us to her even more.

"I'll leave you here," I said, kissing John's face. "I'm going exploring."

He watched as I stood up and moved behind Molly whose ass was pointing towards the elevator door. She continued to suck on my husband but took a glance back when I threw her dress up over her ass.

"You don't mind, do you?" I asked, kneeling behind her.

"I don't mind at all," she said coolly.

John looked over her shoulder with wide, lust-filled eyes, letting out a moan as Molly returned to his hard cock and I peeled her panties down over her ass.

She was totally unabashed as the panties slipped from between her legs, falling flimsily to her knees and resting across her calf.

I looked forward into that perfect dot of an asshole, sat above her waxed rose petals that glistened with due.

"Well, look at that," I swooned, opening her ass cheek wider with my hand.

Molly looked back again. "Like what you see?"

I didn't answer. Instead I inched my head forwards and kept my gaze on her until I could hold it no longer.

When my mouth kissed her soft mound and my nose pressed against her ass she let out deep moan, then I heard the sound of her lips smacking again over the tip of my husband's cock.

She sucked on him with greater vigor, as though my busy lips were fuelling her pace. I pointed my tongue and guided it around the outside of her puss, tickling the edge before plunging deep and getting a real taste of her.

"Oh, Gail," she cried, and hearing her say my name really got to me.

I ran my tongue up out of her pussy and circled it around that perfect asshole of her, listening to her moans become deeper as she enjoyed the forbidden pleasure.

"Tell him what I'm doing," I said, peering over her ass and into my husband's eyes.

"Your wife is licking my asshole," Molly said, and the sentence bounced off the metal walls.

John swallowed and looked over her shoulder at me. I gave him a wink and then plunged my tongue forwards against the tight knot of hers, waggling myself inside just enough to tease her.

"You like that, huh?" John said, looking down into Molly's reddening face.

She nodded. "I do."

She jerked John and leaned forward to kiss him now. I watched the two of them embrace and felt a chill of excitement shimmer through me. I stabbed again at Molly's asshole, sliding around it and then rolling back down over her flesh and around her pussy again.

I curled two fingers into her honey pot, driving them deep and listening to the breath leave her as I started to work into her.

"That feels so good, Gail," she groaned, taking a break from my husband's mouth.

I worked back and forth and then placed my tongue back on her ass, feeling it pulse as she became impossibly excited.

She shuffled her knees wider and I pulled her ass open with my free hand, watching it move as I plowed my fingers in and out of her warm core.

I could feel my own desires rising now and was desperate to be satisfied myself, so before I brought her off I stood up and began to undress.

The both of them turned to watch and I felt suddenly on show, transforming the moment into something a little sultrier.

I pulled my sweater up slowly, exciting myself as the fabric slid over my stiffened nipples. I wasn't wearing a bra and I felt the air hit my chest when that fact was finally revealed to them.

"Looking good, Gail," Molly swooned, lying back against my husband who was idly squeezing her tits.

I tossed the sweater to the corner and then turned my back to them, sliding my yoga pants slowly over my mature ass and inching it down until it was at my ankles.

I kicked off my sneakers and dragged the legs of my pants off until I stood in front of them in only my thong. I curled a finger at John and beckoned him over.

"Where do you want me?" he asked.

"On your knees." I pointed to my crotch. "Face: here."

John was excited as he stood up and Molly moved aside to give him some room. He started to remove his pants and Molly helped him, stepping out of her own panties and letting her dress fall back down to hide her sodden pussy.

She started to unbutton his plaid shirt too. I leaned back against the cool, metal door to watch, rubbing gently at my pussy and teasing myself for John's arrival.

Molly pushed his shirt back off his shoulders and ran her fingers through the hair of his chest. She gave his nipples a kiss and a lick and then gave him another French-kiss before surrendering him to me.

John took a couple of steps towards me, his big cock swaying on his crotch like he was dowsing for water.

He crouched before me and I looked down, sliding the crotch of my panties over to reveal myself to him.

"There's a good boy." I said wryly.

John stared forward and went for it. I felt his warm breath first of all, then the soft stubble of his chin and then his rough tongue as it tickled over my clit.

I let out a wail of delight that had been waiting to be released. Molly watched from the corner, putting a hand beneath her dress and spinning her fingers over her clit, seemingly unable to let the moment pass without celebrating it.

I watched her as John ate from me. She moved the straps of her dress off her shoulders and down her arms. It fell in an instant to reveal her naked, perfect body, all unblemished and pure.

I bit my lip and watched her squeeze her tits as she stared at me, then I followed her hand down as it nestled between her legs and she fingered at her soaked lips.

Molly walked over and John finally saw her naked. He put an arm around her ass and pulled her beside me so that both of us were naked against the door of the elevator.

She pushed her feet into her boots and leaned back, turning her head to mine and looking down her nose at my lips. I bridged the gap and started to kiss her, holding John's head onto me and grinding against his lashing tongue.

When I looked down at him I could see him working his cock as he ate on my pussy, no doubt turned-on by the sight of his wife and our neighbor getting a little more familiar.

"Don't forget our new friend," I said to him.

Molly looked down as John shifted positions, pushing her boots astride and then clamping his maw onto her hot pussy.

She moaned in delight and John stared up at her, looking between the two of us as his busy tongue worked out of sight.

He'd pull back and toy her flesh with his finger and then clamp himself back onto her, sucking lovingly on her folds and tickling his tongue around her stiffening clit.

"You should feel him inside you," I whispered, close to the ear of Molly.

"Is he good?" she groaned.

"The best." I looked down at him. "John. On your back, honey."

He reclined eagerly, falling back and letting his dick slap up against his toned stomach.

"Have a seat," I said, kissing her again and offering him to her.

Molly stepped forward demurely, curling her hair back over her ear and stomping a boot at either side of John's torso.

He watched her descend and I dropped to the floor to hold his cock upright and guide him into her. It was hot to see her tight pussy spread over my husband's cock and the ensuing, satisfied moans from the pair of them made me flood with juices all over again.

She swallowed the whole thing inside her to the hilt, putting her hands on John's stomach and bouncing carefully in a kind of leap-frog pose.

"She really knows how to work it," I swooned, watching her bounce on him like a porn-star. That perfect ass of hers curved around and under her legs and I started to play with my pussy as I watched her treat John to something I wasn't capable of.

He looked down his body in disbelief at the source of his pleasure, his hands by his side as he allowed Molly to treat him.

"You look like you need something to do, honey," I said, walking to his upper-half and facing Molly.

I slid down my thong and Molly looked up at me as I squatted over John's face, kneeling above him and planting my pussy right onto him.

She leaned forward and knelt too, sitting on John and rocking her hips back and forth to stir his slick length inside her. He ate messily beneath me, holding Molly's hips as she rode him and chomping against my sensitive groove that I rubbed on his face.

I was like a woman possessed as I grinded over him, feeling the climax approach and blossom further as Molly leaned her head forward to kiss me. We were like a triangle of sinful lust, each pleasuring the other in a cyclical bout of ecstasy.

I moaned and Molly kissed and licked at my lips as they opened, watching me close as the euphoria spread over my face.

"I'm coming," I cried, and the sound bounced off the elevator walls.

John continued in earnest, tonguing and stabbing at anything and everything that I put above him. On several occasions I'd slip lower so that he could tongue my asshole and it seemed to provide the perfect tonic to push me over the edge.

I closed my eyes and squeezed my tits, letting out a breath of hot, gushing excitement and rolling my eyes back as I faced Molly.

She rocked quicker on John as a result, as though my climax had inspired her. Her chest flushed red and her cheeks blushed too.

She didn't announce it but I could tell from her heated movements and gasping breaths that she was coming too.

"Good boy, honey," I encouraged; proud of John that he'd managed to make the both of us come together.

Molly rode out her climax, putting her hands together on John's stomach so that her cutesy tits bunched together between her arms.

I fondled the nipple and then leant in to suck it, garnishing her climax with my gentle tongue as it circled her areola like it was my prey.

"Oh, fuck!" she said finally, and the words left her with a grunt. It must have been bubbling inside her.

She gasped her eyes open and looked across at me, shaking her head in disbelief as though she was jealous that John was mine.

"Enjoy that?" I asked.

She continued to shake her head, blowing a jet of air up her face and then wincing slightly as she pulled up off John and her stomach tightened. His cock slapped back against his stomach, all slick and wet with Molly's cream.

"Let me taste," I said, kicking a leg off John.

He blinked at the light above as he came back to us, wiping the spit and come from his face and then looking down his body at his cock, all coated in Molly's love.

"No," Molly said. "Don't. I think we can use it."

"Use it for what?" I asked, intrigued.

Molly turned against the wall and pushed her ass out. She pulled her cheek aside with one hand and then tickled the tip of a finger at that perfect asshole of hers.

"Use it for this," she said.

John was on his feet in no time. I'd never been able to take him in my ass, but I was sure a young, adventurous woman like Molly would have no problem at all.

"You want him in there, huh?"

"If you don't object?"

"Molly, I'd love to see you take his cock in your ass."

Molly reached her arms up the wall and kept her ass in place as John got himself ready. I put my fingers to my mouth and spat on the tips, moving to Molly before John arrived and curling my fingers against her asshole.

She moaned as I rubbed the saliva around her knot, sliding the tips of both fingers inside her just a little and feeling her tight muscle grip me.

John walked forwards, looking down at his cock as it moved into position. I decided I couldn't possibly let the moment pass without witnessing it as best I could, so moved under and between John's legs, looking up as he approached to dock.

I watched him push against her knot and Molly looked down at the floor, her brow furrowing in pleasured pain as John started to split her open.

The line of her pussy tightened as John pushed himself in and her flesh pulled back. Her ass relented and opened over his crown, sucking several quick inches of him inside as she let out a satisfied wail.

Her muscle gripped him close and her cum from before slid down his cock as he drove it all the way inside her. Soon his balls were tucked against her pussy. I watched his hands come around her, hugging her close to him and squeezing at her tits.

She began to moan and John did too as he pulled back. I watched his length reappear, looking stiff and powerful as it punched into her ass again and then again, building his pace steadily.

I stared up in wonderment as she took his girth like a professional, easily accommodating him inside her and not even blinking when John started to really give it to her.

He slapped his hips forward against her ass and her tits shook each time he struck her. I started to finger my pussy as I watched but from the look of it John wouldn't be inside her for long.

He set off at a terrific pace and I could hear his moans overshadowing Molly's as his balls pulled up tight to the base of his cock.

"He's close," I warned her.

"You're gonna get it," John said, looking down at me.

"Oh, I want it, honey," I said. It wouldn't be the first time.

He leaned closer to Molly and talked into her ear as he fucked her ass. "You wanna pull it out all over her face? Huh?"

"Ohhh, yes!" Molly confessed, her cheek pressed against the wall of the elevator.

"Do it," I urged. "Jerk him off on my face, Molly."

In a flash the moment was upon us. John built to a crescendo and then pulled himself out fast, but thankfully all of us knew our places.

Molly spun around and dropped to her knees and I sat up, pointing my face to John's cock that Molly quickly grabbed and began to jerk hard.

"Ohh, fuck," John cried, and I could see the pleasure in his expression as the cum arrived in his balls.

Molly beat him quick and then John moaned again, just as the first hot lashing leapt from his cock. I flinched as it fell over my face, licking my tongue around my lips and mewling at its warmth as it draped over me.

"That's it," Molly said, beating him hard and looking joyous as all of our efforts culminated at this point.

The cum spat from his cock messily, spiraling upwards and cascading over me in ropes and drops that covered my face all over.

"That's it," I said softly, feeling his slick love slide inside my mouth and web across my lips.

I started to rub my hand over my face as though I was washing myself in it, reveling in the fruits of our love and putting on a show for the both of them.

Molly reached her lips over to mine and started to kiss me as the last few jets burst from John, hitting my face and hers now as we crouched beneath him.

He stepped back and watched as the pair of us shared his cum between us, kissing it from each other's lips and passing it back and forth on our tongues.

"Fuck," he sighed, staring in disbelief.

The both of us giggled up at him. We may have been separated by age but the three of us were certainly aligned in depravity.

Suddenly the elevator jolted and jerked, and then the numbers started to move on the overhead display.

"Shit!" John said, and his urgency made us realize we should hurry too.

The three of us had no time to dine out on the act, instead scrambling to determine which clothes belonged to who and then attempting to put them on as quickly as possible.

There was a ping and the elevator opened. On the other side of the door stood the woman who lived down the hall from us. She smiled but then a strange expression came over her as we traded places and she walked past us into the elevator.

The elevator door closed to leave the three of us alone in our hallway, and it was there that I realized mine and Molly's faces were still covered in cum.

"Oops," I said, and John and Molly laughed.

I pushed his cum into my mouth greedily while Molly got a tissue from her handbag. She handed me one and then took her keys out and stood at her door, dabbing at her cheek with a tissue.

"Well that was fun," she said, turning the key in the lock.

"Thanks for suggestion," I said, and John blew her a playful kiss.

I took his arm and we walked down to our room, looking back at Molly as she disappeared inside her apartment.

"What a naughty slut," I said, and I meant it as a compliment.

"You can talk," John joked, thumbing some of his errant cum into my mouth.

"Mmm," I cooed, sucking the salty seed off him. "Now what's for dessert?"

THE END

Joining My Husband With The Hot Female Chauffeur : Couples Threesomes 3

"Nice of them to send a woman," I said from the back seat, idly peering out of the window as we made our way to the airport.

The lady in the front seat said nothing, staring straight ahead and calmly moving the wheel.

"How old are you?" I asked, looking into her rear-view mirror.

Her blue eyes flicked to the backseat and she gripped her gloved hands on the steering wheel. "Twenty-three, ma'am," she said.

I continued to watch her as she drove. She was a very relaxed, clearly confident woman, and she had every reason to be. When she'd helped with my bag I'd noticed her toned figure and ass-hugging pants. Her blonde hair curled up out from under her chauffeur's hat. She looked like something out of a damn photo-shoot.

"I'm picking up my husband," I said, not really expecting a reply. "He's been on a business trip for two months. Two months. Can you believe that?"

The chauffeur stared straight ahead.

"What's your name?" I asked.

"Lily."

I turned to the tinted windows and watched the city move by. "Pretty name."

We traveled a few more blocks before intrigue got the better of me and I decided to talk again.

"Ever see anything crazy in the back seat, Lily?"

I watched as she thought.

"I once saw a man do a line of cocaine of a stripper's ass," she said. "Butt," she corrected. "Off a stripper's butt."

"I don't mind curse-words, Lily."

She twisted a smirk and stifled it.

"Well, as I say, I haven't seen my husband in months ..."

Lily seemed to be connecting the two topics of conversation together.

"We might be a bit ... frisky."

"I can handle it," Lily said.

"I'm sure you can."

Her eyes flicked to the mirror again and I stared straight into them, smirking naughtily. Lily looked back to the road and I saw a grin flourish on her mouth too.

"What terminal?"

"Three."

We moved to the off-ramp and swung round under the barrier. I slid across the well to the seat just behind Lily, peering over the divide and looking for my husband over her shoulder.

"There," I said, pointing across her. "The stud in the blue suit." I wound down the window and leaned out. "Richard, honey!"

When he saw me he beamed a smile, dropping his cell in his pocket and picking up his bag. Lily put the car in park and I watched her step out to help him.

As she bent for his luggage he gave her a quick look up and down, noticing that same inviting figure that I had when she'd picked me up from our apartment. He looked to me and raised his eyebrows, then he reached down for the bag.

"I've got it," he said, taking it from Lily's hand and looking to her as she stood up.

"That's Lily," I shouted, leaning out of the window with a smile.

She extended a white-gloved hand and Richard took it, shaking it slowly as he studied her.

"My husband likes younger women," I said.

Lily seemed unflustered. She walked to the back of the limo and opened the tiny boot. Richard joined her and tossed his bag inside, then she opened the door for him.

"Come here," I said, snatching his tie and pulling him onto me.

He stumbled and we both fell across the back-seat, kissing each other passionately and giggling like lovers. You'd never have guessed we were in our forties.

I felt the car lurch forward and we sat up, looking to Lily who had begun the return journey home.

"How was your flight?" I asked, leaning on my husband's big, muscled chest.

"Good," he said.

"Did you get much pussy while you were away?"

He looked down on me and grinned. It's fair to say we had a unique relationship, Richard and I. I was more than happy for him to enjoy himself with other women. My only proviso was that I was kept informed, in perhaps a little too much detail than most people would feel comfortable with. In the past I'd also watched him with other women, but they were rare moments. It's not often that they agree.

"One woman," he said, leaning in to whisper in my ear, "took my entire cock in her throat."

I closed my eyes and squeezed his leg, taking a breath as he whispered naughty things to me.

"Another," he began, "rode my cock so hard that I came in her asshole."

I gasped, and looked to him, slapping his chest playfully. "I never knew you like that."

"Anal?" he said. "What guy doesn't?"

It was then that I looked forward and noticed the attention of Lily, scanning the rear-view mirror intermittently and watching as my husband and I became more and more intimate in the back seat.

I pulled his tie over to me and kissed him, looking forward at Lily and watching her as my husband's tongue found mine.

Her hands gripped the steering-wheel, but it wasn't anxiety that was the cause of her fidgeting, it was intrigue.

"What do you think of her?" I asked now, loud enough for Lily to hear.

Richard looked forward at Lily as she took several calming breaths from the front seat. Richard didn't even need to answer.

"Pull over whenever you can, Lily," I called ahead.

Richard looked to me, confused.

"Just wait," I said.

Lily did as instructed, finding a large bay down a side-street and putting the car in park. She shut off the engine and waited patiently.

"Why don't you come and join us?" I called forwards.

"Ma'am?"

"Come and join my husband and I," I said flirtatiously, pulling at Richard's shirt. "We'd both like you to."

She took a breath and then unbuckled her seat-belt, opening the car door in one swift movement and moving to the back of the vehicle.

Richard and I peered excitedly through the tinted windows as she made her way down to us.

"I want you to fuck her," I hushed, patting his chest. "I want to watch."

He looked shocked. "Now? Here?"

"Yes, honey," I said hurriedly as Lily arrived at our door. "It'll be easy."

The door opened and Lily peered inside. "Where should I ...?"

"Oh," I said, acting surprised. "Why don't you sit right here."

I scooched over and patted the seat between my husband and I. Lily moved over Richard's legs, putting her ass right in his face before sitting in between the both of us. When she was comfortable I stood up and moved across from them, sitting on the seat opposite.

"That's better," I said.

The pair of them were close, but not yet close enough.

"What kind of man do you like, Lily?" I asked.

She took a glance left at Richard.

"I like an older guy," she began. "Confident. Handsome. Blue-suited."

Richard's eyes flashed wide and I started to giggle. Lily joined me. It seemed the pair of us was on the same page. I'd hooked a real live one, alright.

"And what do you look for in a woman, Richard?" I asked. "And don't say: your cock."

He and Lily laughed. I could see beneath the gap in her cutesy suit-jacket that her big tits were jiggling beneath her tight shirt.

"Well," Richard began. "I like a confident woman with curves in all the right places and eyes that you can lose yourself in."

I looked across at him, staring into his gaze. Lily cleared her throat.

"What about Lily, here?" I said.

Richard leaned away into the corner of the seat, draping his arm across the head-rests and raising his knee on the chair.

"She's a real cherry-on-top, isn't she?" he said.

Lily cheeks flushed red at the compliment. When Richard turned on the charm it tended to work incredibly well.

"So what do you say?" I asked. "You and my husband?"

She looked across at me with a stark expression.

"Come on," I said. "Don't act like you're surprised."

Her shoulders dropped and she looked more relaxed suddenly. "I don't usually fuck clients," she said. "But I think I can make an exception."

My smile stretched from cheek to cheek as she revealed the naughty side of her that I'd suspected.

"Show her what she's working with, Richard," I said, crossing my legs opposite.

I wore a short skirt deliberately for the trip. I was hoping to be sat right here anyway, flashing myself to Richard whilst the chauffeur up-front remained oblivious. That was, of course, until it turned out that our chauffeur was a saucy, little minx.

Richard kept his left arm where it was, stretched over the back of the seat, close to Lily's face. With his right hand he unfastened his belt and then popped the button at the waist of his trousers.

"Help him out, Lily," I said eagerly.

She pulled her hat off her head and shook her hair out. It fell down in gloriously shiny locks and the whole cabin filled with the scent of her.

She reached over and fumbled at his zipper, then she slid down off the chair and found herself a seat in the well between the both of us. She tugged at his pants and pulled them down his legs, until it was only Richard's underwear that hid his sizeable modesty below.

"Would you look at that?" I said, eyeing down at her big ass that pointed right in my direction. Lily wore a tight pair of pants that fell deep into the crack of her butt, giving me no illusions as to what was to be found beneath.

Richard was too busy staring down at Lily who had returned to his waist to tackle his underwear.

"She's not wasting any time," he said, glancing at me and then looking back down at her.

I leaned forward and watched as she slowly began to reveal him, sliding her fingers inside the waist of his Calvins and teasing them down.

I watched his hair become thicker as the garment dropped and then I braced myself, seeing the wide shaft suddenly and then the bulbous, pink crown that slid up and out of his pants.

Lily paid them no mind for now, instead working his underwear down his legs until it joined his suit-pants. She removed his shoes and took everything off him before pushing his knees wide and finally addressing his engorged cock.

"Is this all for me?" she asked, looking back at me for permission.

"It sure is," I said slowly, watching close as her hand wrapped around my husband's thickness.

It sprouted up out of his fist and looked somehow more impressive when she started to squeeze her way along it.

"Oh, that's it," he groaned, closing his eyes and letting out a deep breath.

"That's it," I agreed, watching close.

Lily moved her face closer, crouched on her knees like a naughty, submissive slut.

"Take him in your mouth, Lily, honey," I said, trying to be as nonchalant as possible as I gave my debauched orders.

She leaned forwards and Richard watched closely. Lily was careful not to obscure a thing, presenting my husband to me as though I was the camera-man in this whole sordid affair.

I watched his thick muscle keep his cock stiff as she took him, moving her body up onto the seat so that she lay across it with her face hovering over him.

Richard moved her hair aside for me and she gripped him, jerking slowly and opening her mouth wide as she approached the bulbous tip.

My mouth opened with hers as I imagined taking him, then I watched in awe as her lips spread right over him and she pushed him into her mouth.

"Fuck," I hushed, and Richard let out a long, deep sigh of approval.

He leaned his head back and I watched him disappear in her mouth. Lily pressed onwards and her throat began to bulge. My eyes spread wide as her lips eked their way down to the hilt of his cock.

"Jesus. Where'd he go?" I said, giggling.

Lily's eyes smiled and then her mouth unwound over him, revealing his inches quickly before she gasped off the tip of him.

"Now that's deep-throating," I said to Richard, but he was too busy looking down in shock.

"Where'd you find this girl?"

"We're lucky, I guess," I shrugged.

Lily smiled and then went in for seconds, planting Richard deep in her throat and this time keeping him there. She worked her neck over him and he let out a long, satisfied groan.

As she devoured him I watched a group of people approach along the sidewalk and pass our car. One of them turned to the window and fixed their hair. They were completely oblivious to the sinful show that was occurring inside.

When I looked back to Lily she was massaging my husband's balls and beating his cock in her fist. Her mouth sat over him, snarling with her efforts as she looked down with lustful energy.

Her legs were split at the knee with one foot placed on top of the other. It seemed to invite me in and I moved across the well of the cab to get closer.

She watched me approach, beating Richard in her fist but turning her attentions to me briefly.

I moved slowly, not wanting to scare her. My eyes stayed locked on hers but my hands were moving to the crotch of her black pants.

I placed my fingers right over her pussy, feeling the heat from it immediately as I stared into her eyes. She showed no sign of stopping of me. When I started to move my fingers back and forth slowly she let out a sigh and dropped her lips right back over Richard.

He let out a groan and I became more relaxed too, relishing the opportunity now that it was upon us. I didn't want to miss a single beat.

"Treat him, Lily," I said, moving my hand slowly. "Treat him to your mouth."

Richard's hand was on her head now, guiding her up and down as she sank over and over on his length.

Lily started to writhe on the seat, pushing her crotch against my hand as it worked busily between her legs.

I dropped to my knees now and used my other hand to open the button of her pants. When I slid the zipper down I could see the lacy red panties that sat beneath, looking just as inviting as the rest of her.

Lily looked down and gave a subtle nod, smiling afterwards. "Help yourself," she said.

It was like Christmas Eve for me as I scrambled open her pants with the intention of tasting my first pussy. I'd never quite been this involved before when Richard was satisfying his urges with other women.

Lily moved her ass up off the seat as I pulled down her pants, sliding them down her closed legs and then dragging them over the high-heels.

When I was done she put her feet exactly where they were. Beneath the sheer fabric of her panties I could see her pubic hair, set in a little triangle atop her pussy that was just out of sight below.

I placed my hand on her again and felt the flesh move beneath me as my fingers worked her. Her moans became louder but were muffled by Richard's cock that sat again in her mouth.

I couldn't believe what was happening, but I wasn't about to take a break in order to come to terms with it. Instead I moved my face closer to those red panties of hers. They seemed to beckon me forwards like a shining light to a magpie.

I breathed long and hard, trying to subtly let Lily know that my mouth was close. I looked down my nose at her panties and then moved my face, opening my mouth and clasping it over the crotch of her panties instead.

She let out a long groan and I heard the slap of my husband's cock falling against his stomach as Lily turned to watch me.

I opened my eyes and looked up at her, pressing my tongue against the crotch of her panties until they were sodden. I kissed and mouthed over her, teasing her just a little longer.

Lily though, it seemed, wasn't in the business of being teased. Instead she slid the crotch aside and then grabbed the back of my head, pushing me on to her.

My mouth fell against her petals and I was shocked by her forwardness at first. I opened my mouth and tasted her, gliding my tongue up and down her groove as she spoke.

"That's it," she said. "Do you know what your naughty wife is doing?"

Richard looked over. "Is she ...?"

"She's eating my pussy," Lily said, giggling. "And she's good at it, too."

She leaned over and I watched her kiss him. I listened to the smacking of their lips and then joined them, smacking my own against her cutesy little pussy and then pulling back to see what I was dealing with.

Her clit peered out from beneath the soaked, soft-pink hood and below that her pussy flowed, her tight skin coursing down to the wet O that was already beginning to leak a bead of white, thick cream. I aimed my tongue at it, diving inside to get a real taste of her silky sweetness.

"Fuck, yes," she growled, pressing her forehead against Richard's.

"Nice work, honey," he said, looking down at me.

I tongued feverishly, sliding it all the way up and down her and imagining how I liked to have it done to me. Beneath my tongue I could feel her clit stiffen and I decided to give it my fully attention, sucking at it and giving it soft bites with my lips that I pulled tight over my teeth.

Lily was by now back on Richard's cock, slurping her way along it and pumping it in her fist whenever she deemed it wet enough.

"I want to put him inside you," I said, eager to be part of the next act. "I want to see him slide inside you, Lily."

Lily reached down and pulled her panties over her ass. I grabbed them and slid them down over her long, smooth legs.

She moved off the chair and into the centre of the cab, turning to us and stooping so as not to hit the roof.

I got up and kissed Richard, sitting beside him heavily and wrapping my fist over his cock. I jerked him slowly as we watched Lily take off her suit-jacket.

"Look at her figure," I swooned.

She tossed her jacket through to the front of the cab and then unfastened her bow-tie. It hung around her neck like she was in a strip-show as she started to unbutton her shirt.

The front came open and her matching red bra sat beneath. My eyes trailed down the opening of her shirt straight to her pussy. I imagined myself latched onto it again and realized just how naughty I'd been a minute ago.

"Are you gonna join us?" Lily asked now, and I realized she was talking to me.

"Join you?"

She threw her shirt back and then unclasped her bra.

"Aren't you gonna get undressed?"

"Oh," I startled. "Of course."

"Good," Lily said, and then she pulled her bra off her chest.

Beneath sat these perfect, big, swinging tits that held a big 'look-at-me' sign as they wobbled on her rib-cage.

"Bring those here," Richard said, curling his finger to her. I knew he'd like them.

Lily walked across the cab in her high heels, straddling Richard's legs and hanging her tits in his face.

I took my panties off beneath my mini-skirt, then I took off my jacket and pulled my turtle-neck over my head.

I put my jacket back on now, thinking it somehow kinkier to appear clothed but instead be completely naked beneath.

I watched as I sat beside them. Richard sucked on her tits like he was feeding from her, angling his head up with this serene look on his face.

Lily looked down, watching him carefully as his mouth made her nipples stiff. When he took his lips back off her I marveled at just how stiff they were. The jutted out from her flesh like bullets and I couldn't help but ask to sample them myself.

"Come here," I said, and I sat on the chair just like my husband had.

Lily straddled me and I held her ass, feeling the muscled curves and squeezing them as her tits arrived in front of my face.

Richard moved off the chair as I started to suck on her. It wasn't until I felt his hand pushing up my mini-skirt that I knew where he'd moved too.

Lily watched me as I sucked on her delicious nipples, then I let out an aching groan and she looked under herself to see the top of Richard's head, busily lapping at my pussy below.

I mouthed sinfully on her flesh, embracing the debauched little cab that we'd made for ourselves in the back of her limo.

My hands gripped at her ass as my husband teased his tongue over me. I grabbed each of her cheeks and pulled them wide as I groaned, then I had the naughtiest of ideas.

"Don't forget Lily," I said, and my eyes met with hers.

I watched closely as I felt Richard leave me, then I watched her pupils fatten as he arrived at her instead. She closed her eyes and let out a soft groan.

"What's he doing?" I asked, oblivious to the answer I was about to receive.

"He's licking my asshole," Lily whispered, her eyes still closed.

My throat tightened in shock.

"Your asshole?"

"Yes," she said, then she let out a giggle. Another groan quickly followed it. "His tongue is pressing into my ass."

"Richard!" I gasped, faux-shocked.

I heard him chuckle. "It just looked so nice," he said.

"Show me," I said.

Lily looked down and then smiled, kicking her legs off me and leaning over the back of the seat. I moved back and joined Richard. The both of us stared up at that perfect little dot of an asshole of hers that sat just above the creamy, aching O of her pussy.

"Delightful," I said, and I hadn't imagined I'd be so impressed.

"Try it," Richard said. I looked to Lily who nodded again.

I moved forward and Richard stood up walked beside me as I crawled towards that naughty asshole that I had no business being anywhere near.

I held her cheek and moved it aside, creeping my face forwards as though I was about to try some foreign food. My tongue pressed outwards and Lily let out a breath as it touched her ass.

It tasted kind of sweet, but I wondered if that was just the residue of my husband's spit on her. I circled my pointed tongue around her tight aperture, pressing it against the muscle that appeared to have a certain amount of give to it.

When I pulled back to look at it I noticed my husband's big cock hanging close. I looked at it and then up at him. He raised his eyebrows as he looked down.

I grabbed him with my hand and put my mouth over him, sucking at the tip of his cock until it was glistening and dripping with my saliva.

Then I moved my face back to Lily's asshole, pushing the flat of my tongue against it and really working it as best I could. The moans and groans from her above me told me I must have been doing something right.

This time when I moved away from her ass Richard filled the spot. His cock ventured into her and I decided to do something crazy. I gripped the hilt of him and guided him towards her tight ass, holding him there with one hand and using the other to pull him closer.

He pressed against her and I looked to Lily's face for a sign of protestation. None came. Instead her eyes winced closed and Richard continued to press forwards.

I looked down at her ass just as it was gasping over the head of my husband's cock. The pair of them let out a moan for entirely different reasons.

The tightness of her aperture over him must have felt incredible, but the dull pain of his thickness pressing into a place that it doesn't belong must have been uncomfortable. Or so I thought.

I watched her face with concern, then I watched her bite her lip and furrow her brow. Suddenly she pushed her ass back with a grunt, taking several quick inches of my husband and driving all the way down the hilt. I was amazed.

"That's so fucking hot," I gushed, spinning a finger over my pussy. I had front-row seats to an act I'd never witnessed before.

Lily started to bounce back against him at her own pace and Richard kept himself where he was, staring down as his length sprouted again and again from her tight knot.

"He feels so good in my ass," she said.

I watched her toned, elegant, young body take him. The image seemed so surreal. Here was the prettiest woman I'd ever laid eyes on, and yet she was doing the nastiest of things with a guy twice her age while his wife watched. You couldn't write it.

She slapped back against him and pulled forwards a little too far. Richard's cock sprang free and I found myself quickly drawn to it, like an eager ball-boy at Wimbledon who races in front of the net to retrieve errant shots.

I grabbed his dick in my fist and then put my mouth back over the head of his cock, sucking him as hard as I could and working my spit all over his shaft.

I'd never done something so sinful before, but Lily's infectious adventurism was having an effect on me.

She looked down and watched as I soaked him up again, pushing my head onto him before turning him back towards her asshole.

"Fuck her, honey," I snarled, pushing the hot tip of his dick back into her impossibly tight hole.

He pierced her again and she groaned with pained pleasure. I worked my pussy fast and felt it drool with desire as I watched, but I could tell from Richard's erratic pumps that he was close to climax.

"Where do you want his cum, Lily?" I asked, sitting up on the seat with her.

She moaned, fuck drunk. "In my ass."

I kissed her mouth and wound my tongue around hers, feeling impossibly close to her all of a sudden. We were allies in this sinful act and our goal was fast-approaching.

"Give it her, Richard," I said, looking back to him.

His face was a portrait of pleasure. Sweat had dappled his forehead and his expression was stern and determined. His lip curled as he plowed through her tight ring, jerking himself past the muscle over and over until he could stand no more.

I dropped back to my knees and watched as he built to a glorious crescendo. His hips slapped against her ass and his cock emerged faster and faster. Lily let out a long moan that came from her lips in stuttered breaths that Richard fucked out of her.

"Give it her, honey!" I cried, becoming excited by the inevitable conclusion.

He leaned his head back and let out a groan, then he stopped abruptly and looked down, his cock half way out of her

"Yes!" I cried, watching as the hard muscle pulsed strongly inside his length.

Lily let out a soothing moan, feeling the heat pour out of his cock and straight into her asshole.

"Fill me with it," she urged.

I rubbed over her stomach and tits as Richard erupted, groaning out each rope and letting it fall inside her.

When he was done he pulled his cock from her and I dropped to my knees submissively, putting my hair behind my shoulders and then attacking the slick-white residue that sat on his shaft.

I drove him into my mouth and tasted the bitterness of his cum, swashing my tongue from hilt to tip until there were no more traces of his climax. His cock bobbed with each beat, slowly dropping.

I turned now to Lily's asshole, looking almost as perfect as before. There sat a ring of cum around it that beckoned me forwards. My cheeks pressed inside hers and my tongue ventured out again, cleansing that perfect asshole of hers like I was some kind of slave to the both of them.

Lily stayed where she was, looking back and watching. My eyes met hers and I felt more sinful than ever. I looked deep into her soul and she caught the depravity in mine as I eagerly licked the cum from out of her crease.

I pulled back and Lily turned over onto her ass, sitting in the seat and looking down at her big tits as they sat on her chest.

She patted the seats beside her with a smile. My husband fell into one and I fell into the other, sandwiching out beauty between us.

She put her hand around Richard's spent cock and jerked him idly, then her hand came in between my legs and she slowly circled her finger on my clit.

I groaned against her, pushing my ass up off the seat and feeling the sexual tension become released in a hot flurry. She was so good with my clit that I started to come almost instantly.

I gripped her wrist, not wanting her to leave me. I sucked a breath in and held it, closing my eyes tight and shivering as the climax bubbled.

I exhaled and dropped back to the seat. Lily pushed two of her fingers inside me and my pussy gripped them, contracting on the intruders as an ooze of hot cum gradually slid over them.

"Good girl," Lily said, dragging her fingers out of me slowly.

She held them in front of her and both Richard and I watched as she scissored them open. My juices webbed between them. I shuddered excitedly.

She brought her fingers to my mouth and I wasted no time in wrapping my lips over them and cleansing her of my juices.

"You dirty bitch," she said, and I couldn't help but take it as a compliment.

I smirked and fell against her, lying against those big tits of hers. Opposite me Richard did the same and the three of us sat there in the back seat of her limo, in a strangely loving moment. It wasn't often that you experienced such kinship after tonguing your husband's cum from a stranger's asshole, but here we were.

I made sure the next time we rang the limo company that we asked for Lily.

THE END

Helping My Husband With The Hotel Maid : Couples Threesomes 4

My husband Bernard had surprised me with a vacation in the Caribbean that Summer, sparing no expense when it came to our accommodation.

He was a high-flying executive at a big insurance firm that you might have heard of. This was my belated birthday treat that I'd been promised, and it wound up being a real treat indeed.

Bernard and I had quite an unconventional relationship. On the surface we were husband and wife, just like anyone else, but when it came to the bedroom I think our tastes differed quite considerably from what you might deem 'normal.'

It's difficult for most people to comprehend, but I really get off on watching my husband enjoy himself, specifically with other women. It's an added bonus if they're younger than me, but Bernard is lucky. He has that confident, brooding, alpha-male kind of demeanor that seems to attract twenty-somethings like nothing else. Coupled with his success, he could basically have any woman he wants and I never want to deny him that.

Besides, there's nothing better than watching your husband get what he deserves. I've watched countless, tight pussies drop down over his gorgeous cock, and each and every one of them sent a shiver of jealous delight coursing through me.

I woke earlier than my husband that morning, somewhere around nine-thirty after a heavy night. I could see the light creeping in from outside and hoped that a bit of fresh-air might clear my mind before we ordered some room-service.

I looked over at Bernard whose eyes were closed peacefully. A couple of day's stubble sat on his face and with his bed-hair he looked mighty scrumptious indeed. But I didn't want to wake him just yet.

I slinked from under the duvet and out towards the black-out curtains, grabbing my robe and creeping through to carefully pull open the patio door that led out onto the veranda.

The day was already hot and the sun on my face felt warm and satisfying. I blinked at the light and sauntered out across the decking, looking out to sea at the various skiffs and sail-boats that adorned the vista. Palm trees dotted the coastline and fishermen brought in their early-morning catches.

I took a deep breath and pulled my gown tight around me, fastening it and leaning out over the railing that separated our villa from the private beach beyond. I could see several couples sunbathing and others braving an early-morning soak in the sea. It was peaceful out here.

I stayed and admired it all for a few minutes. It's not every day I got to wake up to something as good as thing and I was determined to bathe in it. Eventually I moved back inside to wake Bernard and enjoy the view with him.

I pushed open the curtains as I stepped back inside the room, then I startled as I realized we weren't alone.

At the foot of our bed stood one of the hotel's housekeepers, dressed in a sexy, tight shirt and cutesy shorts that showed off her smooth, caramel legs. When I saw her she was staring at the bed and she jumped at the sight of me, bursting into dialogue not long after.

"Room service," she hushed. "I knocked. Uh, there was no answer."

"That's quite alright," I whispered back, and I walked a few steps closer towards her, studying her face in the half-light of the room.

Her eyes shifted warily to Bernard and I looked back to the bed to see him sprawled out. The duvet had shifted, covering only half of his legs. Above that he lay completely naked, clearly enjoying a very nice dream indeed. His cock was stretched up towards his stomach, thick and inviting. His face stayed peaceful, unaware of the two voyeurs at the foot of the bed who drank in the view.

I looked back to our housekeeper. "A lovely view," I smiled.

She forced a smile and cast her eyes downwards. She must have been in her early-twenties and I'm guessing it wasn't the first time she'd seen something like this. I looked to her name-badge.

"Michelle," I read, and she looked up to me and smiled.

"At your service," she said softly.

"At *my* service?" I smirked, letting my imagination start to run away from me immediately. "Do you like what you see?"

"Ma'am?"

"My husband," I said, nodding to the bed. "Impressive, isn't he?"

Her gaze fluttered back to him before looking back down at the floor. "Quite."

"It's okay, you can look."

She brought her chin up slowly and I looked at that perfect face of hers and her nervous eyes.

"Go on," I urged, nodding to the bed.

Her eyes moved to the left and then so did her head until she was staring at the thick, engorged cock of my husband. He let out a deep breath and shifted his weight. His cock rolled over and settled to the left of his navel. His stomach was rippled with muscle and a smattering of hair covered his entire trunk.

"Looks good, doesn't it?" I said, standing beside her.

Michelle said nothing. As I got closer I could smell her sweet perfume. She was well manicured, as were the entire hotel's staff, but I wanted much more from her than housekeeping or room-service.

"Look at it," I said, standing beside her and whispering in her ear. "So thick and long. Imagine how it would feel inside you."

I moved her hair behind her ear and continued to whisper. "I can tell you it feels good. Would you like to try it?"

Michelle flinched and looked at me with a look of concern and horror.

"It's quite alright," I said. "I'd very much like you to try it. It's a little ... *kink* of mine."

Michelle swallowed hard and looked back at the door for her escape.

"Come on," I said, putting an arm around her. We walked a few steps to the bed. "Okay, I'll start."

Michelle stood at the foot of the bed and I mounted it carefully, crawling up to my husband and putting my face close to that exposed cock of his. I lifted it carefully, as though we were playing a game of buckaroo, looking to his face for a sign that he might wake soon.

I held him upright and bit my lip in Michelle's direction. Her gaze was rapt on his cock, flicking between it and my mouth and waiting for the two to meet. She took a deep breath and her tits lifted her tight shirt as she inhaled.

"Watch," I said, and then I wound my lips down over the smooth crown of his delicious cock.

He filled my mouth and I pressed down slowly, then I heard a sharp intake of breath from above and he shuffled on the mattress, moving my hair aside and looking down.

"We have a guest," I said, holding his cock close to my face.

He looked up over me and saw Michelle watching on. Unabashed, Bernard put his hands behind his head. "Hey," he said coolly, with a gruff morning croak.

Michelle lifted her hand and fluttered her fingers at him. She kept her place and watched, dining out on the view of my husband's cock disappearing back between my lips. He exhaled deeply and sank into the bed, pushing his hips up of it and driving himself into me.

Gradually he pumped up into me and I held my head in place, letting him fuck my mouth as Michelle watched on.

I took him from my lips now and beat him in my fist, looking to Michelle and raising my eyebrows.

"Come join us," I said.

She seemed to think briefly, then, without a word, she removed her white sneakers and put a knee on the bed.

"That's it," I urged.

"Well this certainly beats breakfast," Bernard said.

Michelle let out a nervous laugh, standing up on her knees and looking down at her target.

"Go ahead," I urged. "Come have a taste."

I pointed Bernard's cock in her direction like it was a Popsicle that we were about to share.

Michelle brushed a lock of her brown hair behind her ears and dropped slowly towards him. She was a strange mix of races that I couldn't quite place, but she seemed to have taken the best traits of each one. Her hips were slender but her ass was big and round; her tits were full and pert; her face was smooth and glowing; and her green eyes sparkled in the half-light of the room.

"Good girl," I encouraged as she dropped closer to him. I held Bernard upright as Michelle took her place on the bed.

She looked up at Bernard who gave a nod, then she moved her face over him and I watched as those plump lips of hers surrounded my husband's flesh and swallowed him up.

He groaned and closed his eyes as I jerked the hilt of him. Michelle pressed down as far as she could and I watched in awe as she almost took all of him inside her.

Her throat bulged and gripped him and Bernard rose up on the pillow, looking down himself in quiet adoration.

"It's in her throat," he said, and I felt my stomach tighten with jealous arousal.

"You're a deep-throater?" I asked, amazed.

Michelle pulled up off Bernard, revealing his inches quickly like the flourish of a magic trick. "One of my many skills," she smiled.

"Many skills, huh," I grinned. "I hope we get to see them."

I dropped with her this time and the both of us licked and gnawed on Bernard's cock that was thankfully big enough to share. He stared down his body, as casual as always, enjoying the view of his two beauties as they sought to make his morning.

"Luckiest guy in the hotel," he said, with a hand on each of our heads.

I smiled up at him and looked to Michelle as she went to work. She drank in his cock lovingly, caressing it with her slender, manicured nails.

My hand fell to her ass and I squeezed, jealous of the toned muscle that sat beneath her white shorts.

"I think I need a closer look at that," I said, moving behind her.

Michelle looked back to me and smiled, biting her lip as I reached beneath and unfastened her shorts. She showed no sign in stopping me from venturing further.

Bernard moved her hair aside and watched as she worked him through her lips and hand. She soaked up his pole magnificently but my target was somewhere else now.

With her shorts unfastened I pulled them back and squeaked with joyous arousal as I spied her toned ass. Her panties split it down the middle, arcing up to give two round, full, circles of flesh.

"Damn," I swooned, and without warning I flashed down a quick spank on Michelle's ass.

The clap bounced off the walls of our suite and the both of them jumped. Bernard started to chuckle soon after.

"She's a feisty one, Michelle," he said. "Make sure you watch her closely."

I leaned in to her ass and looked up over it into her eyes as she looked back cautiously. I bit her softly and then held her panties between my teeth, pulling them back and watching her expression turn to a sultry smile all over again.

I dragged her panties back until they were sliding down over her ample ass and I could see in between her cheeks.

The panties fell to her knees and I opened her ass wide with both hands, staring into the tight, little slit and the perfect dot of an asshole that sat above it.

"She looks good honey," I said, staring into that forbidden cocktail.

"Give her a taste," Bernard replied.

I did his bidding, though it was what I'd planned to do all along. I parted her cheeks and drove my face in to her, tonguing a kiss over the puffy lips of her tight pussy.

Michelle cooed appreciatively. She injected fresh vigor into her blowjob and Bernard was rewarded by proxy. The more I tongued at her pussy the more sloppily she toyed with his cock until soon she was beating her spit over it with her fist.

"Don't stop," Bernard urged, and I think he was talking to the both of us.

Each time I pressed my face between her cheeks my nose struck her knot and with no protestation I decided to explore further. I lapped my tongue out and teased underneath at her clit, then I ran it back up along her slit and over her honey-pot, settling finally at that puckered hole of hers.

My tongue tickled around the sensitive edge and Michelle looked back, her eyes wide with arousal and surprise.

"You like that?" I asked, spearing my tongue out and washing it over her again.

She closed her eyes and took a deep breath.

"She likes it when I lick her ass, honey," I said.

"Then keep doing it," he replied casually.

I ran my tongue into her again and pressed against the muscle, jostling it through the tight aperture and getting myself all worked up in the process.

I pulled the belt of my gown apart and sent a hand down to my crotch, pushing over my panties and feeling the heat of arousal rising beneath.

"Oh, fuck! Her pussy looks so good, Bernard."

"Let me see," he said, and he began to move from under her.

Michelle stayed on all-fours, with the top half of her looking prim and proper, whilst her bottom half looked slutty and alluring.

"Look at that," I said, opening her up wide for Bernard and he came behind her and stared forwards eagerly.

"You weren't lying," he said, and I watched him dart to where my face had just been and lick at her out of sight.

She let out a breath again and closed her eyes, moaning as my husband's tongue went to work over her. I watched him and felt my pulse rising, sending the adrenaline through my veins like it was a drug.

I moved away and opened my gown wider, standing beside the bed and looking down as my fingers rubbed at my pussy.

Michelle turned her head to the right to watch me. She stared at my fingers as they worked busily beneath my panties. It was hot to have her watch. I moved my gown back off my shoulders and let it drop to the floor, revealing my mature, womanly body to her.

Her pupils fattened as she saw me and she reached her lips forward as though she wanted me too. Behind her Bernard was pushing his face into her ass and jerking his cock in the process.

"Fuck her, honey," I urged, unfastening my bra. "Let me see you inside her."

Michelle looked back as Bernard moved his face off her and knelt behind, spitting on his fingers and massaging them over the swollen head of his cock.

He jerked his flesh and then took aim. I unfastened my bra and moved behind the pair of them to get a good vantage, watching close as his bulbous crown pressed against her flesh.

Michelle's mouth opened to moan but nothing escaped her yet. I watched Bernard's meaty cock drive its way in and her pussy gripped him close, absorbing him like a welcome guest.

"Oh, fuck, that's it," I cried, pushing my fingers against my pussy impatiently.

I watched for a moment as my husband drove his inches into her pink-chocolate flesh, then Michelle finally let a gasp escape her, followed quickly by several more as she breathed out her release.

Bernard sank all the way and then put his arms around her, kissing her neck as he started to unbutton her shirt.

Michelle was breathing deep, clearly struggling to accommodate him comfortably. I knew exactly how she felt. Bernard was a big guy alright, but I had faith in Michelle. Bernard opened her shirt and straightened back up, holding her ass and pulling out gradually.

I moved around the side of the bed and stood at the head of it, just next to the bedside table. Michelle's eyes were closed as I slid my panties down, but she opened them to the sound of me mounting the mattress.

I sat beside her against the headboard, looking into her face and studying the pleasure as it started to overcome the pain of Bernard stretching her.

I opened my legs wide and put one beneath her, then I moved my fingers to my pussy and teased gently over my flesh, making a big deal of enjoying myself as I watched the pair of them.

Both of their eyes focused on me as I played and there was something intoxicating about having the pair of them watch me. I felt like the kinkiest, naughtiest exhibitionist in the world, but there was something voyeuristic to be had from it all too. Bernard and Michelle were putting on a show for me and I wasn't about to ignore it.

I watched the ecstasy etch its way across both of their faces as they enjoyed each other. Michelle was much tighter than me and I could see that in the look on Bernard's face as he drove himself into her. It looked like he couldn't believe his luck.

Bernard kept his pace and Michelle shook beneath him, her open shirt wafting invitingly until I could take it no more.

"Get on your back Bernard," I said before addressing Michelle. "I want you to ride him."

Bernard pulled back slowly with a grunt, looking down as his cock reappeared, glossed in a film of Michelle's cum.

He rolled over to the left of her, using every inch of the king bed. Michelle rose up on her knees and I arrived behind her, pressing my body against her and kissing her neck.

"We don't need this anymore," I said, pulling back her shirt and tossing it to the side of the bed.

I kissed her again and brought my hands up to cup her bra, squeezing against her tits and gnawing on her neck.

I unclasped her as Bernard got into position and he watched her shapely breasts fall out from the bra. As she shuffled over the bed towards him they shook on her chest, looking magnificent and drawing the eye.

"Wait," I called suddenly.

Michelle stopped in her tracks and I pounced towards Bernard.

"Let me clean him up a little," I said, lying between his legs and grabbing his cock.

I could see her juices coating his length. They were creamy and pearlescent, forming a ring around the hilt of him where he'd pushed forwards as far as he could.

I winked up at Bernard as I wound my mouth over him and the pair of them watched me cleanse him of her love. I looked to the both of them as I drew my lips tight around him and popped them off the crown.

"Much better," I said, tasting her sweetness on my tongue.

Michelle came into position and kicked a leg over Bernard, straddling him and looking down into his face.

My husband stared up, torn between watching her pretty, brown face or her inviting tits with their dark nipples.

Before she planted herself on him Bernard pulled her forward, opening his mouth over the teat of her breast and sucking it until it stiffened.

He bit and teased as Michelle moaned and I got in position behind, keen to see the moment when he breached her flesh again.

I took his cock and worked him in my fist, keeping him busy while he had his fill of her. When he was done Michelle squared up and dropped slowly, giving me time to line up my husband's cock with its target.

I watched open-mouthed as her flesh swallowed him again, hugging him tighter than I ever could. The three of us exhaled in exalted pleasure together.

I let go of my husband and Michelle began to bounce, slowly beginning to show a side of herself to us that was intimate and private. She rode him by gyrating her hips and I watched her big ass flex and bounce as she did so. She was a master of cock and no mistake.

Bernard beckoned her towards him with a finger and my eyes spread wide as they kissed with him inside her. My husband pumped up slowly and held her close, keeping her still as he fed his inches into her lovingly.

The smacking of their lips was getting me hot and bothered and I sent a hand down to coax the juices from my sex. I twisted on my stiffening clit but the view of Michelle's vacant asshole was drawing me in.

I prowled over to the pair of them and rubbed gently at her ass to announce my arrival. My hands went down the crease of her ass and stroked over her asshole, then I massaged my husband's cock before it disappeared again out of sight between her pink slit.

My face dropped on her and I drove a tongue into her butt, teasing the puckered knot all over again and listening to her heady cries of joy.

"Oh, yes!" she purred, thrashing her hair over my husband's face. "She's licking my ass. Fuck!"

"Naughty girl," Bernard said wryly, pushing his cock back up into his new mistress.

I pulled back and stared at her wet ass. The next action seemed only right. I moved my finger towards it and drove it inside, feeling her warmth at first, and then the monolith of my husband's cock sliding against the divide between us.

"Can you feel me?" I asked, looking to Bernard. I tickled back along his cock, pressing against him inside her asshole.

His eyes sparkled and he nodded. "Yes."

I bit my lip and pressed another finger into her, stretching her naughty muscle over my fingers in the same manner that she'd hugged Bernard's cock.

Her asshole squeezed me tight and seemed reluctant to house its new visitor, but Michelle's heady moans told me in no uncertain terms that I was to continue.

Bernard started to fuck her faster and I plowed my fingers into her hot ass, pulling out every so often to stab my tongue into the weakening hole.

Before long Michelle was getting fucked in both holes, with my husband and I working in unison. He'd stab forwards and I'd pull out a little to make way. When he withdrew I'd thrust my fingers deep and press down onto her pussy.

The excitement must have been too much for Michelle. Her breath quickly began to race away from her and soon she was beating the bed with a fist, pushing back onto my fingers and holding her breath to concentrate on the intriguing sensations.

Finally she let out a long, gasping breath and I felt her come on me. Her asshole winked over and over and I watched her pussy swell and bulge over Bernard's cock as the climax flourished.

In the frantic gyrating my husband's cock fell out of her and it was just my fingers left inside her. I watched her pussy gasp and then saw a deliciously creamy string of her cum ooze out of her, expelled with a deep grunt of satisfaction.

"Good girl," Bernard said, looking to her and then me. He raised his eyebrows and shook his head in disbelief.

I pulled my fingers from her big ass and watched as she turned over to lie beside Bernard. Her face was flush with a reddish hue, clearly flustered from her efforts. Her tits heaved up and down on her chest as she took several calming breaths.

Michelle was giggling now, as though she couldn't believe she'd shown us this side to her.

"Sorry," she said, covering her mouth with her hand.

"Don't apologize," I said quickly.

I stalked towards her again and Bernard watched. I worked my way up her body and her expression changed again to one of fearful arousal.

I approached as gently as I could, leaning my lips towards hers until my intentions were clear. Michelle bridged the final few inches and we kissed, long and deep. Her tongue tasted sweet on mine and I fell against her, rubbing my pussy on her leg and squeezing at her big tits.

I felt Bernard move and opened my eyes to see him knelt over the both of us. His fist gripped his cock tight so that the veins bulged along its length, then slowly he started to jerk himself above us.

"Where do you want it?" he asked.

I looked to Michelle. "Any ideas?"

She bit her lip, seeming reluctant to answer.

"Go on," I pushed. "Wherever you want."

"I kinda ..." she pursed her lips and started again. "I kinda want him to cum all over your face."

My mouth hung agape at the suggestion. "You do?"

Michelle nodded, fast and excited.

I looked up at Bernard and gave the order. "Cover me in it."

"Can I do it?" Michelle asked.

Bernard let go of his cock and Michelle moved from under me. I lay back on the pillow as my husband moved himself to the top of the bed and Michelle put herself next to him.

I sprawled out and took a deep breath, looking up as she gripped around his thick flesh and started to pump him through her fist.

"That's it," she purred, looking down and smiling as I got myself ready.

"Give it me," I begged now. "Give me your fucking cum, honey. Pump it out for me, Michelle."

She smiled a dirty smile and upped her pace, looking at my husband's cock as her hand squeezed it tight and rifled back and forth along it.

Bernard put a hand on his hip and cast his head back to the ceiling to let out a groan and when he looked back down at the source of his pleasure he seemed ready.

"Good girl, Michelle," I encouraged, opening my mouth ready for the ensuing torrent.

She beat him fast and Bernard started to suck in breaths and moan them back out. It was so hot to hear his imminent pleasure that I started to tickle my pussy all over again.

"Oh, fuck!" he strained now, looking down at his cock attentively. He opened his mouth in silence at first and then another moan broke from his lips.

Michelle's eyes widened as she felt his cock swell and stiffen, then it pulsed and fired a quick, hot rope across my face that caused me to jump.

I gasped and giggled, letting it fall across my open mouth, then another lashing escaped him before I was ready and landed again on my face.

Michelle continued to beat him and the pair of them looked at his cock as the cum spiraled messily from the tip, jerked free by our eager housekeeper.

"Every drop!" I moaned now, rubbing my fingers around my mouth and pushing his seed inside me.

He tasted bitter and sweet on my tongue but there was more to come. Michelle's fist worked him and he pulsed over and over, firing many more ropes over my face until I was an utter mess of his love.

When he'd finished I blinked warily upwards, then opened my eyes to see the pair of them looking down, amazed.

"Fuck," Michelle gasped.

I laughed and so did Bernard, but then Michelle dropped down on me and started to kiss me. It was gentle at first, her tongue teasing out from her lips to taste my husband's cum, but then she started to open her mouth over him.

"That's it," Bernard said, taking it all in his stride. "Feed it back to her."

Her lips found mine and we kissed. With my husband's cum between our lips the whole thing was ten times more erotic than before. His velvet love helped our tongues glide over each other and soon Michelle's mouth was awash with him too.

Bernard brought his waning cock between us one last time and we licked and sucked him dry, then he fell beside us on the bed in a lump, spent from his effort.

Michelle and I continued to kiss for the moment, sharing each other's bodies one last time before the whole thing drew to a close.

She lay with us for a while, stroking my skin softly while I toyed with her hair, but then she jumped up in a flash and looked at her thick sports-watch.

"Shit!"

Bernard startled. "Huh?!"

"I've gotta go," she said, hopping up and stepping back into her shorts.

"Your panties?" I said after her as she threw her shirt on.

"Keep them. And my bra," she laughed. "I'll be back for them."

Bernard hummed at the thought. "Make sure you are," he said.

"And if they ask, I cleaned your room, okay?"

I blew her a kiss and she smiled shyly.

"Bye lovely," I called after her.

The door closed and I looked over to Bernard who was staring with a big grin on his face.

"Enjoy yourself?" I asked.

"I think you know the answer."

I pushed some more of his cum into my mouth and popped my lips off my finger. "I'm gonna take a shower."

"I'll be in soon."

I walked naked to the bathroom and stared at the debauched, cum-drenched reflection that looked back. I couldn't believe myself sometimes, but moments like this really brought out who I was deep inside. I was a naughty slut and it made no sense to hide it. I hoped Michelle would stick around for a while when she returned so we could enjoy each other again.

THE END

A Salsa Dancer Fucked My Husband While I Watched : Couples Threesomes 5

With us both in our forties we had decided to try something new. My husband Peter and I had been taking Salsa lessons for several months now and whenever we did I found myself impossibly infatuated by our instructor, Sasha.

She was from South-America and had wild black hair and tanned, olive skin that she tried her best never to cover. Her outfits were always revealing and she commanded a presence over the group of inexperienced dancers that made everyone intimidated, despite her youthful appearance.

Peter and I had been coming along great, having advanced through the early stages to a point where we looked almost competent. It'd pass for a sporadic dance in a bar, but we'd probably get found out among other Salsa dancers. As such there was still some fine-tuning to perform and Sasha was more than keen on working out the kinks.

That day she pulled us aside while the rest of the room was running through the latest steps.

"Give him to me, Ellen" she said, holding out a hand for Peter.

"He's all yours," I said, putting his hand in hers.

Peter gave me a quick look of wide-eyed worry as she led him a couple of feet away.

"You have to hold your woman," she said, moving with him. "Like this."

Sasha placed his hand on her ass and pulled him in to her.

"Groins on thighs," she said. "What do I always say?"

Peter cleared his throat. "Groins on thighs."

I giggled as he looked over at me, still panicked. "Don't mind me," I laughed, waving a hand.

"Exactly," Sasha said. "When you dance with a partner it is just you and them in the room. No-one else. So dance like it."

She tugged him tighter and moved faster, flailing around Peter like she was a bird doing a mating ritual. The whole thing was a sight to behold.

Finally she spun her way towards me and placed his hand back in mine.

"Now: *Dance*," she said.

She moved back through the room and I watched her click away in her high-heels, touching each couple and fixing their posture.

Peter turned to me and looked me dead in the eye. "*Dance*," he said, mocking her thick accent.

He pulled me towards him and continued. At first he took the whole thing for a joke but I could notice a difference in him immediately. Our groins rested on each other's thighs and I started to feel the passion in Peter that Sasha had often talked about.

"Is that ... are you ...?" I asked, feeling a stiffness in Peter's tight pants.

He seemed slightly awkward. "Hey, I just love salsa."

"Salsa or Sasha?" I asked with a wry smile.

Peter pursed his lips and continued dancing, looking across the room so as to avoid eye-contact.

"It's okay, you know," I said, turning his chin back to me. "She has a habit of turning everyone on. Even me."

Peter looked back to me quickly now and I shrugged.

"She's hot," I said. "We should invite her over to dinner."

"Not this again," he sighed.

"What?"

"You keep insisting that we invite women over. I'm starting to think you don't like me."

"You know it's not that," I said, still doing my steps around him. "I like you so much that I want to see you enjoy yourself."

He took a deep breath and shook his head.

"Lessons then," I offered. "We'll invite her over to give us some private lessons."

"Will that make you happy?"

"It'd make me ecstatic," I beamed.

We danced out the final twenty minutes and when the class was over I made my way across the room to Sasha who was busy packing up her bag.

"Yes?" she said, turning to me as I approached.

"I was wondering if we could get a private lesson, Peter and I?" I motioned back to him as he walked over.

"Two-hundred for an hour," she replied, barely stopping to think.

"Honey, I'm not sure—" Peter began.

"Deal," I said, before Peter could scupper my plans.

I told Sasha where we lived whilst ignoring the piercing stare of Peter as he burned it into the side of my face. After we'd left he told me what was on his mind.

"What the hell are you thinking?"

"I'm thinking that two-hundred an hour is cheap."

"Cheap?! That's the most expensive lesson of anything I've ever heard of."

"Don't worry," I said. "I'll get our money's worth."

I left Peter to stew on the comment for a few days until it was time for our appointment with Sasha. Right on cue she rang the bell of our little suburban paradise a little before seven in the evening.

"Come on," I motioned to Peter and we answered the door together.

"Sasha!" we both beamed, smiling as warmly as we could. She was wearing a tight pair of pants and a fancy, pink dress-shirt.

"Let's get to it," she said, walking through the pair of us and into the hall. "Where do you want to do it?"

I pointed across to the doorway. "In the lounge is good."

Sasha moved in there with her bag and I gave another smile to Peter, rubbing his arm. "Don't' worry, honey."

We followed her tight ass and watched as she sat her bag down on the seat and turned to the middle of the room.

"This coffee table ..."

"Peter," I said. "Move the table, would you, honey?"

He got to it whilst Sasha pulled a CD out of her bag. "Do you have a player?"

"You didn't bring your own?" Peter said.

"We have one," I said, ignoring him. "One second."

I dashed from the room to grab a CD-player from the kitchen and returned to see Peter watching as Sasha began a routine of stretches.

"It's important to stay limber," she said, sliding her hands down her legs and looking back at us from in-between them. "Stretch."

Peter and I started mimicking her routine, trying—and failing—not to feel awkward in the process. After around five minutes it looked as though she was ready to begin.

She pressed play on the machine and beckoned Peter forwards with a finger.

She pointed at me. "You. Watch." She pointed at Peter. "You. Dance."

Peter shook his head and I knew exactly what he was thinking: *$200 for that?!*

The music started to get upbeat and the pair of them began dancing with Peter holding his own. It was hot to see how far he'd come since we started lessons, and it was twice as hot to see a fine lady on his arm while he enjoyed himself.

He started to get into it and looked over to smile. Sasha turned his head back to her. "On me," she said.

I leaned forward on the chair as the dance became more intimate. She was flailing around him wildly. Every so often they'd break apart and when they came back together things seemed twice as raunchy as before.

I watched Peter and my eyes began to widen as I realized how it was all affecting him. Beneath his tight pants I could see the bulge of his aroused cock, but Sasha didn't seem to care. If anything, she targeted it more.

She grinded along his thigh and pressed hers along his thickness, staring into his eyes with a piercing, seductive gaze that was even having an effect on me.

I bit my lip and swallowed, staring at the pair of them as they became increasingly intimate. My pussy dampened at the thought of her conquering my man. I wanted nothing more than to see Peter enjoy himself and it looked like he was starting to.

He never glanced back at me once. Instead he was fixated by his seductress as the quick music played.

My hand moved between my legs, pushing along the crotch of my tight, white jeans as I looked on. To Sasha I'm sure it was all part of the dance, but to Peter and I it just felt too sexual to ignore.

The music started to wind down and tail off. I narrowed my eyes and continued to tease my pussy, looking at Sasha as she stared deep into my husband's gaze.

"He's very excitable," she said, then she looked over at me. "And he's not the only one."

I smirked and bit my lip as I looked over at her. "That was hot."

"You like it when I dance with your husband?" Sasha said, seeming unfazed.

"I love it," I admitted. "I'd love to see you do other things with him."

Sasha turned to Peter who was quiet for now. It's always better for a woman to negotiate a threesome. The guys just come across as so ... perverse.

"Other things?" Sasha said, bobbing her eyebrows. "Like what."

"Oh, I don't know," I said, standing up and walking over to Peter. "Maybe put this in your mouth?"

Sasha followed my hand as it gripped his hard packet.

"You'd like that, wouldn't you?"

"I'd love it," I said. "And I think Peter here wouldn't mind."

"Do you mind, Peter?" Sasha said, dropping slowly to her knees in front of him but keeping eye-contact. "Do you mind if I eat your cock?"

I gushed excitedly and tried to hide it. Sasha wasn't playing around either. Maybe our motives were obvious from the start.

"I don't mind at all," Peter said.

"Open him for me," Sasha said.

I tugged at his belt and looked in his face as I opened his pants excitedly. Peter was staring down and I could see the anticipation in his eyes as the fiery instructor sat in wait.

"Let's get him out for you," I teased, dropping my hands into his pants.

I gripped that thick shaft of his and tugged him up proudly, pulling him over the waist of his boxer-shorts and offering him up to Sasha for inspection.

She gasped. "Wow. You are a very lucky woman."

"And Peter here is a very lucky man," I smirked.

I tugged his pants down to his knees and pulled the skin back over his cock. Sasha shuffled and tossed her hair behind her shoulders, locking her eyes on the forbidden target.

"Give him to me," she said, opening her mouth and tilting her head back.

I walked Peter forwards and aimed him toward her full, open lips. I felt a tingle of excitement inside myself that was tinged with a strange kind of jealousy. Sasha was younger, fitter, and sexier with a much bigger set of tits. I'd have given anything to be her.

Peter took another step and exhaled as the tip of his cock drove into her patient mouth. She hummed and pushed her head forwards, sliding over several inches of his shaft before winding herself back off him.

I stood at his side, looking down his body as she went to work on him. Her eager eyes would flit between me and Peter. Eventually she moved a hand and placed it on the inside of my thigh, scratching her nails along the white denim.

She pulled off his cock and slurped. "I want both."

My eyes widened as I looked down on her. "Me too?"

"Yes."

I looked to Peter and he looked at me.

"You heard the lady," he said.

Sasha shuffled closer to me. "Take off her jeans, Peter."

I was beside myself. I'd never been with a woman before and losing my lesbian wings to someone as vivacious as Sasha was getting me impossibly excited.

Peter popped open the button of my jeans and pushed them down over my thighs slowly. I wriggled my ass out of them and watched as he bent to my knees and took off my shoes. Sasha moved beside him and kissed at his face as he pulled the legs off my ankles and I stood in only my panties before her now.

"Those too," she said, leaning back on her heels and biting her lip.

He tugged the waist of my panties down and I felt the stickiness of my crotch pull against the fabric. I was almost embarrassed by how wet I was, but when Sasha saw it she seemed impossibly excited.

"My God," she gasped. "You are wet. So wet!"

She hurried forward for a closer inspection and I put one knee across the other.

"Now is no time to be coy," she said, looking up at me. It felt like being scalded in class.

I moved my legs apart and her hand came up the inside of them. She gripped the top of my leg and thumbed gently at my crease, putting her face close enough to smell my scent.

"And you are a lucky man, Peter," she said, and then without another word she opened her mouth and planted it right over my folds.

My mouth dropped open in a silent moan and I closed my eyes, holding her head against me. Her tongue tickled along the groove and I let out a whimper that became a moan. I dropped my head with a look of bewilderment and noticed that Sasha's hand had found Peter's cock too.

He looked at her hand as it briskly stroked up and down his pole. He was leant back on his palm and had started to take off his shirt. Sasha's busy arm had made him lose his focus.

I couldn't believe how masterfully she satisfied the both of us. Her tongue worked busily out of sight and she used her in-built sense of rhythm to pleasure Peter and me together at once.

After a moment she pulled her face off me and looked up into my eyes. "Take your top off," she said.

I unbuttoned my dress-shirt quickly, keen not to disappoint the lady. Despite her being almost twenty years my junior she had a way about her that belied her years.

"Good," she said, and I felt a swell of pride.

I hurriedly tugged it back off my shoulders and she planted herself back on me. I took a moment to pause, closing my eyes and filling my lungs with air. My scalp began to tingle as I breathed quicker. Watching her jerk my husband fiercely was doing nothing to calm me down.

I tossed my shirt back and then unclasped my bra. Sasha pulled her face off me and wiped a hand at her wet maw. She lay back beside Peter and jerked him close to her, looking over the top of his cock and waiting to see my tits. I removed my bra as both of them watched.

"Perfect," Sasha said, and she raced her lips on Peter's dick, keeping her focus on me.

He groaned and I pushed my tits together for our new mistress, licking my finger and toying it around my nipples.

"Come and lay with us," Sasha said.

I dropped to the carpet and unbuttoned the rest of Peter's shirt. He took it back off his arms and tossed it aside, then he held Sasha's head against him as she slid his slick pole back and forth through her lips.

I started to kiss him and then I felt Sasha's hand between my legs. She curled a finger inside me and covered it in my juices, driving against my spongy g-spot as she slurped along my husband's cock.

Every so often I'd blink at the scene before me. We'd known Sasha for months but had no idea she was this naughty. In South-America it seemed they did things a lot differently and Peter and I were struggling to cope with the freedom at which she moved between the pair of us. 'Sexually fluid' was an understatement.

I leaned over and started to kiss Peter as Sasha jerked him. She leaned her other arm over his torso to finger me. Feeling her digits pulse back and forth inside me was intoxicating and each time she thrust upwards I whimpered on Peter, grunting and biting at his lip. If anyone was going to benefit from my sudden increased libido it was him.

"Put him inside me, Ellen," she ordered now, and I opened my eyes to see her standing up. She took off her tight pants without ceremony, showing us her toned, smooth legs that stretched all the way up to that perfect ass of hers.

She faced away from us and turned to the mirror above the fireplace, pulling her thin turtle-neck up over her head to reveal her unbound, naked tits. She ruffled her hair and then turned back to us, looking fucking perfect.

She motioned to me. "Take this off for me."

I left Peter on the floor and walked towards her. When I was close she put her arms around me and gripped my ass, pulling me towards her and leaning her naked body against mine. Our tits pressed together and I felt her stiff nipples on mine. I gasped in faux-shock, looking down my nose at her lips as she moved them close to mine.

"You're a naughty girl, Ellen," she smiled.

I bit my lip and pushed a finger down inside her pants.

"But I think I'm naughtier," she said.

With that she placed her lips on mine and quickly I found myself in the throes of a passionate kiss—the first lesbian kiss of my life. Her tongue felt so smooth and delicate, but equally forceful and commanding. It was a rush like no other.

As we kissed I pushed her panties down and she gripped my hand, putting it between her legs in case I was too timid to do it myself.

I could feel her kempt hair on my wrist as I danced my fingers along her sensitive petals, sliding open her tight pussy that felt as well put-together as the rest of her.

Peter watched from the floor, pleasing himself as he got front-row tickets to my first-time experience.

Finally I broke from the embrace and looked back at him. Sasha's panties fell down her legs to the floor and she stepped out of them, revealing a perfect strip of black hair that lead down to her cutesy pussy.

"You okay there, honey?" I asked, raising my eyebrows at Peter.

"Never better," he said.

Sasha turned to him and waltzed over on tip-toes, her tits bouncing invitingly the entire way. She straddled his torso and looked down on him.

Peter stared up, shaking his head in disbelief at the goddess that towered over him. Her dark-nipples were taut with excitement and her sex was moist with desire.

"Ellen," she said, and she curled a finger in my direction.

I stepped into action as though my superior was about to scald me at work.

"Put him inside me," she ordered.

She locked her eyes on Peter and started to drop her body, bending her knees over him. I gripped his cock and stood it upright, working back and forth and looking to his face to watch the joy etch over him.

His pupils were fat with lust and he kept his eyes fixed on his temptress until the last moment. She sank down and I watched as her perfect pussy pushed over the head of his thick cock.

I looked to Peter again and saw him staring down at the source of his pleasure. Her pussy crept down over him, wrapping him in sinful warmth and slicking up his entire pole as she continued her descent.

Eventually she sat on his waist with his cock buried to the hilt inside her and placed her hands on his stomach, bunching her big tits between her arms.

"I want your cum," she said plainly, looking down into his eyes.

My mouth opened in shock that turned into a grin. I dropped to the floor and put my face close to Peter's.

"You heard her," I said. "Give it her." I kissed his cheek and bit at his ear as she started to rise up off him. "Give her your fucking cum, honey."

Peter moaned and closed his eyes. I kissed down off his face and over his hairy chest, moving down his torso until I was staring down at his cock. Sasha would rise up and I'd see his slick pole briefly, then she'd rock her ass back down on him and swallow him up all over again.

Without too much thought I flung my leg over Peter so that I was facing her. I felt his hands arrive on my ass and he squeezed it, sucking his breath through gritted teeth.

"Sit on my face," he said.

Sasha raised her eyebrows at me and gave a nod. "You'd better do it."

I turned my chin into my shoulder coyly and wriggled backwards to meet Peter's eager mouth. When I was within range I dropped my pussy on him and felt his stubble against the inside of my thighs.

His tongue darted along my groove and I let out a soothing breath, opening my eyes to Sasha's smile as she continued to bounce on my husband's dick.

"Is he good?" she asked.

"You tell me," I said wryly.

Sasha smiled and then leaned forwards. I did too and wet met above Peter, kissing passionately as my husband serviced the pair of us from below.

The motion of Sasha's tongue in my mouth and my husband's tongue along my pussy was too much to bear. Before long I was racing in breaths and holding them and I could no longer concentrate on kissing Sasha. She didn't mind. Instead she kissed me with wet pecks on my cheek and face, licking along me like an animal and pushing her fingers through my hair and against my scalp.

I could feel the climax blossoming inside me, arriving like a freight train that was fighting to be released from within me.

Each movement of Peter's tongue felt huge and I became so sensitive that the littlest of strokes would send me over the edge.

Peter could hear me panting above him. He slapped his hands against my ass and I shrieked from the quick flash of pain. It seemed like a catalyst, because quickly afterwards the orgasm crashed out of me and I writhed back against him.

My pussy pulsed on his mouth, opening and closing wildly as the muscles contracted and relaxed. Each wave felt huge and my head became light and airy. I looked through my weary, fuck-drunk eye-lids at Sasha who was smiling back as pleased as punch.

She bounced harder on Peter now, getting up on her feet so she could jerk her pussy over his entire length. As I came to from the climax I witnessed her prowess. Peter didn't know what to do with himself.

I crept off his face and turned back to see him staring down. Sasha was looking into his eyes like an animal, mounted over him and sliding herself down him again and again.

"Give me your cum," she demanded again, staring forward at him. "Let it all out inside me."

"You heard her baby," I said, breathing heavy. I wiped at his mouth and kissed my juices off him. "Give her your fucking cum," I hushed.

She worked over him at such a speed that I knew Peter couldn't deny her much longer, even if he wanted to. I watched him tense up as his moans rang skyward, becoming louder and longer with each of her descents.

Sasha looked at me and raised her eyebrows. "He's ready."

"Come," I told him. "Come inside her, honey."

Sasha continued to goad him too. "Give it me," she said, and her voice had a sense of urgency. "Give me that fucking load."

It was so hot to hear her accent beg for my husband's cum, but it was even hotter when he eventually gave it to her.

"Give me that fucking—ohh, fuck," she gasped and I noticed a change in the pair of them as Peter's cries became longer. "That's it."

I watched Peter's body undulate as Sasha hovered over him. His cock throbbed and I knew that with each movement it was throwing rope after rope of his hot love inside her.

"Fuck," Sasha groaned, sinking down on him. "That's it. Every drop."

Peter poured out inside her, moaning out each spurt as though it was a great effort. Truthfully I think it had been more than easy to give Sasha exactly what she wanted.

"Yes! Yes! Yes!" she cried, dropping on him again and I again.

I looked to his cock now, all lacquered up with pearlescent cum that rolled down his shaft briefly before being claimed by her hungry pussy for the second time.

"Good boy," she said, staring down with adoration before looking to me. "And good girl."

She put a hand on my cheek and I crept towards her, kissing her as my husband's spent cock settled inside her.

Slowly she pulled herself up off him and several drops of his cum fell back against his body. She raced to his side and then dropped her mouth on his cock, sucking his cum off before taking a grip of it and offering it me.

"Help me clean him."

I didn't need a second invitation. My mouth wound around his cock and I sampled that familiar taste of his cum. He was bitter but amongst it I could taste the sweetness of Sasha's juices, mingling perfectly in a deliciously sinful cocktail.

The pair of us sucked and slurped at Peter's errant spunk until there was nothing left except for the stuff that was deep in her pussy.

Sasha let out a hum of appreciation and fell heavy beside Peter who quickly put his arm under and around her. I mirrored her opposite him and we both lay in his arms for a moment as he breathed heavily between us.

"That was incredible," he said, laughing in disbelief afterwards.

I kissed his cheek and Sasha did the same beside him.

"Don't worry about the payment," she said. "So long as we can do this again."

Peter glanced to me and gave me a private look of excitement, as though we were getting much more out of the deal than Sasha was.

"Are you sure?" he said, but I could tell from his tone he wasn't about to pass it up.

"I'm positive," Sasha said, leaning her head on his big chest and letting out a satisfied sigh.

We lay there for the rest of the session in a kind of post-coital, unspoken bliss. The three of us had gotten exactly what we wanted and there was nothing left to do but enjoy each other in silence. Sasha had a strange way of making a person feel comfortable. I couldn't wait to explore her some more.

THE END

The Nurse Took Care Of My Husband : Couples Threesomes 6

I can remember exactly where I was when I received the news that my husband Kurt had been involved in a car accident. I was just on my way out of the salon after my weekly hair appointment when my cell rang. It was a number I didn't recognize and when I answered the voice sounded very solemn and direct.

They didn't let me see him at first. He'd gone straight into surgery and I was advised that he was in a stable condition and I could visit him in several days. Apparently this was all part of his private health-insurance package, but I was desperate to see that he was okay with my own eyes.

When I finally got word that I was permitted to see him I raced to the hospital right then and there. At the desk I asked to be directed to his room and I practically sprinted down the corridor, pushing straight into his room.

I largely ignored the person in the corner as my eyes flashed straight to Kurt. He was sat up in bed and he beamed a warm smile over at me as I ran towards him with a hand over my mouth, trying not to start bawling.

"You look so *good*," I said honestly. I'd half expected to see a black and blue, bashed up man I didn't recognize staring back.

"They did a great job," Kurt said, opening his arm up so I could lay myself over him.

I held his face and kissed him over and over, staring down into his eyes with a love I'd never felt before.

"What do they say? What's the prognosis? When are you out?" I asked hurriedly.

"Chelsea?" Kurt said, and he looked over my shoulder to the corner of the room.

It was only then that I noticed the skimpily dressed bombshell, stood at the side of a brushed-steel table and carefully placing a selection of pills into a small cup.

"Only a couple more days, honey," she said, smiling

I blinked over in her direction and then looked back to Kurt.

"Who the hell is that?"

"Chelsea," he said. "My nurse."

I stood up and walked over to her, narrowing my eyes curiously.

"You're ... my husband's *nurse?*"

"Pleasure to meet you, Mrs. Junger."

"Kelly," I said. "Call me Kelly."

"Pleasure to meet you, Kelly."

"What are you doing here?"

"I'm a nurse," she restated. "I'm helping your husband with his rehabilitation."

"You don't look much like a nurse?"

"The outfit?" she asked, looking down at her bunched up tits that sat between the open buttons of a pure white top that hugged her close and flowed down over her curves. A short skirt sat below it, barely covering her ass. The high-heels really seemed against protocol.

"And the make-up," I said. She was dressed up like a stripper.

"It's all part of Mr. Junger's health-insurance package," she said, and she walked over to his bed and carefully placed the cup on the moveable table that sat over his body. She gave him a glass of water and carefully held his face, smiling down onto him. Kurt smiled back.

"What the hell is going on here?" I asked, putting a hand on my hip.

"We do things a little differently here at Comfort Medical," Chelsea said.

"More than a little differently," I said. I set my bag down and sat on a chair away from the bed.

"Your husband is one of our platinum members and as such he receives only the most attentive of care."

"Attentive?"

"Yes," Chelsea said, looking back to Kurt and holding his face. "Mr. Junger gets whatever he needs."

He smiled back at her and there was clearly something between them that I wasn't privy to.

"And exactly what has he been needing?" I asked.

"Well," Chelsea began, "part of the package involves a comprehensive after-care treatment. We want to make sure your husband still has all of his ... faculties."

I furrowed my brow. "Faculties?"

"Yes," she said, putting a hand on Kurt's chest as he swallowed down his meds. "We need to make sure everything is in working order, if you take my meaning, Kelly."

"I'm not quite sure I do take your meaning," I said, standing again. "Exactly what have you been doing?"

"Honey, relax," Kurt said, sitting up. Chelsea moved his pillow behind him and stood by his side. She moved the table back from over him.

"I'll relax when you tell me what the hell's been going on here. I've been worried sick."

"I understand," Chelsea said. "But here at Comfort Medical we have a very strict procedure for our patient's care. We want them nursed back to health as quickly as possible, even if that comes with the restriction of family contact. We hope you understand."

"I'm not sure I do understand," I said. "What exactly is involved in this 'care?'"

"Would you like to tell her or should I?" Chelsea said, looking down on Kurt and putting her hand on his shoulder.

"They make sure everything works," Kurt said. "And I mean everything."

I walked towards his bed and put myself opposite Kelly who stood there looking like a damn porn-star across from me. She was probably in her early twenties and I had no idea how she'd wound up with this job. Kurt and I were almost in our forties. I felt kind of threatened.

"What have you been doing to my husband?!"

"Kelly, cool it," Kurt said. "It's because of these guys that I'm alive."

"So start answering me!" I cried, angry and confused.

"Chelsea here has been tending to my needs," Kurt said, affecting a conciliatory tone. "She's made sure everything's in ... working order."

Kurt nodded down his body.

"And ...?" I asked, suddenly curious.

"It works exactly as expected," Chelsea said.

"What's that supposed to mean?"

"It means your husband can still ejaculate," she said plainly. "And there was quite a lot."

I couldn't believe the nerve of the woman, but another part of me found the whole thing intriguing.

"You've been jerking my husband off?!"

"It's not like that," Kurt started.

"It was actually a blowjob," Chelsea interjected.

"What the fuck!?"

"Honey," Kurt said, reaching out for my arm. "Look at me. Look at me."

I felt the bubbling anger inside me turn to a simmer as I turned to him. The range of emotions these past few minutes was exhausting.

"There's nothing personal between Chelsea and me," he said. "It's purely ..."—he didn't know if he should say the word—"... sexual."

I took a deep breath in and pursed my lips. Chelsea was looking sideways at me from across the bed, wondering if I was going to strike out.

Finally I exhaled, trying to let my anger go. "Show me."

"Honey?" Kurt said.

"Show me," I repeated, taking a seat by the bed. "Show me this fucking 'after-care' of yours."

Chelsea looked between my husband and me.

Kurt opened his mouth and wondered how best to approach it. "Are you sure you want to see?" he said. "You might not—"

"Show me," I repeated, sterner now. "I think I have a right to see. I am your *wife* after all."

Kelly cleared her throat and pulled the bottom of her dress down slightly.

"Well," Kurt sighed. "You heard her, Kelly."

Kelly turned away and opened a drawer behind her, pulling out a pair of latex gloves and sliding them over her slender fingers. She fitted them to her hand and snapped them closed, then she carefully folded the sheets of my husband's bed down until I could see his boxer-shorts.

Kurt took a deep breath and the nurse pulled his boxer-shorts down, letting his semi-flaccid cock flop out against his leg.

His cock was gorgeous of that there was no denying. He was clean-cut and big. Chelsea and I watched as the blood slowly started to fill his shaft, stretching the length of his cock until he was at full mast.

"If you'd like me to stop at any moment, just say," Kelly said.

I nodded. It was hard to stay angry at her. I could see she was simply a young woman doing her job, even if her job was a little ... odd.

She turned back and squirted a liquid from a dispenser onto her hands, and then she administered it straight to my husband's growing cock. He took another breath and so did I as I watched those white hands come around him carefully.

She massaged the lubricant over his stiffness and the veins popped along his shaft as it glistened in the light. My eyes widened and my pussy tingled with delight as I watched his fierce arousal.

Chelsea was gentle to begin with. She worked her fingertips up along him and pinched delicately over his head, massaging the tip briefly before finally taking him in her fist.

Slowly her hands pumped over him and I watched them glide back and forth, keeping her grip tight. I could hear the sticky slip and slap of the liquid as it squeezed between their flesh and I felt my pussy begin to swell with desire. I shuffled my chair closer.

Chelsea upped her pace suddenly and Kurt's hands gripped at the sheets.

"It's been a couple of days," she said, looking at me as she worked my husband's dick. "There was *a lot* last time!"

My eyes widened with lust and I felt a sudden desire for more. I didn't want this to end here.

"Wait," I called, and Chelsea stopped abruptly.

Kurt's eyes opened and his grip relaxed on the sheets as he stared down, wondering where the pleasure had just gone.

"Is this all you do?" I asked.

"There is a more *in depth* service," Chelsea replied. "So far, your husband has refused it."

"And what does that entail?"

"To put it bluntly," Chelsea said, "it involved me taking my panties off and sliding your husband's cock inside my tight pussy."

Kurt looked at me warily, as though he was fearful that I'd erupt in a frenzy of anger.

"Is that so?" I said slowly.

"I didn't think you'd—" Kurt began.

"Let's do it," I said.

Kurt looked shocked. "Kelly?"

"Do it," I urged. "I want to watch."

The jealousy twisted in my stomach into something more erotic, feeding off of a deep-rooted, instinctual fear. My husband was mine and the act of offering him up to a more beautiful, younger woman was something most people would find alien, Kurt included.

"Kelly, you know once we've—"

"Do it," I insisted.

Kurt looked to Chelsea who moved around the bed now so that I could see her full figure. She reached beneath her dress and fidgeted, then a pair of lacy, red panties dropped down her smooth legs and she stepped her white high-heels out of them.

"Wait," I said, and I stood up, moving closer towards her.

I wasn't sure of the boundaries. Chelsea looked down her nose as my face came close to hers. I moved my lips forward slowly until they were on hers. I paused as we touched, then I closed my eyes and started to kiss her.

Chelsea started to kiss me back and soon we were embroiled in a deep, passionate embrace while Kurt watched on. As we kissed I reached beneath her skirt, knowing that her naked pussy sat in wait.

I felt the inside of her thigh and then moved my hands upwards, feeling the sticky, loose flesh of her pussy that my husband was about to enjoy. My fingers span on her petals and I worked her clit until it stiffened, then I brought my lips off her and looked down.

I could see her stiff nipples pressing against the bust of her dress. Her cleavage looked inviting, but instead of pouncing I took her hand and led her towards my husband's bed.

"Let's get him inside you," I said, eager to witness it.

Chelsea mounted the bed carefully, putting her knees either side of Kurt's body. He stayed where he was, marveling wide-eyed as the whole scenario unfolded.

Her skirt pulled tight across her ass and I peeled it upwards, sucking a breath through my clenched teeth as I stared at that young, tight butt of hers. She clearly hit the gym often. Her ass was perfectly toned and her pussy was a tight, thin slit, sat beneath a perfect looking asshole. Nothing about her was subpar.

"Look at that," I marveled, using a hand to open her ass.

I couldn't help myself. Without even realizing what I was doing I soon found my face surrounded by the cheeks of her ass as I stared down into her cutesy pussy.

My tongue flashed outwards and she tightened up and flinched as I raced over her pussy.

"She's licking me," she said to Kurt.

"Licking you where?"

"She's licking my pussy," Chelsea said, and it caused me to smile wide.

This time I pressed my tongue right inside her and tasted the cum that was soon to be lathering my husband's cock.

In the meantime she was toying with him slowly, running her latex gloves over his slippery cock and leaning her face towards him.

I started to hear their lips smacking at the head of the bed and I tried my best to mimic the sound with my mouth, biting at her flesh and dining out on the first lesbian experience of my life.

"That's perfect," Chelsea said. "Perfect."

She crawled above his body and I watched her ass move away. I put a finger in my mouth and tried not to think too much about what I'd just done.

I watched from the foot of the bed as she hovered over his manhood. That same jealousy twisted inside me again, but I didn't just want to observe the act—I wanted to contribute.

"Let me put him inside you," I said, moving to the side of the bed and looking under her tight ass.

Chelsea unbuttoned the front of her top until her tits were exposed to Kurt. He reached up and gripped them with two hands, pushing them together and moving his hips upwards in the hope of meeting her dropping pussy.

I reached beneath and took his dick, feeling the sticky lube on my palm as I jerked gently. I watched as close as I could as Chelsea's pussy approached. I had front row seats to my husband's infidelity and I couldn't wait.

As she exhaled, so did Kurt and me. The three of us were in unison as her pussy opened over his hard cock, swallowing the glistening tip and taking the ensuing inches with ease.

"That's it," I groaned in disbelief, watching the beautiful moment closely.

I couldn't let it pass without touching myself. My hand moved down to the crotch of my yoga pants and I let go of my husband's dick so she could sit right down on him to the hilt.

She started to bounce gradually, putting her palms on his chest and squeezing her big tits between her arms.

I moved hastily now, flashing my yoga pants down and off my feet so that I could get to my pussy. I slid my chair to the bottom end of the bed and sat away from it so Kurt could see me. I made sure he was looking when I pulled the crotch of my panties over and started to play with my lips.

"I had no idea you were so naughty," Kurt said, admiring the show.

"You and me both," I said, surprised with myself.

Chelsea looked over her shoulder and hummed appreciatively as my fingers danced over my sensitive petals. I looked down and pushed my ass forwards to the front of the seat, tickling my middle finger up and around my clit.

I closed my eyes and let out a gushing breath, feeling my pussy ache open and spill some of its juices out of itself.

Chelsea had started to bounce faster on Kurt. His hands held her hips and he helped her as best he could, but she seemed not to need it. The girl knew how to work it. She leaned over him and twerked her ass down quickly, slapping her cheeks around his shaft and riding up his length in a tight grip.

I felt another sudden urge inside me that I couldn't contain. As I watched her pussy coat his cock in a film of white I knew I needed to sample it. Chelsea was such a stunner that I just knew she would taste amazing too.

"Let me suck him," I said, standing up and pulling my t-shirt up over my head.

She turned back and her eyes moved down to my tits. She bounced her eyebrows. "Nice , Mrs. Junger," she said.

I damn-near blushed. "Thank you," I said. "May I please have my husband's cock for a second?"

She moved a knee over his body and slipped him out of her. His slick cock fell back against his naked stomach and I gripped the base and held him upright, admiring her cum that covered his entire length.

As the pair of them watched I pointed my tongue out from between my lips and teased it all the way up the side of his prowess. When I reached the tip I opened my mouth and swallowed down over the crown, washing her sweet cum from his cock on my descent. When I pulled up off him he was all cleaned up and ready to be used again.

"Can you turn around?" I asked now. "I want to see it better."

This time I moved the chair to the foot of the bed and Chelsea did as I asked. I don't think Kurt had any complaints. Now he got to see that perfect ass of hers bouncing down on his dick as he relaxed.

She faced her pussy to me and leaned back, then Kurt held his dick steady and she wrapped the petals of her pussy over him one more time.

It was a sight to behold when he pierced her again. Her soft lips rolled down his shaft and his cock disappeared like a magic trick until it was all inside her.

"He has such a nice cock," she moaned. "You're a lucky lady, Mrs. Junger."

"As are you," I said, and I leaned forward off the chair to get a closer look.

I watched the imperceptible movements of his cock and her pussy as she rolled it down him over and over, but I wanted more. I wanted to help the pair of them.

Soon I found myself licking at her occupied hole and kissing her clit as it sat above her open O. My husband's dick squirmed through over and over and I ran my tongue over it as it became unsheathed each time. To be so close to such an unholy union was exhilarating, but I wasn't done yet.

"I want to watch him come inside you," I said, then I got up quickly and moved to the top of the bed. "Can you do that Kurt, honey?" I asked, stroking his hair.

He looked up, smiling warmly. He had beads of sweat at his hairline but his face was a picture of pleasure.

"I'm pretty sure I can do that," he said wryly.

"Good boy," I said, kissing his mouth as Chelsea continued to bounce steadily over his cock. It must have felt incredible to be treated to such a tight pussy out of the blue. I watched from his position for a moment, seeing her ass ride up and witnessing the brief glimpse of her cutesy little asshole each time she bounced on him.

Kurt started to breathe deeper, holding his breaths and feeling the imminent release approach at pace.

"Give it to her, honey," I urged, putting my mouth close to his ear. "Give her your fucking cum."

I left him with those words and moved down the bed again, seeing his cock looking even stiffer as it speared up into the beauty on top of him.

"He's close," she said, twisting a finger on her clit and looking down at the source of her pleasure.

"Do it," I begged. "Give her that fucking cum, Kurt."

He groaned to the finale, pushing up off the bed and sending his stiffness through her. She moaned with him and I watched his balls pull tight to the base of his shaft.

"Fuck," he groaned. "Oh, fuck!"

Suddenly he twitched and then I watched as his cock pulsed and Chelsea hovered on it. The pair of them let out a long, satisfied moan and I was left to imagine what was occurring inside her.

His cock twitched over and over and I pictured his thick, white seed firing into her pussy and coating her core in his love.

It began to slide down over his cock as it fell out of her. When he pushed himself inside more of it ran out of her and I found myself drawn to the forbidden lashings that escaped her.

My tongue licked at his shaft as it continued to convulse, then it squirmed its way out of her and the last few spurts shot up from the tip, scattering across her kempt fur.

I pumped him steadily against her and marveled at the mess. Her pussy glistened in the bright lights from above, along with his sleek cock that looked just as delicious as ever.

Like a starved cum-slut I pounced on the both of them, tasting his bitter love in my mouth as I jerked and sucked on his pole. I ran off him and went straight to her pussy now, tonguing out his cum like I'd done this a thousand times.

She held my head against her and moaned long and deep as I searched inside her for his deposit. My finger probed her and I felt his love burst over me, then it ran out over my finger and I gobbled at it greedily, pushing it into my mouth and then spitting it back over her pussy.

My tongue glided over her folds, massaging her stiffening clit until she started to moan on top of him. Her fingers span quickly on her clit and her pussy gasped wide, expelling more cum from its depths.

Again I tongued at it and then I watched her twitch and spasm as a climax came almost from nowhere.

"Fuck!" she cried, clenching her eyes tight and spinning her finger on her sensitive pearl.

Her stomach tightened and then she let out a gasping breath that turned into a moan. Kurt held her steady and she started to writhe.

She moved her hand away to steady herself on the bed, positioning herself crab-like and hovering above Kurt with her legs wide open.

I moved my face to her contracting pussy and attached myself to it like it was feed-bag, munching on her quivering flesh like I'd been starved of it.

Kurt steadily jerked his cock as I dabbled in the joys of lesbianism. My tongue flurried over her exploding pussy and I rubbed at myself, tasting a mixture of her sweet joy and Kurt's salty cum.

Finally I pulled away and Chelsea gasped a breath, kicking herself off to the side and taking several deep breaths as she leant heavily against the side of my husband's bed.

I stared at her and bit my lip, smearing some of my husband cum over my mouth and licking it clean.

He looked down and shook his head in disbelief. We shared a naughty smile and there was an unspoken bond amidst it. I knew this wouldn't be the last time we did something like this.

"Well, it looks as though you're right," I said, and Chelsea lifted her head and looked at me.

"About what?" she said, breathing heavily.

"Everything seems to be in working order."

She let out a short breath and then hung her head again, trying to regain herself.

"Could we get a moment alone?" I asked.

"Of course," Chelsea said, and there seemed to be a quick return of professionalism as she donned her clothes as quickly as possible, still breathing heavily.

She dawdled at the door, looking back and opening her mouth as if she was about to say something. She seemed to compose herself and said: "Thank you," before leaving.

When the door closed I erupted in a giggle and Kurt started to laugh too. I kissed his face and put my head on his chest again. Inside I could hear his heart beating a thousand times a minute.

"I'm so glad you're okay," I said.

"So am I," he said, stroking my hair.

I stayed right there for a minute or so and listened to him begin to calm.

"Am I on the same kind of health-care?" I asked eventually.

Kurt smiled. "Of course you are. But I hope you never need it," he added.

"I hope I do!" I laughed. "I wouldn't mind another go on that fiery slut."

"Chelsea?"

"Yeah," I said, looking to the door. "She tasted so good."

Kurt looked like an excited kid. "You liked it?"

"I *loved* it!"

"Then I think this is the start of something," he said, playing with my hair as his mind wandered.

It certainly was.

THE END

Arousal Airways : Couples Threesomes 7

I'd managed to keep it a secret from my husband right up until we boarded the plane. I walked in front of him and turned back to watch as he admired the many sexy stewardesses that greeted us on boarding in first-class.

"They really push the boat out," he said, eyeing a woman from top to bottom as we found our way to our private cabin.

You see, Anthony thought his fortieth birthday present was a trans-Atlantic trip to London, and—while that was true—the journey just happened to be as big a part of his treat as the destination itself.

I'd found Arousal Airways after plenty of clandestine searching online. I decided early on that I wanted to treat him to a first-class experience, as neither of us had ever flown that way before in our lives. However, whilst searching for the airline to take us on our vacation I happened upon a very peculiar, unique company indeed.

From what I could discern it appeared to be offering a very specific kind of travel service, the likes of which other airlines couldn't deliver. The language was deliberately vague, but nevertheless intriguing and seductive. They italicized words and phrases like '*package*' and '*in flight entertainment.*' It promised to be a once-in-a-lifetime journey and they were absolutely right.

The plane itself had a long, thin aisle down the middle and either side was a selection of booths, each of them private. We walked down towards number eleven—our booth—and opened the small door that led inside.

"Jesus Christ!" Anthony exclaimed, looking wide-eyed at his mode of travel.

"Pretty special, huh?" I said. I'd seen the cabins online but they didn't really prepare me for the real thing. They were so spacious.

"Mr. and Mrs. Thomas?" a spritely, young woman said, standing in the door of our private cabin in a kinky ensemble of garments.

"Yes?" I said.

"I'm Lucy, I'll be your private stewardess for today's trip. How are we feeling today?"

"Just fine, Lucy," Anthony said, still drinking in the surroundings. "Is that ..." he walked over to the glass fridge in the corner. "We have our own bar?!"

"Of course," Lucy said.

I don't quite think Anthony had yet paid her the attention she deserved. He'd been so busy inspecting the cabin that he hadn't noticed the fish-net stockings that stretched up her long, slender legs and disappeared beneath her mini-skirt. Above she wore a tiny white shirt with this cutesy little sash and a classic stewardess's hat to boot.

"If you want something a little more complex, I'd be happy to *service you*," she said.

That got him. Anthony looked over to the door and I watched his Adam's apple drop out of his throat as the blood rushed to his crotch.

"Is that right?" he said, and he looked across to me to check if he'd heard her correctly.

All I could do was smile, looking away to the floor and then coquettishly across at Lucy who had no-doubt done this a thousand times before.

"That's correct, Sir," she said, taking a step into the cabin in her high-heels and putting on a sultry stage-whisper. "We aim to please here at Arousal Airlines."

She walked out of the cabin and I took a step over towards Anthony, putting my hand on the bottom of his chin and closing his mouth.

"*Arousal Airlines?!*" he said, looking at me, bewildered.

"It took me a long time to find them."

"*Arousal Airlines?!*" he repeated, aghast.

I laughed. "Yes, honey! Arousal Airlines!"

"What in God's name is that?"

I put a hand on his tie and straightened it out. The pair of us had dressed for the occasion in order to sell the whole "first-class" thing to Anthony.

"I figured I'd do something special for my special man's fortieth birthday."

"Just what the hell do they do on here?"

"Well," I began, but a tap on the door interrupted us.

"Your caviar and champagne," Lucy said.

"Perfect," I said, turning to face our private beauty.

"I'll just set it down here."

The pair of us watched as she bent over at the waist and placed the caviar and champagne on a small table by the door. It stood beside our two seats that faced the front of the plane. Opposite was a large, flat-screen television and above it, on the ceiling, was a long mirror that covered the width of the cabin.

"I'll be back after take-off," she said. "That's when the fun begins."

She left us again and, once-again, left Anthony with a head full of questions.

"*When the fun begins?*" he said, almost panicked. "What fun?!"

"Relax," I laughed, kissing his lips and guiding him to his chair. "You just strap in and enjoy the ride."

Anthony poured me a glass of champagne and set the bucket in a sunken part of the table that separated us. He placed the caviar tray next to it. We spooned it onto some of the bread and ate and drank like it was the first time we'd ever done either in our lives.

The safety video played on the screen in front of us, replete with scantily-clad stewardesses going through the motions.

There were intermittent smiles and giggles, the pair of us already spoilt beyond belief. The both of us were unaccustomed to this lifestyle, but it was about to get stranger still.

We watched the city disappear below us as we ventured skywards, oblivious to the delights that awaited us in our mile-high, private cabin. The seat-belt sign pinged and we unbuckled. Shortly afterwards there was another knock at our door.

"That must be Lucy," I smiled.

As the door opened the lights in the cabin turned to a red-hue and some soulful music set the stage for Lucy's entrance.

She shut the door behind her and turned to the both of us.

"First time?" she asked.

Anthony and I nodded.

"I'll be gentle," she said, and she ran her hands down her body and to the inside of her thighs beneath her skirt.

I sat closest to the door and Lucy came to me first. I looked up at her younger body as she straddled my legs and started to dance slowly, thrusting out her curves to the beat of the music.

She must have been in her early-twenties. She had long, blonde hair that looked natural and she had a pair of big, natural tits to boot. They looked ripe as they pressed against the open top of her shirt, giving her an inviting cleavage that was tough to draw the eye away from. Her sash flowed down beside it and her gorgeous, smooth, rounded, cherubic face smiled downwards. Her eyes betrayed her features, giving way to a devilish soul that definitely knew how to be naughty.

Anthony watched close from my side as Lucy writhed over me, pushing up the bottom of my black dress and sitting on my smooth, bare legs.

She writhed across me and I could feel the heat of her pussy beneath her panties as they pressed against my legs. I'd never been with a woman before, but if I was going to pick one to experiment with, it would definitely have been Lucy.

She put her hand on my face now and moved hers to mine. She was so close that I could smell her sweet perfume and if either of us moved forwards another inch our lips would touch.

Lucy smiled and opened her mouth slowly. I saw her pink tongue inside and my mouth became wet at the thought of tasting her. She giggled and pushed off the chair behind me, standing upright. She did a kind of slut-drop move and then kicked out her ass as she span, walking over to Anthony beside me.

"Happy birthday, honey," I said, and he glanced over quickly to see me laughing. He started to laugh too, but the smile dropped from his face when Lucy straddled him and turned his head to face her.

"This is the birthday boy, huh?" Lucy said, unfastening his tie and opening the top button of his shirt.

"It certainly is," I called over the music. "He's forty."

"Forty, huh," she said, biting his tie between her teeth and pulling it out from his collar. "I like an older man."

She stood in front of the both of us and threw the bottom of his tie between her legs, catching it on the other side of her body and flossing it up against the crotch of her panties.

She turned on the spot so that Anthony and I could see her skirt ride up over the top of her fishnet stockings and reveal that perfectly rounded ass of hers. I reached over and took Anthony's hand as we stared, watching her hungry butt swallow the thin fabric of her panties.

Lucy continued to dance and I started to feel more comfortable in her presence. Her energy was infectious and her lack of inhibitions was intoxicating. I let go of Anthony's hand and reached over the table towards him, rubbing at the hard packet that I found at the front of his trousers.

"Is it working?" Lucy asked, watching me rub him.

I nodded. "Certainly is."

She smiled and tossed his tie behind her. She danced in front of us and began to pop open the buttons of her shirt as I rubbed over my husband's thickness.

I stretched him out beneath his pants and his cock made a b-line for his side-pocket, as though it was making a bid for freedom.

Lucy watched him grow, fixing her eyes on my hand as I pinched around his length. She pulled the bottom of her shirt out from her skirt and we both watched as she pushed it back off her shoulders, revealing her black, lacy bra that barely contained her big tits.

She turned away from the both of us now and set her legs apart wider than her shoulders. She kept the stance as she unzipped the side of her short skirt and Anthony shifted his weight in his seat, clearly affected by the sight of this young beauty undressing in front of him.

"Enjoy it," I whispered across to him, pointing my mouth in his direction but refusing to turn my head.

Lucy unzipped all the way down, then she brought her feet together and her mini-skirt fell down her legs, dropping quickly to her feet where she stepped her high-heels out of it.

We watched her ass bounce as she flexed it in front of us to the music, dancing her ass-cheeks in perfect synchronicity. I couldn't imagine having that kind of control over my body.

Anthony and I marveled from our seat as she turned to face us. She walked back over towards me and crouched to the floor. Her hands ran up from my bare ankles, along my smooth calves and then up and under my dress.

My eyes widened and my pupils fattened as she searched up under my skirt—but I didn't stop her. I had framed the occasion in such a way that I felt as though the three of us could do anything in that room and it would be okay. It was like a private booth of sin that we could indulge in without fear of recrimination or judgment.

I felt her naughty fingers curl over the top of my panties and I lifted my ass as she dragged them down. Anthony watched beside me and I heard him splutter a breath as my panties came down from under my skirt.

Lucy looked across to him and bit her lips, bobbing her eyebrows and putting my panties between her teeth after she'd taken them off my feet.

She stood back up in front of us again and danced. I took Anthony's hand again, but I didn't just want to hold it. Instead I moved him to my skirt and Lucy watched, looking proud as I pushed his hand underneath and to my exposed, aching pussy.

Anthony started to move his fingers over my sex, relieving the tension inside me as I felt the juices begin to come to the fore.

Lucy stretched my panties, holding one side in her teeth and pushing the other out playfully with her hand. She tossed them behind her and strode forward to Anthony now, dropping again to her knees and quickly beginning to tackle his belt.

His hand hurried away from my crotch to stop her, but I grabbed his wrist before he could protest. He looked over at me.

"Let her," I said, and I felt the muscle in his arm relax as he exhaled. I pulled his arm back over towards my crotch and he continued. He stared down as Lucy unfastened his belt and pulled his trousers open wide.

I watched as her hand rubbed over the outline of his cock. She was biting her lip and looking ravenous as she stared down, teasing all three of us as she tickled her long nails over his shaft.

I started to squeeze at my tits beneath my dress and my breaths became longer and deeper. Lucy ran a single finger along the elasticized waist-band of my husband's boxer-shorts, pulling them out so that I could see the kempt hair and juicy cock that lay in wait inside.

"Wanna join me?" she said suddenly, looking over to me. I damn-near burst out of my chair.

She shuffled over and I perched beside her on the floor. The pair of us looked up at Anthony who didn't quite know which of us to look at. His face was a picture of aroused nervousness. He'd never been with two women before, but I knew he'd be just fine under Lucy's tutelage.

She pulled his boxer-shorts and trousers down together now and Anthony lifted his butt off the seat so that we could undress him.

His cock snapped out of his underwear and fell up against his white shirt, stiffer than I'd ever seen him before in his life. I felt a strange sense of pride to be showing him off to Lucy like this. Although she'd no-doubt seen her fair share of cocks, I liked to think that Anthony's was one of the nicest.

He was thick and long, with a smooth, unblemished crown and a veined shaft that looked like it could really do some damage in the wrong hands. His shaven balls hung heavy at the hilt of his thickness and it was there that Lucy first targeted.

I busied myself with his shoes and socks first of all, removing them and then dragging his pants and underwear off his ankles.

When my head reappeared it was to the sight of Lucy, holding his cock back against his stomach as she sucked one of his balls in her mouth.

Anthony caught my eye and shook his head in disbelief. It was taking me some time to believe it all too, but rather than stop and digest it all I dived in head first.

I moved over Anthony's lap and pushed his legs open wider, putting my face beside Lucy's now. She looked to me and kissed my cheek with that infectious smile of hers. I turned my face to hers and before I knew it we were kissing. She drove her tongue into my mouth and I tasted her in me. I'd never kissed a woman like this before and there was something tender and alien about it all. When my hand touched her face it was shocking to feel the smooth, gentle jaw of a woman and not that of another man.

I broke from the kiss and smiled, but before we could do it all again she'd turned her attentions forwards towards Anthony's as-yet-unsucked cock.

"Would you like to do the honors?" she asked, holding him in her fist.

"Let me show you how he likes it," I said, and I pushed my brown hair behind my ear and mouthed gently over the top of Anthony's cock.

His hands gripped the arm-rest and his knuckles turned white as I eased my mouth down on him, keeping my grip around his shaft loose so as to glide over him.

"Fuck," he groaned, and Lucy giggled and looked up at him.

She pumped slowly at the hilt of his dick, watching closely as I brought my mouth up and off him. His cock glistened in the low, red light of the cabin and Lucy was drawn towards it now, like a moth to the flame.

"Let me show you how I like to do it," she said.

I knelt before Anthony like a student in training and I watched as Lucy put her mouth over him just like I had. Unlike me though, Lucy didn't stop in her descent. Her mouth continued down his shaft until I was wondering just where the hell Anthony's cock had gone. I leant back to take in the view, cocking my head like a puppy that's just seen a new trick.

Lucy's throat bulged as she pressed the top of Anthony's cock into it, but she didn't gag. Instead she relished the sensation, opening her eyes and locking sidelong at me. She seemed to smile, but it was tough to tell with a mouth full of my husband's hard cock.

"Damn," I hushed, unable to take my eyes off the event.

She pulled her neck off him and revealed his length again like a sword-swallower. Her mouth gasped and she beat him in her hands, then she offered him over to me.

The pair of us passed his cock between us whilst Anthony stared down and watched, wondering what the hell he'd done to deserve our servitude.

Lucy would kiss at one half of the barrel of his cock while I'd toy with the other, sliding my lips up along him whilst she did the same. His slick cock lay sandwiched between us, but there was much more to the Arousal Airways package I'd ordered than a blowjob.

"One second," Lucy said. "You keep him busy."

I looked up at Anthony and kept my eyes on his as I drove him into my mouth, watching the serene expression wash over him as Lucy made some thudding noises behind us.

"Voila," she said suddenly, and I looked back over my shoulder to see a large bed where the table had been. The flat-screen TV had been covered over and the mirror on the ceiling now sat directly above the bed.

She draped herself on the mattress and looked over at the pair of us. "Care to join me?"

I took my shoes off and unfastened my dress, letting it fall to the floor and forgetting completely that Lucy had already removed my panties.

I closed my legs, about to become embarrassed before I remembered exactly what we were doing. Embarrassment seemed kind of ridiculous, given the occasion.

"Perfect," Lucy said, admiring my mature body from her position on the bed. "Have you ever been with a woman before?"

I stepped out of the dress and walked over to her as Anthony watched, still seated across from us.

"Never," I said, and I sat on the mattress beside her.

She leaned in to kiss me, pushing my shoulders down so that I lay across the bed. "We can fix that."

Anthony took up his cock and jerked slowly as he watched. Lucy started by kissing my lips but before long I was feeling the wet pecks of her mouth descending down my body.

She kissed around my tits and over my bra, biting at my nipples before kissing down over my flat stomach and arriving eventually between my legs.

She glanced over to Anthony who was on the edge of his seat, then she closed her eyes and dropped her mouth right over my pussy.

I sucked a breath and groaned, feeling her fresh lips caress my petals as her tongue slithered out and trailed up the crease.

At first she was gentle, meandering around my folds and teasing me. My clit started to swell and the juices rushed to my pussy, ready for whatever was to happen next.

Suddenly she grabbed the insides of my legs with each hand and pushed them open, then she pierced me with her tongue and pushed it up inside me, licking out the juices that she'd worked so hard to produce.

"She tastes good," she said, looking over at Anthony.

He started to unbutton his shirt and came over to join us. He knelt at the top of my body and pointed his cock down towards my mouth. Lucy sucked on my pussy again and when I moaned Anthony put his cock right between my lips.

Lucy's busy lips were delighting me in ways I never thought possible, and it made it increasingly difficult to keep any kind of rhythm over Anthony. Porn-stars made it look so easy. Luckily, he took up the mantle himself.

He started to thrust into me, sending his cock through my open lips and using my mouth like I was his slut. He fucked me slowly at first, looking down his toned stomach as his dick disappeared into my mouth.

Lucy eyed him every now and then as she ate my pussy, running her gaze down from his eyes and over his hairy chest to the big cock that disappeared into my face.

She pushed a finger inside me and rose up on the mattress, looking down as I pushed my ass up off the bed and groaned.

"I want him," she said. "I want his fucking cock inside me."

Hastily she unfastened her bra, then she pulled at the tassels on her cutesy black panties and they dropped off her pussy. In a quick few seconds she was completely naked—and she looked fucking good.

"Have him," I insisted, wanting Anthony to enjoy himself.

I knelt up and guided his hand to hers. Lucy fell back and her big tits shook on her chest as she lay against the mattress.

Anthony knelt over her, his huge cock hanging beneath him and pointing towards her forbidden pussy.

She moved her fingers over herself and used her cum to lather the outside of her flesh as Anthony approached and for a moment I was mere bystander.

"Put him inside me," she said.

I reached around the back of his thick thigh and grabbed his cock in my hands, steering the tip towards her pussy and moving my head to try and get a good look.

Her pussy was a thin slit of flesh with slender lips that folded out like petals of a flower. There wasn't a wasted bit of skin on show. Everything looked as though it was being used to sculpt the perfect, most aesthetically-pleasing pussy that I'd ever seen in my life, and Anthony's beautiful cock was about to sample it.

I looked between his legs and helped steer him, watching him arrive at her aching O and listening to her heady moan as he stretched her open and breached her.

I rubbed my pussy as I watched, taking my bra off so that the three of us were now completely naked, save for Lucy's slutty sash that hung around her neck.

Anthony pressed himself all the way inside and the pair of them synchronized their breaths, gasping deep and long while I watched.

I moved away for a better view, seeing my husband stare down into the face of his new lover as they shared an intimate connection.

Something about watching them was a turn-on. Being a voyeur, watching on the sidelines like that, was like being a hidden witness to their love—however short-lived it might be. It was hot to see the unadulterated pleasure in Anthony's eyes as another woman gave him a sample of something I couldn't give him. She was younger, hotter, *tighter* than I could ever be and watching him enjoy her was intoxicating.

I leant back on my knees and started to work my fingers over my pussy, putting on my own show for the pair of them as the plane's engine hummed behind the sensual music that now played in our private cabin.

When my eyes opened the pair of them were staring at me, but Anthony was still busy thrusting away inside her. His ass worked back and forth, moving like a champion race-horse as he claimed his prize.

I felt the rumblings of climax in the background of my emotions, building slowly inside me as my fingers span on my pussy. As hot as it was to watch, it was also kind of hot to *be* watched, and having the adoration of a young woman like Lucy was giving me a confidence I didn't know I possessed.

"God, I want that pussy," she groaned, holding my husband's ass and pulling him into her. "Look at that fucking pussy, Mr. Thomas."

"She looks fucking good, doesn't she," he said, and the pair of them was staring straight into my wet flesh as my fingers strummed over it.

I brought a hand to my tits and squeezed at my nipples, moaning and letting the moment completely devour me as I gave in to my body.

"Don't you cum yet," Lucy said, and my eyes blinked open to see she was talking to me. "I want you to cum on my mouth," she said. "I want to work that orgasm out of you."

I hummed appreciatively. "Sounds good to me."

"Come here," she said, patting the mattress.

My husband pulled back and his cock slid out of her pussy, covered in a film of white cum. On my way over to the bed I dropped to his cock and sucked her juices off it. Lucy watched, smiling wide-eyed. She seemed to like the image of me tasting her wetness on my husband's cock.

"Good girl," she cooed, watching me lick my lips when I'd had my fill. Anthony looked wryly at me as though he was fond of the slut I'd become.

I got down onto the mattress and kept my legs wide open. There was nothing to be coy about now, and as if to prove it Lucy got on all fours and pointed her amazing ass straight at my husband as she dived for my pussy.

"Here's what I want you to do, Mr. Thomas," she said, but while she spoke she stared right at my sex. "I want you to tongue my tight little asshole—do you see it?"

"I see it," Anthony said, biting his lip as he stared into her.

"I want your tongue in it," she insisted. "And then, once you've teased me open, I want that big cock inside my ass. Can you do that?"

Lucy looked up at my shocked expression and the two of us shared a moment. We both knew she was giving Anthony something that he'd probably only ever dreamed of. What guy could possibly refuse the tight, perfect asshole of a woman like Lucy?

"I can do that," he said.

Lucy closed her eyes and clamped her lips over my pussy. They seemed to display an experience that she couldn't possibly have garnered in all of her years. They danced over me as though she knew exactly what I needed. She'd pull back and suck on my stiffening clit and then, just as I yearned for it, she'd drive a finger into my core and it'd squeeze on her and beg her to stay inside.

As she busied herself on me I watched over the curves of her butt as my husband pleased himself between her cheeks. His eyes would close as he tongued her, then he'd pull his face back and open her ass with a hand, staring in to admire his handiwork before venturing forwards to do it again.

"He's licking my ass," Lucy moaned, talking into my pussy.

Her mouth clasped over it again and I watched Anthony bring a hand up to her ass and work it out of sight.

"Oh, fuck," she groaned. "Fuck that's good."

"What's he doing?" I asked. I had a pretty good idea, but I wanted to hear her say it.

"He's finger-fucking my tight-asshole," she said, describing it better than I ever could have hoped.

"Good boy, Anthony," I smiled, and he looked over her ass at me.

He sucked a finger and pushed it back into her ass, opening her wider and wider in anticipation of his girth that was sure to shock her.

I held her face on me as she ate my pussy, fluttering her fingers over my pussy until I was about ready to burst.

"Now!" she said, looking back to Anthony. "Now. I'm ready."

He rose up and I saw his rock-hard cock again. He eased himself down and pointed his cock towards his target, leaving my imagination to conjure up the image of this beautiful dick spearing through her gasping ring.

She moaned long and deep and I felt the vibrations of her cries against my over-sensitized pussy. Anthony pushed into her and the moan deepened, then she clasped her lips over me to muffle her cries.

He eased himself in deep, sheathing his length in her asshole in ways that I couldn't even imagine. The idea of taking that big dick of his in my ass was a daunting prospect, but Lucy seemed to be managing him excellently.

"That's it," she grunted, pulling her face off me for the moment. "That's good. Fuck it. Fuck my ass."

She seemed possessed by the act, suddenly animated and finding an appreciation for ass-fucking that I didn't know a woman could muster.

She looked back to him and started to bounce, hitting her butt against Anthony's hips without him even having to move.

The look on his face was priceless. He was staring down, wide-eyed as he watched his cock disappear over and over into the asshole of our private stewardess. I could practically see him vying to commit the whole thing to a kind of photographic memory so that he could recall it in the future in great detail.

"Does he feel good?" I asked.

"So fucking good," she moaned.

Anthony gave her ass a slap and she squeaked, groaning like an animal before putting my pussy back on her face.

She dived right in and sucked me harder and deeper, thrashing over my cunt and transferring the energy of Anthony's thrusts straight onto me.

"Fuck," I hummed, throwing my head back and feeling the climax fighting to get out.

"Come on my mouth," Lucy snarled, as though she knew exactly what was happening. "Come on my mouth, you dirty bitch."

The insult stung me in just the right place. It was a shock to be degraded like that, but I couldn't deny the assessment. I was a dirty fucking bitch alright.

"Yes! Yes! Yes!" I groaned, matching my words to the thrusts of my husband.

Lucy pushed two fingers into my pussy and it gripped her in a firm embrace, refusing to let her go. My muscles squeezed her and my vision swirled in magical colors.

Anthony gasped and thrust against her, slapping his hips rhythmically against her ass and pushing her face onto my stiff clit.

I shivered and my thighs closed on her head briefly, trapping her in my honey-pot as it ached out its juices.

She lapped up everything I had to offer, slithering her tongue over the escaping juices and drinking them down. Whatever she didn't swallow was cast back up against me and smoothed across my flesh with her massaging tongue.

"Now you, Anthony," she cried, looking back to my husband. "Come. Come in my ass."

I was still emerging from the throes of my own climax, but I didn't want to miss my husband's. That would have been like walking out of the room just as he was about to blow out his candles.

I hurried myself beneath her, turning upside down and wriggling up under her perfect body until my face was staring straight up at her pussy. My husband's balls slammed against it and I watched the barrel of his cock disappear into her forbidden asshole as he pumped away.

Lucy's head hung down and she bit the inside of my thigh, teasing a tongue over my pussy every-so-often, but oddly sympathetic to how sensitive it had become now.

I watched her pussy flex and gasp as she moaned and it looked for all the world like she was coming too.

Anthony blasted himself through her ass and I watched him twitch as his own climax approached. His balls pulled away from her, rising to the base of his cock as his cum prepared to leap for freedom.

"I'm gonna come," he groaned, and the pair of us became excited at the prospect.

"Come with me!" Lucy said, confirming my suspicions as her pussy gasped and her ass pinched and gasped on my husband's girth.

He thrust quickly to climax and then his rhythm stopped. From my vantage I could practically see the cum surge from the bottom of his cock, all the way up the underside before flooding into Lucy's asshole.

"Yes!" she cried, and then Anthony's breaths returned, quick and fast as the lashes flowed out of him.

"Oh fuck!" he groaned, and I lay silent beneath, watching the whole thing like the naughtiest kind of voyeur.

He pumped slowly, pushing his throbbing cock through her tight hole as the ropes of cum blasted from his crown.

She pressed her face into the mattress and moaned into it. It dampened her cries and Anthony worked himself through her slower now. The pulses from the base of his cock grew farther apart until they stopped completely. All that could be heard was the soft music and Lucy's gasping breaths.

Anthony pulled out and I got the shock of my life. His cum fell out of her and cascaded messily on to my face. I gasped at first, but soon-after the sensation of his warmth on my skin started to feel good.

I don't know if either of them knew what had happened, but I didn't care. I started to rub it over me, feeling the velvet texture against me and moaning as I pushed it into my mouth. It seemed strangely right to not let the fruits of our labor go to waste. Thankfully Lucy was on the same wave-length.

"Oh, gosh," she marveled, looking back. "Fuck, that's hot."

She sped her movements, kicking her leg over me and then turning her body so that her face was close to mine.

She dropped on me and started to kiss my mouth and Anthony jerked his spent clock slowly above us, looking down on yet another unforgettable image.

We kissed his cum between us, smacking our lips greedily as Lucy pushed the errant drops that had landed around my face towards our mouths.

"That's so fucking hot," Anthony hushed above us, catatonic as he looked down.

We shared his spunk like sex-starved lovers, worshipping his offering and passing it between our mouths until there was hardly any of it left.

Lucy kissed me and tasted him and our tongues wrestled over each other. My husband's texture felt incredible in her mouth and I vowed that this wouldn't be the last threesome we experienced as a couple.

Finally he fell between us and Lucy and I draped our bodies over him, staring into each other's eyes across his hairy chest. We'd bonded in a way I'd never imagined.

"How are you enjoying Arousal Airways?" she asked.

"Already looking forward to the return leg," Anthony laughed, and our heads bounced on his chest as he did so.

Lucy smiled into my eyes and pursed her lips. "Ready for your in-flight meal?" she asked.

I giggled. "I think I've already had dessert."

She laughed and got to her feet. I moved closer to Anthony and the pair of us watched as our one-time lover got dressed back into her slutty uniform. She didn't seem to mind too much that the rest of my husband's seed lay deep in her ass.

"I'll be right back, you two love-birds," she said.

When she'd left I kissed Anthony's face and then his mouth. He breathed a long, deep kiss into me and I felt our relationship blossom inside the two of us, as though we'd unlocked a hidden-room of love and adoration that had needed the most unusual of keys.

"Happy birthday," I smiled.

THE END

Treating My Husband To My Ex-Girlfriend : Couples Threesomes 8

My husband Topher and I were socialites who often found ourselves mingling in similar circles. In many ways it was inevitable that I'd meet her eventually, but what wasn't so certain was what we'd wind up doing when we eventually did meet.

Gisele was an old flame of mine from my more adventurous days. I'd dabbled with the same sex in my early twenties, experimenting with the women after some rocky relationships with guys. I thought I'd give girls a shot—why not?

Topher and I were madly in love, despite him being twenty years my senior. We'd met not long after my amicable parting from Gisele. Her and I had careers that pulled is in opposite directions. Her modeling and my city-job didn't exactly marry well, especially as her work often saw her jet-setting to foreign climes and sun-kissed beaches. Maybe we could have made it work—I don't know—but what I do know is that what I had now with Topher was something I didn't want to give up.

Pool-parties were a staple of our life-style. There was something fun about kicking back and relaxing with people outside of their work-hours, and in this setting there was no call for suits and stuffy offices. It was the great leveler. Everyone was just their body, and very little else. It made it much easier to talk to people comfortably.

"Topher and Valerie, our very own power-couple," Lance said, laughing with open arms as he found us amidst the crowd.

"Great party," I said, smiling at Lance who wore an open white shirt and shorts.

"Thank you for having us," Topher added, slapping his back. The pair went way back.

"Are you kidding?" Lance said. "Who wouldn't want you two here?"

Lance eyed a woman walking past and shook his head in disbelief. "These new European models that I'm hiring ... hot *damn*!"

Topher laughed and I took a moment to admire the beauty he was referring to. She had long, smooth, bronzed legs leading up to her cutesy ass that was barely wrapped in her bikini. Her sunglasses made her even more mysterious and alluring.

"Hey," Lance said, leaning in closer and whispering. "I've saved you two a private cabana behind the pool-house over there if you need to get away for a few minutes. If you know what I mean?"

I could feel myself blushing as Topher laughed.

"Who knows?" my husband said, looking sideways at me with a twinkle in his eye that made me melt like always. I guess it was fairly common knowledge that the pair of us liked to enjoy each other at the strangest of times. In fact it was only last month that we'd been caught in the bathroom of one of our friends' parties. There was something thrilling about it all and Topher just brought the craziness out of me.

"Listen, I'll let you guys go," Lance said, standing on his tip-toes and looking around the crowd. "Oh and Valerie, there's someone here that you might remember."

He left us with that statement and Topher looked to me and raised his eyebrow.

"I don't know who he's talking about," I said, defensive as my mind wandered.

"I guess I'll keep my eye on you," Topher said wryly, putting a hand on my ass and pulling me close to him.

He looked down and kissed my lips and, like always, everything else just dropped away for the moment. I think that was always the danger. Sometimes I'd forget myself and not realize that other people might be watching as I fondled his cock. I had to restrain myself.

We mixed amongst the crowd, grabbing canapés and champagne at will until we were feeling as though we were on the same level as the rest of the revelers.

The sun beat down relentlessly and every so often I'd take a dip in the pool, sinking into the cool water and back-stroking my way across the water in order to tease some of the other guests. I'd worked hard on my body and sometimes it was nice to let other people enjoy it too.

After a length of the pool I trod water at one end, looking up around at the guests, some of whom looked down at me and smiled, raising a glass.

I waved a hand and then scanned the water to see who else I was swimming alongside. That's when I saw her. At the far end of the pool in a dazzling white bikini was Gisele, walking demurely down the stairs and into the azure-blue water.

I bit my lip as I watched, instantly running a hundred encounters with her through my mind. I felt my stomach drop and my throat tightened. It had been years since I'd seen her, and she hadn't change a bit. Likewise, my feelings hadn't changed either. She still got me worked up like no woman ever had before.

She must have spotted me long ago, because when her eyes met mine she gave a familiar smile without a shred of surprise.

I was frozen at one end of the pool, watching as Gisele swam over, bobbing her head steadily out of the water like a predator toying with its prey.

"I thought you might be here," she said, coming in close.

"Didn't figure you'd be the type," I said, shifting my gaze around the pool to see if anyone was watching. "You used to hate these things."

"Don't worry," she said, looking around too. "I'm not gonna start finger-fucking you right here in the pool."

For whatever reason I tried to bat back her casual reference with one of my own. "Might be fun," I said, narrowing my eyes. Thankfully, she laughed.

"So, your *husband* is here?" she said.

"He's around."

"Oh, just around?"

"Somewhere." I scanned the pool, finding him with Lance and a couple of his models.

"Looks like he's downgraded," Gisele said, looking back to me and sending her gaze down under the water.

I tried my hardest not to blush. Getting compliments from a woman as attractive as Gisele would make anyone hot under the collar.

"I'm happy with him," I blurted.

"Sure you are," Gisele countered. "But I know you still think about me."

The murmur of the party faded around us as I lost myself in her eyes. It was like it was five years ago all over again.

"Lance tells me you and your husband can be pretty ... adventurous?"

I swallowed. "Now why would Lance tell you a thing like that?"

"I'm signed with his label," Gisele said. "You didn't hear?"

"Lance mentioned something."

"So what do you guys get up to?"

"I—I'm really not sure—"

Gisele laughed, loud enough for a few bystanders to send their gaze this way briefly.

"Come on," she said. "The things me and you have done together and you can't tell me the tiniest little detail?"

I stayed quiet.

"Does he put it in your ass too?" she said.

"*Gisele!*"

She laughed again, quieter now as she put her arm over my shoulder and against the side of the pool. "Ever invited another girl along?"

Just then there was a huge splash and we both turned to see Topher emerging from the water that broke over his handsome face as he resurfaced. His hands pushed through his hair and he started swimming over towards us.

"Shit," I said, unable to keep it all to myself. "Tell him we're old ballet friends."

Gisele pulled a face as Topher stopped swimming and came within ear-shot.

"Honey," I smiled. "I'd like you to meet—"

"Gisele," she said, extending a hand. "Your wife and I used to be lovers."

I pursed my lips and looked to Topher for his reaction. He was utterly unfazed.

"*Gisele,*" he repeated. "Sounds exotic."

"I guess I kind of am," she said, looking between me and Topher.

"Lance was telling me you're on his label?"

"For my sins," Gisele said. "He really knows how to work a gal."

"I bet," Topher said, smiling like a child as he looked between the two of us. I think he enjoyed the tension as much as Gisele did.

"So, Valerie was telling me all the things you two like to get up to."

"Oh was she?" Topher asked, smirking.

"We used to do the craziest of things," Gisele continued.

"I'm not sure Topher wants to hear—"

"Do tell," he said, excited.

"Well," Gisele said, swimming closer to Topher and draping herself over him to whisper. "We used to fuck each other in the *ass*."

Topher gasped playfully and looked to me. I wasn't quite sharing their debauched enthusiasm.

"We have so much in common," he joked.

"Let's bring things down a notch, guys," I tried, but I couldn't help but find it kind of hot when Topher put his arm around her.

"I think we should take it *up* a few notches," Topher said, looking to me with a wild look in his eye and then to Gisele. I could tell his plan before he even spoke.

"No way," I said, shaking my head.

"Come on," Topher said, and Gisele slowly started to catch up.

"What's being suggested here," she said, eagerly.

"My husband here appears to be wanting a threesome."

"Oooh," Gisele said. "I haven't fucked a guy in a while."

"I haven't been with two women in a while either," Topher said casually.

"Jeez, guys. You're acting like we're just gonna start fucking right here in the pool."

"That wouldn't be a bad idea," Gisele said.

"No need," Topher interrupted. "Lance gave us a private cabana out-back."

"He did, did he?" Gisele said, both curious and a jealous.

I could feel the moment running away without me. The idea of Gisele and Topher together was heaven to me, but I wasn't sure if I could separate my emotions from the experience.

"Baby?" Topher said. It all hinged on me.

I looked around the pool at the major players that surrounded us. They all stood comfortably amongst their peers, doing whatever came naturally to them. You didn't get successful by caring about what other people thought. Shit, half the people here would probably high-five us if they knew what we were about to do.

"Tell you what," Gisele began. "I'll go back there now and if you two decide to come join me then I won't have to masturbate on my own."

Gisele leaned in to Topher and gave him a kiss, then she moved towards me and kissed my lips too.

"See you there," she whispered, holding my face before swimming away.

Topher and I watched as she emerged from the pool, her white bikini showing her skin beneath it. She didn't seem at all shy as she turned to grab a towel. She might as well have not even been wearing the bikini top. Her nipples were showing through the now-sheer fabric and she made no effort to hide them.

"Damn," Topher said, looking to me. "So you've fucked her?"

"I have," I said cautiously.

"We should do it again."

"*We* should, should *we*?" I asked, pulling him towards me for a kiss.

My hand searched beneath the water and I found his cock. It was exactly as hard as I thought it would be.

"Someone's getting ahead of themselves," I said, putting my forehead close to his and doing that thing again where I forgot we were in public.

My hand started to rub over his big cock as I thought about the pair of us fucking Gisele. I pinched my fingers around him and talked close to his ear.

"You'd like to see me with her, wouldn't you?"

"Definitely."

"I'd like to see her with you," I said and Topher pulled back to look at me and make sure I was being serious.

"What would you like me to do to her?" he asked, and over his shoulder I saw Gisele walk around behind the pool-house.

"Everything," I said. "I'll let her be your plaything while I watch."

Topher's pupils fattened with lust. "I want the both of you," he said.

"You can have us. Let's do it."

Topher pushed off the wall behind me and swam steadily away on his back, facing me with a grin. I smiled and followed him. He emerged from the pool, completely uncaring of the thick mast that jutted out from his swim-shorts.

I walked carefully up the steps, looking down at my black bikini and making sure everything was in order. My nipples were stiff with arousal but Gisele had pretty much normalized the sight of tits at this party. No-one batted an eye.

Topher held out his hand and I took it, walking around the pool and trying to shake the feeling of all the eyes on us. Truthfully it was only Lance who spotted what was happening. He raised his glass to Topher who gave him a thumbs-up and laughed, bumping his shoulder to mine as we walked away from the pool.

The cabanas were part of a set. There were four of them in a line behind the pool-house. They were big enough for a large bed, television and en-suite. It was kind of like a hotel-room in Lance's expansive back-yard.

"We're the second one down," Topher said, walking to the door. He put his hand on the handle and looked to me. "Ready?"

I nodded.

Topher opened the door and pushed through the white curtains within, entering the wood-clad room. He was immediately struck by the sight of something that I couldn't yet witness.

I closed the door behind me and pulled the curtains away. Inside of the room, sprawled across the bed and propped up on her elbow, lay Gisele. She was completely naked.

"Starting without us?" Topher asked, walking over to the bed and putting a knee on it.

"My bikini was wet," she said, looking perfectly comfortable.

Topher didn't know where to look. Gisele's perfect, softly-sculpted face stared at us. Her tits sat on her chest invitingly, held there by some kind of magic and looking pert and magnificent. Down below her flat stomach sat the thin line of black, kempt hair, trailing down to the folds of her pussy that she made no effort to hide. Perfect as always.

"You guys look pretty wet too," she said.

Topher stepped back off the bed and pulled at the tassel of his shorts, unfastening the knot and pulling the waist out.

"You too, Valerie," she said, staring.

Topher pushed his shorts down and his giant, hard cock sprang upwards, sat amidst his shorn hair. Gisele did a double-take.

"Fuck!" she marveled, losing the cool air that she'd been working on. She leaned forwards on the bed for a better look. "I can see why you switched back to men."

Topher stood proudly, staring with the pair of us at his big cock. The thick veins pumped up its length, feeding the life into it. Gisele barely looked when I dropped my bikini top.

I moved a hand over my tits and walked closer to Topher as Gisele watched from the bed, unable to hide her sudden arousal.

"Lucky for you I'm in a sharing mood," I said, dropping to my knees and holding Topher's leg close to my naked chest.

Gisele watched, opening her mouth slightly as I put my face closer to him. She wanted to see it as much as I wanted to do it.

Topher stepped out of his shorts and turned to me and I wasted no time in opening my mouth over the bulbous, smooth, cut crown of his cock.

He sighed and Gisele sucked a breath through her teeth as she watched me feed on him, sending his thickness straight to the back of my throat.

"Good girl," she cooed.

Topher held my head, enjoying the sensation and relishing the chance to put on a show. He knew how good he looked for his age.

I popped my lips off him and beat my fist over his cock, turning to see Gisele begin to play too. Her hand had found her pussy and she was spinning her fingers on her clit. My husband and I watched close as the juices began to flood from her pink O. She splayed them back up over her flesh until it glistened invitingly.

"Have a taste," I said, to Topher.

Gisele locked eyes with him, looking suddenly attracted to men all over again.

Topher put his knee on the bed and prowled forwards. His body cut a magnificent frame as he crawled over the mattress. His muscled ass bounced and flexed and I watched it close as he approached.

Gisele opened her legs wider and smiled down at Topher who smirked upwards as he put his mouth in position.

I watched the look on her face as her mouth opened wide to gasp, then she closed her eyes and sank into the cushion as I heard the smack of my husband's lips on her pussy.

I dropped my sodden bikini panties and stepped out of them, rubbing at my pussy and biting my lip as I walked towards the pair of them and joined them on the bed.

Outside could be heard the slow murmur of the revelers, interspersed with cheers, laughter and splashing as the party continued without us. In our cabin of sin though, all that could be heard was the wet kisses of my husband as he ate lovingly on Gisele's beautiful pussy.

"Come here," she said, curling a finger at me. "Come and watch him."

I knelt my way towards her and she put a hand on the small of my back as I turned to look down on Topher.

His body stretched away behind him and his eyes smiled at us as his mouth worked away out of sight. I imagined it was me between her legs, tasting her familiar flesh all over again like I had years before.

Gisele's hand dropped lower and she moved under my ass, finding my damp pussy and working her fingers over me in that delicate, passionate way of hers.

I closed my eyes and sighed, remembering vividly how good she was at fucking. I was so comfortable with the both of them, but Gisele had the inside-scoop on exactly what felt good to a woman. Despite this, Topher seemed to be doing a pretty fucking good job down there.

"That's perfect," she groaned, using one of her hands to push his head onto her while the other pressed through the wet muscle of my pussy.

My stomach tightened as she drove two fingers inside me, stretching me out and using the resultant cum to slip her fingers more quickly over my flesh.

"Come here," she said, moving me over her.

I straddled her hips and leant over her, draping my hair over our faces as we met to kiss. My lips wound around hers and our tongues wrestled as my husband ate her pussy below. As he moved I felt his hair stroke the insides of my thigh and it hammered home what was going on down there.

"He's good at that, huh?" I said.

"Very," Gisele whispered.

Suddenly I gasped in shock and Gisele's eyes widened with excitement.

"What's he doing?" she asked, knowing that his lips were no longer on her flesh.

"He's—" I wondered if I could say it. "He's eating my ass."

Gisele breathed deep. "Naughty."

She held my neck and looked at the pleasure in my face as my husband's tongue circled my muscle, teasing around the sensitive flesh.

"You like that?" she asked, squeezing the air from me.

I nodded, my face becoming hot and red.

"Eat her ass, Topher," she said loud, snarling at me and relishing the effect she had on me.

She let go and I moaned, dropping to kiss her passionately as Topher's busy tongue continued below.

After a few minutes of working my asshole he made his way up the bed, stroking at Gisele's pussy as he came beside the both of us.

"I'm not interrupting am I?"

"Not at all," Gisele said. "You're right on time."

Topher knelt at the head of the bed, positioning himself so that his cock came between the two of our faces.

"Mmm," Gisele moaned. "That's it."

She started to play with my pussy again, working my stiff clit and mouthing at the underside of my husband's delicious cock.

I dropped my face to sandwich him between our mouths. We kissed messily and I let my spit roll around the barrel of his flesh where Gisele slurped it along his length, moving back and forth as though she was devouring a corncob.

I stared down on Gisele's lust-filled face as my husband's cock pushed between our lips. In that moment we shared an intimate release of our old love and it reminded me of our previous sexual sessions together. Times when she'd stare into my eyes as I came, goading me on by calling my name.

Topher reached over the back of me and found my ass again. It was wet, just as he'd left it, and he toyed his finger around the outside.

Gisele worked up from my pussy and then her eyes dazzled with a sparkle as she felt my husband's fingers working at the other hole.

"Put it in her ass," she said, and on command my husband drove one of his fingers through the tight muscle.

I ached a groan that Gisele seemed to relish. Spit fell from my mouth across Topher's cock and Gisele's perfect face.

"Yes, that's it," she cried. "Take his finger in your ass, you dirty bitch."

I whimpered at her insult. I found myself strangely proud at the moniker. I certainly *was* a dirty bitch, but no-one had ever said that so explicitly.

Topher drove his finger back and forth as Gisele started to work at my pussy, nudging my swelling clitoris with her fingers and bouncing Topher's dick on her tongue.

My husband pulled his finger out and gave my ass a slap so hard that it rang off the walls. I sucked a breath and straightened upright, giggling afterwards. I loved the pain of a sharp spanking.

I let out a long breath and looked to him. He smiled and leaned over to kiss me as we towered over Gisele together.

"Ready for his cock?" I asked, looking down on her.

She was a picture of excitement. "I hope so," she said. She seemed to have some genuine trepidation about fitting his huge girth inside her.

"I'll be gentle," Topher said, and I walked my way up Gisele's body to make way for him.

"That's the last thing I want," Gisele said, humming appreciatively as my pussy came into view.

I sat over her face and used the headboard to steady myself.

Topher yanked her under me, dragging her down the bed and resting her ass on his thighs. He worked his cock into her and I looked under at her face as she winced a groan.

"Fuck!" she cried, and I knew immediately that his big cock was now stretching her open.

"Feel good?" I asked, looking down my body at her.

I wriggled my way back on her to hover my pussy over her face again.

"It's perfect," she groaned, and at the end of her impassioned wail she enveloped her lips over my pussy.

I breathed in deep and grinded over her mouth, feeling her tongue slip out from her mouth and move roughly over my flesh. She found my clit and worked across it and I started to gasp and pant immediately, as though the ecstasy from each of them was being transferred to me unfiltered.

I knew Gisele was tight and my husband sounded like he was discovering that too. He was grunting away behind us, no doubt in disbelief. I leaned back to him and moved my hand behind his head to pull him against me. He bit my shoulder and I looked down over my tits into the face of Gisele who was busily lapping my folds and trying not to squeal with delight.

"Fuck her pussy, baby," I cried, grinding my hips over her face.

Gisele's eyes rolled back and she struggled to concentrate her efforts on me. Instead she started to moan, but to feel each groan against my wet petals was just as intoxicating as the sensation of her tongue.

The vibrations of pleasure bounced off me and I started to writhe excitedly, pushing my folds onto her crying mouth and making her maw wet with my juices.

"Take this cock," Topher grunted, rocking in and out of her.

I made my way off her and turned to watch. I noticed her chest was dappled with red blushes, the same ones that I'd noticed years ago when I first watched her climax.

His fat cock looked impossibly slotted inside her and her flesh was pinching him tight. The lips of her pussy spread and I stared at her swollen clit that peered out at the top of her pussy, just beneath her kempt fur.

I stared to rub it with my fingers, bending over her and sucking on her nipples as she groaned with delight.

Topher kept his pace and my husband and I watched as Gisele became a different woman. The orgasm gripped her and the cool persona dropped away as she gasped and trembled, becoming suddenly endearingly vulnerable as the pleasure tore through her.

She gripped the sheets in her fist and pulled forwards, dragging her pussy off my husband's cock and rolling over to grunt in satisfaction.

I pulled back and rubbed at her pussy and her hand quickly came and gripped my wrist, holding me off her. She quivered with delight and stretched out on the bed, arching her back and wailing with delight.

"Nice work," I said to Topher.

He laughed and took hold of his cock, moving Gisele's cum along it as he worked it in his palm. "What can I say?" he shrugged.

"Give me that," I hushed, dropping my face to him. "I want to taste."

He relinquished control and I put a fist around him, pointing the tip of his cock up to my mouth. I gasped deep over his crown and pinched my lips close, pulling back and slurping Gisele's sweet cum off him.

"Mmm," I hummed, and Gisele finally seemed to return to earth.

"Fuck!" she cried, blinking at my husband's dick as though it didn't belong on this planet.

"You're one lucky girl."

I popped him out of my mouth. "I know."

"Let's get his cum," Gisele said. "I want to see it. It's been so long since I've seen a guy come."

"I'm sure he can help you out," I said wryly, looking to Topher. "Any objections?"

"None from me," he laughed. "Where do you want it?"

Gisele opened her mouth to speak and stopped. She smiled broadly and then tried again. "All over her face."

Topher raised an eyebrow and looked to me.

I shrugged. "Cover me in it."

I lay down on the mattress and Topher knelt beside me, his cock bobbing over my body and pointing towards my face.

Gisele prowled behind him, taking his cock in her fist and starting to beat it slowly as the pair of them looked down on me.

I bit my lip and closed my eyes, moving a hand in between my legs and playing with my pussy as the pair of them watched me. It felt hot to play for the both of them.

"That's it," Gisele said, looking down at my hand. "You too," she said. "I want you to come, too, Valerie."

She pumped Topher slowly, building her speed almost imperceptibly as his slick cock moved through her hand. I watched her control his flesh, pinching and pulling in a way that elicited these heady moans from my husband.

"Tell me when you're close, honey," I moaned, knowing that his imminent arrival was sure to get me off too.

"That's it," Gisele snarled, talking to his cock. "Cum all over her pretty fucking face. I wanna see it."

"Give it me," I begged, writhing in the sheets as I felt the euphoria build inside me.

My fingers pinched against my clit, sandwiching it and jerking it between the tiny movements of my middle-finger.

I could feel the wetness of my pussy flooding to the fore and I watched close as Topher's balls pulled tight to the hilt of his cock. Gisele upped her pace.

"He's so fucking hard," she swooned, beating over his stiff length.

Her delicate hands looked amazing as they massaged over him and I soon I could hear his breaths get away from him as he approached the inevitable climax.

My fingers worked faster too as he breathed and I waited for the words that would release the shackles of my orgasm.

"Yes, baby," Gisele moaned, looking at his cock expectantly as she jerked him.

"I'm—" Topher began, and I gasped in anticipation. "I'm gonna come."

"Fucking come," Gisele ordered. "Come all over her fucking face."

She beat him hard and watched close, keen to see him make a mess of the beautiful picture below.

I flicked my fingers quickly and held my breath, concentrating on the powerful sensation that had built to gargantuan proportions inside me.

"Here it comes," Topher said, and the words fell out of him with a moan.

His quick breaths became groans that grew louder as I trembled, then suddenly I felt the crashing heat of the first blast as it leaped from his cock.

"Yes!" Gisele said, excited. "Come on her face, that's it."

When the warmth struck me it was like a catalyst. The orgasm instantly blossomed inside me, pouring out in gasps and convulsions as his bountiful seed cascaded across my ecstasy-riddled face.

I opened my eyes to watch the next batch spurt free, pumped by the eager, tight fist of Gisele who snarled down from above, looking into my eyes and studying the passion that she'd missed all these years.

My chin shook and I pushed my fingers against my pussy, moving another hand to my face to rub his cum all over me and push it into my mouth.

"Yes!" Gisele squeaked excitedly. "Eat that fucking cum."

The ropes became spurts now as Topher emptied his balls. Gisele let go of him and raced her face to mine, keen to join me in my bubble of bliss.

She started to kiss me and lick across my mouth, tasting my husband's seed and sharing it with me in a sticky messy embrace.

Topher watched in awe. In all his years I think this was something that was finally new to him. He held his cock and jerked it slowly, pinching the last few drops onto Gisele as though she deserved some too.

I held her face and licked at the errant drops, then I opened my mouth over hers and felt the silky cream of my husband as it spread between us.

"That's incredible," he said, watching close as we played with his spunk.

Gisele giggled and I laughed too, as though we were back in my old apartment having just made each other come, only now my husband was sharing the intimacy.

"You taste good," she said, looking to Topher.

"How would you know what 'good' is?" I cried, mock offended.

"I know good when I taste it," she said dreamily, then she dropped her lips to mine and kissed me again.

Topher fell heavy on the mattress and took a deep breath. Gisele looked back at him, then she looked to me and smirked.

"There's still some left," she said playfully.

I watched her amazing ass point towards me as her face dropped over Topher's spent cock. He moaned and laughed as she slurped on his dick, cleansing him of the last of his seed as though she was a hungry animal.

She smiled back and wiped her mouth, then she fell beside him and looked over his body at me.

"That was something," she said.

"Not your average pool-party," Topher said. He slapped both our thighs and heaved himself up, climbing down and off the mattress before walking to the en-suite.

The door locked and Gisele shuffled over the sheets, playing with my hair.

"Just like old times," she said softly.

"Not quite," I said.

She pushed some more of his cum towards my mouth and when I opened my lips over her finger she started to kiss me again.

"You really love his cum," I laughed.

She shrugged. "It's a delicacy for me."

"Perhaps we can get your more familiar with it," I said, tickling her skin with my nails.

"Perhaps," she said, smiling. I think she'd already made the decision. I know I had.

THE END

A French Maid For Me And My Husband : Couples Threesomes 9

French Maids, it turns out, are remarkably easy to attain. A simple website search was all it took to be presented with a catalogue of mistresses at my disposal. Of course, sex was never explicitly stated, but the implication was definitely there.

My husband James would be forty at the weekend and I planned to give him something unforgettable. Our love-life often got an injection of spice every now and then and this seemed like the perfect tonic. Besides, I'm sure after almost twenty years of marriage James wouldn't mind trying out some fresh, younger pussy. It was my gift to him.

"Matilda," I said, reading the name of the mistress who'd taken my fancy.

She was blonde and looked to be in her early twenties, with a devilish smile, hinting at a hidden naughtiness that her cherubic face didn't convey. The naughty smirk seemed to penetrate me completely, sparking a desire inside me that didn't know I possessed. I *wanted* Matilda.

"Good morning, my love," James said, walking into the kitchen in his robe.

He came around the table and I quickly clicked to another tab in my browser.

"What are you doing on that so early?" he asked, kissing my head and squeezing my shoulder.

"None of your business," I said, tongue-in-cheek.

He smiled and moved to the counter. "Coffee?"

"Please."

I looked back to James as he busied himself, making a fresh batch for the morning ahead. Beneath his gown I could see his firm ass and I followed it up to those broad shoulders of his and his perfect, handsome features. His hair was ashen in places, but rather than take away from his look it seemed only to add to it. He had a confident, commanding way about him that made me melt.

I pulled my gown tighter around me and divulged my fantasy for a moment, imagining myself watching as Matilda took his robe off and swallowed his huge cock submissively.

"What?" James said, noticing me staring.

I blushed, turning away and curling a lock of hair behind my ear. "Nothing."

I could feel his gaze on me for a moment longer and I idly clicked open the local news website, pretending to be busy investigating something. I think his impending birthday had slipped his mind.

James didn't pry any more. I think he knew it was for the best not to. By the time the weekend came around he'd all but forgotten about my odd breakfast browsing.

"Happy birthday," I said on Saturday morning, waking him with a kiss.

His eyes opened dreamily and focused on me. He smiled broadly. "Thanks, honey," he said, pulling me into him.

We shared each other's warmth as he held me and I kissed his cheek, staring into his sleepy face adoringly.

"Your present is arriving later," I said, trying to hold it all in. I wanted to blurt it out and tell him, but it wouldn't pack the same punch.

"What is it?" he asked, stretching.

"Wouldn't be much of a surprise if I told you. Get yourself a shower and I'll make your breakfast."

I left him in bed and gave him another kiss, walking downstairs and rustling up a hearty breakfast. We'd certainly be burning the calories off later, that was for sure.

He emerged in the kitchen around thirty minutes later, just as I was plating up. It was around ten o'clock.

"Smells amazing," he said, eyeing the platter laid out on the table. "And it looks even better."

I pulled out his chair and presented his seat with a flourish, as though he was royalty.

"I'm being spoilt today," he chuckled. He didn't know the half of it.

We ate together and then I left for a shower as James settled in the lounge, idly clicking through the channels and oblivious to the treat that lay in store.

"Your gift will be here soon," I said mysteriously, standing in the doorway of the lounge.

"Can't wait," he said, and I found myself becoming impossibly excited by the big reveal.

I skipped upstairs to our shower and threw off my robe, staring at myself in the long mirror that stood beside the cubicle.

I turned sidelong and admired the curves down my body. I wasn't as young as I used to be, but thanks to a strict regime of exercise and healthy-eating I'd managed to keep a good figure. My ass was rounded without an ounce of cellulite and my big tits looked as firm as ever.

I framed my pussy in a triangle with my hands and smoothed them over it, feeling the slight stubble from several days of growth.

I ran the shower and started tending to it, shaving close and leaving a little triangle of fur just above my clit. As I shaved I stroked over my flesh, imagining my husband and our mistress admiring my handiwork. I wanted to look my best for both of them.

All told I spent around and hour in the bathroom, waxing, shaving, plucking and doing all manner of grooming in order to prepare myself.

When I emerged downstairs I felt like a new woman.

"What's all this in aid of?" James asked, sitting on the sofa and gawping as I approached in my robe and full make-up.

"I just want to look the best for my husband on his special day," I said, walking to the couch and kneeling before him.

He stifled his smile, perhaps not wanting to get ahead of himself.

"Open your legs," I said.

James did as requested, flicking the television to a music channel before tossing the remote aside.

"Happy birthday," I breezed.

I pushed his gown open at the bottom and James sank into the couch, leaning back as I revealed his naked cock.

It was flaccid for now but no less impressive. He was well trimmed and I could see the arousal begin to flow into him immediately as I picked up his cock in my hand.

"This is *my dick*," I said, putting him in my mouth and letting him blossom.

I pushed my mouth all the way over him as he groaned, moving my lips to the hilt and pulling back when his cock started to stiffen inside me.

It grew with each pulse, throbbing larger until I could only feed half of it into me before it hit my throat.

"Good boy."

James breathed heavy, sighing and groaning as I toyed with his slick length. I wanted to get him worked up enough in time for our guest, who would be arriving imminently.

He leant forward now and held a hand on my head, guiding me up and down along his cock and watching close as I gave him my performance.

I wound my lips down him, throwing him into my mouth before sensually sucking my way off and beating my spit back over his length.

He was clean-cut and smooth, with a picture-perfect cock that wouldn't be out of place in a promo image for a porn film. I delighted in covering it in my spit. It felt like an honor to wield him.

"Fuck, honey," he groaned, looking down wide eyed and smiling at me.

I gave him a brief smile back and then spat on the tip of his cock, working my saliva over him until his whole length was drenched.

I dropped him back against his naked stomach with a slap, then I bit down his length softly and arrived at his clean-shaven balls, sucking one through my lips and rolling it around.

"Fuck," he groaned again. "Happy birthday to me."

Suddenly there came a knock at the door and James sat bolt upright.

"She's here," I said, pulling his gown back over his stiff cock and standing up.

"Who?"

"Your present," I smiled.

"What?!"

I walked to the door and opened it to see our guest looking just like the picture. Beyond her sat a car at the front of our driveway with the driver staring down into his lap.

"Matilda?" I asked.

"My pleasure," she said, with this cutesy French accent that matched her attire.

"Come in," I said, looking up and down the street and hoping that no-one was mowing their lawns.

I beckoned her inside and she stepped over the threshold and into the hall.

"He's just through here," I said. "Nice and ready."

Matilda smiled excitedly. "Would you like me to do anything?"

"Do you have anything you *don't* do?"

"Not really," she shrugged, and then I saw that devilish smile that had wooed me in the first place.

I couldn't help but giggle, reaching an arm out to touch her wrist. "Good."

"He's in here?" she asked.

"Yes," I said. "It's his birthday. Can you—uhmm—let him do whatever he wants?"

"Of course," she said, giving a cutesy curtsy.

I offered her into the lounge and she stepped through. Inside there was silence.

"Happy birthday," I shouted, following Matilda into the room. Sho joined me in the celebration.

"Happy birthday," she said, giving James a twirl.

He swallowed hard and stared at me from the couch with bulging eyes.

"What the hell is this, honey?"

"Your gift," I said. "This is Matilda."

"Hello, Matilda," James said, standing and walking towards me. "Do you mind if my wife and I have a quick conversation?"

"Of course," Matilda said, and James walked out of the room.

"Just one second," I smiled, following him, embarrassed.

"What is it?" I asked, joining him in the hall.

"I could ask the same thing!" he hissed.

"It's your present, honey."

"What kind of present is that? What am I supposed to do."

I gripped the lapel of his gown and tugged him towards me. "Whatever you want."

"Anything?"

"Anything," I repeated. "You get a pass today."

"Honey, are you sure about this?"

"I'm looking forward to it," I smiled. "I can't wait until she sees you."

I took a fistful of his cock beneath his gown and gave it a squeeze, leaning against him.

"Are you—will you be...watching?"

"More than that, I hope," I said excitedly.

"Fuck," James said, putting a hand on his forehead and taking a breath.

"Happy birthday," I said again.

"You're serious about this?"

I nodded. "I wouldn't have ordered her if I wasn't."

"Ordered her?!"

"Look, never mind all that," I said, patting his ass as I pointed back to the lounge. "She's in there waiting and our time is running out. Get in there!"

Pep-talk complete we walked back into the room to find Matilda perched on the couch.

"Sorry about that," I said.

"Quite alright," Matilda said. "James, would you like to take a seat."

James looked to me again for approval and I nodded. He walked back to the couch and sat beside Matilda. He looked nervous but I was sure it wouldn't last.

"Would you like to sit beside him?" she asked.

I moved to the couch too and sat to the right of James, leaving him between Matilda and me.

"Right," she said. "Let's see what we've got here."

Matilda sank to the floor where I'd been only moments earlier. She tugged at the thick tassel of his gown and pulled him open quickly, freezing and looking up to me and then James.

"My, oh, my," she swooned.

"Good, isn't he?" I asked, leaning in to kiss his face.

Matilda picked it up and examined him like it was an alien artifact. James was semi-erect, but such was his size that even his half-stiff cock looked impressive.

The second her gloved fingers started to dance over him he began to awaken again. The thick vein stretched up his length and breathed life back into him until he was at full mast, poking out from the top of Matilda's fist.

She pumped her hand over him, clenching her jaw tight and relishing the groan that escaped my husband's mouth as she took to task.

"That's it," I purred, kneeling up on the couch and kissing his face and mouth as he cried in pleasure.

He kissed me back but I could tell that his main focus lay in the blonde, twenty-something beauty that sat between his legs, jerking his cock like she wanted him to explode right there and then.

"What do you want?" I whispered. "Tell us."

I kissed him again and opened my gown, bringing my tits to his face. James turned towards them and started to suck on my nipples, making them stiff in his mouth and sending a ripple of pleasure through me. I groaned and felt the wetness arrive at my pussy.

James gasped suddenly and moaned against my breasts and I looked down to see Matilda's mouth over his cock. She had pressed down over him so far that I could only make out the hilt. I wondered if he'd gone soft from the nerves, but Matilda suddenly pulled back and I marveled as his entire thick length revealed itself.

"Damn," I hushed, amazed.

She smiled up at me, her eyes welling with tears from her efforts. She giggled and slurped some saliva back into her mouth before going back over him and doing it all over again.

James hand gripped around me, holding me close to him for support as his leg straightened inexplicably and he held his breath. She popped back off him and the both of them exhaled, long and hard.

"That's fucking hot," I cooed, spectating her handiwork. I had no idea she'd be so talented.

She sank back over his cock and I kissed James again.

"Happy birthday," I whispered, and then I gasped as I felt a hand between my legs.

I looked down to see Matilda continuing her blowjob, but with her other hand planted between my thighs. Her gloved hands smoothed over my velvet flesh and she split my lips to tease her way inside me, turning her fingertips damp.

I held James close as we shared her expertise between us. Her fingers moved nimbly and with purpose over my flesh, teasing up to my clit which started to stiffen in an instant and peer out from beneath its fleshy hood.

"Tell her what you want, James," I moaned, trying to remind myself that this was his special day and not mine.

He stared down at Matilda who locked her gaze on him with a mouth full of his hard dick. She slid back over him steadily and revealed his length like a sword-swallower.

"Tell me, James," she said, her accent tinged with a mouthful of saliva.

"Can—can you lick her pussy?" he tried.

"Honey!" I gasped.

"You want?" Matilda asked, looking at both of us.

"If you want to?" James asked, looking to me.

I shook the trepidation from my mind. "Of course," I said, remembering whose birthday it was. "I'd love that."

Matilda rolled over onto her back and held herself in a kind of reverse-crab-stance, her face pointed upwards from the sofa cushion beside James while her legs stretched out and she propped herself up on the floor.

"On my face," she said, beckoning me with a finger. "Come on."

I looked to James who smiled, holding his cock in his hand and jerking it steadily as I started to move into position.

"I've never done this before," I said, curling my hair over my ear and staring down as I placed myself over her.

My robe fell open and I looked down on Matilda's ensemble, seeing her smiling face disappear beneath me until all I could see was her firm tits and tight body, wrapped in that maid's outfit.

"On my face," she ordered again, and as she spoke I felt the vibrations of her words against my pussy. I was relieved that I'd neatened it so fastidiously earlier.

I sank down, holding James's shoulder for support and then feeling the unmistakable sensation of Matilda's mouth as it planted on my pussy.

Her tongue emerged immediately and the alien-like sensation washed over me. I moaned with delight and James beat his cock faster, looking at the pleasure in my face and biting his lip as he stared down at Matilda.

"What's she doing?" he asked.

"She's tonguing my pussy," I moaned, relaxing onto her even more and closing my eyes.

Matilda sucked and licked on me and then moved her hand between her legs, pushing down on her ruffled ballerina-like skirt and smoothing her hand over the crotch of her panties beneath.

"Look at that," James said softly, watching her play as she ate my sex.

My eyes gasped open and I blinked down at her. She seemed to be enjoying this as much as the both of us.

James moved away and I rested my hand on the back of the couch as he stood up. He stepped in front of the both of us and looked up along Matilda's body, giving himself the perfect view between her legs and mine.

He pulled open his gown and let it drop to the floor. His body was muscled and hairy in all the right places. His pecs tightened as he took grip of his cock and jerked it as he ogled his new French beauty.

"Does it look good?" I asked.

He nodded. "I can do anything, right?"

"Uh-huh," I moaned, grinding my pussy across her face. I didn't know it would be my treat too.

I watched as James moved eagerly forwards, crouching next to Matilda and reaching up under her cutesy little skirt.

My jaw dropped as I saw her panties emerge, sliding down her thighs as James's face lit up with a smile and he shook his head in disbelief.

I felt a pang of jealousy that I tried to quash before it took root. I had to remind myself that I was deviating from the relationship too, but something about James's undeniable satisfaction at seeing Matilda's younger, tighter pussy had got to me.

"Yes," Matilda groaned, opening her legs as the panties fell down to her ankles.

I smothered her again with my flesh, but she combated my attempt to silence her by ravenously munching at my pussy. My face contorted in pained pleasure and I watched as James delicately removed her panties and positioned himself on all-fours between her legs.

He moved into her and I watched his eyes close as he worked his tongue on her sex, listening to her moan beneath me. We were like a conga-line of hedonism, with James satisfying Matilda whilst she, in turn, treated me.

I pushed my gown back off my shoulders and threw it to the floor, smiling at James as his eyes opened to look at my naked body, squatted over his new mistress.

I looked down on her tight, tense stomach as she kept the pose. I couldn't have stayed there as long as she did. She had the endurance of youth on her side.

"Come down here, honey," James said now, beckoning me with finger.

I flung my leg over Matilda and dropped to the floor. She moved up to sit on the couch, keeping her legs open and looking to James for her cue.

I looked between her legs at the tight, perfect slit, sat beneath her impeccably manicured fur. She glistened from James's spit.

"Get in between her legs," James said, patting my ass and giving it a squeeze. "I want to watch you eat her out."

"What will you do?"

James put a foot on the couch and then stood on it, holding his cock proudly. "I'm gonna fuck her mouth."

Matilda giggled gleefully and wrapped her lips over his cock as he arrived, jerking the exposed hilt with those velvet-gloved hands of hers.

James started to move his hips into her and I watched his cock disappear into her throat, her neck bulging as she took everything he had to offer.

Her eyes glanced down and she patted her pussy impatiently, pulling him from his mouth and turning to me.

"Eat my pussy," she snarled, and James seemed to delight in her new-found confidence as I played sub to her whims.

James stood like a Greek God on the sofa, his muscled body looking like a sculpted marble statue and his monolithic cock jutting out powerfully. He fucked Matilda's face and I marveled at how readily she took it, letting him into her throat with ease and taking it all in her stride.

James pulled out now, breathing heavily and looking down with a demeanor I'd never seen before. He stooped to her top and tugged at it roughly. Matilda looked fuck-drunk as she looked down her body at me, her mouth dripping with spit.

"That's it, you dirty bitch," James said, sinking into his role with worrying ease. He ripped down the front of her top and he pert tits hurried over the bust.

James dropped to his knees and clamped his mouth over her, sucking on her breasts as Matilda held his head on her and encouraged him.

"Spoil me," she groaned, and I found myself putting more effort into my pussy-eating, so as to earn her praise.

"That's it," she groaned, looking down to me as James rose back to his feet. "Eat my fucking pussy, you dirty bitch."

Again James seemed to relish her vulgarity. He turned her chin towards him and slotted his cock back home inside her, holding her head and fucking it like a crazed animal.

My eyes bulged in shock as I saw this primal side of James. I was intoxicated by his animal-like approach. It was as though he had become someone else. It scared and delighted me in equal measure as I sat awestruck at the beast I had unleashed.

He pushed the shaft of his cock against the groove of her open mouth now, running his length back and forth along her lips as she faced down at me between her legs.

"Tell her what to do, Matilda," James said, spotting her eyeing me.

I pulled my face back off her flesh and looked to her from my position on the floor, like a subservient dog awaiting an order from its master.

"Eat his ass," she said.

I swallowed nervously but James didn't appear to share the trepidation. Instead he dropped to the couch and sat on it, lifting his legs back and baring his clean, pink asshole. He'd groomed there too.

"I've never done that," I said.

"Let me help you," Matilda said.

She leant forward and took a fistful of my hair, gripping hard enough for me to feel a pang of pain in my scalp.

I leaned into her to give myself some slack and she guided me as I moaned, right to the ass of my husband who was beating his cock as he waited.

"There," Matilda said, moving her hand to the back of my head and pressing me onto him.

I had no choice now but to surrender. My lips touched his forbidden knot and I tongued over it, feeling the humiliation twist in my stomach, but having it dampened by the impassioned groan of James who appeared to love the new sensation.

"Ohhh, fuck, honey," he groaned, and Matilda sat on the couch with him.

She kissed his face as I ate his hole and I was forced to watch, seeing the two of them share each other while I did the dirty work below.

My tongue stabbed against his hot ass and poked a little ways inside, waggling as best I could. I decided that if I was going to do it, I would do it properly.

My hands parted his ass wider and stretched his hole as Matilda took his cock from him, beating it and looking down on me like a proud mistress.

"Good slut," she said, biting her lip as she stared.

I scrunched my brow and stabbed out my tongue, washing it over him in an attempt to defy her and show her how much I enjoyed my new task.

Matilda fought back by mounting my husband reverse-cowgirl-style and I had to watch as that perfect pussy of hers descended down his body and approached his thick cock.

"Put him inside me," she insisted, and I pulled my face back to grip his stern dick, holding the hilt and aiming the tip right to her wet honey-pot.

"Good girl," she said with a wry smile.

I watched in awe as her petals spread over the crown of my lover and listened to his groan deepen as she dropped down on him further. She sank the entire way, claiming each and every inch of him until she was perched on his balls.

"Oh, yes!" she wailed, throwing her head back and shaking out her hair. She looked down into my eyes again. "Keep licking," she said.

I hurried back to my husband's ass and tongued it as she started to bounce. My face was impossibly close and I could see her cum start to coat his cock, circling the hilt in a film of white as she lost herself to his cock. I'd had it many times before and couldn't be mad; James's dick always felt incredible.

Matilda held his legs and gyrated on him, stirring his length inside her as she watched down on my handiwork. I pointed my tongue and teased it around the sensitive, pink rim off his ass, and then finally she gave me a fresh order.

"Eat my pussy," she breathed. "Eat it while your husband fucks me."

James's hands were wrapped around her, gripping each breast and groping her as she treated his pole to her wetness. Her outfit sat bunched around her midriff, her tits exposed above and her pussy below.

Her tight slit gripped him close and I tongued tentatively at it. I kissed and licked, tasting her sweetness as it draped over my lover's cock and gave him more pleasure than I ever could.

Matilda was like a student of sex and I was a mere novice in comparison. I had the experience in years, but not in practice. I was sure she'd delighted many a man—and woman—in her short time on this earth. You don't get this good at it otherwise.

She started to bounce quicker now and I listened to the tone shift as James's groans become more desperate in intense. I knew better than anyone what that meant.

"He's close," I hushed.

"Keep licking," Matilda said, closing her eyes and losing herself to him.

I pressed my face to the union of sinful flesh, smothering everything I could without a care now as James's balls pulled up close to the hilt of his cock.

"Fuck!" he groaned, becoming more animated as Matilda rose him faster.

A long, satisfied wail escaped him and Matilda started to moan too. I pulled my face back and watched the hilt of his cock throb, delivering a bout of his seed deep into her pussy out of sight.

"Ohhh, yes, baby!" she groaned, looking down and pulling back her clit-hood. She patted her stud with a finger. "Right there."

I moved forward and teased my tongue over her swollen pearl, slipping it down to feel the continuing pulses of James's muscle as he fired out his load.

"That's it," she groaned, and suddenly I tasted a bitterness.

I pulled back and saw his viscous cum escaping, sliding down over his pole and leaving it glistening.

"Eat it," she said, and I started to tongue and suck at the errant seed, mopping up as best I could like a good little fuck-slave.

"Good," she said over and over. "Good."

I slurped and swallowed down the fruits of her labor, then she eased herself off him and hovered in place. This time she didn't even have to say a thing.

I planted my face onto her pussy and felt the warm flesh envelop my maw. My tongue probed her as she pushed and I felt my husband's cum flow into my mouth. I gulped with abandon, feeling it slide down my throat before another serving eked its way from her satisfied pussy.

"He's not done," she said, stepping off his cock and taking it in her hand.

Her gloves moved over him, spreading his cum back and forth and keeping him bolt stiff.

"What now?" I asked, surprised she wanted to continue and equally surprised that James was still able to.

"Turn around," she said.

I span on my knees and looked back over my shoulder.

"Bend over."

I did as requested, pointing my ass to the pair of them.

"Do you like the look of that, James?" she asked, standing up and sitting on my back to face him.

I took her weight and bit my lip, rolling my teeth over it as I anticipated her next move.

"Do you like the look of that *tight* asshole?"

The words came as a surprise. Before I had time to gasp I felt her drop a mouthful of spit straight down onto my tight, virgin asshole and soon she was smoothing it around with her fingers.

"Do you want this?" she said to James. "That hard cock of yours still needs a treat."

James stood up as her finger probed me and I groaned, furrowing my brow and wondering if I was really about to go through with this.

I heard him kiss her behind me.

"I fucking want it," he said, and I had to remind myself again that it was his birthday.

"You hear that?" Matilda said. "He wants this fucking asshole."

Her finger pushed inside and she pulled it out slowly, spitting again and pushing her saliva into my ass.

"Do it," I said defiantly, not wanting her to give her the victory or refusal.

"Oh, honey," James purred, then I felt something decidedly bigger pressing against my knot.

He forced his length through the muscle and it spread slowly over him. James groaned and I grunted, wincing as I felt a pang of pain when the muscle stretched.

He popped through the hole and sank a ways inside as Matilda swooned: "He's fucking in!"

I didn't need her to tell me that. The pain was immeasurable but it was over fast. I breathed deep and relaxed around him, then James started to bounce into me as our mistress goaded him.

"That's it," she purred sat on my back. "Kiss me."

The two of them embraced behind me and I listened to the smacking of their lips as James's hard cock thrust back and forth through my tight aperture. I felt the pleasure of it, peering out from behind a curtain of pain.

I focused on the sensation, feeling him tease my insides with his magnificent cock and suddenly I was yearning for him like never before.

"Harder," I cried, looking back and snarling.

"You hear that?" Matilda said. "I think she fucking likes it."

James shifted gears and dropped into me faster, working his cock through my tight ring until it was jerking his entire length.

"That's it," Matilda said, watching him slip inside. "Are you gonna come again, my love?"

James must have nodded.

"Oh, you naughty boy," Matilda said, and she kissed him again.

He bounced into me and I felt him stiffen and swell. I hadn't expected it all to happen so soon, but suddenly he was right on the edge again.

"Fuck!" he groaned, becoming louder. "I'm gonna come."

"Come!" I urged, and Matilda joined me.

"Come in her fucking ass," she purred.

"Come in my fucking ass, baby. Yes!"

James fell silent and then a deep, guttural groan escaped him. He throbbed and I felt the strange, sticky sensation flood into my asshole.

"Let it all out," Matilda said through clenched teeth.

She kissed his neck and chest as he wailed out his release, slowly rocking through my ring and sending violent blasts of cum deep into my body. I was surprised he had so much left to give.

I eased forward off him and my asshole winked shut, trapping his deposit deep and giving me a warm feeling in the pit of my stomach.

Matilda sat up off my back and stood beside James who was proudly showing his cum-glossed cock.

An idea seemed to strike her but I was one step ahead of her depravity. Before she spoke I dropped back to James's cock, putting it right back into my mouth and cleansing him of the pure, white cum that coated his length. My first anal session and my first taste of ass-to-mouth. Not bad. Matilda looked impressed.

"Good girl," she said, stroking my hair as I tongued around the tip of my husband.

I pulled him back out and smiled up at the both of them. "Happy birthday," I giggled.

James smiled back, staring straight into my eyes as Matilda draped herself over him and kissed his cheek. He was mine again,

but I wouldn't be averse to sharing his delicious cock again in the future. Matilda was only an e-mail away.
THE END

Surprising My In The Tub : Couples Threesomes 10

Five-year anniversaries are pretty tough to buy gifts for. I know my husband William well, of course, but for some reason an expensive bottle of whiskey didn't quite cut it.

For over a year now I'd wanted to spice things up between us and William—being a man—was never going to turn down the idea of threesome, especially when the additional person just happened to be my best friend Jan, who I knew he liked.

Jan was that girl in your group that was always game for anything. She had a bubbly, excitable personality and could make even the most mundane of things seem interesting. I'd always say it was the blonde in her. In contrast I was a little more reserved, but that didn't stop me from cutting loose once in a while. She always said that was the brunette in me ...

Getting Jan involved was simple. The conversation went a little bit like this:

"I was thinking of surprising my husband for our five-year wedding anniversary," I said.

"What did you have in mind?"

"Well, I want to treat him ... to another woman."

"Count me in!" Jan said.

"I haven't even asked you yet," I laughed.

"But you're going to."

"That's not the point."

"So count me in!"

It was as easy as that. In the following minutes we talked over exactly how we'd do it and whether there were any rules or boundaries.

I'd decided that I wanted to share Jan with William completely, and whatever she felt like doing in the moment would be absolutely fine by me.

Jan was clapping her hands with excitement. I could tell that she was already imagining a whole host of ways to take care of him.

Eventually we decided that we'd surprise him in the bathtub. Our bathroom's tub was huge and William and I had had it fitted just for us. We enjoyed a long soak together and the water-jets had a way of really relaxing you. They were perfect for winding down after a hard day's work.

"How do we lure him to us?" Jan asked, fearful that we might spend an hour alone in the tub together.

"I'll make a pathway of candles," I offered.

"Perfect. Although ..." Jan looked me up and down and curled her lip. "Spending an hour alone with you in the tub might not be the worst of ideas."

I slapped her arm playfully and gave her a sideways smirk. Jan had a figure to die for. Her waist was tiny, her ass was full and round and her tits were these big play-things that she never balked at putting on display. I definitely admired the gal.

She was still looking at me when I'd stopped smirking.

"What?" I asked, looking down myself. "I got food on me or something?"

"I bet you're an animal in the sack," she said.

"I don't know about that."

"I can't wait," she said, shaking her head in disbelief.

"Well it's this weekend. You won't really have to wait."

"Do you want me to bring anything?"

"Like what?"

"Oh, I don't know ... dildo? Butt-plug? Anal beads?"

"Jan!"

"What?" she said, incredulous. "You're giving your husband a threesome and suddenly I'm the dirty one?"

I guess she was right.

"You have all those?" I asked, curious now.

Jan nodded.

"I think we'll be fine"

"If you think so, Meg" Jan said, twisting her mouth and raising an eyebrow.

"You have a butt-plug?"

Jan laughed. "Fine, I'll bring it."

"No," I said quickly. "No, it's okay."

I left Jan with that and for the next few days I tried to keep things a secret between my husband and me. The only thing I had to hope was that he didn't have a surprise in store for me too.

Our anniversary fell on a Friday, but I knew that if William was going to do anything, he'd do it on the Saturday. It made the most sense as he'd be at work on Friday and I know he likes to make a day of things. So, that Friday afternoon, around five o'clock, Jan came to visit.

"Well hello, beautiful," she said, as I opened the door.

She leant in to kiss me and I could smell the sweet, floral perfume on her neck. She was wearing a tight pair of jeans and a wife-beater that her tits were practically falling out of. I invited her inside and she walked across the threshold, swinging a white plastic-bag in her hand.

"What's that?" I pointed.

"Just some things, Meg" she answered mysteriously.

"*Things?* You didn't bring your toys, did you?"

"Ugh, why not?"

"Because," I said, as though that answered things.

"We might as well experiment a little," she shrugged. "Not every day that you have a lesbian encounter with your best friend."

"Lesbian encounter?"

"You didn't think I'd just be fucking your husband, did you?"

"I don't know, I hadn't really—"

"I'm gonna get my tongue right in your ass," she giggled, leaning up against me and tickling my ribs.

"Jan!" I jumped, batting her away and laughing. "You are *not!*"

She calmed down and gave me that look again. "We'll see."

Before I could warn her away her attention moved elsewhere, like an excited puppy exploring the outdoors.

"Oooh, the candles," she said, looking to the sets that lined the stairs.

"Does it look good?"

"It looks dreamy," she answered. "Very intriguing."

She started to walk up the stairs and I followed behind her, watching her ass bounce in her jeans.

"You think he'll follow them?"

"Who wouldn't," Jan said.

She rounded the corner of the hall and used the candles as a guide all the way to the bathroom door. When she got there she looked back to me.

"You've really pulled out all the stops," she said.

I joined her in the doorway and looked at the bubble-bath that I'd created only moments ago. I'd scattered rose petals across the foam and several scented candles lined the tub.

"You think he'll like it?"

Jan turned to me and raised an eyebrow. "What man *wouldn't* like coming home to two naked women in the tub?"

"Good point," I conceded.

We walked into the green-tiled, romantically-lit room. Without a word Jan put down her bag and pulled her tank-top up over her head. Her huge tits dropped out of the bottom of them and she moved straight to the button of her jeans.

"What are you doing?"

"Getting in," she said, nodding to the tub. She stopped her hand at her zipper. "Did you want to undress me?"

I was dumbstruck as I stared at her. I'd never known anyone take so effortlessly to something as huge as this. My gaze fluttered down to those big, inviting tits that sat on her chest and then back up to her face. She smirked.

"Come on," she said, walking forward and holding my wrist. "I know you want to."

"Jan," I sighed, but I let her move my hand anyway. It settled on her breast and I let out a breath.

"Go on," she said. "Fool around."

Subtly my hand squeezed and I watched Jan's face light up. She stared down at my slender fingers as they made an impression on her tits.

"You're getting me all worked up," she cooed, and then I felt her nipples begin to stiffen beneath my palms.

She let go of my hand now and I kept it in place, fondling her soft skin and relishing the impact my touches were having on her. Knowing that I was turning her on was having an effect on me.

"Here," she said, and she started to pull my shirt up over my stomach.

I thought about stopping her but it seemed senseless delaying the inevitable. I knew we'd be getting close today, but I had no idea it would start before my husband was even home.

I lifted my arms above my head as the shirt rose. Before I could even get it over my head I felt the kisses of Jan on my chest, pecking away just above the lining of my bra.

"Wait," I said quickly, tossing the garment away and looking down. She was smirking up at me with these devilish eyes.

"I'm waiting," she said, not moving.

I said nothing and Jan tested the waters, keeping her eyes on me as she started to kiss at my chest again. I sighed, pretending that I was reluctantly resigning to it all.

Jan's eyes moved to my tits now as she slid down my bra, still kissing until she met my nipple that was already hard.

"Look what's happening here," Jan said, pulling my bra down further and staring inside. Compared to her my tits were a little more on the humble side, but having someone's mouth around them got me going nonetheless.

She started to lick around the raised stud and I shuddered with delight, throwing my head back and dining out on the pleasure that she gave so effortlessly.

"Let's get this out of the way," she said, unclasping my bra.

I let it fall forward off my shoulders and stared down at Jan as she pounced on me again. This time I buried my hands into her luscious blonde locks and scratched her scalp as her tongue wound around me again.

My hands ran down over her bare back and I looked down at the delightful V of her ass, finding myself wondering what it looked like without the pants covering it.

"When does he get home?" Jan asked.

I looked to the clock on the wall. "In around ten minutes, usually."

"Hadn't we better get in the tub?" Jan said.

She stood upright and went back to her jeans. Her fingers slid down the zipper and she wriggled her hips out from the tight fabric, causing her tits to sway hypnotically as she did so. The jeans came off her ass and she stepped out of them. Her panties formed the perfect curve over the top of her thighs and her body looked incredible.

"Are you joining me?" she paused.

"Yeah—uhh—of course."

I popped the button of my pants and Jan came towards me. "Let me do that," she said.

She slid down the zipper and started to pull at the waist, sinking to her knees as she did so. I brushed my brunette hair behind my ear and bit my lip as she wriggled the pants down to my ankles. I raised a foot and Jan carefully took the pants over the heel before doing the same to the other leg.

I watched as her face moved between my legs and then she kissed at my panties, pressing her lips against the fabric.

My jaw tightened and I swallowed hard. Jan's nails slid down inside the waist of my panties at each side and she pulled them down with a smile. This was it.

"Look at that," she swooned, and she smiled as she looked up at me.

I had to remind myself to enjoy the occasion. I was so busy being nervous that I'd forgotten how unique an experience this could become.

Jan didn't waste her time in planting her lips back on me. She kissed me deep, just beneath the kempt triangle of fur that I'd sculpted for this very moment.

My eyes closed and a whimper escaped me as I felt her tongue slide down along my crease and tease towards the tight O of my pussy. It was the first time a woman had ever been down there.

"You taste good," she said excitedly, looking up and then sucking a breath over her teeth as she started at my freshly wet petals.

Her face was on me again, licking deep. This time I put my hand at the back of her head and kept her there, staring down her slender back and watching her feed on me.

She kissed at my flesh noisily, then I felt one of her fingers tease its way inside and she moved up to my clit, tonguing the hood and awakening the pearl beneath.

"Shall we get in," she said, looking up with a sparkle in her devilish eyes.

She rose to her feet and I blinked quickly as though I was awakening from a dream.

"Y—yeah," I answered awkwardly.

"Relax," Jan said, and she kissed my mouth. I could taste my sweetness on her tongue and I had to admit that Jan was right: I did taste good.

When I pulled away slowly she moved to her own panties and threw them down her legs like it was nothing. I watched as she bent to the floor and delved inside her bag, removing an unmistakable brushed-metal butt-plug.

"What are you doing with that?" I gasped.

Jan gave my butt a slap and put one leg in the tub.

"You're putting it in my ass," she said plainly. "Get in."

Jan slid into the bubbles, humming contentedly as the warm water flowed over her skin. I followed her in, listening as the bubbles cracked around us and the water sloshed beneath. Jan settled herself on one of the seats in the corner and I sat across from her.

"What are you doing all the way over there?" she said. "You gonna fuck me with your feet? Get over here."

I shook my head as I switched seats, moving in beside her. When I was close enough Jan put an arm around me and pulled me nearer. I could feel her naked body against mine and it felt good.

"That wasn't so hard was it," she said, looking down her nose at my lips.

This time I kissed her, moving forward and draping my lips over hers. Jan was quick to return it, flipping me into her spot and mounting me. She rose up and her soapy tits hung in my face, her knees split across my thighs.

"Go on," she said, seeing the delight in my eyes as her big tits swung in front of me. I think she knew I liked them.

I put a hand on each one and started to squeeze them. Jan moaned excitedly, throwing her head back and sending a hand plunging into the bubbles beneath.

I watched her elbow begin to move and there was little doubt as to what she was doing. Her expression changed suddenly to one of unadulterated pleasure. It looks as though sexual gratification was one of the only things she took seriously.

"Are you...?" I asked, knowing the answer.

"Here," she said, and she took one of my hands and sent it beneath the water with hers.

I was on her pussy in an instant. Yet another one of my firsts had been broken. Jan pushed my fingers along her petals and then put me inside her, moaning loud when I entered.

She was warm and wet and as she groaned I could hear her cries return off the walls, bouncing on the dark-green tiles and ringing throughout the house.

She threw her head down and stared at me with this animal like gaze. "Here," she said, and she handed me the plug.

"What do you want me to do with that?"

Jan turned around and stood up. I watched the water and bubbles drip off her to reveal her glistening, round ass. She bent forward and I stared in wide-eyed wonder as it split open to reveal her perfect, pink dot of an asshole, sat right above her delicious looking pussy.

"I want you to slide it in my ass," she said, looking back and using a hand to hold it open.

"Jan, I'm not sure—"

"Come on, Meg," she interjected. "You didn't ask me to do this so you could chicken out at the last minute. Come on. Stick it in my fucking ass."

My eyes bulged with surprise at her sudden strict enthusiasm. She was right of course. I was going to do it. I wanted to.

I leaned forward and brought the wet metal to her tight knot. She looked back and shook her hand on her ass and I touched the tip of it to her muscle.

"That's it," she said, closing her eyes.

I bit my lip and pushed, marveling as the aperture opened over the metal, keeping a close grip on it as it started to widen.

"Yes!" Jan grunted.

"Is that—do you want it—"

"All the way," she said. "Fucking plug me."

I kept on pushing, watching her swallow the metal and hide it out of sight inside her. Her ass spread wide over it and then it popped through to the sound of a heady breath escaping her.

"Uhhh," she groaned, satisfied. "That's my girl."

I stared at the bejeweled base of the plug that put a circle over her hole. It was so naughty to think of what was hidden out of sight beneath, and even naughtier to know I'd put it there.

There came a sudden noise at the door of the bathroom and I turned quickly in the water to see my husband standing in the frame.

"William!"

He dropped the bag he was carrying and stared at the sight before him.

"What ...?"

His eyes were fixed on the twinkling plug that sat in Jan's ass. She was staring back over her shoulder at him with a smirk on her face.

"Happy anniversary," she said. "I see we had the same idea." Jan looked down at the dropped plastic bag and I saw a packaged butt-plug peering out.

"What the hell is this?" William said.

Even though it had been my idea I felt inexplicably guilty. Jan was unwavering in her debauched frivolity.

"Take those clothes off and come and join us," she said.

William dragged his eyes away from Jan's ass long enough to look at me. "Meg?"

"It's your treat," I said. "I wanted to give you something special for our fifth anniversary. We've been wanting to spice things up."

"Pretty spiced, right?" Jan said, holding her ass open and shaking it in the foam.

"With this?" William said, running an outstretched hand across the scene before him.

"Don't look a gift-horse in the mouth," Jan said, and she turned around and draped herself over me. "Come on," she said, at her most seductive now. "Come and wind down."

She kissed me and then looked to William's pants. "I bet he's got a big cock waiting in there for us, hasn't he?"

I realized the game she was playing and did my best to join in.

"Oh, it's big," I said. "I can hardly fit it in my mouth. I'd need someone to help me suck it properly."

William seemed to awaken. The confusion on his expression lifted and you could visibly see the arousal begin to pump around his body. The bulge beneath his suit-pants grew.

"You know, come to think of it," he said, walking forward and unbuckling his belt, "I really think we could do with an extra pair of hands."

Jan moved excitedly to the edge of the tub, putting her hands on the rim like an impatient pet waiting for its food. I joined her at her side and the pair of us watched as William unzipped.

"Here it comes, Jan," I said, nudging her excitedly.

"I can't wait to see his big—ohh—ohhh fuck, look at that!" she swooned, cutting herself off when William pulled his thickness up over his boxer shorts and put it on show.

He shook it and pumped his hand along it slowly as Jan reached out for his pants, tugging them down his legs and taking his boxer-shorts with them.

He started to rip his tie off and unbutton his shirt, feasting on the fantasy before him as though it might disappear at any moment.

"There's a good boy," Jan said, reaching forward and taking his cock.

Strangely I didn't feel a single ounce of jealousy. I'd known Jan so long and we'd shared so much over the years that this just felt like another example, albeit one that I would be reluctant to recall to our other friends.

"Come here," she said to me, and she tugged William forward. She brought her other hand around my shoulders and held my chin, angling his cock right towards my lips.

William stepped into me and I felt his flesh slide through my mouth. I'd sucked his cock so many times before, of course, but having Jan there feeding it to me gave it this added tinge of eroticism that our previous exploits had sorely missed.

"Eat that fat cock," she said, pumping the hilt as I rolled my tongue around the tip.

"Oh, fuck," William groaned. Only a few minutes ago he was on his commute home from work and now this.

He put a hand on his ass and started to rock forward at the hips, passing his cock through my mouth. His muscles flexed in the light of the bathroom and I reached out a hand to scratch down the front of his washboard abs.

Jan started to kiss my face and then she moved closer until she was gnawing on the inches of my husband's cock that I couldn't swallow.

I pulled him out from my lips and gasped. Jan quickly arrived on my mouth, kissing and biting at my lips before the pair of us returned to William's juicy cock.

This time Jan pulled it towards her own mouth and she wrapped her lips over it. I watched it disappear inside her and then marveled as she pressed on, taking his entire dick until her throat started to bulge.

She pulled him out and turned to me with a smirk. "Impressed?"

I started to laugh. "You'll have to teach me."

"It's not so hard," she said, and she passed his cock back to me like it was plaything.

I opened my mouth and Jan pressed the back of my head forwards. He hit the top of my throat and I doubled over, but Jan kept pushing. I felt my gullet open and suddenly he was in my neck.

I pulled back off him quick, my lips stringing with saliva as I turned to Jan who watched on like a proud parent.

"See!" she said.

She held my cheeks with both of her hands and kissed me. I smiled and bit my lip, impressed with myself. I'd managed to deep-throat, if only for a second or two.

"Now are you gonna get in here or what?" Jan said, looking to William.

He flung a leg over into the warm water and the pair of us moved back to watch him sink in.

"That feels good," he groaned, easing into the tub.

The bubbles cracked again and started to dissipate, leaving the petals floating on the water. Beneath you could see the blurred naked flesh of our sinful bodies. No amount of cleansing would wash away what we were about to do.

Jan moved across to the side of William and I took her cue and joined her opposite. My hands wandered beneath the water and I found his cock with Jan's hand already around it. I moved down as she jerked him and I started to squeeze his balls, teasing my fingers underneath his sack and touching his ass briefly. I knew he liked that.

"Meg here was telling me how amazing your cock feels inside her," Jan said, talking close to William's ear in breathy tones.

"She was, was she?" he said, raising his eyebrow at me as I pressed my finger on his ass.

"Think you can give me a sample?"

"I'll give you more than that," William said.

Jan pushed through the water to the far side of the tub and she breached the surface with her soaked ass, showing that glistening wet plug of hers and the delightfully tight crease that sat below it.

"Have at it," she said, staring back. "You don't mind, do you Meg?"

"Not at all."

William stood up and the water rushed off him. I sat behind and watched through his legs as he squared up behind her. His balls hung beneath him and beyond them his long cock aimed for its target.

"Fuck her," I urged, eager to see it.

"You tell him, Meg," Jan said.

"Put that fucking cock in her cunt," I tried.

"Oooh, Meg," Jan said, taking a moment to look back around my husband at me. "I *like* it."

Suddenly her grin turned to a moan and I looked beneath to watch her tight pussy sheathing my husband's cock, inch by inch.

"That's it, you fucking slut," he said, surprising me with how kinky he was. Jan tended to bring that out of people.

He slid into her and I stared in wonder. Without even realizing it my hand had found its way to my pussy and it was pushing up and down the channel of flesh with vigor.

William began his strokes and the water started to splash along the tub, driving to one end and rushing back to the other as he hit his rhythm.

"Fuck me! Fuck me! Fuck me!" Jan urged.

I decided I couldn't just sit there and watch the whole thing. I crawled forward along the floor of the bathtub and moved beneath the pair of them, sitting on the bottom so that my head was just a little ways above the water line.

"Room for one more," I smirked, reversing beneath them until my face was right underneath the action.

"Always," Jan said, looking under her body at me.

Her tits shook on her chest as she stared downward and gave me a knowing smile.

"Go on," she said, nodding subtly.

She was like a snake charmer the way she had me at her whims. Ordinarily I was a good girl, but Jan was very convincing.

I stretched upwards and planted my mouth over her clit, listening to the delighted sounds escape her immediately.

"Oh fuck," she cried. "She's sucking my clit. She's sucking my fucking clit, William."

"Eat that pussy, Meg," William cried, encouraging me. "Eat that fucking pussy and watch me fuck her."

His hips clapped against her ass and my tongue slithered over the sinful union until William had another sudden idea.

"Reach in that bag down there, Meg," he said. "Get that butt-plug."

I did as commanded, grabbing the plastic and tearing it off the sex-toy. I wondered if William wanted it in his ass but his intentions became clear soon after.

"Put it in her ass, Jan," William said, and he pulled his cock out from her aching sex.

Jan turned quickly and reached for the toy, taking it from me and then gripping my face with her hand.

"Open wide," she said, and she put it in my mouth.

I sucked on it and felt a strange allure. The moment was so depraved and naughty that I wished I could have bottled it: my husband stood over us, jerking his big cock while Jan fed a butt-plug into my mouth. It was just the craziest thing.

"On your knees," Jan ordered.

I put myself in position just like she had and soon I could feel the metal against my virginal knot.

"Oh, fuck-yes," William said, and he crouched beside Jan as she started to feed it into me. "That's it."

Jan pushed and I felt my hot asshole widen over it. The sensation was alien and a little painful, but the more it stretched the more I enjoyed it.

"Keep going," I insisted, but I don't think Jan had any designs of stopping anyway.

She pressed it all the way until my asshole relaxed over the narrow neck.

"Butt-plug sisters," Jan said, and when I turned back she kissed my mouth as though I had been accepted in her naughty sorority.

"Where do you want this cum, ladies?" William asked, stroking himself above us.

"Hmm," Jan thought. "I think I want to pull it out all over Meg's face. What do you think?"

William looked to me. "That sounds delightful, Jan. Meg?"

I'd never taken a face-full of cum before either. Shit, we'd broken so many barriers today that this barely seemed forbidden.

"Do it," I said. "Cum all over my fucking face."

"*Meg*," Jan swooned. "I'm really liking this new you."

I leaned back against the edge of the tub and Jan crouched close, jerking William above me as I rested my head back. I could smell the lavender of the candles when I closed my eyes.

"That's it," Jan said. "You relax and let me take care of you."

Jan's fingers arrived at my pussy and her left hand jerked fiercely at William's cock as she pleased the both of us. I'd never known a person so gifted in the bedroom. Jan probably couldn't keep a beat while singing, but she could sure jerk the hell out of my husband's hard cock while she fingered me.

Her touch was something else. I guess women know how women like it, but Jan seemed like an expert in knowing exactly when I wanted a finger inside me and exactly when I wanted to have my clit toyed with.

"Oh, fuck, that's it," William said, and my breathing started to match his and Jan drove us to climax.

I sucked in a gasp of air and then several more, staring up at the ecstasy-filled face of my husband as Jan's hand pumped along his shaft.

"He's fucking close," Jan said, looking to me. "So are you."

She slid two fingers inside me and I groaned loud, then her thumb came to my clit and she smothered it, pushing the flesh over it until I was a shuddering mess of glee.

"Come all over her fucking face," Jan said, looking to William now. "Give her that hot fucking load."

Her arms worked quick, fed by some kind of hidden reserve of energy that Jan kept aside for moment's like this.

"I'm fucking coming," I strained now. My mouth opened wide and my eyes closed. I felt my pussy tighten on her fingers.

"Yes," Jan said. "Oh, look at that."

I sucked a breath over my teeth and then heard the sudden release of my husband above me. He let out a deep, guttural grunt that seemed to enliven Jan.

"Here he comes," she said. "Shoot that fucking load."

William ached a groan and then a sudden flash of heat blasted over me, accompanied by another coo from Jan.

"Oh, yes!" she cried. "Fucking cum on her fucking face. That's it. Give her your fucking cum."

I blinked quick and stared through my lashes as another fierce jet spiraled off the tip of his cock, pumped free by Jan's steady rhythm.

It flailed in the air and crashed over me, joining its friend that had roped itself all the way from my forehead to my chin.

"Oh, look how much fucking cum he's got for us," Jan said, still beating it out of him.

My pussy gripped and relaxed, gripped and relaxed, pressing against her fingers until she pulled them out of me slowly.

Without warning she tugged at the plug and the sensation of that exiting me gave the orgasm the kind of cherry-on-the-top that I'd been sorely missing.

"Fuck!" I cried, spluttering as yet another fierce lashing crashed across my face.

Jan started to laugh and then she brought her face to mine, letting the last few escaping arcs web across our faces.

"Good boy," Jan said, blinking up at William who was staring down as though he'd just awoken from a dream to discover it had all been real.

"There's a ton," he said, surveying the destruction below.

Jan giggled and held my face and I started to laugh too. Her tongue slipped over my cheek and she took up some of his seed, moving it down to our mouths where we both kissed.

"Take this plug out of my ass," Jan said to William, keen to give him something to do.

She eased her ass above the water and William pinched at the flat end, pulling it as Jan and I passed his cum between us.

"He tastes good," she said, and she was right. It definitely had a sweet tinge, like an exotic dessert.

Jan let out a breath as the plug popped free from her ass. Before William could move she'd grabbed his wrist, bringing his hand and the plug to her mouth.

She tongued the tip and then sucked over the brushed-metal, giving a naughty flourish to an already crazy set of events.

"Well that was fun," she said, idly fingering the cum around my face and pushing it into my mouth.

"It was," I breathed, blinking and trying not to get him in my eye.

Jan licked around my lashes and cleansed me of the troubling drops of spunk, moving down to kiss me again as though she didn't want me to go hungry.

"Did you have fun, William?" she asked, knowing the answer.

"Are you kidding? All of my fun is on your beautiful faces right now."

"Aww," Jan mocked. "We are beautiful, aren't we?"

She turned to me and kissed me again, only this time it felt more passionate. She took a deep breath and pressed her body against me, pushing her tongue on mine.

When she pulled back she blinked as though she'd forgotten herself, then she stood up from the tub and gave William a kiss too. He didn't balk at her cum-lined mouth.

"Thank you, handsome," she said, stepping out of the tub. "I hope I've showed you guys a thing or two."

"Definitely," I said, exhaling and shooting a jet of air up my face.

William looked down and smiled. "We definitely have some things to explore."

"Well, if you need me," Jan said, toweling off and excusing herself.

She walked from the room naked and turned back at the door.

"You two have fun now."

I bit my lip and shook my head at her.

"Bye, Jan," William said.

He sank into the bath and put his arm round me, kissing my head.

"Happy anniversary," I said, gently tickling his cock beneath the water.

"Yes, it was," he said. "It was."

THE END

Watching My Husband Fuck The Waitress : Couples Threesomes 11

Our European city breaks were always the perfect tonic. Despite their expense they were an experience that you couldn't really put a price on. To immerse yourself in a different culture entirely was a thrill and it was part of the reason that my husband Jason and I were so compatible.

We shared the sense of adventure and the yearning for new experiences was a vein that ran through both of us. There wasn't much we wouldn't try. That weekend Jason and I were in Paris. A cliché I know, but what we wound up doing in the city of love was far from your standard romance.

We'd been there for one day already and it had been action-packed. I'd taken Jason up the Eiffel Tower, to the top of the Arc De Triomphe and the top of the Sacre-Coeur. Between those three sites we'd basically looked out across the entirety of Paris and it was quite a sight to behold.

That morning we'd kept things a little closer to ground-level, visiting the Moulin Rouge and the Louvre where we stared at the Mona Lisa. Jason said he definitely thought she was smiling. I said I was sure there was something occurring out-of-sight below that was giving her that curious grin.

"I was thinking we could eat at the restaurant downstairs?" I said to Jason as we returned back to the room of our five-star hotel.

"You haven't steered me wrong so far," he said, his hands behind his head as he lay on the bed.

I crawled across to him and gave him a kiss, lying against him and putting my head to his chest.

"It's got great reviews," I said.

"Honey, eating anywhere with you is a pleasure."

I slapped him playfully and looked up at his smirking, handsome face. He looked down at me and chuckled, putting his arm around me and pulling me close. I could hear his heart beating in his chest when I put my head to it.

"And maybe afterwards we can come back up here for an early night," I said suggestively.

"An early night, huh?"

"I don't plan on us sleeping."

"Mmm, I like the sound of that."

"We can do anything you like."

I rolled over onto my stomach and lay my chin on his midriff, looking up at him and kicking my feet behind me. Jason and I had been together almost ten years, but there were still places in the bedroom that we hadn't ventured.

"Like what?"

I batted my eye lashes and thought. "If you play nice maybe you can put it in my ass."

Jason's eyes lit up at that.

"Or maybe we could invite someone to join us," I suggested.

"Wouldn't that be fun?"

"Guy or girl?"

"Girl," he answered without hesitation.

"Of course," I said, putting a hand on the inside of his leg.

"Well I'm not gonna want another guy, am I? This is my fantasy, not yours!"

"Who says I don't want another woman too?"

Jason raised his eyebrows. "You do?"

I shrugged. "I don't care. As long as you're happy."

"I'll be happy fucking you," Jason said.

"Not interested in a one-time pass?"

"Not in the slightest."

I laughed. "We'll see."

I hadn't quite expected the opportunity for Jason prove it to arrive as soon as it did.

We dressed for dinner. I wore a red dress with pearls and a red clutch, trimmed with gold that matched my bracelet.

Jason was impeccable as always. He'd had the hotel press his trousers and iron his crisp white shirt. In his black suit and polished shoes he looked about as close to James Bond as you can get, complete with the black hair and suave, sophisticated demeanor.

"Shall we?" he asked, walking from the bathroom and holding out his elbow to me.

He always made me laugh. I took his arm and the pair of us left the suite. They'd upgraded us when we checked in and honestly we could have easily stayed in the room and enjoyed the city from the balcony. It was incredible.

Downstairs the restaurant maintained the thread of class that the hotel oozed. A piano twinkled and the chandeliers sparkled above as we waited inside the doors of their plush Michelin-starred eatery.

I gave the maitre d' our names and he guided us to a table near the centre. It was round with a crisp white table-cloth and ornate chairs at opposite sides. The wine-glasses were big balloons stuck on the end of a spaghetti-like stem and the cutlery was a shimmering silver.

"Hey," a familiar sounding female voice called. "I'm Sam and I'll be your waitress this evening."

"A fellow America," my husband said, and I could tell he was immediately enamored. Something about meeting someone so familiar in an unfamiliar place gave you an immediate connection that you otherwise might not share.

"Yes, sir," Sam said, smiling at the both of us with dazzling white teeth. She looked cute in her white shirt and short, black skirt. I wasn't sure about the black tights and the flat shoes, but her face drew the eye way more than her clothes. It was so fresh and inviting.

"Short for Samantha?" I guessed.

"You got it, Ma'am. Here's a couple of menus for you guys."

Sam seemed much more casual and friendly than the rest of the waiters and waitresses. I was guessing her fluency of English was one of the big things helping her stand-out here.

"Will you be having wine?" she asked.

Jason looked across at me. "I think so," he said.

"One for the lady to decide," Sam smiled.

"We'll be having wine," I said, looking at Sam alluringly. I hadn't even had a drink yet but I found something about her intoxicating. She seemed naturally flirtatious to the both of us.

"Perfect," Sam said, handing me a menu. "If the lady would like to pick something out, I'll be back soon."

She turned on her heel and walked briskly from the table, her blonde hair in a tightly wound bun behind her head. She walked with purpose and confidence, smiling to her fellow members of staff who wore stoic expressions instead.

"What do you think?" I asked.

Jason hummed. "I'm thinking muscles," he said.

"Of our waitress," I added.

He looked up from the menu. "Oh. *Oh.* I wouldn't uhhm—"

"Come on," I said, nudging his shin with my foot beneath the table. "What do you think?"

"She's cute," he said, not looking up from his menu. "Pretty."

"She's *hot*," I corrected.

Jason looked over his menu at me finally and stifled a smile. "I think you like her more than I do."

"Come on," I said, leaning in closer and whispering across the table. "Don't tell me you wouldn't like that tight pussy over your dick."

Jason's eyes bulged and he swallowed, looking around the restaurant for anyone in ear-shot. It was clear immediately that he'd gotten an erection. I didn't even need to look.

I smiled knowingly and then Sam came back over, bouncing on her toes close to our table.

"Made a decision on the wine?"

"We're celebrating," I said. "Can we get a bottle of Crystal?"

"Certainly," Sam said, removing our wine glasses. She scooted off again for the champagne glasses.

"Look at that ass," I said to Jason, teasing him.

I saw his eyes shift towards our departing waitress.

"Caught you!" I said.

He laughed and shook his head, looking back down at his menu.

Sam returned with two champagne flutes that she set down on the table, then she hurried off again and came back with a stand for our champagne bucket. She popped it effortlessly and silently, emitting only a minor hiss. She caught my eye and smiled, then picked up my glass and poured some out.

"Would madam like to try?" she said. I could tell that was something they made her say.

"Madam would," I joked.

Sam was about twenty years our junior but she had such a casual way about her that you'd never really notice. It was only her tight body and unblemished features that set her apart from forty-somethings like Jason and me.

The rest of the meal went by in much the same fashion. Sam would return to our table between courses and we'd share some flirty dialogue while I teased my husband. Whenever she spoke directly to him I'd watch as his throat became dry and his cheeks flushed red. He was definitely into her and Sam, I think, was game too. I had to know how far she'd go.

"Dessert?" she said simply, returning to the table after we'd finished our final course.

"Anything you can tempt us with?" I said, looking across as Jason as the words left my mouth.

"I'm sure there is," Sam replied, equally flirtatiously.

"Do you think we could take dessert in our room upstairs?"

"Of course," Sam said. "We can fix that for you."

"And my husband was wondering," I began, and I saw him turn tight in suspense, "if you'd like to join us?"

He looked across at me in horror and then up at Sam.

"I—" he began.

"I finish in ten minutes," she said simply. "I'd be happy to."

I was taken aback by how casual she was about it all. "It might not *just* be dessert," I added, keen to make things abundantly clear.

"I hoped as much," Sam said. "What kind of dessert would you like?"

I rolled my tongue over my teeth and stroked my foot up the side of Jason's leg. "I think a can of whipped cream will suffice."

Sam giggled. "Right you are. I'll add all of this to your bill. Your room number?"

"Four-four-five," I answered.

"Oooh," Sam swooned. "I'll be up as soon as I can. Sound good?"

"Sounds perfect," I said. I could see the excitement in Jason's eyes but he was reluctant to let it all out just yet. "Doesn't it honey?"

"It certainly does," he said, and thankfully he managed to give off the confident allure that I knew he was capable of. When it came to it I knew that Sam would be like putty in his hands.

She turned to leave and Jason called her back. "Oh, Sam," he said.

She hurried back to the table. "Yes, sir?"

"Keep that outfit on, will you?"

She looked down herself and nodded. I think there was something about the whole 'servant' look that turned Jason on more than anything.

"Right you are," she said.

We finished the last of the champagne and left our seats, walking out from the restaurant that was oblivious to the sinful little deal that we'd just brokered.

When we were clear I let out a breath and leaned against Jason, laughing. "Did that just really happen?!"

"I think it did," he said, equally giddy. "Are we gonna ... have a threesome?"

"We just might," I said, holding his arm and pausing the conversation while we walked past a smartly dressed couple.

We hurried into the elevator and when the doors closed we gushed like teenagers to each other.

"Did you see how cool I was?" I burst, leaning against him.

"You were perfect," he beamed. "And did you hear me tell her to keep her outfit on?"

"I did!" I jumped, before remembering we were in an elevator. "You were so smooth."

I leaned against his lapel and planted a kiss on his lips. "Ready for the both of us?"

"Of course."

"It'll be great."

"Are you ready for her?"

"Oh, yes," I answered, sure of myself. "I think we can show you a thing or three."

Jason laughed and then took a deep breath. "You sure you're okay with this?"

"Didn't you see her? I wanna fuck that little minx just as much as you do."

He laughed as we exited the elevator and rounded the resplendent corridor to our room. He slid the key in the lock and we pushed through together, babbling like best friends.

"What should we wear?" I asked

"I think we're fine as we are, aren't we?"

"Are you gonna answer the door?"

"I think you should," Jason said. "I'll just be on the bed here, all casual like."

"And then the pair of us will come in and get straight to work."

"Fuck," he said, jumping on the bed. He could barely contain himself.

"Nice and hard?"

"I'm stiff as a rock just thinking about it," he said. "Look."

I stared to his suit pants and saw the impressive bulge across the front of them.

"She's gonna like that," I said softly, sauntering across the thick carpet towards him. I put a knee on the bed and rubbed at his stiffness beneath his pants.

He hummed contentedly, looking out briefly across the twinkling lights of the city and the Eiffel tower before looking back to me and smiling.

"Thank you for this," he said.

"It's a gift to both of us, remember."

Just then the door knocked and Jason's eyes lit up. "She's here!"

"Relax, honey," I said, kissing his lips and leaving him on the bed.

I skipped to the door, feeling the soft carpet through the bottom of my stockings. I opened the door to the sight of Sam peering at my emerging face and then smiling wide as she realized it was me. She'd let her hair down and one hand was giving it some volume.

"Hey," she said, and from behind her back she pulled a can of whipped cream. "Dessert?"

"Get in here," I said.

She walked past, smelling of sweet perfume mixed with the fruity scent of her conditioner.

"My husband is waiting on the bed."

"Well, hello," I heard her say ahead of me as she walked through the lounge and into our bedroom. "What a view."

She looked briefly out of the window but then turned to Jason who lay on the bed with his hands behind his head and his feet crossed. He was still wearing his tux.

Sam shook the can and turned to the both of us. She popped the lid and squirted some into her mouth, laughing over it as she swallowed it down without a care.

"Yum!" she cooed.

"Wanna eat that off something else?" I asked, narrowing my eyes across at her.

"Sounds like fun."

"Pull out your cock, Jason," I said, not wasting an ounce of time.

His hands moved down to his belt and he unbuckled himself. I could see that his packet was stiff inside. Sam interjected before he could show her.

"Can't I pull it out?" she asked.

"Of course," I said. "How rude of me. Jason?"

He let his hands fall by his side and Sam took off her flat shoes. She mounted the bed and crawled across. Her short black skirt pulled tight over her bubbly ass. She had an athlete's frame and her butt looked like it had been toned with squat-work.

"Let's see what I'm working with here," she said, and unabashed she went straight for her target.

She opened his fly wide and reached down into his pants, swooning as she felt his thickness and pulled it up out of his pants.

"Oh, fuck-yes," she said. "That's what I was hoping for."

Jason had a lot to be proud of. His cock was one of the biggest and nicest I'd ever had. It wasn't ridiculously huge but it definitely left a lady satisfied.

Sam shook the can in her hand and squirted a dollop of cream out onto Jason's cock. She stooped her head and licked along it, then she arrived at the bulbous crown and planted it straight into her mouth, fighting to get all the cream that she could.

She hummed at her decadent behavior and slid back off him, leaving a trail of cream along his shaft that she quickly tended to with her tongue until it was all gone.

"Perfect," she said.

I was still watching her from the foot of the bed. She had such a confident, mesmerizing way about her that I'd kind of forgotten that I'd intended to join in too.

"My turn," I said, and I put a knee on the bed. My red dress drifted up over my black stockings and I pushed my ass out as I crawled behind her, but my target wasn't Jason. It was her.

I slid her dress up over her ass and she turned her head quickly. At first her face was a picture of shock, but she soon remembered herself. She narrowed her eyes and looked through her lashes.

"You gonna be naughty back there?" she asked.

"I intend to be," I said, rubbing at her ass that was covered in her tights.

She hummed contentedly and moved back to Jason's cock putting it back in her mouth and rolling her tongue around him.

He took a sharp breath through his teeth and groaned, looking through his lashes at me as I started to tug down her tights.

With some effort I slid them underneath her skirt and down her pale, smooth legs. Eventually I peeled them off her cutesy, painted toes and then I was back behind her, staring into the cleavage of her delicious ass.

"Hand me the cream," I said.

Sam's jaw dropped open in faux shock, but she did as I asked.

I took the can and moved my face close, kissing one of her cheeks gently and looking at the strap of fabric that pulled across her panties. I moved my lips to her crotch and gave it a kiss, listening to her gasp ahead of me.

"What's she doing?" Jason asked, looking to Sam.

"She's taking down my panties," Sam said, although I hadn't yet.

With her passive instructions made I reached beneath her dress and grabbed the waist of her tiny panties. I pulled at them and the fabric slipped off her crotch and fell down off her ass. I pulled it down and stared at her tight, perfect, symmetrical slit. Above it sat her tiny dot-like asshole, all hairless and impeccable. I'd have been envious if I wasn't so turned on.

"Eat her pussy, honey," Jason said, getting into the spirit of things faster than I thought he might.

I shook the cream and squirted a slither of it down over her ass and pussy. I pressed my face against her and listened to her moan as my tongue scooped out the sweet cream. I raced over her asshole and down to her pussy, tonguing at everything along the route and filling my mouth with the decadent cream.

I heard Sam moan ahead of me, her cries muffled by the thick packet of my husband that was wedged inside her mouth. She slurped him through her lips and I heard the spit filling her mouth as she spoke.

"Eat my ass and pussy, Mrs. Casper," she groaned. To hear her use my name like that gave me a thrill like no other.

She plunged my husband's cock back into her mouth and by now the whipped-cream seemed unnecessarily calorific. I tossed it to the carpet and planted my mouth back over her ass, tonguing at that perfect dimple of hers and slithering down to tease inside her aching honey-pot.

Sam gave out appreciative moans and groans for each one of my exploratory licks. I'd never eaten pussy before—or ass for that matter—so it was reassuring to hear that I was doing something right.

My tongue teased inside and I tasted her sweetness. She tasted good enough without the cream anyway and soon I was parting her lips with my fingers and licking over her pink flesh. My mouth enveloped her slit and I teased my tongue out, targeting her clit.

My husband took off his suit-jacket, throwing it to the floor before Sam rose up and got to work on the buttons of his shirt.

He unfastened his bow-tie and I rose up on my knees to join her, putting my arm over her shoulder and watching her undress him.

"Good girl," I hushed, biting at her ear.

She shuddered a playful groan and giggled, then she turned to me and started to kiss my lips. Before I knew it was making-out with a woman twenty years my junior who I'd only met about an hour and a half ago. This was certainly a vacation to remember.

She looked back to Jason and pushed his shirt open. Her hands found his pecs and she gushed as she squeezed them, giggling and looking back at me.

"We're gonna have some fun," she said.

"I already am," I said, and I nuzzled my head into her neck and put a hand up her dress.

She leant forward and started to kiss my husband on the mouth like he was her lover. I watched his eyes close and his tongue push through to meet hers. Her hand was quickly around his cock and I thrust my fingers up inside her to match her rhythm.

"That's it," she purred, pushing her forehead against my husband's and looking at her hand as it pulled back and forth over his flesh.

I could feel her wetness sliding over my fingers as I probed two inside. I clapped my palm against her as I beat them into her, listening to the juices of her pussy echo inside her snatch.

"Let's get this shirt off," I said now, sliding my fingers out of her wetness and looking over her shoulder as I unfastened her pressed, white blouse.

I pulled it back off her arms and she broke away from my husband momentarily. My hands were quickly around her body, putting a breast in each hand and pressing my chest to her back.

Her tits were smaller but perkier than my own. I unclasped her bra and she took it off her shoulders, tossing it aside and draping her arms over my husband to kiss him again.

My hands were on her breasts again, sliding over her pink nipples until they started to stiffen against me.

"Look at those tits," Jason said, and he leant forward and eased Sam back.

He held her in his powerful arms and I moved from behind her, holding his head and bringing him to her tits like it was a gift to him.

He wound his lips over her and encircled her raised studs with his hungry mouth. Sam moaned to the ceiling, her eyes closed as she relished the sensation.

I stood away from the bed now and watched the pair of them. It was like a page from the Kama Sutra seeing them in their pose. Jason's big cock sprang up from between them both, resting against Sam's skirt that covered her modesty for now. My husband fed on her tits with aplomb, uncaring as I undressed beside them.

Sam's eyes finally opened and she turned to me just as I was unzipping my dress. It fell to the floor to reveal my black bra and panties, with the garter-belt to hold up my stockings.

"Now that's a woman," she growled, biting her lip. "Come here."

I walked over towards them and their eyes were on me now. I put a knee on the bed and returned to my spot, then Sam reached around my back and unclasped my bra.

"Look at those," she said. My husband didn't need a second invitation.

The bra fell away and my big tits sat on display for the pair of them. Sam took my husband's cock in one hand and put the other on my breast, jerking him and squeezing me as she closed her eyes. It was as though she wanted the mixture of both sensations at once: a hard cock in one hand, a soft tit in the other.

I watched her slender fingers take control of Jason's cock, getting him in the mood and filling his weighty balls with huge load of spunk that we were sure to enjoy together.

"We need to get those pants off," I said, looking to Jason.

Sam obliged by kicked her leg over him and leaning back to give him a view up her skirt. His eyes were on her immediately, keen not to waste the opportunity as he stared at her perfectly kempt slit.

"You like that?" I asked him, coming behind her again and pulling up the hemming of her skirt.

She groaned before I even touched her and when my fingers split her flesh Jason hurried his movements, as though he couldn't wait to be rid of his pants and back to us.

He tossed them aside and came forward on his knees, his huge cock swaying like he was dowsing for water.

"Put it in her pussy," I said sternly, looking down over her shoulder.

She lay against me with my arms under hers and I started to squeeze her tits as Jason readied himself.

He pumped his cock and wiggled between her legs, pushing her skirt up until it was around her midriff. Sam split her knees wide and lay back against me.

"Fuck her," I said.

"Fuck me, Mr. Casper," she mewled.

Jason grabbed underneath at her ass and pulled her up to rest on his thighs, then he pushed his cock down and found her sticky wetness, slipping inside slowly.

My mouth hung open as I watched his inches disappear out of sight and I looked down to see Sam's face. Her brow was furrowed but the look on her face was one of pure unadulterated pleasure as she took each and every inch that he had to give her.

"Good girl," I said, rubbing her stomach as though I was massaging Jason's cock beneath.

I eased myself out from under her and Sam stayed in position. She stretched out her legs until they were around Jason's back, leaving her ass on his thigh and giving him a view right down on the action.

Well I couldn't leave her mouth vacant like that, especially when it kept falling open to moan. She looked so pretty.

I peeled my panties down over my ass and stepped out of them, then I flung my leg over her face and knelt myself down on her.

She took to it instantly, moaning up at my pussy and then giving me a huge, open-mouthed kiss. I hummed contentedly, as though I'd just sunk into a hot bath.

When I opened my eyes again I saw Jason smirking back. "Enjoying yourself?"

"Uh-huh," I nodded, rolling my bottom-lip through my teeth and starting to grind over Sam's moaning face.

She pulled at the folds of my pussy with her lips over her teeth, tonguing into me and tasting the pooling cum that had already arrived in my sex.

"Come here," I said to Jason, curling a finger and beckoning him forward.

He leaned close and we performed our very own Eiffel Tower above our new lover as we kissed, with my husband deep in her pussy while mine sat on her face.

We kept that up for several minutes until Sam had me right on the edge of climax. I couldn't speak for Jason but I was about to explode. My pussy was charged with eroticism, so sensitive now that each of her licks felt enormous. I was swollen beyond belief.

"I'm gonna come!" I cried suddenly, and I watched Jason's pupils dilate as he looked on.

My eyes closed and the color swirled across my vision. I gasped and exhaled and then I felt the tremor course through me and strike my pussy. The waves of euphoria exploded outwards as Sam tongued up into me, sucking, licking and biting in just the right way.

"Come on my face," she cried, licking at my contracting pussy as my juices eased out of me.

She slurped them down and spread them back across my flesh as my husband continued to plow into her, but his main focus was on me now.

I put both hands on her tits and bunched mine together between my arms, groaning out my release and then falling off her to stretch myself out on the bed as the aftershocks trembled through me.

Quickly I was back to her, kissing her mouth lovingly and tasting my own juices that lay smeared across her maw.

"That was hot," she giggled, but a sharp pump from Jason snatched the laugh from her.

"Give it us now, honey," I called, putting myself alongside Sam. "Give us your cum."

Sam turned to me and we kissed as my husband's big cock reemerged.

"Taste yourself," I said, nodding to his dick.

Sam turned immediately and wrapped her lips over him as he arrived, slurping her sweet nectar off his cock with a smack of her lips.

"I taste good," she cooed.

"I know," I agreed.

Jason smirked as he looked down, beating his cock over his two beauties as though he owned us.

My hand worked down the front of her flat stomach and I found her soaked pussy. Her clit was stiff and she needed only a little bit of jostling before she was primed to climax herself.

"Yes, Mrs. Casper," she whined, gripping my wrist and keeping me there.

She started to take these deep breaths and her tits seemed to swell as her climax approached. It was glorious to watch. Her chest blushed red and her whole body tensed as she ached out her release. Her sexuality seemed so raw and on display.

Jason was enjoying it too, I could tell. He was working his hand over his big cock and the veins inside it were thicker than ever. He looked ready to pop.

"Come for me," I hushed, and both of them thought the request was for them.

Sam let out a yelp and exhaled, shuddering and opening her mouth wide in silent moan.

Jason was more audible, building his pumps to a flurry and then grunting wildly as the first rope of hot cum leapt from his cock and fell across the both of us.

Sam let out a delighted groan as the warm cum hit her tits and I continued to slide my finger along her soaked groove as my husband delivered his next lashing.

This time he pointed it closer to our faces. I flinched as it struck my mouth, then I hummed contentedly and licked my tongue across my lips to taste the bitter-sweetness.

Sam moaned alongside me, her orgasm flowing out of her as she undulated in the sheets. Jason watched down above us, pumping along his cock and making a real mess of the both of us as more and more of his hot love poured out.

It fell across our faces again and I put a hand to her jaw and turned her face towards me. We kissed and the cum found its way between the embrace until soon our tongues were wrapping around it.

Sam was unabashed as the mess flowed over our faces, kissing me with more passion than I'd ever seen from her. It was as though the kiss was a display of gratitude for everything we'd given her that evening.

The final few webs arced over us and Jason's groan told us he was spent, kneeling there breathless with his cock steadily dripping the last of his seed.

Sam turned to him and raced her mouth down over his cock again, claiming the errant cum and keen for it not to go to waste.

She turned to me with a full mouth and looked to my lips. I met hers again and felt the velvety texture spilled over into my mouth, sliding between our tongues as we kissed it back and forth until it was all gone.

"That's so fucking hot," Jason said, looking down and shaking his head in disbelief.

The pair of us started to giggle.

"Sorry about the sheets," Jason said.

"Not my problem," Sam said, and she gave me another deep kiss.

Jason fell beside us and we lay there in silence, apart from the deep breathing. The three of us were utterly spent and utterly contented. Sam had given us a world-class service and my husband had given her a big tip in return. Paris was everything we hoped, plus a little more.

THE END

My Husband's Salon Treatment : Couples Threesomes 12

"He'll be here soon," I said across to Liz, finishing up on Carol, a regular client who sat in front of me in the salon chair.

"Does he know?" Liz said, sweeping up the trimmings of previous customers.

"Not a clue," I beamed.

"What's happening?" Carol asked.

"Well," I smiled, running my tongue over my teeth. "It's his birthday and Liz and I are going to give him a treat he won't forget."

"Damn," Carol swooned, "that sounds interesting."

"You don't know the half of it," Liz said. She'd worn this tiny black skirt for the occasion and looked a picture.

Liz and my husband had only met once before at a work party, but I could tell immediately that they liked each other. My husband Sean is a handsome guy. His hair is this ashen-grey, giving him a texture that I'd love to replicate in the salon. He has these warm blue eyes and an inviting smile that makes you confess things you shouldn't.

Liz is young and feisty. She made no bones about her feelings for my husband and I found the whole thing flattering. She'd openly talk about him in the salon as we went about our day, asking me more intimate questions when no clients were around. I'd half-promised to show her exactly what she wanted to know one day. Well today was that day.

"What have you got planned?" Carol asked, looking in the mirror at me as I stood behind her.

"Oh, one or two things" I said, tongue-in-cheek. "He'll leave here a happy man, put it that way."

"I'm thinking I should stick around," she said.

I laughed. "No spectators. It's just Liz, me and my husband."

Carol was cool with it all. She'd been a client of mine for years and knew that I was an open-book when it came to many things, but staunchly closed on others. I'd decided that Liz could join us, but nothing more than that.

"You'll have to tell me all the juicy details when I'm next here," she said.

"Deal," I agreed.

Carol paid and shook her head with a smile as she lingered at the door. "I hope he knows how lucky he is."

"He will," Liz said, standing all prim-and-proper in her tiny dress and tights. She looked like butter wouldn't melt in her mouth, but I knew better. Liz had confided in me about her escapades since I'd employed her last year. Despite being only nineteen she had this wealth of depravity that I was almost jealous of. She found herself in the damndest of scrapes, and here I was putting her in another.

Carol pulled the door closed and walked off down the sidewalk. I dropped the blinds on the two huge windows that sat either side of the door, spotting Sean pulling up in his car across the road as I did so.

"He's here," I said to Liz.

She jumped quickly on the spot. She'd been more excited about this whole thing than I was.

"So, run me through it again," she said. "We get him in the chair and then …?"

"I'll be washing his hair. You'll be pulling his cock out."

She bit her lip. "And he has no idea?"

"None," I smirked. "He thinks he's just getting a special haircut for our dinner reservation tonight."

"I love giving surprises!"

"Shh, he's coming!"

Liz ran for her broom and grabbed it just as Sean arrived at the door. I opened it for him and he stepped. He wore a long business coat and had his suit on beneath. With autumn well underway we had a lot of clothes to remove, but the shop was warm. He took his coat off immediately and hung it on the stand, looking around.

"It's quiet," he said, not noticing as I closed and locked the door behind him.

"I cleared the schedule," I said.

He looked to Liz who was concentrating far too much on her broom as she passed it over the lacquered wooden floor.

"Hey—uhmm—Liz, is it?" he said.

She looked up and smiled. "Hello, Mr. Connors."

"Sean," he said. "You can call me Sean, please."

"Hey, Sean," she said, giving him a flirtatious wave.

Sean swallowed uncomfortably and pulled at the collar of his shirt.

"You can take your jacket and tie off, honey," I said. "They'll only get in the way."

He turned back to the coat-stand and pulled his suit-jacket off his back. I turned to Liz and gave her the thumbs-up. Her eyes were sparkling with delight as she watched him open the collar of his shirt and pop open a couple of buttons.

"Where do you want me?" he asked, turning to us.

"Well I think we should give these locks a wash before we give you a trim," I said, running my fingers through his hair.

"You're the boss," he said.

"Come sit in the chair."

I walked over to the black, leather seat that sat in front of the basin. The basin was its own island so you could move around it—something I'd insisted on when we had the place refurbished.

"*The chair*," my husband smiled. "Sounds like the name of a challenge."

"It might be," I smiled, looking again to Liz who was doing her best not to giggle.

She moved around the room, sweeping and clicking her high-heels along the wooden floor. It was hard not to pay attention to her. I'd never known anyone look so good with a broom before.

"Lie back," I said to Sean.

He sat in the chair and sank against the back of it, putting his head into the groove of the basin and staring up at the ceiling.

"Comfortable?" I asked, turning on the water and checking the heat against my hand.

"Umm, *yeah*," he said, sounding surprised.

"Relax."

I put a towel around his neck. Sean's eyes closed warily. I guess the whole thing was pretty new to him and guys aren't good at letting their guards down.

I ran the warm jets of water into his hair and started to massage his scalp. He let out a deep groan and I flashed my eyes to Liz as it filled the salon.

Her mouth hung agape as she heard it. It sounded decidedly erotic and I could tell Liz was excited by it. I don't think it'd be the first groan we heard from him that day.

"Relax," I said again slowly, as though I was a hypnotist.

Sean rolled his shoulders into the leather and let out a calming breath, seeming to sink into the experience and embrace it. I knew then that I had him.

I pushed my nails through his black and gray hair, teasing my long nails against his scalp and treating him to an experience that he'd been sorely missing. Ordinarily Sean would head into a barber's for a five-minute cut, but I think he was beginning to see how he'd been missing out. Never again would he pass-up an offer from me for a cut at the salon.

He hummed another appreciative groan and I motioned silently to Liz to come over. She placed the broom quietly against the wall and walked cautiously across the floor, keen not to let the clicks of her heels ring out too loudly.

Sean was too deeply relaxed to notice. When Liz arrived over him he didn't even open his eyes. Instead he lay there with a contented smile on his face, his eyes closed as I massaged is scalp.

I nodded down to his belt and Liz put herself beside his waist, looking down and preparing herself to unleash him.

"Now since it's your birthday," I said, watching his smile broaden, "I've decided to give you access to our most exclusive package of all here at the salon."

I gave Liz a signal and her hands moved to his belt. Sean's eyes flashed open and he looked straight up at me.

"The platinum package, sir," I said, my mouth twisting in a smile as I relished the look of confused panic on Sean's face.

He realized far too slowly that if both my hands were on his scalp then someone else's hands must have been on his belt buckle.

He looked down his body, keeping his head still. Liz smiled up at him, unlocking the buckle of his belt and sliding it open.

"Wh—what?" Sean said, and he tried to sit up.

I shut the water of and held his shoulders down, dropping my head to whisper close to his ear.

"It's my husband's fortieth," I said calmly, "and I'll be damned if I'm not going to give him a present to remember."

He swallowed and looked back to me.

"Now relax," I said again. "Liz and I are going to treat you to something you'll never forget."

She used this as her cue to pop the button at his waist. Sean tried to move again but I kept my hand on his shoulders. He didn't seem to be putting up too much of a fight.

"It's okay," I said. "You have a pass today. Enjoy it."

"A pass?" he asked, flashing his gaze quickly between me and Liz. She was unzipping his pants slowly and building the tension inside both her and Sean.

"Today you can do anything you want. Liz knows the deal, don't you Liz?"

"A one-time ticket to ride," she said, putting it in a way only she could.

"A one-time ticket," I repeated. "Happy birthday."

At that Liz reached into his boxer-shorts and pulled out the stiffening muscle inside. I think my hands on his scalp had already got him half-way there, and Liz's eagerness to see his cock was doing the rest.

She stood there in her short, tight dress, her face a picture of unbridled joy as she marveled at the thick length of my husband that was finishing its growth in her hand.

He looked down and I put my hands on his shoulders, bending down to talk into his ear again. "Let her do her thing."

I squeezed at the tension beneath the towel, massaging him briefly before turning the water back on and continuing to tickle his scalp.

Liz was holding his thick cock like a baton, jerking it gradually up and down and looking into the face of my husband as she did so. She was no longer looking to me for approval. Instead the moment felt like something intimate between her and my husband. She was like a snake-charmer gradually wooing her subject.

I could see Sean visibly begin to relax again. His shoulders flattened back against the leather chair and his eyes closed as Liz pumped over him. Sean's cock was beautiful, if you could say that about a cock. It was just the right length and girth—like a golden ratio for dicks.

Liz was smitten by it. She stared down and watched it move through her hand, giving it long, slow pumps to begin with as he reached his full size. She pointed her thumb up the underside of it and stroked over him, moving his skin over the muscle.

"Mmmm," he groaned again, submitting completely now. I knew it wouldn't take much effort.

Sean wiggled his butt in the chair as Liz got more comfortable too. She put another hand around his length now and pumped both of them over him, wielding him like a huge sabre.

She knelt to the floor now and took a look at me for one final request of permission. I closed my eyes and gave her a nod. I think I was just as keen to see her suck his cock as he was. She'd certainly talked a good game when it came to blowjobs in the past.

Liz really started the thing off with a bang. She dropped her mouth over him and Sean tightened up and squeezed at the arm-rests. Her mouth ran over the head of his cock and rolled down the shaft. I watched him disappear inside her as she swallowed him, taking inch after inch after inch. Just when I was sure she was done she pushed down further until her lips were right around the hilt of him.

Sean's eyes opened and he stared down to confirm his suspicions. By this point I'd stopped massaging his head. I shut the water off and watched, wondering just where exactly Sean's cock was hiding.

"Are you seeing this?" he asked, looking back to me.

Liz pushed a lock of her blonde hair behind her head and bounced her eyebrows at the both of us.

Sean let out a chuckle but it was snatched away by Liz as she crept out her tongue and teased it at the underside of his cock. He groaned long and loud, letting his head fall back against the basin and looking up to me.

"Where did you find this girl?!"

Liz unwound him from her mouth, peeling her lips back over him to reveal his slick length. She was like a sword-swallower or close-up magician.

"You never told me you could do that," I said, dumbfounded.

"You never asked," she shrugged, squeezing and pulling at Sean's cock.

"Do it again," I said, nodding to him. "Let me see it."

Liz smiled and tossed her hair behind her shoulders again, sinking her lips over him. This time I moved back and watched her throat thicken as she took him inside it. It bulged with his girth, looking like a snake swallowing its prey.

"What other secrets are you hiding?" I said, stepping back again to admire the whole scene.

Sean's knuckles were white as he held on tight for the ride. Liz pulled back and his wet cock slipped from her again, but this time she snarled at it like an animal and switched gears, gripping it in her fist and pumping her saliva over him.

He slipped through her wet grip as she pinched her way to the crown, putting the tip of him inside her and kissing his glistening cock like she was sucking an ice-pop.

"That's good," I said slowly, moving my hand down to touch at the crotch of my pants. Watching Liz move was like a treat unto itself. She had such a commanding way over Sean, as though she was a mistress of cock and he was yet another subject.

Finally Sean's eyes opened and he stared down again to witness the devilish little nymph that was giving him the ultimate birthday present.

Liz looked to me now, spotting my hand working between my legs. "Come and join me," she said.

I stepped back towards her and moved around the other side of the chair, positioning myself opposite.

Sean looked down, his hair wet and dripping. He took the towel from his neck and rubbed quickly, drying off the brunt of the water. Then he sat up to enjoy the incoming treatment from his wife and his mistress.

I knelt opposite Liz and she pointed the tip of his Sean's cock towards me, offering it as though it was a spoonful of foreign food.

"Try it," she said.

I pushed my brunette locks behind my ear and moved in timidly. I'd sucked his cock before—of course—but I'd never had him in my throat. Liz had made it look easy.

I pushed down over him and stifled a gag as I felt his thick tip hit my tonsils. Quickly I pulled back, gasping and spluttering.

"I don't have a gag reflex," she said, taking back control and pushing her lips down over him again.

He sank straight into her throat with ease, bulging her gullet wide. She pulled back and his cock was awash with her spit, looking big and delicious.

She aimed it back to me and instead of trying to match her party-trick I took a grip of Sean and gave him every other move in my repertoire.

I twisted two hands up and down his cock, spitting on the tip and using it to lubricate my grip. The embrace was tight and wet and I knew Sean loved it. I got a kick out of watching his knuckles whiten again as he gripped the hair. His fingers pushed into the leather and he groaned as though the release was cathartic.

"You girls are something else," he cried.

"Undress for him, Liz," I said casually, still beating his cock and sucking on him.

Liz didn't miss a step. She stood up and walked to the foot of the chair, staring down at Sean who watched her intently.

I slurped along his cock as she pulled the dress off her shoulders, unzipping the back of it and then letting it fall to the wooden floor.

Beneath she wore a set of black, lacey lingerie, covering her tits and flowing down over her flat stomach to wrap between her legs.

She kicked the dress aside with her high-heeled shoes, standing astride in front of Sean. He looked her up and down and so did I. My hand beat idly as I looked at her slender figure. She was curvy in all the right places. The lingerie held her big tits perfectly and as she turned slowly you could see her delightful ass, made rounder by the cut of her garment that turned her cheeks into two full circles.

"Is that what you want?" I asked, looking up into his eyes.

"I want you both," he confessed. "Can I have that?"

"It's your birthday," I said. "You can have anything you want."

I went to stand next to Liz. I unfastened the buttons of my white blouse and pulled it out from my tight pants. I was dressed a little more professionally than Liz, but she was young enough to get away with turning up to work in all manner of ensembles.

I made it half-way down my blouse before Liz came to help. She took the task from me and continued unbuttoning me, facing her ass towards Sean who took the opportunity to ogle it some more. He grabbed his cock and started to jerk himself as he watched us both.

"Look at that," I motioned, and Liz turned to see.

"My, oh, my," she said. "I love watching guys jerk."

Sean pumped his cock through his fist with fresh vigor, putting on a show for the both of us now. Liz undid the last couple of buttons without looking, keeping her gaze on Sean's thick length instead.

She walked behind me and took the shirt back off my shoulder, showing Sean my white bra that contrasted hers.

Her hands came under my arms and she gripped at my tits, pushing them together in their cups and bouncing them for Sean who smirked back. Liz unfastened my bra, smoothing her hands back round to my front and pushing them up under the garment.

Her cool hands touched my bare tits now and I leant my head back against her. I turned my lips towards her and she pulled me closer, kissing my mouth. I'd never kissed a woman before. There was something even more sensual about it than kissing my husband. Her smooth lips felt different.

She dragged my bra off and then moved her hands down to the front of my pants, still holding me in a hug. I could feel her big tits pressing against my back as she unfastened my pants and pulled them wide, teasing the fingertips of each hand down inside my panties.

"That's it," Sean said, yearning to see more.

I bent as demurely as possible and unfastened my shoes. Liz stepped away from me and took the attention of Sean again, slipping the shoulder-straps of her lingerie down over her arms. The garment was almost sheer and in the right light you could make out the darkening flesh of her nipples beneath.

Sean was rapt on her. When I stepped out of my shoes and stood back up I could see him looking to her tits as she did a writhing movement in front of him. I was captivated too. Gradually she peeled down the lingerie, moving even slower as she revealed her stiff nipples.

"Perfect," Sean gushed, watching the picture of her tits become complete in front of him.

I dropped my pants and stepped out of them in just my white panties, tip-toeing around the back of Liz now to mimic what she'd done to me.

I put my hands under her arms and gripped her tits, squeezing the flesh and feeling her nipples stiffen against my palms. She seemed to dine out on the moment much more comfortably than I had. She groaned to my touch and brought her hand behind me to pull me closer to her.

"Yes," she hushed. "Play with these big titties."

I felt the juices flood to my pussy as I surrendered to her order. Suddenly the dynamic in the shop had changed. I might have been in charge when it came to cutting and styling hair, but Liz seemed to wear the trousers when it came to matters of the flesh. She was so at-ease with it all.

I squeezed and pinched to the nipple, looking intermittently to Sean who was still jerking his cock. He started to unbutton his shirt and Liz seemed incapable of merely watching. She strode towards him when the hair of his chest became visible and she pushed the shirt back off his shoulders.

Sean hurried out of it and she dropped his lips to him, kissing him deep and passionately as I stood in place, wondering what the hell I'd unleashed.

The sight of her kissing him as he jerked his cock turned me on more than I thought it would. The idea of sharing Sean was something that had scared me, but now that it was happening I found myself strangely enjoying it all. Liz was giving him something I couldn't.

I pushed two fingers over the crotch of my panties and groaned as I felt he juices slide out of me inside.

I walked forwards and Liz vacated Sean's mouth. He tossed his shirt aside as I put my mouth to his, kissing him deep before putting my forehead against his.

"Enjoying yourself?" I asked, knowing the answer.

He opened his mouth to say something, but all that came out was a whimpering groan. I looked down to see Liz wrapping her lips around his cock again, then she moved off him and trapped his length between her big tits.

She pushed them over him, roughly working within the limited parameters of the salon chair. She jerked him from the side, wedging him up between her big cleavage and sucking at his cock whenever it came free.

I held Sean's head against my tits while he watched, but then I started to share the animal-like primal eroticism that was flowing out of Liz. I gripped my breasts and pushed them towards Sean's face and he opened his mouth hungrily to wrap his lips over them.

He sucked and fed on my nipples as Liz held him in the soft embrace of her big tits, jerking him between them and yearning for the cum that was building in his balls.

I moved down from Sean's face and around the back of the basin behind, standing over Liz. I took a fistful of her hair and pushed her down over Sean's cock, moving her head over him and jerking him in her throat.

With her under my control I started to become more empowered. I'd been caught off-guard by the initial depravity but now I felt at home in it. I yanked her head up by the hair and Liz grunted in pain as she stood quickly.

I pulled her over towards the basin and Sean turned to watch, surprised by my sudden power-play. I took her hand and put it on the rim of the round basin, then I did the same with her other hand.

"Get up, Sean," I said.

He slid down off the chair and stepped out of his pants and boxer-shorts, standing proud with his big erection that jutted out from his body. It was surreal to have my husband naked in the place I worked, but it wasn't the oddest thing about the day.

I gripped Liz's hair again and saw the delight in her eyes as she felt the pain. I had my suspicions that she might like it rough, but this was confirmation.

"Come over her and fuck her, Sean," I said.

I took a grip of her lingerie and yanked it down, listening to it rip and watching her ass wobble as I teared it away.

I yanked again and the thing came free, leaving her naked now apart from her high-heels. She pushed her ass out and posed against the basin, looking to Sean who was walking behind her now. I stepped out of my panties and took a grip of his cock as he came close.

"Get it in her tight pussy," I snarled, pumping my fist over him and pointing him towards his target.

Liz looked back over her shoulder. "Fuck me, Mr. Connors," she said. Sean didn't correct her this time.

He shuffled forwards and I stroked the tip of his cock back and forth along her wet pussy. I could feel how soaked he was when my fist touched her swollen sex. She was ready alright.

I held him close and helped him inside. I was a party to his adultery, making the whole things even more sinful than I could have imagined.

I pushed forward and let him go, listening to her cries of pleasure as his burgeoning inches sank up into her.

"Good girl," I said, holding her neck. I bit at her ear and squeezed her throat as Sean pushed inside.

Liz let out a groaning scream of pleasure, forcing it out through her throat that I squeezed tight.

"You like that? You like this big fucking cock inside you, huh?" I asked.

"I do!" she screamed. "He feels so fucking good in my pussy."

Sean was gripping at her ass, pushing his hips against her butt and slamming himself deep each time. His flesh clapped against her as he built his rhythm and I looked down to watch him disappear through the crack of her ass.

"Are you gonna take him?" I asked, twisting my fingers over my pussy now. "You want to take his fucking cum?"

"Uh-huh," she nodded. "I want it."

"Where do you want it?" I asked, eager to hear.

Sean slammed away behind, grunting and groaning as he jerked his cock through her tight body. Liz gripped him much more firmly than I ever could.

"I want it on my fucking face," she growled, looking to me.

For a moment I was caught off guard by her serious enthusiasm.

"You do, huh?" I asked, taking hold of her cheeks in my hand. I squeezed her face and kissed her lips, rubbing my pussy with increasing vigor.

"I fucking want it," she begged. "I want his fucking cum on my face."

"You hear that, honey?" I asked, keeping my eyes on Liz's moaning face.

"I heard her," he said.

I looked to him and he smiled back. I stood up and put my naked body against his, kissing him as he fucked her.

"Do it," I insisted. "Let me pull your cum out all over her. Do you want that?"

Sean nodded.

"Would that be a good birthday gift?"

"It'd be fucking perfect," he said, lunging his lips forwards and kissing me deep.

His tongue wound around mine and he upped his tempo, slamming against Liz's ass and causing her to scream so loud that her voice bounced off the walls.

"She's fucking coming," Sean said, breaking from the embrace and looking at me with a proud smile.

"Is that right," I asked, stepping back to Liz. "Are you coming on my husband's big, hard cock?"

"Yes!" she cried, slapping at the porcelain basin and grunting hard.

She bent over more and Sean shuffled back. She was at a right-angle now, her ass pointed straight towards him.

I bent to my knees and finger-fucked my pussy as I watched the pleasure wash over my assistant's face. I could see the climax captivate her. Her body tightened and then relaxed in undulating waves. Her groans matched her trembling knees and Sean's groans told me that her pussy was busily contracting over his thick length.

"Are you close, honey?" I asked, looking to him.

"I'm close."

"I want to share it," I said, looking at Liz's pleasured expression. "I want to pump it over the both of us."

I seldom let my husband shoot on my face but Liz's sense of adventure was contagious.

"Give it us," I urged to Sean. "Give us that full-load. I want to feel your fucking cum on my face."

Sean clapped through her tight pussy and then pulled out. Liz moved quick and fast, as though she knew all-too-well that she might miss the moment.

She spun to her knees and put her face close to mine, rubbing her pussy and looking to Sean who had started to beat his cock in front of us.

"Give me that," I urged, reaching out for it.

He loosed his grip and I took him up, beating fast and yanking him forward.

He walked onto us so that his cock was only a couple of inches from our faces and Liz and I braced ourselves.

"Are you gonna shoot it?" I asked, knowing the answer. "Are you gonna cover us in that fucking cum?"

"I want it," Liz cried. "I fucking want it, Mr. Connors."

I saw the signs in him as I had many times before. His eyes were closed and his muscles were tensed. His hand was open in this strange paralyzed state as his mind concentrated on the sensation that was building inside him.

"Give us your fucking cum, honey. Give us that fucking load!"

"Oh, yes, Mr. Connors," Liz joined, fucking her pussy so hard that I could heard the squelching of her juices inside. "Cum on our fucking faces."

I pulled at his stiff cock and then I felt it throb and stiffen further still. His eyes opened and he looked down as he let out a groan.

"Oh, fuck!" he cried.

"Shoot that fucking—" the first blast bounced out of his cock and splashed over my face. I flinched, then embraced it. "Oh yes! Cum! Cum! Cum!"

I beat over him and his cum sprang messily from the tip of his dick, leaping into the air and cascading down onto the gasping faces of Liz and me. She opened her mouth and hummed contentedly as the warmth struck her.

"I want every fucking drop," I grunted pulling hard and feeling the spasm in his length as each rope was released.

He blasted jet-after-warm-jet of spunk, firing it out of his balls in a volume that I'd never known from him.

"Oh, honey!" I gasped, marveling and looking to Liz to see her face awash with his pearlescent seed.

She was rubbing it against her face and then moving the same hand down to her pussy to smother it with his sinful seed.

I licked over my lips and watched another lashing unwind from his dick, spiraling over the pair of us. He tasted bitter and sweet all at once. I turned to Liz again to see her looking at me.

She lunged for my mouth and we kissed, sharing my husband's slick seed between the both of us. My tongue slid over hers, lubricated by the fruits of our labor.

My pumping slowed now and I started to concentrate more on our kiss. There was precious-little cum left inside Sean's balls and his long, satisfied groan told me he was spent.

I put both hands around her as we kissed, washing his cum over her and passing it between our mouths.

She pulled back and held me, licking at his seed as it hung on my nose and lip. She tongued over me and Sean watched above, gently working his cock.

"Good girls," he said, and I felt proud to have pleased him. The evidence of it was cast across the both of us.

Liz and I continued to kiss until there wasn't much left of Sean to taste. I looked up to him finally and opened my mouth to take him inside one last time.

Liz stroked my hair behind my shoulders and rubbed at my pussy as I sucked on Sean's length, sliding my lips off him and leaving him spent. He looked down, bewildered.

"Did you enjoy your present?" Liz asked, still slowly toying with my stiff clit.

"It was certainly a birthday to remember," he said, laughing.

"Good," I smiled, turning back to Liz and pecking her cheek.

I stood up and took Liz's hand, lifting her to join me.

"Honey, there's a bathroom out back," I said, pointing to the door with the 'Private' sign on it.

He gathered his clothes and moved away to tend to himself. When he'd gone I turned to Liz and walked back over.

"I hope that was al—" she began, but my lips were on her before she could finish.

I kissed her deep, sliding my tongue over hers and relishing the embrace. It felt much more sinful now that my husband wasn't there. I pulled back and Liz seemed bashful.

"You're a beautiful woman, Mrs. Connors," she said.

I wondered just what I'd started ...

THE END

My Husband Fucked A Hot Hitchhiker : Couples Threesomes 13

"Only two-hundred miles to go," Callum said, reading the sign as we whooshed by.

"I guess it's time," I said mysteriously.

"Time for what?"

Callum held the wheel tight and glanced over briefly, watching as my hand crept down to my bare knees and lifted my skirt slowly.

"Oh boy," he said, desperately concentrating on the road ahead.

The road was thankfully quiet and, more importantly, straight. He didn't have to do much, which was just as well.

"I was thinking," I began, sliding my hand into the hot crotch of my panties and working down along the groove, "that you could set the cruise control on for a couple of minutes."

"And what can you do in a couple of minutes?"

I reached my hand across the centre console and squeezed at the bulge in his jeans.

"I can think of something," I said.

Callum cleared his throat and smiled. "Don't let me stop you."

He pressed a button on the steering-wheel and set his speed, looking down to my hand as I unfastened the button of his pants.

"Let me get in there," I hushed, brushing my brunette hair behind my shoulders and turning my baseball-cap backwards.

Callum and I had been married now for almost a decade and we delighted in spicing things up in the bedroom. You had to keep things interesting, but at just the right pace so that you weren't out of ideas after a few years. There were plenty of things the two of us hadn't done together and I looked forward to trying them out in the coming years.

Callum's father would lend us the keys to his lakeside lodge once a year every summer. We'd head up there for a debauched weekend of fun, passing the time having sex and trying all manner different positions as we whiled away the weekend. It was there that I first tried anal; there that I first took a facial and there that I hoped to try out some of the new toys that I'd stowed away in my bags. Now though, I was keen to get Callum's appetite nice and whetted for the weekend of fun to come.

Callum lifted his ass of the seat as I tugged at his jeans and slid them down. I could see his white Calvins beneath, hiding that delicious cock of his that I'd fallen in love with the first time I spied it.

I pulled down the waist and it popped out, already stiffening from the notion of his roadway blowjob.

"Fuck, honey," he said, slapping on the wheel. "You know just how to get me going."

I smiled as I dropped my head to him, pulling out his long, sleek cock that belied his forty years. The thing looked like it followed a strict moisturizing regime. It was unblemished and clean-cut, with thick veins just beneath the surface that stretched upwards towards the taut, soft-pink crown that I eyed now.

"That's it," he said steadily, looking down his chest as my mouth approached.

I jerked him slowly in my fist and then stuck out my tongue, circling it around the head of his cock and listening to him exhale in a long, satisfied groan, akin to sitting down after a hard day.

"Oh, that's fucking good, Lill," he said, putting a hand on the back of my neck and squeezing.

I teased around the bulbous head, flaying my tongue on the underside of his cock and smiling at the groaning reaction that escaped him.

My mouth finally pressed over him and I felt his stiffness slide inside me, feeling hard against my tongue and cheeks.

"Damn, I hope we don't crash," he joked. "Imagine they find us like this."

The macabre thought made me giggle and I pulled back off him, smiling up into his face. He winked down and then reached over to my side of the car, moving his hand down along my spine.

He eased downwards and I went back to work on his stiffness, thrusting it into my mouth as I felt him pull up my skirt. Truth be told I'd put it on especially for the journey. Easy access was the order of the day. Shit, if I could have convinced Callum to wear his kilt I would have.

His hand moved down into my ass and he pushed the thin strip of fabric back against me, teasing down my cleavage until he arrived at my asshole.

His fingers pressed against it, massaging around it and then teasing a little further down to arrive at the puffed lips of my excited pussy.

I cooed delightedly at his touches, doubling down on the blowjob and thrusting his cock deeper to show my appreciation. I pressed him against the top of my throat and Callum forked his fingers either side of my pussy, squeezing at the flesh in-between and getting my panties all sodden as they settled in the crease.

"Is that all for me?" he asked, sensing the moisture against his fingertips.

"Always," I said, pulling him from my mouth.

My tongue encircled the head again but then I slid forward off him as he braked suddenly.

"What the fuck?" I asked, pushing off the centre of the car and sitting upright.

"There was a hitchhiker," he said. "She looked hot."

I sat upright and turned around, looking out of the rear-window to see the long, blonde locks of a twenty-something hitcher, thumbing a lift in our direction. I had a crazy thought.

"We should pick her up," I said.

"I didn't see where she was going," Callum said.

"She's on our side of the road. Don't worry, she won't interrupt your blowjob."

Callum slowed down and took a sweeping turn in the empty road, driving back down towards the blonde woman who moved to pick up her huge bag.

"Do me back up, would you babe?" he said, nodding down at his cock.

I reached over and put him back in his pants, then I straightened myself out and wound down the window as we pulled up opposite our soon-to-be passenger.

"I'm Kim," she said. "Y'all going to Michigan?"

"Sure are," I beamed. "I'm Lillian and this is my husband Callum."

She looked beyond me at Callum who raised a hand in her direction. She looked to be around twenty-something. She had long, blonde hair and an infectious smile. She seemed bubbly and adventurous, if the huge backpack hadn't already given that away. She wore a pair of trail boots with thick socks and tight yoga-pants. Her t-shirt pulled across her cute little tits.

"Toss your stuff in the back," I said. Callum drove a pick-up and we had plenty of room.

Kim walked to the back of the truck and I looked in the wing-mirror at her shapely ass bouncing as she did so. She had a skip in her walk that seemed to aid in the bounce. It was mesmerizing. I didn't usually go for women, but I knew straight away that I'd make an exception for Kim.

"You were right," I said, looking across at Callum. "She's *hot*."

She jumped in the backseat behind me and closed the door, belting up and then stretching out a hand between the two of us. "Nice to meet you," she said.

Callum took it and gave it a shake, and then I did the same. He started up the engine and turned again, heading back along the corridor of road that lay between the tall, verdant trees.

"What the hell are you doing all the way out here?" I asked.

"My last drive came a bit out of their way to drop me off. Said it was the best they could do. You're the first to drive past in almost half an hour."

"Well, you're lucky," I said. "My husband and I are quite the adventurers."

"Oh, yeah? Me too a little bit. I'll try anything."

"We're heading up to Torch Lake," I continued.

"My Dad's place," Callum added. "We're not that rich, don't worry."

Kim laughed. "Well, me neither."

We drove through a couple more miles and I started to imagine Callum's cock, sitting unsatisfied in his pants. Blue-balls was the worst, he'd told me that. The more I thought of it the wetter I became and soon I was wondering exactly what Kim meant by the phrase: "try anything."

"You consider yourself a free-spirit, Kim?" I asked, looking at her in the wing-mirror.

"I guess so," she said.

"You know when we spotted you we were doing something pretty adventurous ourselves."

"What's that?" she asked, leaning forward.

Callum gripped the steering-wheel tighter and steeled his sights ahead.

"I was treating my husband here to a risky blowjob."

"No shit?" Kim said.

"No shit," I said, proud of myself that I'd had the balls to tell her.

"Well don't stop on my account," she said.

I turned on the seat and looked back to her. "You really meant it when you said *free-spirit*, huh?"

"Well I'm certainly not a liar," she said.

"You don't mind if we—"

"Lill," Callum said, sternly.

"I don't mind," Kim said. "Knock yourselves out. It'd be kinda hot."

"You hear that, honey?" I said, leaning back over the divide and gripping his packet.

Callum wrestled against a smirk. "I heard that."

"We've tried all sorts of things," I said, looking back to Kim who was leaning forward and hoping to get a peek.

"Me too," Kim said, perching right on the edge of the back-seat. "But I've never done that."

I opened his jeans again and delved inside, finding his cock just as hard as I left it. I pulled it out of his jeans and Callum stared ahead.

"Damn," Kim said, spying it. "He's a big boy, huh?"

"All the better," I said, leaning back over the divide. This time I faced my body towards the back of the car, keen to give Kim a good view as Callum's cock disappeared through my lips.

She watched on as I steered him towards my wet mouth, opening my lips over him and humming contently as his stiffness filled me again.

"That's fucking hot," Kim said with relish.

I peeled my lips back off him and looked in her direction. "You should try it."

"I want to," she said, staring longingly at my husband's gorgeous dick.

I hadn't meant for her to explicitly try it with my husband, but Kim was keen to misunderstand me and I was keen to let her.

"You hear that, honey?" I asked, pumping his cock through my fist. "Those young lips around your dick ... you want that?"

He let out a sigh. "I'd *love* that."

"Wanna come up-front, Kim?" I asked, stroking slowly now and looking right at her.

Her eyes were sparkling with lust as she watched me close. "How about you two come back here?" she said, then she looked ahead through the windscreen.

I looked up at Callum. "Fancy pulling over?" I smirked.

"We're making good time," he said.

I stared in disbelief and then watched the smile crack on his face as he started to laugh.

"Are you kidding?" he laughed. "Of course I wanna pull over."

I gave his thigh a playful slap. He started to decelerate as we approached a pull-in and he steered the pick-up into the vacant rest-stop beside the road.

I unbuckled hastily and so did Callum, turning off the engine and jumping from the car with his cock flailing. The road was still empty as the pair of us entered the driver's rear side. My husband went first, sitting in the middle seat beside Kim.

"Nice to meet you," she said again, only this time she was staring down at my husband's swaying cock as he shuffled beside her.

I closed the door and leaned forward, watching as her hand came out to meet my husband's hard cock. It was the first time I'd ever seen anyone else tackle him. It was a strange kind of thrill to witness someone else pleasing him.

Callum lifted his arms and put them around the back of both of us, looking down his body as the slender fingers of Kim wrapped around him.

"I can feel his heartbeat," she cooed, looking across at me with that same sparkle. Her pupils were fat with excitement.

"You can feel it better against your tongue," I said, keen to see her swallow him.

Callum watched as she shuffled her butt back against the door and stooped her head towards him, curling a lock of that perfect blonde hair behind her ear.

She moved her mouth like she didn't want to make a mess, carefully placing her lips over him and then driving down his thickness slowly.

I'd never seen a blowjob up-close and personal before and to watch my husband's strong cock twitch in her mouth was a pleasure to behold. My pussy came to life in an instant as Kim sucked a deep breath through her nose and pushed him deeper.

Callum groaned and then pulled me in towards him, motioning for me to join our new friend at his cock. I wasn't going to deny him.

I slid back against the door too and moved my head down his chest, putting it close to Kim. Her eyes opened slowly and she spied me, taking his cock from her mouth.

"How rude of me," she said, offering the slick pole to me.

My husband watched on with drooping eye-lids, the pleasure on his face immeasurable. As long as one of us was busily toying with his shaft then I don't think he could have too many complaints.

Kim held the hilt of him in my direction as I spread my mouth over him, putting on a show for Kim now too as I unraveled my tongue around him and popped the top of his dick from my mouth.

Kim moved in to gnaw at the base and soon the two of us were working in unison. My wet mouth would stir around the tip of him whilst Kim would feast on the base, slipping her tongue down towards his weighty balls and sucking them into her mouth to the sound of my husband's pleasured groans.

"Fuck," he said eventually, tossing his head back. "Why didn't we do this sooner?"

I pulled him from my mouth. "Because we didn't find someone as devilish as our new friend, here."

Kim rolled my husband's balls in her mouth and eye-smiled at me.

Callum moved his hand down over my back again and started to slide his hand over my mound, doing the same to Kim opposite me who started to groan against his cock.

"Do you want him?" I hushed, talking across his wet length.

"I want him *everywhere*," she cooed, and that seemed to suggest more than just her pussy.

I pulled my way off Callum now and moved to the front passenger-seat, fiddling at the sides and finding the lever that slid it forwards. With a clunk and a clank I pushed the seat towards the dash, then I moved to the driver's side to do the same. I don't think Callum would mind too much that his precious seat-calibration was all out of whack.

"That should give us more room," I said, eyeing the new floor-space that had been revealed.

I sat back against the back of the passenger-seat, opening my legs wide and showing my husband the crotch of my panties.

He stared down and Kim took a look over too, watching as I moved the crotch aside and bared my wet, thin lips to the pair of them.

"Are you gonna play with that while I suck him?" Kim asked.

I worked my fingers down the slit and teased them inside as I stared. "I'm gonna play with it while you *fuck* him," I corrected.

Kim's eyes spread wide with delight and Callum seemed to perk-up too. It would be the first taste of new pussy that he'd had in years and he had every right to be excited. Kim looked like she'd be nice and tight for him.

"On one condition," I said, raising a finger. "I want to see it slide inside."

"You stay there," Kim said, patting Callum's thigh.

She stooped on her feet, keeping away from the roof of the car as she shuffled off her trail-boots. She pulled her thick socks off her feet to reveal her dainty, painted toes then she went straight to the waist of her yoga-pants.

"Let me do that," I urged, moving forward off the floor and crawling towards her.

Kim stayed in place and rested her hands to her side, watching as I started to slide her yoga-pants down her leg to reveal her thin panties.

"Damn," Callum said, watching her tight ass become uncovered. It must have looked good because he gripped his cock and started to work it as he watched, as though he couldn't let the moment pass without ceremony.

She leaned between the front seats and pointed her ass back to him, with only the thin strip of fabric cutting through the middle of it.

I tugged her pants down her leg and off her slim ankles, tossing it aside and then stroking both hands up and putting my face close to her ass.

I looked back to my husband and rubbed her round cheeks, spanking it so that Kim let out a playful wail as her ass wobbled in front of Callum.

"That looks perfect," he said, and I couldn't help but agree.

"It looks delicious," I said, turning back to it and planting a soft-kiss on the reddening cheek.

"Maybe it tastes delicious," Kim said, looking back over her shoulder at me with her infectious smirk.

I felt a sudden surge of excitement pull through me, as though I'd just remembered that all of this was real and that it was actually happening. The thought of her ass sitting in front of me, waiting to be claimed made me giddy.

"Let's see," I breezed, as though eating a woman's ass was something I did regularly.

I slid her black panties down off her ass and listened to Callum groan as her puckered knot revealed itself above a hint of her pussy curving away beneath.

"Mmm," I groaned, opening the cheek with my hand and showing my husband.

He pumped his hand over his cock, keeping himself stiff as I stretched out my tongue and moved it closer. Callum leant forward on his seat and stared as the point of my tongue made contact.

It tasted sweet and I forgot about how sinful it was as I pressed my tongue flat against her and waggled it. Kim let out a deep groan, as though she loved getting her ass eaten.

I teased around the rim and then slid under, tickling inside her petals and sampling the cream that was ready to break out of her.

"Fuck, that's good," she groaned, looking back again.

She moved her hand and held my head against her and I felt particularly devilish as she did so. Soon my face was pressed between her crack while my husband enjoyed the show. I felt a pang of lusty depravity.

"Sit on him," I urged now, pulling away. "I want to see his cock open you up."

Kim reversed towards Callum, keeping her ass pointed in his direction as she sat back. Callum held his cock steady and he guided himself towards her pussy.

Kim mounted the seat and leant back against his chest, opening her legs as Callum's hands came up her front and gripped at her tits that sat beneath her t-shirt.

I rushed to his aid and pulled his jeans down his legs, removing them like I had Kim's and then grabbing her t-shirt and wresting it up her arms and off her.

My husband popped her bra open before I even had chance to admire her bound tits and soon I was staring at her cutesy tits and stiff, pink nipples.

"You are a little minx," I beamed, moving forward and opening my mouth over her appetizing breasts.

I rolled my fingers around her nipple and felt it stiffen in my mouth as she gasped and groaned like a giddy teenager.

Callum's cock flayed beneath her, looking powerful as the veins breathed life into him and the muscle at the hilt throbbed.

I gripped him and held him upright, then Kim dropped her naked body down steadily until her pussy draped over the crown of his dick.

I watched her swallow him up, listening to each of them groan and joining them as though it was happening to me too.

My pussy spasmed and I felt some of my wetness leak out of me as I aided my husband in his adultery. It didn't feel the least bit wrong. It felt as though we were each helping one another get what we wanted in that moment.

I leaned back and stared now, watching her body descend on him as his cock slid up insider her tight body.

She arched back on him and her ribs eased out beneath her tits. Her hand came over her shoulder and she held the back of my husband's head as he kissed at her neck and shoulder, groaning as she sheathed him in her wet, warm embrace.

"That's fucking hot," I whispered, rubbing beneath my skirt.

I pulled my tank-top over my head and downed my panties, keeping my skirt on for the moment as I watched the pair of them.

My fingers spun on my clit, working it stiff as she began to bounce. The V of her pussy dropped over his length and I watched her hands begin to work over her clit that sat just below the triangle of kempt fur above.

She knelt over him, her legs either side, and she began to bounce slowly, grinding up off him and then dropping down over his stiffness that soon became coated in a film of her pure-white juices.

"Fuck, she's tight," my husband strained, as though he was warning us that he might bolt at any second.

I got on my hands and knees and crawled forward, staring at the sinful union of their sex organs as they writhed against each other.

His cock looked more powerful than ever as it sprang through her tight O over and over and his balls hung beneath, looking deliciously inviting.

I honed in, gnawing at the shaft and tasting the cream that she'd spread over him. She was as sweet as ever. I made a point of my tongue and teased it down, washing it around his stubbled balls and then circling back up before kissing just below her clit.

I kept my face there, inexplicably drawn to the very point at which the two of them fused together. My tongue flitted between her pearly stud and my husband's balls, winding up and down along the route each time as she bounced steadily.

"Lick my pussy, you naughty bitch," she gasped, looking down into my eyes as they met hers.

There was something thrilling about being degraded like that and I think Kim knew it. I kind of wanted to get back at her, and I had just the way of doing it.

"Let me put him in your ass," I hushed, sucking on Callum's balls so that a huge groan escaped him—one that made him sound like he was all-for the idea too.

"You want that?" Kim asked, looking under her arm at Callum.

"I'm not exactly gonna say 'no,'" he grinned.

She rose up steadily and I gripped the hilt of Callum's dick before it could slap back against him. I moved the tip back an inch and Kim sat back down, letting out a long, pained groan as the tip of him made contact with her tight aperture.

Her mouth hung open and her brow furrowed as she sank, but like a good little slut she slowly began to open over him.

"Good girl," I encouraged, peering under and watching the head of Callum's dick disappear inside her.

She spread over him and then he surged inside a few inches to the sound of Kim's quick intake of breath.

"Damn," I swooned, leaning back to look at her wet, vacant pussy and her stretched asshole. "Looks like that pussy is all mine now."

I leaned forward and started to feast on her petals, fondling at my husband's ball as she dropped on him and took him all the way up to the pit of her stomach.

Finally she let out a grunt that made it sound as though the worst was over, then gradually she started to bounce on him, jerking him through her tight sphincter with only one goal in mind.

My fingers worked busily at my pussy as I ate her soaked cunt, tonguing my way into her and smooshing her flesh against my face as I did so.

She held the back of my head on her as she rocked over my husband's dick, looking down into my eyes with relish as my tongue toyed around her pussy.

"You're good at that," she groaned eventually, her eyelids fluttering and her body tightening.

She rocked faster and started to moan and I soon spotted the unmistakable signs of climax begin to wash over her.

"Yes! Yes! Yes!" she groaned, bouncing like a champion jockey.

Her asshole peeled over my husband's cock again and again, sliding over his contours with a keen grip.

"Cum in her ass," I ordered now, knowing that the both of them were close to orgasm.

Callum's balls were tighter now, turning walnut-like as I massaged them into his body. His cock seemed stiffer than ever and his gasps sounded more primal and urgent.

Kim too was groaning and moaning, her pussy gasping open as I tongued it before then winking shut. I probed a finger inside and felt the contraction against it, then she let out a wail and really started to go for it.

Her face looked strewn with pained pleasure as she groaned onwards, looking down into me and then back at Callum whose eyes were closed as he focused.

"Shoot it in my fucking ass," she snarled.

"In her ass, honey," I chimed in.

"I'm fucking close," he grunted.

I rubbed his balls and shaft, matching the movements of my hand on my own pussy as I felt my cream leak out of me. Suddenly he rose to a crescendo and then he let out a huge, unmistakable cry that could only mean one thing.

Kim's bounces stopped suddenly as she felt the blast of sticky heat arrive fiercely in her asshole.

"He's fucking coming," she beamed, looking down at her pussy as though she could see it pouring into her.

I pushed two fingers inside her pussy and felt the throbbing of his cock on the other side of the divide. Each pulse inside her matched the groans that lurched out of him. He filled her with six or seven delicious ropes, coating her insides in his white love until there was nowhere else for it to go.

"Lick it out of her," Callum said now, still wheezing and rocking slowly.

He put his hands beneath her ass and lifted her up off his pole. Cum dribbled down his cock and her asshole spluttered open as he lifted her. Bubbles of pearlescent spunk popped on her ring.

I lunged forwards, caught up in the moment. I tongued at his seed, tasting the salted-caramel of his release and slurping it into my mouth like a good slut.

"Good girl," Callum said, and I felt a pang of pride as I pleased him.

I tongued under her, washing her asshole clean and then kissing her pussy with my cum-strewn mouth.

I licked around her one last time, slurping everything I could out of her ass as she squeezed. When I was full of his seed I moved up her body, holding it in my mouth and letting it pool under my tongue.

When I arrived at her face she squeezed my cheeks, studying my mouth and lips before smiling at the white deposit that I held inside.

Her lips met mine and we French-kissed, moving his love between us and passing it from one mouth to the other like the dirty bitches that we each knew we were. Callum panted behind us, oblivious to what was happening.

She held her lips on mine as she moved down onto the floor of the cab, letting his spunk pass between in messy strings that she slurped back up.

"Damn!" Callum said, awestruck by the display of depravity before him as he spotted it.

Eventually the cum has all but dissipated—swallowed or dripped away down our naked bodies. Callum stroked steadily over his spent cock as he watched us enjoy each other.

"You know," he said, looking between me and Kim. "There's a spare room at the cabin ... if you wanted?"

Kim looked to me for approval and all I could do was beam a smile.

"Would that ... be okay?" she asked warily, looking again like the vulnerable go-getter that we'd picked up.

"Are you kidding?" I said. "I haven't finished with you yet."

I leaned forward and kissed her again to show my approval and we went from there. The rest of the weekend was one big adventure. In the days we'd relax, maybe taking a walk around the lake before dining in a nearby restaurant, but at night the time was ours to be naughty all over again, and we didn't pass it up.

Kim was our fuck-slut for the weekend and she brought out a side to me that I wasn't sure existed before. Callum was one lucky guy.

THE END

Hotel Sex : Couples Threesomes 14

There was something clearly different about 'Hotel Sex' from the moment we arrived. The women on reception wore lingerie, the bell-hops wore buttless chaps and the concierge wore a bow-tie and very little else.

"Are you sure this is the right place?" Nate said, leaning in to whisper.

I giggled, looking to him and then noticing the bobbing pecs of the barman who was putting on a display for his raucous female customers.

"I think this is the right one."

Nate's birthday was soon but I'd be lying if I said I wasn't just as keen to sample the place as he was. Some friends of ours had mentioned it years back and we vowed to visit soon-after. We weren't too precious over each other when it came to matters of the flesh. As long as we were back in each other's arms after everything was said and done then we were both happy.

A threesome was something neither of us had done but it was something I certainly wanted to try. I'd spoken to Nate beforehand and he'd told me that was exactly what he was looking for too. Going to the south of France to get it might seem a bit extreme, but we figured we could combine it with a holiday, you know? Fine wine, fine cuisine and fine, fine ladies.

I tipped the bellhop after he'd set down our bags. I was intrigued to see where he was going to put the money, given his limited options. Before I could watch he'd slid back out of the room and it was just my husband and I.

The room seemed like your fairly average affair at first glance, but it had its little nuances that let you know exactly where you were. Along with the soap and shampoo sat little bottles of lubricant. As well as the room-service menu there was also a 'Hotel

Sex' special menu that featured adult toys of every variety. In the back of it was what we came for: the room-ordered mistresses.

"Here it is!" I chirped, holding it up to Nate who was admiring the view out over the beach.

"So the old bastard was telling the truth," he said, coming over with wide eyes.

"You can pick them!" I said, amazed.

Nate took the magazine from me. "*Monica*," he read. "They even have bios! '*I enjoy long walks and deep-throating.*'"

"You're kidding," I said, snatching it back from him.

I read through it and confirmed it with my own eyes. "And very reasonably priced," I said.

Nate peered over my shoulder and we looked across the pages together.

"See anything you like?" I asked.

"I was thinking someone blonde."

"Oh, were you?"

I smiled back at him but Nate's eyes stayed focused on the page. "There," he said. "Her."

His finger came down on a lady called Anjelica. I read the bio aloud.

"'*I came here to sample the sun, but stayed to sample the tourists. I enjoy both men and women and there's nothing that I'm not into. If you're looking for a night you won't forget, then you'll get exactly that with me.*'"

"Sounds intriguing," Nate said. "Look, she's Croatian."

He pointed to the little flag beside her name and I noticed that each woman had one, along with their height and sexual preference. Anjelica was bisexual, as were most of the women there. I couldn't help but get turned on as I imagined what she might do to me.

"You want this one?" I asked.

"If that's okay?"

"Of course," I said. "Look at her!"

I moved to the phone and picked it up.

"Now?!" Nate said.

"Why not? We don't just get to have one, you know."

He laughed as though he couldn't believe his luck and then someone picked up on the other end of the line.

"I'd like to order Anjelica, please," I said, strangely comfortable with how surreal it all was. "Ooh, *'extras'*" I repeated, bobbing my eyebrows at Nate.

"*Extras?*"

I covered the mouth-piece and whispered into it, keen not to let him hear. I wanted to leave some of it a surprise for him.

"Yes, that's everything, thank you."

I set the phone back down and Nate was still looking across, wide eyed.

"*Extras?!*"

I giggled. "You'll see."

"When is it?"

"She'll be up to our room in an hour."

"This is certainly kicking off the vacation right, huh?" he said, unfastening his shirt. "I'm gonna jump in the shower."

The pair of us got showered and dressed. It seemed senseless to put all of our clothes back on afterwards, so instead I opted for a black, one-piece lingerie that my husband had bought for me last Christmas. He wore a tight pair of boxer-shorts and nothing else. Nate didn't need it. His sculpted body was a testament to his commitment in the gym.

"Two minutes," he said, looking to the clock on the wall.

"Maybe she'll"—there was a knock on the door—"be early," I finished.

The excitement on both of our faces was palpable. On the other side of the door stood the woman who was going to unlock a whole new experience for the both of us.

"Ready?" I asked, looking back to Nate. "You look ready."

He took a breath. "Do it."

I opened the door wide and on the other side stood Anjelica, looking exactly like she had in the picture. She had this beaming, infectious smile.

"You dressed for the occasion," she said, extending an elegant hand to shake. "Nice to meet you. I'm Anjelica."

I took her hand and invited her in. "I'm Tori," I said.

Nate rushed forwards, extending his hand too. "Nate," he said. "It's a pleasure."

"It looks like the pleasure will be all mine," she said wryly.

Her accent had this eastern European tinge to it that tickled down my spine every time she spoke. Something about the way her mouth moved made me imagine it in a host of other places. I think we'd made the right choice.

She wore long black stockings and a fur-lined white coat that she removed the second she came in. Beneath it she had on a black bra and panties that drew the eye with its swirling lace and sheer look.

"So how do we begin?" I asked, looking to her for guidance.

"Like this," she said, and she stepped into me and planted her lips on mine.

We kissed deep and her hand came to my ass, squeezing at it while I sampled her mouth. She tasted sweet and addictive, like candy.

As she pulled back I looked into her dazzling hazel eyes then across at my husband. His jaw was almost on the floor. Beneath his tight underwear I could see the thick slab of flesh that was getting ready.

"Now you," she said, stepping towards him.

I was still giddy with the excitement of our kiss when she wrapped those same lips over my husband. He closed his eyes and pushed is fingers into her glossy, blonde hair, pulling her slender body close to his. She looked good draped against him.

Anjelica wasted no time in sliding her hand down to the thick packet of my husband. She rubbed along it and he groaned into her mouth.

"Excited already?" she smirked, pulling back.

"Who wouldn't be?" he said, looking between the both of us. "Two beautiful women in one room, dressed like that!? Damn!"

Anjelica giggled now too, pushing her hair behind her ear and looking down as though she was slightly shy of showing such emotion.

"I—uhmm—ordered the 'surprise'" I said, looking to her and hoping she knew what I meant.

She turned away from the both of us and bent forwards. Our eyes darted to her round ass and I noticed the box-shape in the centre of her butt, pushing against the panties.

"A buttplug!" Nate guessed instantly.

"A buttplug," Anjelica said, spinning playfully back around. "And that's just to warm me up."

Nate was beyond excited. I'd known him for years and I'd never quite seen the sheer elation that cast across his face before now.

"You really are spoiling me."

"It's for a birthday?" Anjelica guessed.

"Sort of," I said. "It's a treat for both of us."

"Is it now?" she said, looking at me in a new light. "Tell me, Tori. Have you ever eaten pussy before?"

She asked the question so frankly that I wondered if I'd heard her right.

"Never," I confessed.

"Well that is something we will have to change. Get on the bed."

She had this commanding yet alluring way about her. To look at her and listen to her soft voice you would think her meek and vulnerable, but the words she chose and her delivery of them made me act without hesitation.

I moved to our hotel bed and sprawled across it, rolling onto my back to notice Anjelica and my husband sharing another moment together.

Her hand went down inside the back of his boxer-shorts and she squeezed his buttocks. I watched her fingers start to move down there and then I listened to a gasp from Nate.

"She sure is playful," he said, looking back to me.

"What was she doing?"

Anjelica smiled over his shoulder at me. "I was fingering your husband's asshole."

"Oh," I said. "I've never really done that before."

"That's why I'm here," she said. "To give you a taste of the things you've never had or done."

She moved to the bed and lay beside me. I could smell her flowery perfume and conditioner and her lips came close to mine again.

We kissed and I ran my hands over her smooth skin, moving down curiously towards the protrusion in her panties. I pressed against it and she closed her eyes tight, sucking a breath and pulling her lips off mine.

I watched the expression on her face awaken in pleasure and her eyes opened to look at me again. "Have you ever had anything in your ass before?"

"A finger," I said.

"Nothing more?"

"Nothing more."

"Nate," she said, turning to him. "You've never put anything other than a finger in your pretty wife's pretty asshole before?"

"I haven't," he said, laughing.

"You have very boring sex in America," she declared.

I'd have been offended if she weren't so god-damn delightful.

Nate walked over and joined us on the bed, kneeling over the both of us with his stiffness still stowed away in his briefs.

"Shall we introduce your husband to the party?"

"We should," I said, tasting her lips again. I could scarcely keep myself off her.

Anjelica sat up and put herself in front of Nate who looked down, taking deep breaths as though he was practicing a kind of stoicism. Knowing him like I did I think he was tempering his enjoyment. It was unbecoming to come in the first few minutes of a threesome.

"Let's see what we've got here," she said, rubbing her hands across his packet.

Nate threw back his head and groaned, surrendering to the unadulterated joy of it all. I couldn't help but giggle at how much he seemed to relish it.

Anjelica curled her long nails over the waist of his boxer-shorts and pulled him down, revealing the kempt hair that sat sculpted above his clean-cut cock.

It rolled out and bounced upright, looking more impressive than I'd ever known. The thick veins stretched up him and Anjelica seemed immediately smitten.

"He looks delicious," she said, looking to me. "May I?"

"You may," I said, watching on eagerly. I wanted to see how she tackled him.

I knelt up on the bed for a better view, looking down on Anjelica as she moved her lips over the smooth head of my husband's cock.

They slid over him and he let out another moan of pleasure, looking down now and watching his inches disappear inside her eager throat.

When she was at her capacity she wriggled her neck on him and pushed down further, eager to fit as much of his cock into her mouth as she could.

I watched her neck bulge as her hand worked at his balls, massaging them and rolling them in her fingers like they were stress relievers.

My hand moved mechanically to the hot crotch of my panties as I watched. I hadn't even noticed that I'd done so until Anjelica pointed it out.

"You're not as shy as you look," she said, flicking her pointed tongue at my husband's freshly wet cock as she spied my hand.

I bit my lips and continued to smooth my fingers over the front of my panties, pushing the fabric against my dampening groove and coaxing my clit to stiffness as I watched her enjoy him.

Her lips pulled tight around his shaft as she slid him out of her mouth, kissing her lips off the tip and tickling the sensitive underside. Her hand started to jerk him over her and then she lay back on the bed, moving her other hand between my legs and rubbing at the inside of my thigh.

I moved my hand away from my crotch slowly and hers replaced it, rubbing my panties and keeping the rhythm along my husband's cock as she did so.

I looked across and met Nate's eyes. We leaned towards each other and started to kiss while our mistress satisfied the both of us.

"Take off my panties, Tori," she said.

I looked down from her face and over her cutesy tits and flat stomach, all the way down to the black panties that covered her modesty.

She lifted her ass off the bed expectantly and again I couldn't deny her. I moved my hands to the waist of her panties and started to slide them down, realizing in an instant that this was the first time I'd ever undressed a woman.

Anjelica moved back to my husband's cock as though the whole thing was par-for-the-course. She drove him back into her mouth as I pulled down her panties to reveal her completely shaven, smooth pussy. If my pussy looked as perfect as hers I'd have shown it off too.

She kept her ass raised as I pulled the panties down over her stocking and off her ankles. When I was done she split her knees wide, unabashed at showing me exactly what she had to offer. I could see the soft-pink slit and just the hint of pussy lips meandering down the sides. There was a glisten to it that drew the eye, as though it was sparkling like a gem-stone.

Beneath her pussy sat the round, bejeweled base of her butt plug, hiding the last of her modesty beneath it.

She pulled his cock from her mouth and looked to me. "Taste it," she said. "Let me be your first."

I dropped down to lie on the bed, looking forwards at her pussy. They seemed so alien up-close like this. It was easy to forget that I had one of my every own between my legs, gradually getting wetter now at the thought of how slutty I was about to be.

Above me I could hear the slurping kisses of Anjelica as she devoured Nate and every so often he'd let out a groan of enjoyment.

I nestled between her legs and started kissing up her thigh as I approached. It looked so inviting and Anjelica wasn't shy. Her fingers started to rub her clit as I approached and her slit started to move too. I could catch the glimpses of her wetness inside and I licked my lips in preparation.

I kissed softly at first, curious at how it might feel on my lips. It felt no different to anywhere else to begin with, but as I probed deeper I tasted the sweet cream of her pussy on my tongue.

Anjelica moaned as though she'd been waiting for this moment since she arrived. Her fingers scissored her pussy open and I licked my tongue along everything she showed me. I tried to imagine how I'd like to be done to me. My kisses became more wet and erratic. I started to suck and pull at her flesh and soon I was lost in the moment.

"Be my slut," she growled, gripping my hair and holding my head on her.

I started to writhe my ass, pushing my pussy against the mattress impatiently as I fed on her. The horniness built inside me until it started to unlock a new side of me. I was aroused beyond measure and it felt unfair that Anjelica should be the one having all the fun, especially as I'd paid for her.

I took my lips off her and stood up on the bed like a new woman. Anjelica looked up at me with a smirk, as though this was the person she'd yearned to unlock inside me.

"Do it," she urged, as though she could hear my thoughts.

I thrust my panties down my leg and stepped out of them eagerly, straddling her and dropping to my knees. I walked myself up her body until my pussy was over her face.

"That's what I fucking want," she snarled, and she clamped her mouth instantly over my kempt groove.

Her lips worked over me just like I'd imagined them to. She licked and flayed over the sensitive flesh, probing into me and going further beneath me than I intended.

Nate stood up now and put his cock close to me. He didn't say a thing, but he didn't have to. There was no way I was going to leave that throbbing, dangling cock of his unclaimed in front of my face.

I raced my lips over him and felt my competitive streak begin to emerge. I was sure Anjelica had no designs of making it a competition, but I couldn't help but try to best her. I tried to give Nate the sloppiest, nastiest blowjob I could muster.

"This is my fucking cock," I drooled, letting my spit fall over him and then smother it over his cock with my tongue. Before long his entire length was shrink-wrapped in my spit.

"Treat him nasty, Tori," Anjelica said, her words muffled by my thighs.

She gripped at my ass and pulled my pussy against her as though she couldn't get enough. Her tongue pressed against my clit and then she moved down until she was settled on the most sinful place of all.

I cooed delightedly as I felt her start to massage my tight asshole with her tongue. I should have known earlier that her questions weren't innocent.

"What's she doing?" Nate asked, noticing the change in me.

"Her tongue," I gasped. "Her tongue is in my ass."

"I knew you'd like it," Anjelica said, then she teased herself back into my knot again, pushing against it as though she was fighting her way inside.

I started to push my hips forwards and back, running my ass and pussy over her mouth and using her like she was an object. She didn't seem to mind. In fact the smacking of her hand against my ass told me that she was actively enjoying it.

Each spank of hers made me buck like a bronco, as though she were jockeying me from beneath. I started to jerk my husband with the same frenzy, pulling at his cock and listening to the debauched cries bounce off the hotel walls.

I kicked my leg over her and looked down at the wet face as she gasped upwards. I dropped quickly, kissing and licking around her mouth as though I was both tending to her and thanking her for a job well done.

"I want you to pull this thing out of me now and we can give your husband his treat," she said.

Anjelica rolled over on all-fours. My husband pinched the clip of her bra and it dropped down her arms. Her small, perfect titties sat beneath her and my husband squeezed at them.

"You want *me* to pull it out?"

"Yes," she said. "Maybe Nate would like to see it."

Anjelica used one hand to open her ass and looked back over her shoulder at the both of us. Nate was just as keen to see it as I was.

"Here goes," I said.

My fingers teased over the flat head of the bejeweled toy, pulling back and marveling as her muscle started to open wide over the egg-like plug.

"Look at that," Nate said, slowly jerking his cock.

Anjelica looked way too pretty to be this dirty. It felt as though a choir was missing its heavenly lead-singer. Instead of her angelic voice we were bearing witness to her devilish ways.

"That's it," she groaned, biting at the top of her arm. "Do you see it, Nate?"

"Oh, I see it."

He jerked his fist along his cock and Anjelica watched him, as though she was eager to see him enjoy himself at the sight of her. I think she found the idea of people getting excited by her a thrill. The way she concentrated on my husband's expression as he watched me pull the plug from her ass made me think this was as much as a delight to her as my tongue on her pussy.

"Keep pulling," she said, and I watched the shining metal emerge from her perfectly clean asshole.

It popped free and her butt stayed open a little way.

"Tongue it," she said, looking back to me.

I didn't need her instruction this time around. The second I saw her perfect little hole I just knew I had to lick it like she had licked me.

I stabbed into it, listening to the cry of pleasure shoot up out of her lungs as her head hung down beneath her.

"That's so fucking good," she groaned, and I licked my way around her asshole like it was my job.

Nate kicked his leg over the both of us, standing over her and jerking like he was about to unload all over her back.

"Fuck my ass, Nate," Anjelica growled. "Put him in my ass, Tori."

Nate bent forwards, winking his ass at me now too. I took a grip of his cock and pulled it back, smudging his head against her pink, forbidden hole.

"Let's get this big cock in her ass," I said, jerking him and forcing him against her aperture.

He shuffled on his feet, bouncing the mattress as he got into position. I found myself concentrating more than I imagined, lining up the thick, bulbous crown with her impossibly small ass.

"Are you ready for him?" I asked. I think I knew the answer.

"Put him in my ass," she groaned. "Put him inside my ass."

"There it is," I said, slapping my husband's butt as though it was his cue.

He dropped down and I watched her muscle spread over him, sucking tight to his cock and taking him with an ease I was envious of.

"Yes!" she groaned, her voice clenched in pain. "That's it!"

She slapped at the mattress as Nate continued his descent. I fed his inches down into her, massaging his cock until there was none of it left to touch. His balls bunched invitingly against her pussy and I couldn't help but press my face to them.

I sucked on his hanging fruit, rolling them in my mouth as Anjelica's muscled relaxed around its new tenant.

"Now fuck me, Nate," she groaned.

Nate pulled back and started to work his cock through her and I marveled at the sight of it all. I had front-row tickets to my husband's first experience of fucking ass—and what as ass it was.

He dropped into her over and over, groaning as her tight muscle jerked him inside her. It pinched around him like a ring and pinched from tip to hilt, as though it was working the cum from his balls.

I eyed my husband's pink asshole that suddenly looked much more inviting than it had in the past. Before today it was just something that was there, but now it was something to heighten the pleasure. I knew how good it was from Anjelica's deft licks and touches and I knew it would be the same for Nate.

"Stop there," I said, stroking over his back.

Nate did as requested. I moved my face between his muscled cheeks and tickled my tongue out just as before, sampling his flesh and delighting in the coo of appreciation that escaped him.

"She's licking your ass too?" Anjelica asked, as though she was well-versed in the noises people made when someone tongue-fucked their ass.

"She is," Nate confessed.

"You are a very naughty woman," Anjelica said. "Maybe you'd like to lick your husband's come from my asshole too?"

That whole sentence took some devouring. Not only was Anjelica requesting that my husband come in her ass, but she was also requesting that I lick it back out of her.

"You want me to come in your ass?" Nate asked.

"I do," Anjelica said. "Unless Tori has a problem with that."

I massaged my tongue over my husband's asshole again and then gave it a slap.

"Do it," I purred.

"Get beneath me," Anjelica said. "I want to eat your pussy again."

I slid beneath her legs until I felt her kisses on my pussy again. I looked up into her slender, elegant snatch again and saw my husband docked away behind it.

Her asshole pinched over him and every time he pulled back it stretched out from her, as though it didn't want him to leave.

"That's it," Anjelica purred.

Her tongue worked over me and I became impossibly excited. I could feel the ecstasy building inside me and it seemed to be fuelled by the sinful sight that was mere inches above me.

My husband's powerful cock plowed into her over and over. Her pussy hung open and drooled out her juices and I caught them on my face, lurching forward to kiss them back against her.

I could hear the clapping of his hips against her ass, along with the smacking of her lips as she pulled and licked at my swollen flesh again.

Anjelica moved a finger inside me as she toyed with my clit, massaging along my soaked tunnel and giving me something to grip. I could feel the contractions begin and soon I was gasping in air to feed the climax.

My head prickled and turned light and above me Nate continued as though nothing had changed. His pace increased and I watched his cock slam into her harder. His balls pulled up tight to his shaft. Anjelica continued to finger fuck me, tickling her tongue to my clit as the orgasm undulated out of me.

"Oh fuck," I groaned, pushing my pussy up to her face.

My husband used her asshole to jerk him, slamming through her at a pace that I knew I would never be able to endure.

Her ass had looked so untouched before now, but I could see that Anjelica was experienced beyond her years.

"Come in my ass," she groaned, sensing that Nate was close.

He moaned above, letting out a guttural cry that coincided with the slowing of his thrusts.

I watched as his cock pulled back, throbbing above me as he dispensed his seed inside her. The moment was upon me before I had time to prepare.

I was still breathing hard when he pulled his cock all the way out of her. I was breathing so hard, in fact, that when I gasped for air I instead met the first drooling rope of Nate's cum, pouring out of Anjelica's asshole as she pushed it out.

I flinched in surprise at first, then raced my mouth forwards, opening it wide and catching the rest of his seed as she pushed it out of her with a grunt.

Ordinarily something like this was way beyond my level of comfort, but I had a trust in Anjelica that I didn't think I would. She oozed out his white cum like a perfect little porn-star and I ate it like her perfect costar.

My husband had stepped back to watch, not wanting to let this moment pass. It wasn't every day that you watched your wife swallow the cum that you'd fired into another woman's butt.

"Good girl, Tori," he said.

He moved his hand to her ass and probed deep with his finger, dragging the remnants out of her and watching as they poured over my mouth and face.

"Oh, fuck, yes," Anjelica cried, biting the inside of my leg as I put the cherry on the top of our cake.

"Give me those fingers," Anjelica urged, as though it was a competition in naughtiness.

Nate came around the bed, his cock still hard and bobbing as he put his hand close to her.

Anjelica grabbed his wrist and wrestled her lips over his fingers, sucking the cum off them and smacking her lips like it was the tastiest thing she'd eaten in weeks.

Finally she kicked her leg back over me and rushed her face to mine, licking at the cum that had missed my mouth and guiding it back towards the target.

She used her tongue to push it inside me and soon the both of us were kissing again, only this time the seed of my husband was complimenting the moment.

She washed it around my mouth with her tongue and I could feel the silkiness of it all over me. We passed it back and forth, giggling like old school-friends as my husband watched on in awe, steadily working his spent cock and no-doubt committing the moment to memory for whenever he next needed to jerk his cock.

"That's the nastiest thing I've ever seen," he said, sounding impressed.

"You need to get out more," Anjelica said, smiling at him with glossy, cum-drenched lips.

She moved off the bed and left me, dropping at my husband feet and giving his cock one last sensual suck.

He groaned and I watched as he stood there with his dick buried in her throat. I played with a lock of my hair, running my tongue over the slippery cum that coated my mouth and teeth.

"Will that be all?" Anjelica said, turning a knee in and looking between the both of us.

"For now," Nate said.

Anjelica grabbed her bra and panties and put her coat back on as though nothing had happened. She blew us a kiss. "Welcome to Hotel Sex."

We both watched her leave, the two of us disheveled and sweat-dappled as though we'd just survived a natural disaster. A whirlwind of sin had spun wildly in a room and left a trail of sinful destruction in its wake.

"Day one!" Nate said, sitting on the bed and shaking his head.

"I know!"

"When you ate my cum out of her ..." he shook his head and blew a jet of air up his face.

"I'm naughtier than I thought!"

"Good," Nate said. "Think I can put this in your ass later too?" He gripped his cock and shook it.

"No harm in trying." I smirked. It felt as though some of Anjelica's adventurousness had rubbed off on me. My husband was in for a real treat.

THE END

The Marriage Counselor Fucked My Husband : Couples Threesomes 15

Mine and Vince's relationship had been suffering for several months now and the both of us wanted to do something about it.

He'd been saying he just didn't find sex as exciting as he used to, despite me practically throwing myself at him in the months before our counselor meeting.

A part of me had started to feel less sexy than I used to, but Vince had assured me that he was still attracted to me like always. It really played on my mind.

I wasn't the most adventurous of people. I talked to some of my girlfriends about it and they suggested all manner of unsavory sexual activities that I didn't think I'd be able to pull off. I'd never done anal before, or BDSM, or anything too far outside the parameters of what you would call 'regular sex.' Eventually one of my friends had suggested we see a marriage counselor who might be able to help.

"There's nothing wrong with our marriage," I protested. "It's just the sex part of it."

"She helps with that too," Shawna said. "Sometimes she *really* helps."

"Vince and I are fine, relationship-wise."

"You're not listening, Cassie. It's not *just* the relationship part. She'll suggest things for you to do, or try. Maybe even show you a thing or two."

"Show me?"

"Hey, it doesn't hurt. I heard one story where she—"

"Who is this woman, anyway?"

"*Ms. Vickers*," Shawna said, narrowing her eyes when she said it.

"Why are you saying it like that?"

"Like what?"

"*Ms. Vickers*," I mimicked. "She sounds like a Dickens character."

"You'll see when you meet her."

"*If* I meet her."

Shawna shrugged. "What have you got to lose? You see her and it helps or you see her and it doesn't help."

"The hundred dollars an hour is one thing"

"It's worth it," Shawna said. "In fact, if it *isn't* worth it, I'll pay you back."

"Jeez, you sure are confident in this Ms. Vickers."

Shawna raised a finger as she corrected me. "*Ms. Vickers*," she said, pronouncing the name with a flourish. "And now you really don't have anything to lose."

"Fine, I'll do it. But keep your money. I trust you."

"You won't regret it," Shawna said.

I booked in with her a couple of days later, talking on the phone to her secretary. I'd spoken to Vince about it earlier in the day and he seemed willing to try.

"Whatever you think will work," he'd said.

It was mid-afternoon on a Friday when the pair of us drove over there together. We'd each taken the afternoon off work, which I guess is a good sign. If we were willing to make these kinds of sacrifices it showed we were both willing to try and make it work.

We checked in and sat in the waiting room. It had this airy, modern feel to it, looking recently refurbished in clean colors of white and grey, with plants and bookshelves to give it the professional feel.

Vince and I sat on the grey couch and waited for the previous hour to be up. The room was empty and we were quiet. You could almost make out the words of the voices inside the adjacent room. Eventually a couple in their twenties emerged, smiling from ear-to-ear. Behind them *must* have been Ms. Vickers—or *Ms. Vickers*, should I say.

She had on a white blouse and a maroon suit-jacket and matching tight pants that hugged her petite, forty-something physique. She wore thick, black-rimmed spectacles and her golden-brown hair was tight in a bun, with a few loose lockets curling down in front of her face.

"Take care," she said, waving her long-nailed fingers at the couple as they made their way to the door. They joined hands and smiled back at her as she bit her lip. She took a breath and then moved her attention over towards us.

"Mr. and Mrs. Thomas?"

"That's us," I said, standing.

My husband stood up. "Vince," he said. "Nice to meet you,"

Ms. Vickers sized him up wryly.

"Nice to meet you too," she said before looking to me. "And you're ... Carrie?"

"Cassie," I corrected.

"My apologies. Do come inside."

She offered the pair of us into her office. It was bright and airy with a sweet, floral tone hanging in the air. There was a big, grey chair opposite a grey sofa and a desk in the back corner with an open laptop on it.

"I don't get much time between sessions," she said, sliding something into a drawer and shutting it. "Please, have a seat."

Vince and I sat on the sofa, the pair of us palpably nervous.

"You can relax," she said, sitting down in the chair. "This isn't a witch-hunt or a blame-game. It's just open, honest talking. No secrets."

We nodded.

"So how can I help you today?"

I looked to Vince and reached across for his hand, holding it tight.

"Go on, honey," I urged.

"It's ... it's kind of uncomfortable saying it here," he struggled.

"Don't you worry about that," Ms. Vickers said. "There's no such thing as uncomfortable in this room. We are all open with each other in here, okay?"

"Okay," he said, swallowing. "It's the sex."

"Good," she clapped. "We can start from there. What is it about the sex? Too much? Too little?"

"It's fine really, I mean—"

"Come on, Vince," she interjected. "Honesty in here, remember."

"It's ... *stale*," he said.

It felt kind of rough hearing it again.

"And what are your thoughts, Cassie," Ms. Vickers said. "Is it stale for you too?"

I looked down at my feet, pointing my toes inwards and tapping my heels to the floor. "A little," I admitted finally.

Vince looked across in surprise.

"Vince, you seem taken aback?" Ms. Vickers commented.

"I—I had no idea we both were—uhmm—"

"Communication," Ms. Vickers clapped. "That's why we're here. Now ... what can we do to help that?"

Vince and I looked at each other and then at Ms. Vickers. "We were kind of hoping you could help with that," Vince said.

"Good," she beamed. "I was hoping you'd say that."

Ms. Vickers moved to her desk and picked up a note-book and pen, returning to her chair. She crossed her legs and bit the end of the pen in a sexy-secretary kind of way. I don't even think she knew she was doing it. Vince shuffled in his seat, adjusting himself.

"What have you tried so far?"

"We haven't really tried anything," Vince said.

"Okay," she said, narrowing her eyes. "Describe what regular sex is for the both of you."

"Well," I began, clearing my throat. "I'm on birth-control, so it's usually missionary sex followed by an—uhm—internal ejaculation—"

"Creampie," Ms. Vickers said. "We don't have to be all prim-and-proper in here."

"Okay—err—followed by a creampie," I finished.

"And is that fairly typical, Vince?" she asked, making notes and looking over the rim of her glasses at him.

"Yes," he said. "Sometimes we have sex from behind."

"Anal?" Ms. Vickers asked plainly.

"No. We've never done that."

"Okay," she said, scribbling something down on her pad. "Ever thought of deviating from the creampie aspect?"

"Deviating?" I repeated.

"Having Vince come somewhere else," she added.

"Like where?"

"Vince?" Ms. Vickers prompted.

"On your ass or your ... breasts."

"'Tits' is fine, Vince," Ms. Vickers said. "What do you think of that?"

"Why would he come on my tits?" I asked, confused.

"Because it's fucking *hot*," Ms. Vickers said.

"It is?"

"Have you ever done it?" she pressed.

"Well, no, but..."

"So how do you know?" she asked.

"I guess I don't."

"Right," she said, pleased with herself. "And that's also what this is about: trying new things. Experimenting!"

"You think that'll help?" I asked.

"Definitely," Ms. Vickers said. "Try as many different things as you can. Just try. That's all you can do. And then after all that, if you don't like it, well at least you tried. Do you think you can do that for me?"

The pair of us nodded.

"Great," she said. "Now Vince, take out your cock."

The expression dropped off my face. I turned to Vince and furrowed my brow, unsure of whether I'd heard her right. Ms. Vickers was looking down at her pad, making a note of something.

"Sorry, I'm not sure what you just said," I pried.

"I asked your husband to take out his cock," she said, putting down her pen and pad. "The experimenting begins now."

"I—I don't see how—"

"We're going to spice up this dreary sex-life," Ms. Vickers said. "If you want to."

"I want to, but this seems a little extreme. Doesn't it Vince?"

Vince was staring at Ms. Vickers with this odd look in his eyes.

"Vince?" I asked again.

Without saying a word he stood up and dropped his pants, pulling down his underwear until his big cock was visible, hanging there on his waist.

Ms. Vickers was unperturbed. Instead she sucked a breath through her teeth and swooned with delight.

"My, oh, my," she said, running her tongue along her pristine teeth.

"Vince!" I cried, shocked. "What the hell are you doing?"

"Spicing things up," he shrugged.

"That's the spirit, Vince," Ms. Vickers encouraged. "Cassie, you need to relax and roll with it."

"Roll with it?!" I protested. "This is crazy."

"Get him hard," Ms. Vickers said. "If you can?"

Those three added words lit a fire inside me. Suddenly my own determination to get Vince stiff superseded my sensibilities.

"*If I can*?!" I repeated.

Ms. Vickers smiled, as though she knew that it was the exact words that I needed to hear.

"Sit down, Vince," I said, keeping my eyes on Ms. Vickers.

He did as ordered, dropping his bare ass to the couch and leaving his flaccid cock sat on his lap. I picked it up in my hand and started to move over it.

"*If I can*," I said again, shaking my head as I dropped it towards his beautiful cock.

I opened my mouth over the tip and worked my tongue around him, listening to his groan above me as I felt the blood begin to rush into his length. As he grew I moved my head back, tickling around the sensitive crown before finally revealing his stiffness to Ms. Vickers.

"Impressive," she said. "But I didn't say stop."

I twisted my mouth at her, trying not to grin. There was something about her that was both alluringly sexy and overly forward all at once. She had an enviable confidence that both Vince and I seemed to enjoy.

I dropped my mouth back over Vince and realized now that I was sucking his cock just for her. That felt like a pretty huge leap in the 'adventure' stakes. The thought of that—performing for someone else—had an unforeseen effect on me.

"Well, this is already looking rosy," Ms. Vickers said, looking to Vince who let out a brief chuckle.

"How do you feel, Cassie?"

I pinched my lips off him and looked to her, holding his spit-drenched cock next to my face.

"Honestly?" I asked.

"That's why we're here."

"I feel kind of turned on."

"Good," Ms. Vickers said. "So do I. We're going to use that. Keep going."

I pumped my fist along his gorgeous, wet cock, wrapping my lips over him again. Ms. Vickers uncrossed her legs and opened her knees as she set down her note-book.

Out of the corner of my eye I could see her pulling up the skirt of her maroon dress until I could make out her black panties beneath. She started to rub over the crotch of them and squeeze her tits.

"That's it," she said steadily.

I looked up at Vince to see him staring right across at her.

"Don't stop," Vince said now, looking down to me.

I put myself back over him and hummed contentedly, feeling my pussy becoming wetter and wetter as the three of us started to give in to one another.

Ms. Vickers dropped forward off her chair and prowled across the carpet to the foot of the couch.

"This is what I mean by spicing things up," she said, curling her finger towards me.

I dropped off the sofa too and knelt besides her, sitting at the feet of Vince who looked down at the both of us. He couldn't believe his luck.

Ms. Vickers brought herself over to me and I looked to her, noticing that her face wasn't stopping as it moved towards mine.

Suddenly her lips touched mine and we started to kiss. At first it was a shock, but the soft, velvet touch of hers felt good against mine. Our tongue's entwined and I pushed my fingers into her hair, scrunching it in a fist as she gripped my ass.

Finally I pulled back, looking into the dazzling green eyes and then across at my husband who had started to stroke his cock without prompting.

"Good boy, Vince," Ms. Vickers said.

She pulled the clasp from her hair and shook her head, letting her perfect locks flow downwards.

"We should treat him," Ms. Vickers said, licking her lips in my direction.

She shuffled closer to the couch on her knees and I did the same. Her hand gripped around Vince's cock and I watched his face as another woman touched him in a place I thought was only meant for me. Rather than jealousy I felt a deep, burning arousal, as though I wanted to see more. Much more.

Ms. Vickers jerked her fist along his cock and angled it in my direction as I got comfortable beside her.

"After you," she said.

I curled a lock of my blonde hair behind my ear and moved my mouth over the head of his cock. I felt Ms. Vickers' hand come around the back of my neck, guiding me down onto my husband's length until my mouth was full of him.

The tip of his cock probed gently at the top of my throat and I fought against the gag, calming myself with long breaths.

"Good girl," Ms. Vickers said. "We're really getting somewhere, huh?"

I pulled my head off his dick and gasped, looking to Ms. Vickers and smiling.

She smiled back at me and then dropped her mouth over Vince's cock. My jaw dropped open and I looked up to his face, studying the nuances of confused pleasure that flashed across his expression. He knew that it felt incredible, but looked unsure as to whether her could relax and enjoy it.

"Is that good, Vince?" I asked.

He nodded.

"It *looks* good," I said, keen to relax him further.

I moved up his body and started to kiss him softly on the lips.

"Does she suck your cock good?" I asked, pecking kisses at him. Vince nodded.

"I bet her lips feel so good around that beautiful, perfect cock."

"Good, Cassie," I heard from below. Ms. Vickers was impressed. "Now take off his shirt."

Ms. Vickers got to work removing his shoes and pants and I unbuttoned Vince's shirt until he was naked on the sofa, surrounded by the both of us.

"Aren't we a little ... *dressed?*" I asked.

"We *are*," Ms. Vickers said. "Vince, would you like to take your wife's clothes off?"

"Of course," he said, pushing himself up off the sofa.

He stood there with his huge cock hanging out from him like a welcoming draw-bridge. His hand took a grip of my t-shirt and he pulled it up over my head, pushing my tits together in my bra. I started to groan in delight, thrusting my pelvis towards him as my crotch turned hot.

"Keep talking," Ms. Vickers encouraged.

"Can we talk to you too?" I asked.

"Of course," she said. "Whatever you feel comfortable with."

"Okay, Ms. Vickers," I said, wriggling my pants down over my ass. "Let's see what you've got under there."

She smiled broadly with a tongue in her cheek. "You're the boss," she lied.

She pulled her suit-jacket back off her arms and tossed it to her chair, then she started to unfasten the buttons of her blouse.

"Let's watch this honey," I said, turning him towards her.

I moved behind him in only my bra and panties now, pressing my naked flesh to his bare back and bringing my hand around the front of him to hold his cock.

I jerked him steadily as Ms. Vickers popped open each button of her blouse, pulling it off her shoulders and causing her big tits to wobble in her bra as he did so.

"Look at those," I hushed into Vince's ear. "Look at those pretty tits, honey."

"Almost as good as yours," Vince whispered back.

Ms. Vickers unclasped her bra and tossed it to the couch quickly too. She bunched her tits together, stroking her thumbs over her stiffening nipples. She was still in her dress and high-heels as she walked over to join us again.

"Let's take this off," she said, opening my bra open with ease.

I gasped in faux-shock, watching without moving as she pulled the garment from me. Her face went straight to my tits and she started to suck on my nipple, grabbing Vince's cock and jerking it as she did so.

He cupped one of her tits and started to squeeze it, shooting a glance to me and smiling. Ms. Vickers had transformed things immediately. This was more fun than I'd had in years.

"Get her out of those panties, Vince," Ms. Vickers said. "Get on your knees and do it."

Vince knelt at my feet and looked up my body, putting his fingers over the waist of my panties. Everything felt like the first time again. I could feel the nervous arousal building inside me.

Ms. Vickers unzipped the side of her pencil-skirt and stepped out of it. Beneath it her black panties and garter-belt cut a perfect fit around her shapely ass and her black tights looked good around her legs.

Vince pulled my panties down as Ms. Vickers started to rub at her crotch. She watched intently as they fell, revealing my kempt pussy-hair that I'd had no intention of showing off that day.

"That's a pretty pussy," she said, rubbing her own as she watched me. "Does it taste good too, Vince?"

Vince looked up again and locked his brown eyes on me, moving his mouth underneath me and clasping his lips over my pussy as he maintained eye-contact.

I closed my eyes and gushed a moan, almost doubling over as I felt the sumptuous licks and flays of his tongue against my sensitive, primed flesh.

Ms. Vickers walked over to face me, trapping Vince between the both of us as she put her lips back on mine and started to kiss me.

Our tongues wandered over each other's again and the sensation felt incredible. I'd never had anyone touching me in so many amazing places at once. The movements of her tongue started to match my husband's below.

"Fuck, yes!" I moaned, pulling my lips off hers.

"Good boy, Vince," Ms. Vickers said. "We just needed a little prompting here, didn't we?"

I could hear the smacks of Vince's lips as he sucked on my pussy, teasing his tongue up my soaked crease and tickling at my swollen clit. I'd scarcely ever been this turned on before in my life. It felt as though any one of his licks was going to send me over the edge.

"Keep eating that pussy," Ms. Vickers said, positioning herself at the side of us.

She brought her hand down the front of her body, pushing her fingers into the melee of Vince's mouth and my wet slit.

I felt her split me open and Vince's tongue worked with her, then she hooked two fingers deep inside me, probing them through my tight O.

"Fuck!" I cried, as my pussy contracted and gripped them instantly.

"Keep on licking, Vince," Ms. Vickers said, slowly sliding her digits through me as Vince fought to get in at the sides of her hand and beneath her fingers.

I tried to calm myself again, breathing deep through my nose and then slowly out of my mouth.

Ms. Vickers mouth came in close to my ear. "Let go," she hushed softly before changing her tone to a growl. "Come on his face."

I felt my body spasm at her words, and soon the contractions were radiating out of me, as though my pussy was now voice-activated.

"Good girl," Ms. Vickers encouraged, and I felt a certain amount of pride at having pleased her.

"Keep going, Vince," she said, rubbing at his head.

Vince's eyes were closed as he feasted on my flesh from below. I opened my eyes wide and looked down, noticing that his hand was still busily pumping over his thick cock as his mouth pressed up against the filled O of my pussy.

"Oh, Vince," I whispered. My love for him blossomed in that moment. I'd never had him give me such a gift before.

Ms. Vickers slipped her fingers quickly out of me, bringing them to my mouth.

"Lick off your cum," she ordered.

I barely blinked, racing my lips over her fingers and tasting the velvet cream in my mouth as I gasped through the ecstasy. Vince kept busy below.

"Good girl," she said again before looking down to my husband. "Let me feel those lips on me too, Vince."

Ms. Vickers sat on the couch and peeled her panties under her big ass quickly, leaving her garter-belt and tights on.

She opened her legs wide and I looked to her immaculate pussy. Before Vince had a chance to move I settled between her legs, dropping to my knees.

"Can I try?" I asked, still shivering with lust.

"Definitely," Ms. Vickers said, impressed. "You're a fast learner."

I moved my face between her legs and nibbled at the inside of her thigh, feeling my pussy tremble as I heard the heady groan shoot from her throat.

"Oh, Cassie," she mewled, holding my head on her as I took my first taste of pussy.

It was sweet and creamy and her flesh felt good pressed against my face. I knelt on all fours and fed on her, putting my arms beneath her thighs to lift her ass up slightly off the couch.

"Does that look good?" she said suddenly, and I realized she was talking to Vince who was stood behind me. I looked back to see him staring right into my ass.

"As incredible as always," he said.

"Go with it, Vince," she said.

Vince dropped to his knees and moved his face into my ass. Suddenly I felt that perfect tongue of his, settling in an unholy place. My mouth opened in awe and I looked up at Ms. Vickers who nodded down.

"How does it feel?" she asked.

I put my head against her thigh and grunted. "Good," I groaned.

Vince's tongue wandered around my asshole like he was making a map of it. He tickled around the untouched, sensitive muscle and probed a little ways inside, fucking my ass with the tip of his tongue.

"Vince, you're an animal," Ms. Vickers announced with a giggle.

I pulled my face off her thigh and looked back to her pussy, taking a breath and attempting to both feel a gargantuan sense of untold pleasure *and* deliver the same all at once.

My mouth opened again over Ms. Vickers pussy and I tried to transfer the ecstasy through me. The harder Vince's tongue worked around my ass, the harder mine worked around Ms. Vickers' pussy.

Before long she was taking these huge breaths and holding them, her jaw shaking as I sent her right to the edge of climax.

She squeezed at her tits and kept herself on the edge for as long as she could. Vince was taking these long licks across me that started at the wet O of my pussy and finished in a circle around my puckered knot.

"Yes!" Ms. Vickers gasped finally, exhaling deep and becoming animated.

She writhed on the couch, reaching out to grip the cushion and then grasping my head. Her crotch ground up and down over my mouth as she lost herself, snarling and moaning like an animal in its death throes.

"Eat my fucking pussy," she cooed, and I continued to do just that, feeling the undulating contractions of her muscle against my adventurous tongue. But if my tongue was adventurous then Vince's was downright frontier-breaking.

He moved off my ass finally and I brought my face off Ms. Vickers' pussy, turning around to take a look at my husband who was quite the ass-fiend.

"Now it's your turn, Vince," Ms. Vickers said, blowing a waft of air up her face. "Sit up here, Cassie. I want to see him go in you."

I moved up onto the couch, lying on my back and staring up at Vince as he stood over me. Ms. Vickers took a grip of his cock and gave it a few jerks, but it looked like he didn't need any help at all. He'd been stiff as a rock since this whole thing started.

"Let's give it her, Vince," Ms. Vickers whispered, walking him forward and guiding him towards my waiting snatch.

I opened my legs wide and looked down as his cock disappeared from view. Instead I looked to Ms. Vickers who was concentrating hard on the two things as they collided.

She sucked a breath as I felt the bulbous crown of my husband begin to feed its way into me. My pussy spread over it as I moaned. He felt more aroused than I'd ever known him, as though he was sliding a hard, plastic toy deep inside me instead.

He was so stiff that I could feel each ridge and swollen vein as it slipped through my muscle. My pussy gripped tight around him, as though it was just as welcome to have him as I was.

"Look at that," Ms. Vickers said, pushing Vince's ass forwards and giving me several more of his delicious inches.

He started to pump slowly and my tits wobbled on my chest with each thrust. Ms. Vickers started to watch those too, rubbing herself as she did so.

"Where do you want to come, Vince?" she asked, her mouth close to his ear.

He looked down at the source of his pleasure as his cock surged through me.

"On her face," Vince said quickly, as though the thought had been with him for a while. "On both of your faces," he added.

"*Honey*," Ms. Vickers swooned. "Any objections to your lovely husband coming all over my face, Cassie?"

"None," I answered, a smile broadening on my lips.

Vince pumped himself through my core and Ms. Vickers' hand disappeared down behind his back. I watched his eyes close and his mouth drop open as he stopped moving suddenly.

"What's she doing?" I asked.

"Her finger ..." Vince hushed.

"My finger is in your husband's asshole," she said.

"You like that?" I asked, startled.

"Honey, all guys like that. They just won't admit it," Ms. Vickers answered.

Vince let out a brief laugh, then he let out a groan.

"Besides," Ms. Vickers said, looking to her clock. "It's gonna help him come quicker."

Vince started to fuck me again, finding his rhythm as Ms. Vickers massaged his prostate with her slender fingers.

"Good boy, Vince," she said, her mouth close to his ear. "You tell me when you're ready, okay? Tell me when you're ready to shoot that fucking cum all over our faces."

Vince let out a long groan, hearing the sinful words of Ms. Vickers bouncing off the walls of her otherwise professional-looking office.

"Are you gonna come for me, Vince, honey?" I asked, biting a finger and looking at his pleasure-strewn face.

"Yes, baby," he answered.

His brow dappled with sweat as he continued to fuck me. Ms. Vickers fingers worked busily out of sight then his breaths got deeper and his cries became more desperate and wild.

"I'm fucking ready," he said, and it was like an alarm had gone off.

Ms. Vickers took her finger out of him and dropped her back to the front of the couch. Vince pulled his big cock out of me and I quickly slid down through his legs to sit beside Ms. Vickers too, staring at Vince's cock as he took a grip of it and jerked.

"Cum on my face," Ms. Vickers grunted, looking up and tossing her hair behind her head.

"Cum on my fucking face, Vince," I added.

We opened our mouths beneath him like chicks feeding in a nest and Vince's groans reached their peak.

"Oh, fuck!" he cried. This was it.

I could see the visible throb of his cock as his balls pulled upwards, then he let out another deep moan that was accompanied by a cascade of cum that blasted from the tip of his cock.

It fell down over me in one long rope, hitting me from forehead to mouth and causing me to flinch.

"Yes!" Ms. Vickers cried, opening her mouth as Vince angled the next blast towards her.

It shot from his crown with just as much force, bouncing off her forehead and landing on the couch before another jet of cum eased out with less force. She caught the gooey dribble on her tongue and then I opened my mouth for my second dose.

"Give her all that fucking cum," Ms. Vickers said, smothering her fingers around her mouth to spread his offering around her.

I groaned as another lashing fell from him, draping over me like icing on a bun. It felt warm when it touched my skin and even more exciting when it started to slide down off my face.

Vince pumped over me now, letting the final few ropes fall onto my face until I was awash with his pearlescent seed.

I could barely see but Ms. Vickers was on hand, licking across my lashes and cleansing me of my husband's love.

The pair of us started to kiss with Vince's cum webbing between us. Ms. Vickers would pull back to inspect me before licking her tongue across me and moving it to my mouth, as though she was trying to feed it all into me.

The kiss was smooth and salty-sweet. Vince was still breathing heavy and groaning as Ms. Vickers pulled his cock forward and started to kiss it.

I kissed the other side and the two of us fed messily on his spent length, cleansing him of the errant cum that hadn't quite been launched clear.

Her lips smothered mine and it was one of the naughtiest, most debauched things I'd ever done in my life—but I loved every fucking second of it.

"Mmm," Ms. Vickers hummed. "Enjoy yourself?"

"Yes!" Vince and I exclaimed in unison before laughing.

He looked down on me, dropping to his knees and holding my chin.

"That was fucking hot," he said, kissing my lips softly.

"And that's just a *taste* of what's possible," Ms. Vickers said. "Should I book you another appointment?"

Me and my husband looked to each other with glistening eyes.

"I think so," I said, watching Vince as he nodded.

"Definitely," he confirmed. "I think there's a lot more we can do."

"Oh, there is," Ms. Vickers said, clapping her hands together and standing. "Next week at the same time?"

"If you're free?"

"I'll make myself free for you two love-birds," she said, tip-toeing across her office in her cutesy garter and tights. She took a hold of her pen in a funny grip, not wanting to get any cum on it.

"And ... you're booked in!" she announced, dropping her pen. "You can change in the room you were waiting in. It'll be empty. I promise."

"Thank you," I said, standing up.

"Just doing my job," Ms. Vickers said.

Vince gathered up our clothes and I opened the door slowly, peering through the gap to find the room thankfully empty.

"Thanks again," Vince said. It felt odd to both be leaving the room naked, given how we entered it.

"See you soon," Ms. Vickers said, sitting her naked ass on her desk and crossing her legs.

We left with that perfect, seductive image of her, excited to see her again next week. Our sexual awakening had only just begun.

"*Ms. Vickers,*" I said aloud, mimicking Shawna again. She'd certainly earned the inflection.

THE END

Searching For Anal : Couples Threesomes 16

It had long been a sexual fantasy of my husband David. Everyone has one and I guess the very fact they're fantasies mean that they're not easily achievable, but as fantasies go, anal sex was much more probable than most. Whenever he and I had tried I just couldn't do it, no matter how much lubricant we used.

I don't know if it was psychological at this point, but I'd basically decided that my ass was a one-way street and there was no getting inside there at all.

David didn't mind, of course. We'd been married for years and there was all manner of other things we could do together. Still, the elusive anal dream of my husband was one that I'd been keen to satisfy ever since I'd discovered his predilection.

I was at a point now where I'd begun to consider renting the services of another woman for the explicit purpose of stuffing David's cock in her ass. With his forty-fifth birthday looming it seemed like the perfect present.

"What?!" David cried. We were sat on the sofa late one night when I decided to broach the idea.

"Just for one night."

"Melissa, that's crazy," he said, his brown eyes wide.

"Come on," I urged. "I know how much you want this."

"Not if it means cheating!"

I laughed. "It's not cheating, honey, I'm giving you permission. Besides, I'll be there too."

"You will?"

"I'm not gonna give you your wildest desire without being there to see the look on your face."

David shook his head and chuckled. "This is pretty unconventional as far as gifts go, you know?"

"Don't worry, I've got you something more traditional too."

"An ass-fuck and a box of chocolates?"

I giggled and fell against him on the sofa. "So what do you say?"

"It sounds like you want this more than I do!"

"I didn't think it'd be this hard to get you inside someone's ass."

"Inside *whose* ass?!"

"Well," I began, narrowing my eyes as if this was some huge part of my plan, "I've heard that The Blue Rhino offers a few *extras*."

"The Blue Rhino? Isn't that a strip-club?"

"Don't act like you don't know," I said, nudging him.

"They do that there?"

"Apparently."

"According to who?"

"I have my sources," I said. "And they're very reliable."

"Hmm," David said, staring off into the distance.

I kept things to myself for the next few days while I put together my plan for him. I'd phoned The Blue Rhino and confirmed—with many an innuendo and suggestive phrasing—that they did indeed offer additional *services*. The girl who they'd recommended to us was called Justice: a short, blonde fire-cracker of a woman, so they said.

On Friday evening I downed the stairs of our home in my red dress, walking into the living room to find David who was absent-mindedly reading. At first he didn't look up, but when he finally did he couldn't look away.

"What the hell is this in aid of?" he asked, closing his book.

I kept my smile as I walked slowly over to him, dropping to my knees.

"What—what are—ohhh, okay," David said, becoming less startled as I began to open up his pants.

"Is this my gift?" he asked.

"Not quite," I answered with a smirk, pulling out his cock. It took very little effort to get him stiff. David was always a ready-to-go kind of guy.

"Oh, Melissa," he groaned, looking down on me as I opened my lips over that beautiful cock of his.

I hummed contentedly as I wound my lips down over him, filling my mouth with his arousal and smoothing my hands over his stomach.

In my figure-hugging dress I felt so sexy, and I liked to think I injected that same confidence into the blow-job as David started to groan above me.

"Oh, honey, that's so good," he said.

Steadily I wound my lips up off him, flicking my tongue around the submerged crown of his cock as I withdrew.

I popped my lips off him audibly and then stood up briskly, putting both hands on my hips.

"Put something nice on," I said. "We're going to The Blue Rhino."

"You—we—we are?"

"Happy birthday!"

David sat there for a moment, his hard cock stretching up out of his pants as he processed the request. In a flash he jumped from the couch, hopping back into his pants and making for the stairs.

"Ten minutes," I said.

He raced upstairs and I sat on the couch, biting at my lip as I imagined how the evening might play out. I had a couple of reservations but I was sure I'd overcome then when the time was right.

In around fifteen minutes David came down the stairs, dressed in a smart camel jacket and black jeans. He wore a thin charcoal sweater beneath and his black hair was swept back to one side.

"Looking good," I said, standing and taking his hand. "Shall we?"

"Now you're sure about this?"

"David, I'm sure," I said. "I want to see that big cock of yours buried in an ass before the night is through."

He laughed. "Jeez, Melissa!"

I let him out through the door first and gave his ass a slap. I was feeling particularly horny myself that evening and it was just as well.

We parked up in the lot of The Blue Rhino and walked to the entrance, getting the nod from the door-staff who invited us inside.

The club itself had a trim of soft-blue lighting around everything, with a spotlight on the stage that, at that moment, had a fiery beauty writhing around on it.

Men off varying dress lined the centre-stage, tossing their bills and clapping. The girl on stage seemed to be enjoying herself just as much as them.

"Where shall we sit?" David asked, looking around the club.

"We've got a booth," I said, and I gave a nod to the hostess who skipped over with a clipboard.

"Mr. & Mrs. Sutherland," I said.

"Right this way," the hostess answered promptly, guiding us through the tables. She looked cute herself, but she also looked far more clothed than her colleagues.

She presented a booth that seemed almost too big for two people. The back of the chairs ran high around three sides of the rectangle, almost touching the ceiling. The centre was empty where you might usually expect a table. I noticed a curtain on one side that looked as though it could enclose the booth if necessary.

"Can I get you anything to drink?"

"I'll have a double-vodka and cranberry juice," I said.

"Bourbon and ice," David said.

"I'll be back with your drinks," the hostess said, disappearing into the darkness of the club.

The both of us took a moment to look around. The place looked brand-new.

"So this is nice," I said, looking around. "I hadn't expected it to be so ..."

"Up-market?" David added.

"Yeah! It looks real classy."

"Apart from some of the guys around the dance-floor," David said, leaning forward and peering back to the centre-stage.

"Well we won't be mingling with them," I said. "We have our very own girl."

"Huh?!"

Just then the hostess returned with our drinks, setting them into a recess in the back-rest of the seat that we hadn't noticed.

"And would you like Justice now?" she asked.

My husband looked to me and then at the hostess. "In general?"

"Our girl," I laughed, slapping him. "Her name's Justice."

The hostess waited patiently, smiling.

"Yes, I think we'll introduce ourselves now," I said, knowing that David had been stiff as a board less than an hour ago.

"Justice?!" David said, turning to me as the hostess left us.

"She's a fire-cracker."

He took a gulp of his drink. "How do you know that?"

"It's what the guy on the phone said," I shrugged.

"So you don't even know what she looks—"

David's mouth shut tight as a blonde girl of around twenty-years-old made her way to our table. She wore a kind of one-piece bikini, connected by a strip of fabric that joined her panties to her sheer black bra. There was more skin on show than clothes and on closer inspection I was fairly sure I could see her nipples beneath her top.

"Hey," she smiled, holding out a hand. "I'm Justice."

I extended a hand and Justice took it, giving it a kiss and looking down my arm as she did so.

"Oh, my," I blushed, and Justice started to giggle.

"You must be Melissa," she said. "So this must be David."

She extended her hand to him and shook it gently.

David stared wide-eyed like a kid on Christmas morning, looking at Justice and wondering what he'd done to deserve a girl almost half his age.

Justice leaned in to whisper to David and I leaned in too so I could hear. "So you're the one who's going in my ass?" she said.

She pulled back with a smile and David looked to me, shocked.

"You are," I nodded. I felt a pang of nerves but it felt as though we were in safe hands. This was Justice's world and when she closed the curtain on our booth I knew she was the one for us.

My husband's hands gripped his knees tight. He leaned forward and took off his jacket and I grabbed it from him, draping it across the empty seats next to us.

Justice turned to us and started to dance with the background music, writhing slowly and using every inch of that cutesy body of hers to hypnotize us.

She turned away finally and the both of us looked to her ass. It was bisected by the thin strip of fabric that ran down the middle and when she bent forward you could make out the darkening of her flesh around her hidden asshole.

I looked to David and noticed his intense, excited focus, then he turned to me and shook his head in disbelief. I moved a hand over to squeeze his leg and steadily moved it to his crotch, finding his cock already beginning to stiffen in his pants.

Justice turned back and saw where my hand was planted. "Starting early, huh?" she said.

I smirked back and David blushed, but he made no attempt to move my hand. Instead he reclined further in the chair until you could see the thickness of his bulge pressing against the crotch of his jeans.

"Oh, he's ready?" Justice said, winding her hips towards us.

She straddled David's legs and put her tits in his face as she continued to dance to the music. Her eyes stayed locked on him as though she was fixing him in a trance. I kept my hand on him and watched her, mesmerized. I could feel my pulse beginning to race as she charmed my husband and the jealousy I'd feared never emerged. Instead I wanted to see more.

She rose up on him and pressed her tits against his face. I watched the fabric move over David and he closed his eyes. My hand moved with greater purpose over his cock and I started to feel myself becoming wet as I watched.

Justice danced her way off him and then, surprisingly, she moved her attentions towards me. She straddled me in the exact same way, jiggling her cutesy tits in my face. Unlike my husband I wasn't as well versed in the attentions of women. I found my hand coming behind her to hold her ass, touching her gently.

I turned to look at David who seemed excited beyond measure. His pupils were fat with lustful intrigue and he turned his body to face us.

I could scarcely concentrate on running my hand over his thickness now. Instead I grabbed David's hand and brought it up under my red skirt, putting him against my crotch.

Justice leaned away and looked down her body, watching David's hand move out of sight.

"Am I allowed to do that?" she asked.

"Please do," I said, becoming more confident than I imagined.

She put her hand on the inside of my leg and then slid up my thigh, crossing paths with David's hand as he moved out.

Soon I could feel her slender fingers against the crotch of my panties. She rubbed and continued to bounce in front of us, moving to the rhythm of the music and teasing the wetness from my crotch.

Before now I hadn't really considered the prospect of me enjoying myself so much. My attentions were on David and his forty-fifth birthday, but Justice was proving to be a gift for both of us.

She kept her hand on me and moved between the both of us now, crouching slightly and putting her other hand on David's crotch.

She rubbed along the both of us as though she was our own private mistress and somehow—behind the safety of the curtain—we felt a privacy that I didn't think could be found inside a strip-club.

"No-one will bother us," Justice said, allaying my fears further.

I reached over and started to unbuckle David's belt and Justice moved her hand away briefly. She teased along the groove of my pussy slowly, using the back of her nails to gently tease me as I unleashed my husband.

I unclasped his belt and unpopped the button on his pants. Justice started to breathe more heavily and she stared down at my husband's crotch, eager for the reveal.

I pulled the fly of his pants open wide and then delved inside, finding his cock stiff within. I was eager to show Justice how gorgeous it was and when I pulled it out I looked straight to her for the reaction.

Her jaw dropped low and she gushed a laugh, looking to me. "That thing's big, huh?"

I nodded. "Will it be a problem?"

"Oh, no," she said confidently, wrapping her hand around him.

She jerked up and down him slowly, her long-nailed fingers almost touching her thumb. She gave it her full concentration and there was something hot about her being so careful with him.

"Are you gonna take those panties off?" she asked finally, looking to me.

"I—uhh—"

"Take them off, Melissa," David added, as though he was somehow now a veteran of this.

I reached underneath my dress and pulled at my panties, slipping them over my smooth skin and pulling them down off my ass.

Justice smirked and watched the tiny garment emerge and drop down towards my red high-heels. I kicked them off to the floor and looked to her.

With one hand still steadily jerking my husband's dick she used the other to push open my knees. Gradually I parted my legs, causing the skirt of my dress to slide up over my thighs. I didn't know how much of myself I was revealing, but when Justice gasped I guessed that she could see my kempt groove.

"Damn, that's a pretty pussy," she said.

Without a word she let go of David's cock and dropped to her knees, putting herself right between my legs.

I felt self-conscious at first, but it looked as though she was never going to take no for answer. She moved forwards, pushing back my dress further and biting at the inside of my thigh.

"Oh, shit," David said, leaning forward and watching as Justice's lips approached my wet pussy.

"Take those pants off, lover," Justice said, glancing up to David.

He stood up as ordered, keeping his gaze on Justice as she approached. I could feel her breath on me as David dropped his jeans to his ankles.

He pulled off his shoes and shook himself free of his jeans. His huge cock swayed as he did so, but his eyes were unwavering as they watched her.

I let out a groan as I felt her lips race over me. Justice immediately started to feed on me wildly, racing her mouth and tongue over me with the same gusto as the high-tempo music of the club.

"Oh, fuck," I groaned, pushing my head back against the seat.

I felt kind of guilty that I'd brought David here for his birthday and here I was reaping the rewards too. David didn't seem to mind. He was busy stepping up onto the seat, holding his huge cock and pointing it towards my face.

"Suck him," Justice said, taking her lips off me and staring up my body.

I turned my head and opened my mouth, welcoming David back inside and humming contentedly on his arousal. The sensation of his hard cock in my mouth felt incredible and the added bliss of Justice's tongue racing over me was heavenly. I'd never pleased someone while being pleased myself. It was intoxicating.

"That's it," Justice mewled, biting the inside of my thigh. "Get him nice and wet for my ass."

She stood up now, leaving my crotch a wet mess of her spit and my own juices. She put her face close to mine as I sucked over David.

"Get it all the way in," she goaded, pressing the back of my head.

I moved forward as far as I could, feeling him probe at the top of my throat. I pulled back off him with a gasp, dropping my mouth off him and then marveling as Justice took up the mantle.

She gripped my husband's balls and yawned her mouth over his glistening tip, driving him way deep. I watched her throat bulge and witnessed a miracle as the entirety of my husband's cock disappeared.

"My God!" I swooned, looking up to David to see if he shared my surprise.

His mouth and eyes were about was wide open as each other. He closed them both and grunted, delighting in the tight sensation of Justice's throat.

She slurped off him, smirking as she started to jerk him in her hand. She looked to the both of us, knowing that her party-trick had impressed.

"Ta-daa," she said, and the three of us laughed, easing any remaining tension. "Keep him hard for me would you?" she said. She stood up and moved back through the curtain into the club.

She slipped from the booth and I went straight to my husband's cock. I pumped my fist over him and watched close. Something about watching his flesh move over that hard muscle made me more excited than anything.

David lifted his sweatshirt up over his head and he stood naked now, holding my head as I steered my lips back towards him.

Justice slipped back inside the curtain and swooned. "Well done," she said.

She came back over to his dick and the both of us sucked and licked at him, bouncing him between our lips and giving him his first taste of his prize. I knew for a fact he'd never had two women suck his cock before and even though this wasn't number one on his list of fantasies, I knew it made the top-ten.

After a moment Justice started to dance again, standing up and winding herself in a circle like some sort of enchantress.

My husband and I watched her again. There was something about her that was hard to ignore and whenever she moved she commanded attention.

When she rotated away from us we noticed a bejeweled circle hidden beneath the strap of her panties now.

"A plug?" I hushed.

"That's right," Justice said, overhearing. "It's how I get ready."

"I'd never thought of that," I said.

"Fingers will do it too," she said, rushing close to me.

She looked down her nose at me and then started to kiss my lips. There was something mesmerizing about her that I couldn't put my finger on. She was like a goddess of sex, sent from the heavens to draw out the fantasies that we didn't even know we held.

I kissed her, grabbing her ass with greater purpose and pulling her against me. I pressed my body to hers as David stepped down off the seat finally. He stood close holding both of our asses and pressing our bodies together even tighter.

When Justice moved her lips off mine she moved them straight to David's, kissing him and thrusting her tongue into his mouth.

She messed with something on her garment and then pulled down the front of her top, revealing her perky tits to the both of us.

David's face moved straight to them and I watched as his tongue raced over her hard nipples. He sucked her and she threw her head back to moan, seeming to genuinely enjoy his touch.

There was one vacancy left on her chest and I moved my face to fill it, latching onto her other nipple and sucking her along with my husband.

"Double trouble," she cooed, holding my head against her. "Suck my titties! Yes, that's it."

My husband and I did as she requested, as though it was some kind of competition to see who had the best tongue-work.

"Ohhh, fuck, I'm ready," she said. "I'm ready for his cock."

"In your ass?" I asked.

"That's why I'm here, isn't it?"

She moved back to the centre of the booth and turned away from us, bending over at the waist and peeling her panties back down over her big, athletic ass.

We watched the full circle of the plug become revealed, perfectly covering her asshole. Below it were the soft petals of her pussy that looked to glisten in the light of the booth.

"She's so wet," I gasped.

My hand jerked over David's cock idly, watching as her hand moved to the base of her plug. She started to pull it back and we watched in awe as her asshole widened over it. She groaned throughout, reaching a crescendo at the widest point of the toy. Her cries turned almost to relief as she popped it free, placing it on seat close-by and then holding open her cheeks with one hand.

"Ready, David?" she asked.

I stared into the black hole of her ass and nudged my husband forward. "Go get it," I said.

He stared forward and swallowed as though the occasion was momentous. He took his cock in his grasp and pumped slowly, pointing it towards his target.

I walked closer, not wanting to miss the moment of sinful collision as the two were introduced.

"Stick it in my fucking ass, David," she snarled, her head almost touching her ankles.

David moved forward and I watched him dock in to her. The tip of his cock became sheathed in her hole and the pair of them groaned. I found myself groaning too, watching keenly as he forced his dick deeper into her asshole.

It kept a tight grip of him, welcoming him home as though he belonged there the entire time. I looked to his face finally and saw an expression of borderline euphoria. He'd waited a life-time for this moment and I was glad I could be there to witness it.

"Now fuck it," Justice encouraged. "Don't be shy."

"Fuck her, David," I urged, my lips close to her ear. "Fuck her ass."

He started to thrust into her and I found my hand moving inexplicably to my pussy as though it had a life of its own. I rubbed along it, hitching up my skirt. Quickly I unzipped myself, stepping out of my dress so I could get at my aching groove easier.

I flicked my fingers on my clit, dunking them deep inside me and watching as my husband fucked her ass like he owned it.

The three of us were moaning and groaning, forgetting completely that we were in the centre of public strip-club.

"Come here, Melissa," Justice said now, patting the seat beside her.

I moved to the front of the two-cart-train and Justice and my husband jostled to a new location. He stayed inside her, but now she was staring straight forward at me as I sat on the seat.

"Turn around," she said. "We need to get you trained too."

I turned away from her and then felt her unclasp my bra. I helped it off my arms and her hands cupped my big tits as I did so. She was almost standing upright now, bending at the hip only to allow my husband to angle himself through her tight aperture.

"Good," she groaned. "Those tits feel so fucking good. Almost as good as your husband's hard cock. Does it look good, David?"

"Uh-huh," he said.

"Does your cock look good going inside of my ass like that?"

"It looks so good," he confirmed.

"You wish it was your wife's asshole though, don't you?"

"I do," he groaned, and then Justice pushed me forwards and I put a knee on the seat in front.

"You wish it was this, don't you?"

She parted my cheeks and showed my forbidden, virginal knot to David. I bent over and looked back over my shoulder to see him staring into it.

"You wish it was in here," she whispered, then she moved her face forward and put it straight between my cheeks.

"Fuck!" I cried, feeling her wet tongue lash over the forbidden muscle.

"Tell him what I'm doing," she said, her voice muffled by my ass.

"She's—ugh—she's licking my ass."

"I'm getting her ready," she added.

Her tongue wound around my muscle and I felt her nose press against me every time David bucked forwards and slammed his hips against her butt.

He kept his rhythm, watching as her tongue flashed over my puckered ass. She began to press it just a little way inside and I was surprised to feel it gradually begin to relent and relax. In a few minutes she was stabbing more of her tongue inside me and then suddenly it hit me. The reason I'd never been able to take a cock inside there before is because we weren't giving it the time it deserved.

Justice teased me wider and then she introduced a finger, slipping it through my knot and giving the both of us words of encouragement. I took it with ease.

"Good girl," she said, as though she was older than me. "That's perfect. That's what you needed, huh?"

"Uh-huh," I groaned, opening my ass with a hand and groaning.

It felt so good to have her finger teasing inside me and I could only imagine how good it looked to David.

"Would you like that ass?" she asked, looking back to him.

"I'd *love* that ass," he said.

"Take it," she said. "She's ready."

Justice moved her face away from me and when I looked back it was David who was squaring up behind me now.

"Give me that," Justice said, and she took a hold of his cock. She draped her mouth over him, unperturbed by where it had been. She sucked him hungrily and then spat onto him, working her saliva over him and pulling him towards my waiting ass. I felt the crown of him touch me and he pressed forwards.

"Go on," Justice said. "Get it."

My asshole spread open over him and David groaned in approval. I gasped in shock, feeling that thick, hard arousal of his going into me in a whole new way.

"He's in my ass," I announced, keen to let everyone know.

"He is," Justice smirked, rightly proud. "All the way now, David."

He moved forward until there was no more left to give. I opened my eyes and giggled. "I've done it!"

"Good girl," Justice said.

I could feel the alien-like cock tickling deep in the pit of my stomach. It was a whole new kind of pleasure.

She crouched to the carpet and scrambled herself beneath us, sitting on her ass and looking up at the sinful melee. "Now fuck her," she said.

David started to pound into me, giving me his inches slowly at first before my asshole got used to the rough jostling.

Justice reached her mouth up from below and soon I could feel her smother my pussy. The whole thing was crazy. The coupling of her gentle tongue on my petals mixed with the rough bluntness of David's cock hammering me was a match made in heaven. I started to hold my breath and concentrate on the two opposing sensations and in that heady mix I lost myself.

I started to squeak with pleasure, feeling the climax arrive inside me and flash through my body.

"Come for me," Justice said, talking right onto my petals.

She licked at my contracting core, teasing around the gasping O of my pussy with her pointed tongue.

David was becoming more frantic behind me too and I could tell form his breaths and mannerism that he too was on the brink.

"Are you ready, David?" Justice asked, as though she knew too. She'd probably seen her fair share of orgasms.

"I'm close," he hushed, his mind elsewhere.

"Then come," she insisted. "Come in your wife's ass."

"Oh, fuck!" David cried.

Suddenly I felt the spasm of his length, as though Justice's words were all he needed. With my asshole squeezing him in the throes of climax he started to empty, bursting inside me like a balloon.

I felt the flashing heat of his cum and I groaned at the sensation. Justice hummed from below, watching the base of his cock pulse and release its mess out of sight.

"Give her that fucking cum," she moaned, and David started to fuck me again.

His cock continued to fire off its ropes and he pushed them deeper as he made love to my ass. Each of his thrusts was met with encouraging moans from Justice who seemed to enjoy watching as much as she did participating.

"That's it," she purred. "Now give me it."

David pulled back out of me and my asshole pinched off him. I felt a trail of his cum escape and then I heard the messy, yawning groans of Justice as she caught it on her face below.

"Yes," she cried. "Give me that fucking cum!"

I found myself pushing a little, vying to give Justice the cum she yearned for. My asshole exorcised a few more sticky ropes and they fell down onto Justice who rubbed them around her mouth and ate whatever slipped through her lips.

I kicked my leg over and turned around now, keen to watch that pretty face of hers as it smothered itself in cum. Her maw was covered in a glistening coat of spunk and David jerked himself over her, pinching off the last few drops of cum that she opened her mouth wide for, like a hungry chick.

He shook off the last bead and it fell right into her open mouth. She moaned and then curled her finger towards me.

"Kiss me," she said.

I didn't hesitate. I dropped to the floor, putting one hand on her lower jaw and the other on the top of her head. My tongue licked over her face and then I pushed it into her mouth, humming along with her as we felt the velvet seed of my husband pass between us.

We kissed long and deep and I felt the depravity of the occasion baptize me. Above us David jerked steadily and watched. His gaze was unwavering and for good reason. It wasn't often that you watched your wife kiss your cum out of the mouth of a stripper.

"Perfect," Justice said, collapsing back on the carpet as though that was all she needed.

She stayed there a moment and I stood up, walking to my husband and greeting his cock with my fingertips. I bounced him and smiled at his face. It looked like he thought about kissing me and then changed his mind.

"I'll be okay," Justice said, her eyes still closed. She started to giggle.

"Enjoy yourself?" I asked her.

"Did you?" she countered.

"More than I ever thought."

Suddenly she skipped to her feet, as though a thought had electrified her.

"You took it in your ass so well!" she said, bouncing on her toes.

"I didn't think I'd ever be able to."

"You just needed some encouragement," she said, and she licked her lips slowly. "I'm gonna go clean up. I'll give you two lovers some privacy."

Justice grabbed her tiny lingerie and skipped from the booth naked. She didn't seem to mind that the place was filled with clients outside. Who knows, maybe it got her more requests.

"Fuck!" I cried when she'd left.

David put his arms around me and hugged me close, swaying as he laughed. "What a fucking birthday!"

"Enjoy yourself?"

"What do you think?"

"I think your enjoyment is still inside my ass."

David gave my butt a squeeze and then a slap. "Not for the last time."

"I hope not," I said, smiling wryly. "I think it's my new favorite thing."

"Justice or ass-fucking?"

"She's a close second," I giggled.

THE END

My Husband Likes Them Bigger : Couples Threesomes 17

Me and my husband Simon had a pretty active sex-life. The both of us had decided against children, which meant our professional and social lives could flourish more than most people can afford them to. Simon was the manager of a haulage company and I ran my own realty business.

We liked to keep things exciting. We dressed up for each other, tied each other up and did all manner of things to make it more interesting. One thing we'd never tried though was a threesome.

"One day," I'd tell him often. It wasn't as though he was begging to get another woman involved, but I knew from our past that it was one of his deepest fantasies.

There was something else I couldn't give him either, but Simon would never dream of bringing it up. I knew for a fact he liked women with big tits and that, unfortunately, was something else I couldn't provide.

He told me he loved my body and I believed him. A guy doesn't get as stiff as that without being turned on and he was regularly ravenous when it came to giving me head. But whenever I'd caught him ogling another woman or ventured into the saucy search-history of our home computer, it was always big breasts that seemed to be the object of his affection.

Recognizing what Simon was into was easy, but delivering his fantasy had been impossible. For years I'd been open to the idea of a threesome, but it had never truly seemed possible. That was, until busty, I.T-whizz Cassandra walked into my life.

I'd interviewed her for the job a couple of weeks back and she was already getting a reputation. Even in the interview she'd had this devilish smile and I remember being taken aback that she'd left so many buttons open on her blouse. As we talked I realized that it was merely her personality shining through. Her resume was damn impressive so I could ignore her revealing attire and flirtatious nature ... for now.

I had around twelve members of staff at this point and it's safe to say that Cassandra was the one I most looked forward to seeing each morning. She would wear these different outfits every day that really stood out among the ties and blazers and women's suits. She always added an extra flourish, even if it was just red lipstick with red shoes, she always did something.

As such I'd started to admire her far beyond her work capabilities. I think it was starting to show by how increasingly flirtatious our daily chats had become. I'd find reasons to approach her, just so I could talk to her.

"Which one of these ink cartridges is better?" I asked, and Cassandra jumped to her feet, showing a keen interest.

She drifted over in her high-heels and tight skirt. Her long, painted-nail fingers delicately grabbed each cartridge in turn, scrutinizing the names that were embossed on the plastic in tiny letters.

"This one will pump it out at a better rate," she said. "It'll go all day long, if you like that sort of thing."

I giggled, feeling my professionalism wane. "I *do*."

"Good to hear," Cassandra said and I started to blush.

I looked around the office to see if anyone had noticed the exchange. Thankfully they were all far too studious.

"If you need anything else ..." she offered, a sparkle in her eye.

"I'll keep you in mind."

I turned back for my private office holding the cartridges and trying to hide my smile. I thought of Simon and felt a slight guilt, as though the conversation alone had been some kind of infidelity.

I closed the door and sat at my desk, biting my lip as my brain whirred. I glanced through the glass and saw Cassandra chewing the end of her pen as she stared at her screen. Her gaze suddenly shifted to me and I looked away immediately, picking up the phone. I had no idea who I intended to call, but mechanically I found myself ringing my husband.

"Gina? Honey?" he answered, rightly concerned. I never rang him at work.

"Hey ... what are you up to?"

"Why? What's wrong? Are you okay?"

"I'm just feeling kind of ... horny," I confessed.

"Hold on," Simon said, and I heard a sudden flurry of activity. "You're horny? Now? At work?"

"Uh-huh. Where are you?"

"Well I'm"—I heard a door close—"I'm in my office now."

"Alone?" I asked, drifting my hand down my body.

"Yeah. What's gotten into you?"

"Nothing yet," I breathed.

"Where are you?"

"In my office."

"At work?!"

"Yes."

"And you're horny?"

"Is that a problem?"

"No! God, no."

"Are you touching yourself?" I asked.

"I can ..."

I told him my movements as accurately as possible. "I'm sliding my skirt up over my tights."

"Oh yeah?"

"I can feel the heat of my pussy against my fingers."

"You're touching yourself?"

"I'm stroking it ... beneath my desk. No-one knows."

"Fuck, honey," he exhaled. "You're getting me worked up."

"Save it for me later. I want that big, stiff cock."

My words started to excite me. I took a breath and felt my tits pushing against my tight shirt. Beneath my panties my pussy started to swell with arousal and I felt myself becoming wetter.

"It's hard and ready for you now," Simon said. I can feel it, honey."

I groaned into the receiver, and looked out to Cassandra. She was staring right through the glass at me. Her desk was positioned such that she was one of the only people who could see into my office without getting up.

This time I didn't turn my gaze away. Instead I continued to talk to my husband but I looked right at her.

"I'm rubbing my fucking pussy, baby," I hushed. "I can feel how wet I am on my fingers. I'm ready for you."

"Shit," Simon cried. "I wanna fuck you so bad, honey."

"I've been thinking," I moaned, whimpering intermittently. "I've been thinking we need to spice things up."

"Tell me what're you thinking, Gina," Simon groaned back.

"There's a new girl here ..."

"A new girl, huh?"

"I want her to join us. I want her to please you."

"You know I'd love that," Simon said.

"You know what else?"

"What?"

"She has a nice, big set of juicy tits."

"You're spoiling me."

I rubbed hard over my panties, feeling my clit stiffen. Cassandra watched through the glass, still biting the end of her pen. She seemed unable to take her eyes off me.

"She's watching me now," I confessed.

"Right now? Really?"

"She's watching me from outside. I think … I think she knows I'm touching myself."

"Be careful, honey," Simon warned.

"What should I do? How do I get her interested? I've never picked up a girl before."

"Invite her in," Simon said.

"You—you don't mind?"

"As long as you don't fuck her until I get there," he laughed.

"Come by later, okay?"

"To your office?"

"Yeah," I said, smirking. "I want to fuck you here today."

"Then I guess I'll see you there," he said.

I gave Cassandra an upward nod and beckoned her with my finger.

"I'll see you soon," I said, and hung up.

Cassandra got to her feet and brushed her hands down the front of her blouse. She took a look around the office and walked to my door, knocking from outside.

"Come in," I said.

She slipped through the door and closed it quickly behind her as though she knew the nature of me summoning her.

"Yes?" she asked.

Beneath the desk I continued to tease myself slowly. "Take a seat."

Cassandra brushed her tight pencil skirt beneath her ass and sat down.

"I—I don't quite know how to ask this," I began, feeling nervous suddenly.

"Whatever it is: yes," Cassandra said.

I was taken aback. "You know this might not be work related."

"I know," she said, squeezing her legs together.

I tested the water. "Do you ... like women?"

"I like *everything*," Cassandra said, giggling. The relief inside me was palpable.

"Good."

"What do you have in mind?" she said. "I'm always looking to go the extra mile."

"My husband ..." I began, judging her reaction. The sparkling of her eyes told me it was okay to continue. "My husband is stopping by later after hours if you'd like to help us with a ... *work issue*."

Cassandra's mouth twisted in a wry smile. "I would love to help you with that issue."

Skirting around the topic with vague innuendos was kind of fun. Something about not explicitly stating the nature of his visit was keeping my pussy drooling.

"Stay behind after work," I said. "My husband's coming by later."

"Okay," she said, taking a deep breath.

She stood up and walked back to the door and I eyed that bubble-butt of hers. I couldn't wait to undress her, but unfortunately I had to.

After she left I tried to keep myself busy, but the time dragged by slower than ever. I'd shot Simon a message to let him know what was up and he'd replied with a photograph of a huge bulge in his boxer-shorts.

'*Save it until later*,' I messaged back with a wink.

Cassandra was barely at her desk for the rest of the day. She continued working just like normal, moving around the office and tending to everything technical. I wondered if this was just another day for her.

Inevitably the clock ticked around to five and I ventured back out to the office to address the staff.

"Great day, guys. See you all tomorrow." I felt as though they knew, somehow.

Some of them looked up from their desks while others prepared to leave.

"I'm gonna stay behind," Cassandra said. "I've got some things to tend to."

I could feel my cheeks becoming hot with embarrassment again. "That's fine," I said.

I walked back into my office, my heart pounding. I took a deep breath and looked back out to see the office slowly clearing. Cassandra stayed in place, busily typing something at her desk.

Several people waved through as they left and I waved back, moving my mouse and pretending to work. Truthfully I'd barely done a thing all day. I was just too excited.

Around thirty minutes after the last person had left I saw Simon come into the office. He took a look at Cassandra as he stood behind her at her desk. Her back was straight and her shoulders square as she typed with this perfect posture. Her tits looked even more inviting than usual and Simon made sure to get a look as he passed her.

He looked away and caught my gaze, bulging his eyes. He slipped inside the door and closed it.

"Is that her?" he gushed.

I nodded.

"Shit, honey!"

"Come here," I said, and I stood up from my chair.

I moved around my desk and gripped his tie, pulling him towards me and planting a deep, sensual kiss on him. I took a grip of his package and squeezed.

"You really can't wait, can you?" he said.

"Can you?"

"I've been hard as a rock all day."

"Now's your chance to let it all out."

"What are you gonna—" Simon began, but he stopped talking when I opened the office door.

"Cassandra," I said. "Would you like to join us?"

My husband was in shock. I was too but I was trying my damndest not to show it. Cassandra stood up from her chair obediently and sauntered to the front door of the room. She twisted the lock.

"Good thinking," I said to myself.

She walked back through the office, relishing the attention of my husband and me. I think the both of us were staring at her bouncing tits. Her blouse was unbuttoned so far that I could see the bottom of her red bra cutting across her chest.

"You must be the husband," she said, extending a hand.

"Simon. And you must be Cassandra," Simon said, and he took her hand and kissed the back of it.

She bunched her shoulders together and giggled. "What a gentleman."

"Not always," Simon said wryly.

"So how do you want to start?" Cassandra asked.

"We've never really ..."

"I don't mind leading," Cassandra said. "You're not my first."

"Where did you find this girl?" Simon swooned.

"I think it was just meant to be," I said.

"Relax," she said, and she took my husband's hand and guided him to the chair on the opposite side of my desk. "You're in safe hands."

I thought she was going to give him a lap-dance but instead she walked over to me. She took off my glasses and set them carefully on the desk, then she put her long nails through my hair and tickled my scalp.

I took a breath as I felt her touch on me. Her sensuality was infectious and I could feel my heart pounding immediately.

Her face moved into mine and she kissed me as Simon watched from the chair. Her lip-gloss tasted sweet and so did her tongue. I'd never kissed a girl before but something about how delicate her lips were was making me regret not having done it sooner.

"I don't mind watching," Simon said with a smile.

Cassandra turned to him. "Oh, we'll get to you," she warned.

The roles had reversed now and Cassandra was playing boss to her two inexperienced students. Simon and I were much older than she was but she had a confidence that belied her years. I guess some people just *have it*.

Cassandra walked forwards and pushed my shoulders back until I felt my ass touch the desk. I took a glance at Simon who was adjusting himself in the chair. He flicked his fingers over his crotch and I watched his stiffness change position, settling up along the inside of his thigh.

"We'll get to that soon," Cassandra said, seeing me look at him. "But I want you first."

She kissed me again and as she did so she unfastened the buttons beneath my suit-jacket, one-by-one. She pulled the bottom of my shirt out from my high-waisted skirt.

"Mmm," she cooed, pushing my jacket back off my shoulders.

I looked down at my tits and I couldn't help but compare them to the bursting bra of Cassandra that sat opposite.

"I want these," she groaned, and she leaned her head towards me and started to kiss my bare chest.

Simon was rubbing more vigorously over his cock as he watched on, but my attention was centered on our mistress as her mouth moved over to the cups of my bra.

She bit the fabric and stared up my body. I felt a sudden embarrassment at how enraptured I was by her, blushing and feigning to turn away but looking straight back the second she planted her teeth over me again.

"Let's be naughty," she whispered. My shoulders shuddered at the words.

She pushed back my shirt now and then squeezed herself between my legs, letting my skirt ride up over my tights like it had done earlier that day.

She started to kiss me again and her hand came in between my legs, rubbing against the mound in my panties and awakening me instantly.

All of the sexual tension of the day started to release itself the second I felt her touch. I took a deep breath and moaned, gripping the edge of the desk as her tongue explored around my mouth.

She teased a nail along the inside of my panties, tickling the forbidden flesh beneath before pulling her lips away from mine and smiling.

"I want to taste you," she said.

The sound of Simon's belt unfastening cut-through my shocked reaction to her statement.

"Don't mind me," he said, and he repositioned his chair so he could get a good view up my skirt.

"I can give you two things to watch," Cassandra said, and she unzipped the side of her skirt.

She pushed it down her body and—of course—she was wearing a garter belt and stockings. I expected nothing less. The look on Simon's face told me that her ass must have looked just as good as I imagined.

"Sit up on the desk," she said to me, and I inched my ass onto the cool wood.

Cassandra slid her nails up along my tights to where they stopped at the middle of my thigh. She kept her hand there and brought her lips to me, kissing my soft flesh and biting her way up towards my pussy.

I stared down, breathing hard and watching her slowly approach. I never imagined my first lesbian encounter would be witnessed by my husband. Shit, I never imagined having a lesbian encounter at all.

He was pulling his cock out opposite me, his eyes switching between Cassandra's mouth and her shapely ass.

I gushed a moan when I saw his stiffness. I'd wanted it all day, but now what I wanted most of all was Cassandra's mouth on my crotch. She wasn't going to disappoint.

Her lips moved nearer and I could feel her breath draping over my panties as he centered herself between my legs.

Simon looked around, trying to get the best view. I looked down to see her tenderly mouthing at the fabric of my panties and then she moved the crotch of them aside with her fingers and took a taste of me for real.

"Yes!" I groaned, holding her head against me.

At first she was gentle, pulling at my flesh with her lips over her teeth but soon she was pressing her mouth into me as though she enjoyed the sensation of my pussy spreading on her mouth.

"Oh, fuck, honey," I groaned. "Do you see?"

Simon worked his cock in his fist and stared into the melee, delighting at the view.

"Oh, I see it," he said, excited.

Cassandra pulled her face off my pussy and wiped at her lips with a smile. She looked up at me and then back to Simon, noticing his cock for the first time.

"Don't play over there all alone," she said. "Pull your chair closer."

He did as ordered, shuffling closer until Cassandra could reach out to him too. She put a hand around his cock quickly and Simon let it go, giving her charge of his stiffness.

She looked into his eyes for a moment as she slid her hand up and down his hard cock. He couldn't believe what he was seeing. She moved her head to him and gave the tip of his cock a kiss. "I'll be coming to you soon," she whispered.

She kept him in her grip as her lips moved back to my pussy. She opened wide and lashed her tongue over me and then started to eat my folds lovingly.

I couldn't believe the scene we'd created. My husband had only been here for a few minutes and we already had a tableau of sin laid out before us, but the one thing we both wanted was yet to be revealed.

From Cassandra's position between my legs I could see right down that fat cleavage of hers and I started to imagine what Simon's cock might look like as it lay sandwiched between.

She gave his dick a few quick pumps and then released him, standing to her feet and unfastening my bra.

"Take off her shirt, honey," I called to Simon.

He stood up and his pants fell down his legs. He took off his shoes and socks and slid out of his pants, pulling up his boxer-shorts to cover his cock again before taking off his shirt.

He came behind Cassandra and unfastened her buttons as she worked to unclasp my bra. She pulled it down off my shoulders and bit her lip when she saw my stiff nipples, sat atop my ample tits.

"I *love* them," she cooed, and as if to prove it she moved forward and gave each of them a suck.

She giggled and as she stepped away Simon opened her shirt wide and pulled it back. She let him take it off her and I stared at the majesty of her bound tits. They looked so full and round.

Simon's hands came around to grip both of them and he kissed her neck as he squeezed.

"Oh, fuck," Cassandra moaned, reaching a hand behind to hold him against her.

She looked at me with a smirk as he toyed with her, as though she enjoyed being watched like that. The exhibitionist in her was in bloom and she seemed fully aware of it. I was only just beginning to come to terms with how hot I found it whenever my husband gave her his attention.

I watched his hand squeeze her tits with satisfaction, finally getting his hands on the prize that I couldn't give him. I started to rub my pussy as he played with her and Cassandra noticed my sudden heightened lustiness.

"You like it when he plays with me, huh?" she said.

I nodded, too demure to admit it vocally.

"He likes big tits, right?" she said.

"I do," Simon said, still gnawing at her neck.

"Then I'd better give you them, hadn't I?"

Cassandra sat in my husband's chair and unfastened her bra. She perched on the edge of the seat, spreading her high-heeled legs wide.

"Come and guide him to me, Gina," she said.

I hopped down off the desk and took off my skirt, adjusting my panties so they covered my pussy again.

I curled my fingers down inside Simon's boxer shorts and dragged them down. His cock popped out of them, bouncing and looking as majestic as ever amidst his toned body.

He stepped out of his underwear and I took hold of his cock, pulling him gently forward towards Cassandra who was licking her lips in anticipation.

"Put him here," she said, and she opened her mouth and touched her tongue with her finger.

My husband and I watched as his cock neared her mouth and Cassandra opened wide, ready to dock him inside her.

She looked up to the both of us and smiled, then focused on the approaching tip of Simon's cock. I placed the underside of him right on her tongue like she'd requested, then her mouth shut over him and she closed her eyes.

All three of us groaned as she sucked over him. She inched her lips down him and swallowed as much of his cock as she could whilst I squeezed gently at his balls.

She didn't use her hands at all at first, instead rocking her head over him as though the whole thing was a game. As she did so her tits bounced in her bra and her brunette hair started to unwind behind her until it flowed down over her shoulders.

I held my husband ass and moved my hand with the thrusting of his hips, pushing him in and guiding him back. He fucked her mouth like she deserved his cock and Cassandra took it like an absolute champ. I don't think this was the first time she'd had her face fucked like that.

She hummed and moaned on him and I marveled as the spit from her mouth started to drool out of her in messy strings.

I rubbed them back up against my husband's balls and his whole packet turned slippery with her saliva. It looked glorious.

"Shit!" I gasped, rubbing at my pussy now.

Finally Cassandra gasped back and hurried her hands behind her body to the clasp of her bra. "Get him between my tits," she said.

I looked to Simon knowingly, but not for long. Cassandra finally dropped her bra and the pair of us stared at the amazing sight that greeted us. They seemed anatomically perfect, as though someone had figured out the exact nipple-to-breast ratio and put it to practice on her.

"Put him here," she said, opening her cleavage.

Simon walked forward and Cassandra leaned back a little. She pressed her crotch against his legs and settled his cock between her breasts. Her hands pushed them together and she squeezed him in the embrace of her soft tits.

"Yes!" Simon groaned. "That feels so fucking good."

I felt of a charge of excitement at seeing his satisfaction.

"Fuck them, honey," I said, and I spat into the union of flesh, watching it dribble down into her cleavage.

Simon started to rock through her and Cassandra kept her hands in place, keeping him from slipping free.

His dick slipped through her, emerging stiff and glistening with spit. He kept himself between them and held her shoulders to give himself a better purchase.

"Fuck those tits," Cassandra snarled, sucking her spit through her teeth and then letting it drop out of her mouth right onto my husband's cock.

"I want to see him inside you," I said, looking down on her. "I want him to fuck you."

Cassandra's naughty smile broadened, as though this had been her goal all along.

"Then take my panties off," she said.

Simon took his cock from her cleavage and watched as I took the waist of her panties and pulled it down. She helped me unfasten the suspenders and I left those where they were. She looked far too hot in the garter-belt and stockings to deprive her of them.

I pulled down her underwear to reveal her perfectly manicured pussy. There was nary a hair in sight, save for the slit that she'd sculpted above her clit. It looked so perfect, as though she knew it would be scrutinzed.

"Where do you want me?" she asked, keeping her legs open.

"On the desk," I said. "Sit where I was."

She stood up and walked across the floor in her high heels. Her ass looked a picture and I could finally see what Simon had been so excited about.

"Come on," I said, and I took a grip of his cock, as though I couldn't wait to see him inside her.

Cassandra jumped up on the table and opened her legs, leaning back and licking her fingers. She moved them to her pussy and split the petals of her sex invitingly.

"Shove that cock inside me," she urged.

I moved Simon into position and stood close behind him, watching his cock approach another woman's pussy. It was like he was cheating with my permission. There was something thrilling about being their assistant like that.

"Fuck her, honey," I said, kissing his big shoulders and touching the tip of his cock to her pussy finally.

She closed her eyes tight as he pushed forwards and I watched the head of his cock slide inside her. She let out a groan. Simon gripped her hips and pushed forwards, cloaking the rest of his cock in her warm snatch.

"Now fuck me!" she snarled.

"Fuck her, honey," I agreed. "I want to see you fuck her and cum all over those pretty tits."

"Yes!" Cassandra cooed. "Shoot it all over my fucking tits."

It seemed like too much for Simon. He let out a groan of disbelief and then started his thrusts, sending his cock through her tight lips slowly at first but building his strokes the more the two of us encouraged him.

"Fuck that fucking pussy," I urged, unable to take my eyes of the sight. It was rare that I got a view of his cock like this. Usually I'd be staring at the hilt and feeling the sensation of him inside me, but now I could see the exact point at which her lips draped over him.

I could watch the full majesty of his dick as it became creamier and creamier with her cum. She was a mess of excitement and it looked so good on his length.

"Let me taste it," I urged, and I dropped to my knees beside him.

Simon dutifully pulled his cock out of her pussy and offered me it. I was on it like a slut, racing my mouth down over him and humming contentedly when I tasted her sweet cum.

"Taste good?" she asked. I think she knew the answer.

"It tastes amazing," I cooed, licking my lips. "You're full of surprises."

"I *was* full of your husband's cock," she hinted.

I giggled and relinquished control, surrendering him back to her. I reassumed my position at his side and tickled my nails down his back. I started to offer him sinful words of encouragement.

"Cover those big fucking tits," I whispered, my mouth close to his ear.

"Do what she says," Cassandra said, and she was cupping and squeezing them invitingly, jiggling them around. I think she enjoyed playing with them just as much as we enjoyed watching.

I downed my panties now and worked my hand over my pussy, strumming my clit to the glorious sight of my husband fucking my new employee.

"Get it, Simon," I urged, flurrying over my sensitive stud

I started to groan excitedly, mingling my excitement with theirs until the office was flooded with unmistakable noises of sexual euphoria.

It was like a porn-set. Simon was grunting and groaning like a beast and Cassandra and I were moaning in competition, like two female tennis-pros going toe-to-toe.

I breathed heavy and watched him go at it. My lashes fluttered and my chest tensed as I felt the climax approach. I had no idea Simon was going to join me.

"I'm fucking close," he warned.

My eyes sprang open wide. I didn't want to miss this. "Shoot it on her fucking tits!" I cried.

"Do it," Cassandra agreed, staring up into his eyes as though she was daring him. "Cum on these big fucking tits."

The next part happened so organically that it felt like we'd choreographed it months in advance. Simon built to a crescendo of thrusts and pulled himself out with a grunt. Cassandra slid down off the desk and knelt before him and I reached over to grip his cock, just as my own climax rippled through me.

"Fuck!" I groaned, scarcely able to concentrate.

I jerked my fist over him, trying to channel my own excitement into his cock. Simon groaned and shot his first plentiful rope forwards.

Cassandra cried joyously as she caught the warm jet on her chest, bouncing on her knees so her titties clapped together.

"Pull out his fucking cum," she demanded.

I beat him in my fist like my life depended on it. Every time I jerked back Simon would respond with a throb and then another volley of his spunk would leap free.

I watched it hang in the air and drop over her chest, scattering across her fat tits and lacing it like the icing on a cake.

"Look at that," I cooed, still pumping.

I rubbed at my pussy and almost doubled-over. I could barely cope with the excitement of it all and when Cassandra started to massage his cum into her tits I almost lost it.

"Put him back in here," she said, opening up her cleavage again.

I slotted him back between her tits and she embraced him in her cum-blasted pillows. He fired out another rope of his seed and Cassandra giggled as it hit her chin and dribbled down.

She bounced over him and pulled the final few lasings from him. I'd never known Simon cum so much but it seemed to match the debauched scene we'd made for ourselves.

"Oh, fuck!" Cassandra cried, and it looked like she'd never seen so much of it either.

She looked down at her tits in disbelief, assessing the pearlescent sheen that covered them now.

"That was *fucking* incredible," she laughed.

Simon joined her and it helped to ease the tension a little as we transitioned back to reality.

I gave my pussy one last excited rub, teasing my juices along it and staring longingly at those cum-covered tits.

"Get what you wanted?" Cassandra asked, looking to me.

"All that and more," I said.

She stood up and kissed my husband. "Thank you," she whispered, then she moved to me and gave my mouth a kiss. I savored it, as though she was saying goodbye forever.

She broke away and moved to collect her clothes. She looked sexier than ever as she bent over to pick them up, her tits dripping with my husband's cum and her ass curving around to her slender back.

"I'll be cleaning up if you need me," she said, and she gave us one last naughty grin before turning to the door. Naturally both my husband and I watched that fine ass walk out of there before looking to each other.

"You fucking stud," I laughed, slapping his back.

He chuckled and shook his head. "You always manage to surprise me."

I narrowed my eyes at him. "Guess I'll have to think of something even better next time ..."

THE END

The New Gardener Is Our Slut : Couples Threesomes 18

My husband Dillon and I weren't exactly horticulturalists. The garden was something we enjoyed spending time in, but not something we enjoyed tending to. I mean, what's the point? If I'm gonna be venturing outside into the sunshine I want to be enjoying myself, not working!

I get it, some people enjoy it, but Dillon and I were just too busy. It's far better for us to just employ someone. That's where Morgan came in.

Morgan had been recommended to me by a friend and when I finally laid eyes on her I could see exactly why. Janice, the well-to-do housewife from a few doors down, had confessed that while she'd never dabbled with the same sex before, Morgan had given her second-thoughts.

It really piqued my curiosity. If you ever want to recommend someone to a friend, tell them that the person you're suggesting is so hot that you'll start to question your sexuality. It never fails.

So anyway, I'd called Morgan later that day to see if she could fit us in for a week of work. Even her voice sounded sexy on the phone. It had a sultry, cool, casual manner to it that started to excite me. Even though her words weren't explicitly flirtatious, her tone of delivery began to have a strange effect on me.

After getting off the phone I went straight to my husband who was sat tinkering with something in the garage.

"I think you wanna make sure you're out in the garden tomorrow," I said.

He lifted his head and looked at me curiously. "Huh?"

"I've just secured our new gardener, and if what Janice is saying is true, you're gonna wanna see her."

"Am I, now?" Dillon said, smirking.

"I think you'll love her."

"You're always trying to fix me up with women, Sally. Aren't you good enough for me?"

I sauntered over behind him and draped myself along his shoulders. "I know I'm good enough for you, honey, but you've got a big appetite."

My hand slipped down inside his shirt and I tickled at the hair below his navel as I nibbled on his earlobe.

"I think you want it more than me," he said.

"That maybe true," I said, kissing his neck. "Who wouldn't want to see a man like you enjoy themselves?"

"Let's not get ahead of ourselves. She's barely even cut a blade of grass and already you're pimping her out."

"Look, if she's half as flirty as she was on the phone it'll be easy."

"Ha-ha, we'll see," he said.

I left him to his work and whiled away the evening before bed. Morgan said she'd be arriving around nine o'clock and could do a few days work around the garden, sprucing it up. It was fairly low maintenance but some of the raised beds needed attention, as well as the edging of the lawn. I didn't want to get on my hands and knees and do it. I'd much rather see Morgan do that.

By the time she arrived the next day Dillon was already settled outside on his sun-lounger. Our garden got the sun most of the day while being secluded from our neighbors. The odd soccer-ball would fly over into our yard every now and then, but aside from that it was a tranquil spot.

At nine o'clock the doorbell chimed and I moved through the cool marble hall to answer it. I wore a flowing morning gown and slippers. I didn't want to make too much of an effort for her.

I opened the door to be visited by a short-haired brunette in her early-twenties. She wore denim shorts that seemed to finish just low enough to cover her ass and she had on a white wife-beater. From the look of her perky tits she both didn't need a bra, and wasn't wearing one. She had cute, almost elvish features, all dainty-like.

"Mrs. Jasper?" she asked.

"Yes, honey. Lovely to meet you. You must be Morgan." I leaned in to give her a kiss on the cheek.

"Nice to meet you. Where do you want me?"

"We'll get to that later," I smirked.

"Should I come through," she asked, looking down at her clunky brown boots.

"Oh, just go round the side of the house. You'll have to excuse my husband."

"Oh, I don't mind," she said. "I'll grab my things and be right round."

I watched her turn back to her truck. She was an intriguing looking woman, that's for sure. I didn't typically encounter people like her and I think it was that that drew me to her more than anything. She seemed like a slice of sassy-cool amidst our suburban lifestyle.

I closed the door and skipped through the house to the back-door. "She's here," I hissed, all stage-whisper-like.

Dillon looked at me over the top of his book and gave me the thumbs-up. I think he was trying to play it cool. Oiled up and reclined on the sun-lounger he was looking decidedly hot in his tight shorts.

I walked out onto the patio and leaned against the wall, watching as Morgan arrived through the side-gate with her things.

She did a double-take as she spotted Dillon. I doubt she'd have expected him to look as good as he did.

"Dillon, this is Morgan," I said, and she noticed me now too.

"Nice to meet you," Morgan said, and she put down her big, canvas bag to extend a hand.

Dillon got up from the lounger and set down his book. He took her hand and shook it, giving her a lingering look. I found the awkward silence exciting. He knew just how to make a person the right kind of uncomfortable.

"Nice to meet *you*, Morgan," he offered back.

"So—I should ...?"

"We just want a general tidy-up," I said, walking over.

She followed me and we strolled around the perimeter of the yard.

"Just kind of neaten the place up a little, if you know what I mean?"

"Cut back some bushes, straighten the edges, that kind of thing?"

"Exactly, honey. Me and my husband spend quite a lot of time out here in the summer."

"It's certainly the weather for it," she said, making conversation.

"And don't mind us if we get a little *frisky* out here, okay?"

"Frisky?"

"We can't keep our hands off each other some days."

"Oh, I see." Morgan pursed her lips together and started to blush.

"We can temper ourselves I'm sure," I said, sensing discomfort.

"Oh, no," she said quickly. "No, I don't mind at all. Carry on. I'll be practically invisible."

"I hope not," I giggled.

Morgan bit her lip and her eyes lingered on mine for a moment. I knew exactly what Janice had meant when she said she'd started to doubt her sexuality. Morgan was beginning to intrigue me.

She walked back out to grab some more tools and she set to work. I went upstairs to change into something more revealing.

I selected the bikini with the least amount of fabric to wear and when I re-emerged downstairs I soon startled Dillon from his book. I put some music on for us all and walked across the patio to join him on the lawn.

"Damn, Sally," he said. "You might as well be nude."

Morgan looked back from the bush she was tending to feast her eyes on me. The bikini mainly consisted of thin strings of fabric and then a patch of bright yellow to cover the most intimate parts.

"Looking good, Mrs. Jasper," she said, squinting to the sun.

"Thank you," I smiled, taking a sip of orange juice.

I sat beside my husband and he continued to look over at me, watching as my tits settled on my chest, barely supported by the bikini.

"Is this for her or for me?" Dillon whispered.

"I don't mind," I said. "Both?"

He leaned over and gave me a quick kiss, rubbing a finger down in between my legs as he did so. I let out a breath and closed my eyes but he was gone just as soon as he'd arrived.

I was aching to get started on Dillon and Morgan but I thought it prudent to wait a few hours first. I didn't want her to think that the only reason I'd employed her was so she could take part in my sordid game, even if that was the truth. Instead I too started to read, basking in the sun and trying my hardest to lose myself in a book.

I set to work just before lunch. Morgan had made it half-way around the garden and was pruning one of the beds with her back facing us. On her knees and from behind like that was exactly how I wanted my husband to take her, but we'd come to that later.

"Hungry, honey?" I asked, looking across at him.

"I could always eat," he said.

I leaned across to his lounger to whisper in his ear. "I can think of something you can feast on."

I nibbled at his lobe and put a hand on his chest, creeping ever-so-slowly down his body. Dillon gradually set down his book and closed his eyes. By now he was used to my sudden urges.

My hands wandered like a spider further and further down until I was at the waist of his tight shorts. I could see immediately the effect I was having on him. The bulge inside was moving and he was struggling to contain himself. I put a hand on his cock and started to rub, moving it in his shorts so that it started to grow up towards the waist-band.

Across from us Morgan tended to the plants obliviously. My first impressions were that she was a woman-of-the-world, so I was interested to see how she'd handle things when she finally saw the pair of us enjoying ourselves.

My hand dived inside Dillon's shorts and he looked down his washboard abs to the source of his pleasure. I sought out his thick cock and wrapped my hand around him, exciting myself in the process.

What little fabric my bikini had was now being pushed up by my stiffened nipples. I could feel my heart racing in my chest as the arousal built, magnified by the forbidden nature of it all. It felt like such a thrill.

"Morgan, honey," I called, and Dillon startled. "Relax," I said to him out of the corner of my mouth.

"Yes, Mrs. Jasper?"

"I'd like you to come and look at something for me."

She turned back and took stock of the sight before her. Her eyes followed my arm down into my husband's shorts and she seemed decidedly unmoved by it all.

She set down her secateurs and stood up, brushing her gloved-hands down her knees and walking over.

"What have you got to show me?" Morgan asked, walking over with a hand on her hip.

"Dillon, will you do the honors?"

He looked up to Morgan who smirked down at him, setting him somewhat at ease. Slowly he opened his shorts, pulling down the zipper and reaching into his underwear inside.

"It's been a while," Morgan said.

"Since you've seen a guy's cock?" I asked.

Her smirk grew broader. "Since I've been with a couple."

I scoffed in disbelief as Dillon pulled his cock over the waist of his shorts. Morgan caught sight of it and sucked a breath. I looked down to see Dillon stiffer than ever. His perfect-looking cock seemed to glisten in the sunshine, as though it were a beacon drawing us to it.

"That's a nice-looking cock," Morgan said casually.

"Wait till you taste it," I said wryly.

"I wouldn't want to cut in line."

"I don't mind who goes first," Dillon said, and he put his hands behind his head and waited.

"Rock, paper, scissors?" Morgan offered.

"Ha-ha, I like it!"

Morgan set her fist on her palm and I did the same.

"One ... two ... three!" we said in unison.

I shot out two fingers but Morgan held firm, showing her fist.

"After you," I breezed. Either result was a win for me.

I turned on my side on the lounger and watched as Morgan settled beside Dillon. She looked across his body at me as she picked up his cock and started to jerk it slowly.

"I think you like watching," Morgan said.

"She can read your mind, honey," Dillon said.

"You know, Janice told me about you two ..." Morgan hinted.

I raised an eyebrow. "All good I hope?"

"All *bad*," Morgan said. "But bad in a good way. I like bad."

With that she dropped her mouth to my husband's cock and wasted no time in driving her lips straight over him.

Dillon looked between me and Morgan in quick succession. He couldn't believe his eyes and neither could I. I started to wonder if Morgan truly was a gardener or some kind of whore-for-hire.

"Look at her go!" I marveled, feeling my pussy swell with arousal. The mere sight of someone pleasing my husband was something that got me off immeasurably. I started to rub at the crotch of my bikini panties.

Morgan pulled her lips off my husband and took several deep breaths. She'd been almost all the way down over him.

"Your turn," she said, pointing the tip of his length towards me.

I slid down off the lounger and knelt on the plush grass beside Dillon. It felt cool against my knees and when I took his cock it felt hot in my hands. I could feel Morgan's saliva coating him. I started to pump my fist over him slowly and then I looked across at our slutty gardener and gave her a wink.

She squeezed her shoulders together and bunched her tits, gasping as I slipped my lips over the crown of my husband's beautiful cock.

"Ugh! I am being spoiled today," he cried.

Morgan started to kiss his stomach above me, moving her face further and further up Dillon's body until their mouths were on each other.

She kissed him as I rocked my head over his stiffness. I could feel him touch the top of my throat but I didn't have the wherewithal that Morgan did to take him any further. She'd slipped him into her throat so effortlessly that I demanded to see it again.

"All yours, Morgan," I said, kissing my husband's cock goodbye for the moment.

She looked down at it and narrowed her eyes again as though she were preparing to strike. She took off her gloves and tickled her long nails down over my husband's chest. I held his cock upright and she planted herself over him again, pushing all the way down.

"Look at that!" I gushed.

"I am," Dillon said.

I moved up behind him and took in the view that he had. From his vantage he could see the bulging throat of Morgan as it swelled around his girth.

I held his shoulders and kissed his face. "We've got ourselves a pro."

Morgan smiled and peeled Dillon's cock from her mouth. "I don't know about that."

She beat her fist over him and then straddled the bed. Her whole arm worked to jerk him and her cutesy tits bounced beneath her white wife-beater.

"Let me help you out," I said, and I stood up to walk behind her.

Dillon watched me move round the back of her. My hands came through under her arms and I gripped at her perky tits beneath. I could feel the stiffness of her nipples against my palm. Morgan stopped beating Dillon's cock and she looked to my face on her shoulder.

I started to kiss her, fondling her tits and relishing the soft moans that started to escape her. Dillon was stiff as a rock and Morgan's moans made it sound as though she was just as wet as I was.

She took two hands to Dillon's cock now, squeezing up as she moaned. I took a grip of the bottom of her tank-top and lifted it up her body.

She broke her grasp on my husband and I pulled the garment up over her head. I looked to Dillon for a reaction, seeing his pupils fixed firmly Morgan's tits. He shook his head and chuckled in disbelief.

"Mmm," I cooed, tossing her shirt aside and kissing her face again.

I moved down in front of her and she held me gently as I kissed my way towards her tits. My husband started to jerk himself as he watched me tackle her.

I pulled her perky breast towards me and raced my tongue over her nipple. She cooed delightedly as I circled her areola in the embrace.

"Fuck, Mrs. Jasper!"

"Oh, we'll get to that," I smirked.

I moved back up to Morgan's face and kissed at her lips, feeling a sensuality like nothing else. It felt as though we were performing for Dillon and it's fair to say he was enjoying the show. When the pair of us looked back to him he was stiff as a board and waiting for the next act.

I took Morgan's hand and guided her to her feet. We stood at the foot of Dillon's sun-lounger and started to kiss again. My hands wandered down her body and I gripped at that perfect ass that I'd been dying to squeeze since I'd watched her walk to her truck.

It felt round and firm beneath her shorts, but I was desperate to unleash it. Morgan didn't seem shy in undressing.

I moved to Dillon and took a grip of his shorts, pulling them down his legs along with his underwear. When he was free he opened his knees wider and his cock fell back against his stomach. He looked delicious, like he was a centerfold in a women's sordid magazine.

"Have anything in mind?" I said to Morgan, looking between her and my husband.

The sun beat down on his bronzed physique and Morgan studied it, seeming to give the question some consideration.

"I'd love to ride him," she said, nodding to Dillon. "Just like that."

I gave her ass a quick, fierce pat. "That sounds good to me."

She hopped in surprise and her tits bounced on her chest. She giggled and fell into me, looking up at my face first and then beginning to eye my big, mature tits.

Her hand came up to the bikini and she slipped a finger inside the garment, running it down and around my breast.

"You don't have to be coy," I said.

"Oh, I know," Morgan replied. "But sometimes it's fun."

She moved the fabric of my bikini over and bit her lip as she caught sight of my stiff nipple. I watched her tongue flick over it like she was tasting the air. I closed my eyes and took a deep breath, reminding myself that Morgan was here primarily for my husband.

Dillon stood up too now and joined Morgan at my chest, releasing my other breast and feasting on it in exactly the same way, as though the tables had suddenly been turned. I put my hand to the back of both of theirs head, wondering what the hell I'd done to deserve such a treat.

I scanned around the garden and then up at the pure, blue sky. I felt euphoric, as though I might snap from the dream at any moment.

Dillon and Morgan both broke from my nipples and I guided their heads together softly until the two of them began to kiss in front of me. Morgan seemed to like the older man. In fact she seemed to like the older woman, too. I'd have to keep my eye on her ...

I started to jerk my husband's cock as the pair of them kissed. He moaned and pulled Morgan forward by the waist of her denim shorts.

She fell against him and I left them to it for a moment to grab a towel and throw it down onto the lawn. When I looked back I could see Dillon's hand in Morgan's open shorts. They were kissing and he was fingering her with purpose, like a college-student during his first female encounter. I played voyeur for a moment and watched.

Morgan's chin rattled as she gushed a breath and broke away. Dillon's hand emerged from her panties and he brought his fingers to her mouth. I started to rub at my pussy as Morgan took a grip of Dillon's wrist and carefully licked her juices from his digits.

"Take off her shorts, honey," I said to Dillon, biting my lip as I watched.

Morgan saw me playing with myself and then she watched Dillon carefully as he unzipped her further. My eyes were firmly fixed on her. My husband started to drop her shorts and I watched the curve of her milky, perfect ass emerge. Her panties dropped too and soon I was looking at a naked, cherubic beauty. If felt as though she'd been conjured in our garden by some long-forgotten spell.

"Where do you want me?" Morgan asked, unabashed by her nakedness.

"On the towel," I nodded. "I want to see my husband take you from behind."

"I'm not gonna argue with that," Dillon said.

Morgan stepped her boots out of her shorts and walked to the towel. She got to her knees as demurely as possible, as though she were entering a yoga-pose. She put her hands out in front of her and stretched forward, arcing her back to give it the perfect sweep up and over that toned ass of hers.

I moved around to join Dillon, looking down on the opening of her ass at the glistening slit that lay beneath the perfect dot of her asshole.

"After you, Sally," Dillon said, nudging me with an elbow.

"What?"

"Come on," he said. "Try it."

I wasn't about to let him win a dare. I put myself behind Morgan and mimicked her previous movements as I got on my knees. I was on all-fours behind her now and staring into her sinful crotch as she looked back over her shoulders.

"You first, huh, Mrs. Jasper?"

"Me first, Morgan," I said, and I crawled forward into her.

Morgan let out a groan as my face planted itself between her ass. I flicked out my tongue and tasted the sweet cream of her pussy on my lips. It felt so good to smoosh her skin against my face like that and to hear her moaning in response was getting me wet too. She wasn't shy in letting me know how much she was enjoying herself.

I felt Dillon's hand on my bikini panties and soon he was peeling them back over my ass. I continued to lick at Morgan but I was finding it difficult to concentrate, even more-so when I felt the rounded head of Dillon's cock washing back and forth across my aching pussy.

"Ohh, fuck," I moaned, my words deafened by Morgan's flesh.

She reached back and pushed my head into her and I licked out in response, striking her asshole and listening to Morgan hiss in approval.

"Yes, Mrs. Jasper," she cried.

I hadn't meant to tongue her ass but her response only encouraged me to do it more. With Dillon slowly pressing through my pussy-lips from behind I was becoming lost in the excitement of it all.

I moved back down and thrust my tongue through her tight O, feeling the cream of her pussy run over me as my husband teased his cock around my folds. Finally I pulled away and moved around beside her.

"Come on," I said, curling my finger towards Dillon and patting Morgan's ass.

She looked back as Dillon came closer, his huge cock swaying on his hips. The wetness of my pussy coated his tip. I gripped his cock and pulled him forwards, looking down over Morgan's ass and watching the two of them collide sinfully.

"That's what I want," I grunted, sucking a breath through clenched teeth.

I rained another smack down on Morgan's ass and she yelped in pleasure. Dillon pushed forward and I watched her pussy wrap over him like it'd been waiting for him all this time.

He eased forward and dropped the rest of himself into her, getting on his knees behind her and taking charge of her ass with two strong hands.

Gradually he started to rock her back and forth on him and I watched for a moment as his cock drove into the pink slit, emerging with more and more cream strewn across its length.

"Come up here, Mrs. Jasper," Morgan said. "I want to taste you."

I moved in front of her and sat my ass at the top of the towel, opening my legs and giving Morgan the view of my pussy that she craved.

Dillon looked into my eyes as the fiery beauty dropped her head to munch on my mature pussy and I watched back. The second I felt her lips on me I ached a moan. I looked down to see her toying with my flesh, her whole body bouncing as Dillon worked on her from behind.

She pulled at me with her teeth gently and used her lips to nibble along my petals. Every now and then she'd envelop her mouth over me and slip her tongue along my groove in the embrace, washing my juices back along my pussy.

I started to rub my clit as she feasted on me and my husband upped his pace behind, rocking into her faster and faster. Among the chirping of the birds I could hear the claps of flesh as Dillon bucked forward against Morgan's ass. Whenever he thrust deep she'd let out a yelp and I'd feel the vibrations of it across my sensitive pussy.

"Give it to her, honey," I urged, watching as Morgan began to lose herself.

Her focus was on my pussy less and less as my husband gave her that big cock of his. I wasn't surprised. Whenever he'd fucked me it felt so magical that I could scarcely concentrate on anything else.

I could tell by her tightening jaw and staggered breaths that she was close to climax herself. I started to play with myself in front of her as though I was putting on a show, but mostly I was just enjoying the show they were putting on for me.

"I'm gonna come," Morgan whined now, throwing her forehead against her wrist and breathing down into the towel.

"Good girl," I cooed.

I looked to Dillon who fucked her with the prowess of a porn-star. His body glistened in the sunshine with all of his muscles working towards the end goal.

"I want him to come inside you, Morgan," I hushed.

"I want it too," Morgan said, beside herself with pleasure.

Her face was flushed red with arousal and she was lurching her chin forward as she grunted. She embraced the climax and let it capture her without mercy.

"You feel her coming, honey," I said, looking over her ass at him.

"She's so fucking tight," he winced.

"Give her what I want," I said. "Give her what she wants. Tell him what you want, Morgan."

"I want your fucking cum," she growled.

"Tell him," I said.

She lifted her head and looked back at Dillon. "Cum in my fucking pussy!"

Dillon smirked, impressed.

"That's my girl," I said proudly.

I span on the towel and started to inch underneath her on my back.

"I wanna see this," I said. "Up close."

I moved along the towel and looked up at Morgan's slender neck, then her pretty tits and cutesy navel before I finally caught sight of her kempt fur. My husband's cock worked below that, pushing through her wet petals over and over. His balls were tight up against his shaft and he looked swollen beyond measure.

"He's ready, Morgan. Tell him again."

"Come in my pussy, Mr. Jasper! I want to feel that cum inside me!"

Dillon pushed on and I stared up excitedly, watching his cock smash into her quickly. She groaned and Dillon jerked himself through her tight core, building to a flurry of thrusts.

"That's it," I said softly, watching close.

Suddenly he slowed and I watched the orgasm arrive. His cock pulsed and then I heard the groan of Dillon above, all manly and testosterone-laden. He growled like the king of the jungle and then Morgan cooed as she felt his warmth blast into her.

I watched from below, seeing his cock twitch and imagining the pearlescent seed that bursting inside her.

"Oh, that looks so fucking hot," I moaned.

"Fuuuck," Dillon groaned as the throes of climax gripped him.

"It's so warm," Morgan cooed. "Give me it all, Mr. Jasper."

She let out a little yelp and then I felt her kissing my pussy. My husband eased in and out of her slower now, coming and fucking her at the same time. He pushed his love deep but some of it started to flood back, scattering down from her and dripping on my face.

I opened my mouth to it and hummed as I felt the warmth of his love on my cheek and lips. I set a tongue out to search for his seed and then another drop landed in my mouth.

"Mmmm, yes," I hummed.

Dillon moved slowly in and out of her until I could no longer see his cock throbbing at all. When he was spent he pulled back gradually. I'd never had such a good view.

Morgan was kissing and biting at the inside of my thigh as my husband popped himself free of her. I watched her pussy massage him out of her and then a bead of hot cum crept out. Before long it was tear-drop and then it was hanging down from her like a sticky web, targeting my face.

"I love that," giggled, and I opened my mouth to catch the escaping spunk.

Morgan watched down underneath herself as I caught everything that left her. When there was no more left to come she spun on her knees and fell beside me on the towel.

"You two lovers gonna kiss each other?" Dillon asked, looking down and jerking his cock slowly.

He still looked hard but most of all I think he just wanted to witness it. It's not often two women share your cum. I think Morgan was keen too because before I'd had chance to answer him she'd planted her lips on mine.

I ran my tongue around her mouth and passed his cum to her. The embrace was spine-tingling. It gave the kiss this whole new texture that I hadn't anticipated. Our tongues slipped and glided against each other with my husband's love easing their passing. It seemed like the height of sin.

"That's fucking *hot*," Dillon said.

"Now that's a holiday!" Morgan said, laughing as she fingered and errant droplet into her mouth.

I pulled away and wiped at my face, giggling back. I felt suddenly self-conscious of my husband's cum strewn all over me, but Morgan soon put paid to that.

She rose up on me and held my head steady as she carefully licked and kissed his love from me, as though I was a new-born kitten and she was a proud mother cleaning me with her tongue.

Finally she sat back down and swallowed gleefully, biting her lip and looking between the two of us.

"So are you gonna let me get back to this garden?" she joked.

Dillon and I laughed. "For a few more hours, maybe," I said suggestively.

Morgan donned her gloves and nothing else. She moved back to the place she'd left, looking back over her shoulders with a smirk. The fine ass of hers bounced as she got back to it.

"Damn," I said, shaking my head and looking to Dillon. "Any idea she was capable of that?"

"Her?!" he said, laughing. "I didn't even think *you* had it in you."

"Stop it," I laughed. I slapped at him playfully but secretly felt proud of the compliment. "I can still be naughty."

He pulled me close and kissed my lips. "Don't I just know it?"

THE END

The Magical Bouquet : Couples Threesomes 19

My husband Monty and I had worked a stall at the local market for years. We sold fresh produce, plants and flowers—indoors and out—and had even started cultivating our own. A lot of what we offered couldn't be found anywhere else locally and as such we had a constant supply of regular visitors.

Monty was an attractive, mature stud with an easy-going attitude. He always hit it off with customers. I'd noticed the younger women really took a shine to him. I'd ogle as a twenty-something would approach the stall nervously asking for something and within minutes she'd be putty in Monty's hands. I don't think he even realized he was doing it. It just came so effortlessly to him.

He'd talk with such infectious enthusiasm that it was difficult not to be drawn in and he was so engaging that it really made you feel listened to. The cadence of his Scottish accent was like caramel on the ears. Shit, I know that it had wooed me all those years ago.

One of our newer regulars was a girl called Rose. She looked to be in her early twenties and had this shy way about her. At a glance she looked almost like a librarian in her tweed and spectacles, but it didn't take much examining to realize that underneath the bookish exterior there lay a diamond.

I'd seen girls like Rose before. So nervous in the beginning, but given enough cajoling they can open up like a flower, or sometimes a fly-trap. It was tough to know which one lay beneath, but it was fun to speculate.

"Here she comes," I muttered under my breath, spotting her day-dreaming her way over to our stall. "I'll leave her to you."

"Rose," Monty piped up. "What can I do for our loveliest customer?"

She blushed. Monty had her immediately.

I didn't mind the flirting. I figured any way of garnering more sales was a good thing and the old adage suggests that sex sells.

I busied myself with a bit of shop-front aesthetics and listened-in as the pair of them started to talk.

"I'm afraid I don't know much about all of this, but I'm eager to learn," she shared.

"We've all got to start somewhere, my love," Monty said. "Believe it or not, I wasn't born with such wisdom."

I couldn't help but scoff at that and Rose turned to look in my direction.

"Some would say he's still searching for it," I added wryly.

"But I've found so much in the meantime. Like my lovely wife Annabel."

It was my turn to blush. Monty could turn on the charm so easily and so effortlessly. Sometimes I felt as though I wasn't enough for him. I wondered if a girl like Rose might sate the desires that I imagined he had.

When she'd left I sidled up behind him and whispered in his ear.

"She wants you."

"Huh?" he startled. "Who wants who?"

"Rose," I said. "She wants you. *Bad.*"

"She's only human," he shrugged.

I giggled and took a step back to drink him in. In his black and red plaid-shirt, light-blue jeans and flat-cap he looked plucked straight from the heart of his homeland.

"You could have her you know. I wouldn't mind."

"I don't get a say in the *minding*?"

"You don't like her?"

"I didn't say that ..."

I smiled. "You know I've always wanted to see you with someone else."

"I know. I've had years of you telling me as much, you saucy devil, you."

"You're not interested?"

"I'm coming round to the idea. But the more I think about it the more I know that you're my one-and-only." He leant forwards and kissed me on the lips.

The market-place was in full-swing but public displays of affection weren't beneath him. Sometimes he'd pinch my ass while I was talking to customers and we'd all share a joke about it. More secretively he'd move behind me whenever an act of nature caused his cock to stiffen and he'd press his body against me when I leant forward over the display. Those were the hardest to ignore. I'd stand upright again and spend the rest of the interaction with the customer wondering if it was obvious that my pussy was salivating. Monty would trot innocently to the other side of the stall and begin serving someone else while the erection in his pants lay hidden.

We closed the stall around five o'clock in the afternoon, but others around us remained open until nearer seven. We started early but only worked three days a week. In the days in-between we'd supply events with displays and bouquets or ship out orders of produce to local restaurants, but I much preferred the intimacy of the market, and not just with the customers.

As the day wound down I joined Monty at the back of our stall. We always set up in such a way that we got a small modicum of privacy back there. Our stall was set against the wall of a local bank and we kept an area open to sit in and enjoy a break away from prying eyes. Sometimes we enjoyed a tad more.

"She'll be back again tomorrow," I said.

"Who," Monty asked.

I sat on his lap and put my arm around him. "Our lovely little flower."

"Rose? Are you sure you don't want me to leave the two of you alone?"

"Ha-ha, you might regret saying that. I think she has a fiery side."

"Her? I can't see it."

"You're not looking hard enough. You think she doesn't think about you?"

"I hadn't really thought about it."

"I know she does." I kissed his cheek and Monty put his arm around my hips to hold me against him.

"She thinks what it'd be like to have that brooding, Scottish gentleman's cock in her mouth."

"Oooft," Monty gasped, adjusting himself. "I do love it when you talk like that."

I leaned closer and relished the moment. "Maybe she could suck your cock back here while I serve the customers out front."

I could feel him begin to stiffen in his pants and Monty lifted me slightly to allow his erection to blossom.

"Maybe you could come back here and join us," he added.

"Wouldn't that be something ..." I kissed his mouth. "Do you think you could handle the both of us at once?"

"I'm fairly confident I could handle one of you at a time. I'm getting old, remember."

I brushed my hand through his ashen hair and took off his cap. I toyed with a tussle between my fingers and hummed contently.

"Forty-two isn't old," I said. "And besides, I'm sat on something that's making me think you wouldn't have a problem."

"When a woman as beautiful as you shows and interest in an old codger like me then I'm only going to react one way."

"Stop it, you," I said, lifting his chin and looking dreamily into his eyes.

We kissed passionately and I moved across his lap so that I could rest my hand on his bulge. I gave it a squeeze and another noise escaped Monty.

He put a hand on my tits that lay tightly wrapped in a tank-top. I'd often use my assets the same way Monty would use his voice. I'd woo the guys to the stall, but they were often wary. Besides, far fewer men were interested in garden supplies than women in my experience.

"Let's clear up and get home," he said.

Later that night I walked out amongst the large polythene greenhouses that we kept on our land. I wandered from place to place, gathering a selective bouquet of flowers that I hoped to use tomorrow. Rose would surely be by again, and this time I wasn't going to be so coy.

I set the bouquet down close to the front-door so I wouldn't forget it tomorrow and I went to join my husband in the lounge, wrapping my arms around him and fantasizing about tomorrow.

"Let's say *hypothetically* speaking that Rose was available ..."

He stirred and looked down as I nestled against his chest. "Hypothetically?"

"Hypothetically, yes. Let's say she wanted to have sex with you and you had permission to have sex with her."

"Well, if I don't see why we can't have a hypothetical threesome," Monty said.

"With me?"

He laughed. "Of course with you."

I snuggled against him. "I'd like that. I'd be okay with that."

"What have you got planned?"

"Nothing," I lied.

Monty hummed suspiciously.

As predicted, the next day at the stall Rose dropped by again to pick up some fresh vegetables and look over our newest bouquets. She paid my husband and they had another flirtatious conversation.

"You know," I began, and she seemed startled that I should speak to her. "I've got a bouquet I prepared myself out back. I think you'll love it."

"Really?"

"It's just for you. I know how much you like them."

Monty was watching the exchange with interest.

"If you want to come by later I can show them to you?" I offered.

"That sounds nice," Rose said.

"Around five?"

"Sure. I'll be back then."

She sauntered away from the store swinging her bag. My husband walked along the stall and came up beside me. He stared curiously.

"What?" I asked.

"What are you up to?"

"Surely you've guessed that by now?"

"You can't seriously think we're going to have a threesome this afternoon, can you, Annabel?"

"I know we are," I said confidently.

"Oh, so you know, do you?"

"Yep," I smirked. "I've got a secret weapon."

"And that is ...?"

"You'll see."

I walked past Monty and I could feel his gaze follow me. Another customer arrived and soon we were too busy to discuss things. Five o'clock rolled by and my husband and I decided to pack away the stall. We were in our tiny private-quarters when I heard a voice.

"Hey," it called. "Excuse me."

I peered through the slit in the canvas and saw Rose standing there. I became excited immediately. Truth be told in the rush that followed our arrangement I'd completely forgotten about telling her to stop by.

"Rose," I said.

My husband face was a picture but I didn't dwell on it. Instead I pushed through the gap and walked out onto the stall to greet her.

"Come around," I said.

Rose wore a small pair of light denim shorts and some mustard, threadbare knitwear with a cutesy button-up shirt beneath.

"You said you had a bouquet ready?" she said.

"I did indeed."

I reached under the table and grabbed the flowers, then I turned back to join my husband on the other side of the divide.

"Come through," I said to Rose.

Inside Monty was sat at our table with a curious look on his face.

"You know Monty?" I said, and Rose walked through the slit.

"There she is," Monty said. He put on a smile and stood up. "My wife's got a gift for you, huh?"

"They look lovely," Rose said.

I offered them to her and the first thing she did was take a deep sniff. My eyes bulged with excitement as she did so and I looked back to my husband and gave him a wink.

He was still confused but gradually it started to dawn on him. For the past few years we'd been working with several flowering plants that had known aphrodisiacal properties. Our goal was to create a 'Viagra bouquet,' the likes of which you could keep in your home and smell whenever you needed a pep before sex. Rose was our trial subject.

"It smells"—she shifted her eyes to Monty and her pupils fattened—"*incredible.*"

"Ooh, can I smell?" I asked.

Monty watched in horror as I took the bouquet from her and took an equally large breath in through my nose.

I felt my pulse rise instantly and my cheeks turned hot. My pussy started to swell and my clit stiffened. I looked straight to Monty too, drinking in his dreamy physique. He looked so fuckable, stood there in his shorts and t-shirt.

"Now, now, girls," he said, backing off as the pair of us walked towards him like zombies.

"You're so sexy, honey," I uttered.

"I want to fuck you so bad, Monty," Rose said.

"Let's do it, Rose."

"Wait!" Monty cried holding up a hand.

Rose and I stopped in our tracks.

"Hand me that bouquet, would you?"

I smirked and gave him the flowers. Monty inhaled and now the three of us were under its powerful spell.

He set the flowers down in the corner and stood up straight to face us, no longer coy. He had an incredible swelling in his pants that seemed to arrive from nowhere.

"No chance of disappointing you now," he joked.

"There was no chance of that anyway," Rose said, and I watched in amazement as she made her advances on him.

I let her make the first move and so did Monty. He watched her with this commanding gaze in his eye, as though he was daring her to do things to him that she shouldn't.

"Open your shorts," Rose said.

Monty looked over her at me and I gave him a nod. I leaned back against the building and looked along the wall through the gap between the dressing of our stall and the front of the bank. The market was still fairly busy and around us people chattered and shouted between stalls, all of them oblivious to what was occurring at the back of the quaint little market-garden stall.

Monty opened his khaki shorts slowly, teasing Rose who by the looks of it didn't want to be teased. Rather than wait for him she dropped to her knees and started to undress him herself.

Her hands moved quickly and my husband and I watched in amazement. She tore open his pants frantically like she was unwrapping a present, then suddenly she tugged downwards and took shorts and underwear in one.

Monty's hard cock popped up out of his pants, looking stiffer than I'd ever seen it. It looked swollen beyond measure. The veins that normally ran under the skin of his shaft were now pronounced on the outside, to such an extent that his entire cock looked bigger.

"Honey!" I swooned in admiration.

Rose was admiring it too. She was knelt in worship, watching close as my husband's cock swayed in front of her. She stared in a hypnotic trance, focusing intently on the prize she had revealed.

"It's beautiful," she cooed.

"You can—" Monty began, but before he could finish the sentence Rose had struck like a cobra.

She raced her mouth over him and made no effort to be coy. I could hear the smacking of her lips as she drove them over him messily and I watched as his eyes rolled back in his skull.

"Steady on there, girl," Monty said, but there was no way he meant it.

He put a hand on Rose's mousy-brown hair and guided her mouth along his cock. Eventually he looked up to me in disbelief.

As Monty watched me I squeezed at my tits. His face lit-up and I felt myself become more excited as he observed. He kept a hand on Rose's head but his eyes stayed on me. My nipples turned stiff beneath my tank-top and I pulled the inside into my cleavage so my breasts were revealed.

Monty bit at his lip then followed my hand as it moved down over my stiff nipples and to the button of my denim shorts. I popped it open and pushed my hand inside, making a show of how much I was enjoying myself.

Rose was oblivious to it all. She was far too concerned with the stiff slab of meat that my husband had laid out for her. As she ate ravenously my husband and I continued our unspoken foreplay.

She pulled back off his cock and looked up to his face, noticing that he was looking at me. Rose turned and saw my hand buried in my shorts. Her mouth opened in excitement.

"That's hot," she said simply.

Her hand pumped along my husband's hard cock, but her eyes were on me now. She let go of him and then walked slowly over to me.

I looked at Rose nervously and then looked over her shoulder at my husband, worried that he might be offended by it all. Far from it. Monty was studying Rose's ass and jerking his stiff cock.

"Show us what you do, Rose," he said.

The look in her eyes was wild. She'd gone from quiet and reserved to horny and experimental in seconds. It was proof-positive that the bouquet had worked.

"I've always had a soft-spot for you," she said to me.

In an instant her lips were on mine and she pushed her hand into my jeans. I moved my hand out and Rose took charge, thrusting her tongue into my mouth and driving her fingers along my wet flesh.

She kissed down off my face and quickly latched her lips onto my nipples. Her tongue circled the stud and electricity shot down my spine. I shuddered and took a deep breath. Rose was sucking and fingering in equal measure and I could scarcely contain the ecstasy it was bringing me.

The whole time Monty observed, stood there with his cock in hand and pumping slowly. He stepped out of his shorts and pulled his t-shirt up over his head. He was that same guy that I'd fucked a thousand times before, but now I wanted him more than ever. His swollen cock looked so delightful on his hips, as though he'd replaced the appendage with an upgrade. The bouquet had certainly had an effect on him too.

Monty walked over naked, refusing to remove his hand from his stiffness. He stood at my side beside Rose and she looked down from my tits to see his beautiful cock waiting there for her.

"We need to get these clothes off you," he said to Rose.

He pulled the cardigan off her back and she dropped her arms. Monty slid his hands round her neck as if to choke her and suddenly Rose let out a delighted groan.

He unbuttoned her shirt and pulled it back off her shoulders, revealing the milky-white, beautiful body beneath. Rose was slender and angled, but her breasts were ample and rounded like a Grecian marble statue. Her nipples were pert and a bright pink, contrasting her skin and drawing the eye.

Monty must have noticed them too because soon he was kissing his way towards them. Rose stood up and the both of us watched him suck his way around her nipples.

I dropped to my knees to suck on my husband's cock and as I did so I started to unfasten Rose's denim shorts too. She stood there and let the both of us be the boss of her for a moment.

My husband rose from her breasts and started to kiss her lips then his hands came around her throat again. She groaned as he squeezed.

I dropped her denim shorts and made fast work of the tiny green panties that lay beneath. They slid easily over her smooth, slender legs and beneath I could see the ginger-looking fuzz of her pussy-hair.

"Look at you," I cooed.

She was far too busy kissing my husband to notice me venturing forwards. I'd never tasted another woman before, but the scent of the flowers was doing crazy things to me.

I pushed my face to her and felt the hair on my top-lip then I eased my tongue out and listened to her groan above me.

"Yes!" she strained, her voice raspy from my husband's grip.

He looked down to see me suckling under her and nodded with approval. "Well I never," he said, his Scots accent cutting through the scene.

I flexed my tongue over her and tasted the sweetness of her juices. She was just as turned-on as I was. Each of our pussies dripped with lust and none of us could contain our passion. Every rational thought had leapt from my mind and been replaced by debauched instinct.

Rose grunted and moved away suddenly and I looked up with concern, worried that the effect of the flowers had worn off.

"Rose?" I asked, standing beside my husband.

She fell forward against the table and put her hands on its rim, then she looked back over her shoulder.

"Put his cock in me," she snarled.

I looked down along her smooth back and then to the dot of her perfect asshole. Below that were the folds of her pussy and the delightful, glistening O. Its soft-pink hue was like the petals of a flower, drawing the eye in a bid to be pollinated.

Monty walked forward and I moved with him, gripping his cock and leading him onwards. He squared up behind Rose and she awaited his arrival.

"That's it," she said. "That's it. Put his cock in me, Annabel. Get that beautiful plump cock in my pussy."

She looked so swollen. The blood was gushing through her and her pussy-lips looked as though they'd been pumped.

My husband's cock too was dangerously red. The blue veins still breathed life into him and I could tell from the look of it that it wouldn't take long to see him satisfied.

"Here he comes, honey," I warned.

I rubbed the smooth tip of Monty's cock along her folds and listened to the pair of them enjoy each other. My husband moved forward and Rose's beautiful pussy enveloped him. He let out a shuddering groan and Rose's knees buckled.

"Yes, Monty! Your cock feels so fucking good."

"I bet it does," I said, watching him slide inside her beautifully.

I jerked the hilt of him and then pushed his ass forward, letting Rose feel everything that Monty had to offer.

"Good boy," I whispered to him, and Monty turned his head to kiss me.

He started to fuck Rose slowly, but from the noises coming from her mouth I don't think she could stand it any harder.

"Oh, fuck!" she snarled, forgetting that the market was still operating around us. Thankfully the place was always bustling, so the cries dissipated amongst the melee.

"Does that feel good, honey?" I asked.

"So fucking good, Annabel. Your husband has an amazing cock."

"Oh, I know, sweetie," I said, stroking a hand over his muscled chest.

I took down my denim shorts and panties, stepping my boots out of them carefully. I walked away from Monty now, pulling out a chair and sitting at the side of the table, facing Rose.

I set one leg aside purposefully and then the other. Rose looked between my legs and let out a deep groan as she saw my aching pussy.

"You look so turned-on," she said.

"I am. How could I not be?"

"Let me taste you."

Rose pushed off the table and my husband walked behind her, still docked deep inside. She steered him in my direction I slid forward to the edge of the chair, hanging my ass on the rim.

"Eat it," I instructed.

Rose didn't need the prompt. Her face was racing towards my pussy with aplomb. She opened her mouth wide and enveloped everything she could, tonguing out of sight and sending me wild in an instant.

"Good girl!" I groaned, splitting my pussy with two fingers.

She tongued and feasted, looking up at me with this sinful smirk. It seemed so at odds with the reserved manner she adopted whenever she stopped by.

"I think we snared ourselves a slut," I said to Monty.

He laughed. "I think I snared myself two of them."

Rose's tongue slathered my petals and Monty drilled into her slowly from behind. I could feel her racing breaths against my wetness. I used them to gauge her excitement and it soon became obvious that Rose was close to climax.

"Come on his cock," I urged. "I want him to feel you."

"Come, Rose," Monty said, giving her ass a single slap and squeezing a handful of her flesh.

Rose grunted and the climax blossomed. She moaned and bit at the inside of my thigh unable to contain herself.

I started to spin my finger on my clit as I watched. I took several deep breaths and focused on the amazing sensation that built within me.

Rose put her face back on my petals and smothered me with her mouth. She spat on me and made a mess of me. My fingers moved frantically, dancing over my swollen clit.

I started to come too and my husband upped his pace, deserving of his moment in the spotlight too now.

"You feel her h—honey?" I moaned, struggling to talk.

The climax tingled its way up from my pussy and my scalp turned light and prickly.

"I feel her," he said. "She's so fucking tight."

"Are you close baby?" I asked.

Rose was thrashing her hair wildly, and moaning loud. She'd bite and lick at me like a playful animal, and all the while she'd let out these delighted giggles.

"I'm *very* close," Monty said, straining.

"Pull it out on our faces!" Rose cried.

The speed and specifics of her request made me think it wasn't a spur of the moment decision.

"Is that where you want him?" I asked.

Monty pounded away behind. "I'm fucking close!"

He pulled out of her and Rose turned to face him, getting on her knees. I raced to join her and moved my hair behind my shoulders.

Monty groaned, jerking over that big Scottish cock of his. He smoothed Rose's cum along his length quickly, working towards his plump tip and rocking his fist slowly.

"Give it us!" Rose said. "Come on my face!"

"Come honey!" I added.

Monty strained and groaned and then an enormous rope of white cum leapt out of him. It scattered across Rose and I turned, amazed. My mouth hung open in shock and then I turned to Monty in disbelief, just in time to catch the next rope that he angled at me.

It leapt from the tip of him and Rose giggled as it fell over me, stretching right from my forehead all the way down to my chin.

He moved his cock again, pointing it at Rose and she closed her eyes in anticipation. His fist pinched to the tip and another bounteous offering erupted.

Rose and I caught lashing-after-lashing in turn and Monty looked like he might never give up. Each time he let out a groan his cock would throb and throw out a rope of hot spunk that didn't seem to lessen in volume.

More and more of it covered us, with Monty doling out perhaps nine or ten ropes of love. I'd never seen him come so much.

"Fuck!" I gasped, as the last of him spurted out onto Rose's chin.

I laughed across at her and she giggled at me, blinking through the cum that had webbed across her eyelashes.

"What a fucking load," I said, moving it carefully off her eyes.

She blinked as though she was waking from a dream, then she held my chin and studied the mess that my husband had made on me.

She kissed at it, rubbing it over my cheeks with her tongue and then pushing it into my mouth. It tasted of salted-caramel. Rose's tongue smoothed the silky substance over mine and then the pair of us turned to its source.

My husband watched from above as we both tackled him. I took a grip of his spent pole and Rose was quickly on the tip, pushing her lips over him and keeping a tight grip.

"Oh, good girls," Monty said. "You've made an old Scottish man very happy!"

Rose giggled.

"You're not old!" I said again, slapping his thigh.

"Guys my age don't even come like that," Rose said.

I kissed her like she'd done to me, holding her head gently and lovingly licking my husband's cum from her.

The pair of us exchanged licks until we'd each cleaned the other's face of my husband's messy eruption.

"There we are," I said, standing to my feet.

Rose joined me, swaying her hips and looking proud. She leant in and gave my husband a kiss on the cheek.

"Thank you," she said sweetly.

"Any time," Monty said, and I looked at him excited at the prospect.

"I hope so," I said, beaming a smile.

"Would you like to keep the bouquet?" Monty asked.

"I think I'll leave it here," Rose said, finding her clothes. "Perhaps I'll come by and smell it again next week."

"Definitely do," I said.

Monty blew some air up his face. "It'll give me time to recover."

"It'll give you time to fill those balls with cum again," I smirked, kissing him.

"Thank-you, Rose," Monty said, and he took her hand and kissed it.

Rose blushed and started to dress. My husband and I watched her.

"We'll see you next week then?"

"You will," she insisted, buttoning her shirt and shorts.

My husband gave her a simple nod and Rose disappeared out of the tent and back into the marketplace.

My mouth dropped open wide and I stared at Monty. "Can you believe it?"

"If I hadn't seen it, I wouldn't have," Monty said.

"Was it good?"

"Good? It was fucking great."

"It looked like you really enjoyed it."

"Likewise," he smiled.

"If Rose comes back next week then I guess she enjoyed it too."

"She'll be back," Monty said sagely.

I suspected her was right.

THE END

The BJ Fairy : Couples Threesomes 20

"Another one!" my husband said, studying the paper from his chair at the kitchen-table.

"Close-by?" I asked.

"A couple of miles away. Same victim profile: white, mid-thirties, married male."

"You might get lucky yet," I said wryly.

The locals had started calling her 'The BJ Fairy.' The newspapers' descriptor of 'Jewel Thief' didn't exactly get the point across, especially since she never actually stole anything.

It began with sightings and break-ins but slowly the cases mounted. With a spate of forced-entries and nothing reported missing the police were understandably confused. Even the term 'forced-entry' didn't quite fit the bill. In all of the cases she'd slipped in through an open door or window.

It wasn't until one brave soul opened-up and described his ... *ordeal* that the whole thing came to light. He'd been awoken in the night to an amazing sensation, realizing quickly that he was in the midst of a fantastic blowjob. The only problem was that his wife was still asleep beside him.

It transpired that for the past month a latex-clad cat-burglar had been breaking into couple's homes and pleasing the husbands. When the newspapers got hold of it they really went to town. It got so bad there was hysteria around it. You couldn't go a day without talking about it, or overhearing it being discussed in the line for groceries.

There were varying schools of thought. Men pretended to be appalled in public, but talked privately about their desire to be visited by The BJ Fairy. Some women were appalled whilst others found the notion empowering. *Is there really any harm in spreading a bit of joy like that?*

It was obvious immediately why the initial victims had been so coy. Not many guys out there would want to admit to being awoken by the greatest blow-jobs of their lives while their wives or girlfriends slept soundly beside them. Guys can be dumb, but they're smart enough to know they should at least *act* mortified.

As, one-by-one, they started to confess, the true nature of the break-ins became more and more apparent. Housewives would arise from a night of slumber to find their back-doors ajar, or their windows open. They'd walk to the bedroom to confront their husbands, only to be met by their embarrassed, shame-filled faces. Nothing even needed to be said. The BJ Fairy had been.

"Are you still crossing your fingers?" I asked.

"Hey!" Tom protested. "You seemed to want this more than me, last I checked."

I shrugged. "I just think it'd be exciting, wouldn't it?"

"For you?"

"I don't know." I looked off to the corner of the room and tried to imagine it. "To know she's there, spoiling you like that. It's almost charitable, really."

"You think she's a cause for good?"

"It's hardly evil, is it?"

"There are a few relationships on the rocks thanks to the 'Jewel-Thief.'"

"BJ Fairy, honey," I corrected. "And if those relationships are rocky now, then they couldn't have been built on solid foundations to begin with."

"I think you've misjudged other people's relationships," he said. "Not everyone is as care-free as you."

"It's not that I'm care-free about it"—I rounded the table and put my hands around his shoulders—"it's just that I would *love* to see her at work."

"On me?"

"On anyone! Shit, I want her to share some tips."

Tom laughed loud. "You're gonna get sexual advice from a criminal?"

"From a superhero," I countered. "She could start a movement."

"From the newspaper reports she's already started several movements."

"You know what I mean. Don't you find it exciting? It's like waiting for Santa-Claus."

"What makes you think she'd come here?"

"We're in the area, I guess."

"In one of the safest neighborhoods in town," Tom countered.

"Wouldn't that make it more of a challenge?"

"Who wants a challenge? She's breaking into the houses that are the easiest to get inside anyway."

I hummed thoughtfully in response. *If I were a BJ-Fairy, where would I go…?*

There was a chance me and my husband were both right. Maybe she'd arrive in our neighborhood for the challenge and *then* decide to break-in to the house that was most susceptible.

For the next week I made sure our windows were wide-open when we slept. In a time where almost every woman in the area was ensuring their houses were locked-up tight I was actively courting an overnight visit from The BJ Fairy.

Each morning I'd wake and be disappointed that we hadn't been visited. I was like a child sprinting down-stairs on a wintery morning to be met by an empty floor beneath the Christmas-tree. Nevertheless I persevered.

It got to the point where opening the window at night had become part of the habit now. I was doing it without even remembering the reason why. Sightings continued to be reported, but my husband and I remained unsatisfied.

And then, around two months in, we received our fateful visit. It was everything I'd hoped.

I awoke to groans. My eyelids fluttered open to be met by the blackness of the room. It was the dead of night. I looked to the clock, forgetting briefly about the noise that had roused me. It was four in the morning.

"Oh, Caroline," Tom moaned.

I looked across at him and saw the pleasure on his sleepy face. His eyes were closed from what I could make out. I reached across for the bedside light and took several quick blinks to adjust after I'd turned it on.

"That's good," he hushed again.

It was then that I looked down his body, spotting the black-clad figure on the bed. I knew instantly that it was The BJ Fairy. I had to pinch myself.

"It's ... it's ..."

She pulled her head back and unsheathed my husband's hard length from her mouth. She shook out her blonde hair and blinked through the mask that covered her eyes as she licked her lips.

"It's my pleasure," she breezed.

I sat up and the duvet fell down me, revealing the loose, white, silk night-dress that I wore to bed. The BJ Fairy raised her eyebrows and bit her lip, giving me a sultry wink before slipping my husband's cock back inside her mouth.

I've no idea how she'd made it this far without rousing either of us. Somehow she'd crept through the house, crawled onto the foot of our bed, pulled the sheets down and released my husband from his boxer-shorts, all without us realizing.

I bit my lip and watched her and my husband in turn. She'd suck her way along his length and twist her hand in her wake and I'd watch my husband groan in euphoria. He was stuck in the ether between sleep and consciousness. Her soft licks and gentle lips seemed to keep him in that thin avenue of slumber.

"Good girl, Caroline," he said, his eyes still closed.

"You're good at that," I whispered to her.

She raised an eyebrow but didn't stop. She worked over him with greater purpose, taking his entire length in her mouth like she was some kind of magician.

I squeezed at my tits as I watched her. I could feel my pulse rising. My blood pumped the lust around my body. My nipples turned stiff and my curiosities piqued.

I ran my eyes over her body and drank in the rest of her physique. The cat-suit she wore looked like leather or latex. It hugged tight to her body, which looked agile and well-toned. You don't make a name for yourself as a thief without being light on your feet.

She started to move faster over his cock and my husband's groans became louder and more impassioned. Suddenly I found myself worrying. Worrying that this might all be over soon and I didn't get a chance to enjoy it to the fullest.

"You're not gonna make him come now, are you?" I asked.

The BJ Fairy slowed the bobbing of her head and squeezed her lips up over the clean-cut cock of my husband. "What did you have in mind?" she asked.

Just then my husband stirred. I looked to him as his eyes opened and then I waited patiently for him to come to the same realization that I did.

He looked first at the clock, then he looked down his body and then he looked across at me. He pushed his hands into the mattress and sat up in bed, moving away from our sultry home-invader.

"Wh—what? It's ... her!"

The BJ Fairy blew a kiss up the bed. My husband was aghast, but only because he knew that was the correct response.

"Feel good, honey?" I asked.

"No," he protested. "No, I—it—"

I started to laugh. "I won't be offended. It was kind of hot seeing you enjoy her."

"I wasn't enjoying her!"

"Looks like you were to me," I said, and I stared down at his rock-hard cock.

He attempted to pull the duvet back over himself but I snatched it away.

"Don't be shy now, Tom" I said. "This is the moment we've been waiting for."

"You have, huh?" The BJ Fairy said.

"Do you do repeat visits?" I asked wryly.

"They can be arranged."

She rose up on her knees at the foot of the bed, sliding her hands up over her smooth latex body and bunching her tits together.

A silver zipper ran up the front of her cat-suit. It started just above her navel and it was then that I noticed that the crotch of her bodice was removed completely. Her pink-flesh juxtaposed the tight, black suit. Her folds looked wet already, as though the mere act of my husband's cock being in her mouth was enough to get her soaked.

"Look at that, honey," I said.

With her mask on The BJ Fairy wasn't shy. I imagine a costume such as that affords a certain privilege. Who knows what I'd be capable of if I could maintain anonymity?

Her hands ran back down over her curves and she slid them inside her thighs, framing her pussy even more-so. She had a tuft of blonde hair above her clit, sculpted perfectly into a triangle.

"Lie back down, Tom," she said.

As though he was under a spell my husband laid his head back against the pillow, shuffling down the bed and putting his feet between the open knees of our temptress.

"Good boy," I said beside him.

I sat with my legs underneath myself, leaning my elbow against the head-board so I could get a good view of everything.

I took several deep breaths and watched her focus on my husband. She locked eyes on him and then started to walk her knees slowly up his body, straddling him until that pretty pussy of hers hovered over his spit-drenched cock. But she didn't stop there.

She continued to crawl up his body and my husband and I both felt a palpable excitement when we realized her destination.

"Taste it," she ordered.

My husband's pupils fattened as he stared at her soaked slit, mere inches from his face. I watched his maw disappear beneath her and then I heard the smacking sound of his lips accompanied by the groan of our one-time mistress.

"That's it, Tom," I said, studying her body as she writhed on him.

Her hands pushed through his brown hair and she dragged her pussy back and forth. Tom feasted from below, gripping her ass and squeezing against the smooth, black material that bound it tight.

The BJ Fairy looked to me now, staring deep into my eyes as she rode my husband's face. It was as though she was daring me to react—and react I did.

I moved my hand down my silken night-dress and lifted the skirt. My fingers pressed against my pussy as she watched me with a keen eye. I felt every part the exhibitionist.

I leant my head back and groaned as she studied me, then I felt her hand squeezing at my tits as my fingers continued to toy over my folds.

My face turned back to her and she leaned forwards towards me, keeping her crotch on my husband's lapping mouth.

I leaned forward to meet her and kissed those perfect lips of hers. She tasted sweet. Her delicate tongue excited me in an instant.

"He's good at that, huh?" I said, my face close to hers.

"You're a lucky lady."

We kissed again and I searched out the zipper of her cat-suit. I slid it down her body slowly, opening the front and revealing the perfect, womanly abs and rounded tits that threatened to slip out of the open front.

She moved the thin straps of the night-dress off my shoulders and it fell down my body, hanging on to my big tits that she continued to fondle.

"Show me," she said.

"If you show me …"

My husband lapped hungrily and the smacking of his lips and tongue was the backdrop to our debauchery. He feasted hungrily. I knew how good he was at doing that. Every so often The BJ Fairy had to pause to enjoy him. Her eyes would close and her lip would curl as she sucked a breath, then she'd start on me again as though she'd been recharged.

I pulled down the front of my dress and bared my big, ripe tits to her. Her eyes sparkled as she saw them and she pulled open her cat-suit in response.

Her tits sat on her chest, looking as though they'd been sculpted by an artist. In contrast mine were much fuller, but thankfully that was something that she seemed to enjoy.

"Look at those," she said, ogling me.

I looked down at my chest and wiggled my shoulders so my tits swayed for her.

"I wish I could enjoy you two every night," she said.

"We wouldn't want to be so selfish."

She moved away and straightened up on my husband, looking down her body and addressing him now. "You like that pussy?" she said.

"I love it," he said, his voice muffled by her flesh.

She put her hands on her exposed tits and grinded over his face, bossing him with her pussy. She had an amazing body and she knew exactly how to use it.

By now my night-dress was more of a belt than anything. Above it sat my big, exposed tits and below it my thin panties, the crotch of which was fast-becoming sodden.

"Are you gonna fuck him?" I asked.

"I am," she said. "Are you gonna take my spot on his face?"

I watched Tom's eyes dart to me and he bobbed his eyebrows suggestively.

"I *am*," I swooned.

The Fairy moved down off his face and Tom took a quick swipe at his spit-drenched mouth. I leant over and kissed him, tasting her on his lips before I got up on my knees and slipped my panties down.

My dress fell with them and I moved out of them both. I was completely naked on the bed now, staring across Tom at our mistress who was admiring my body with the same verve that I had admired hers.

"You're built to fuck," she said. "If I had a cock as nice as your husband's I'd very much like to put it inside you."

I felt like blushing. The statement was incredibly forthright—that much was obvious—but I couldn't deny the flattery in it. Having a woman tell you she'd love to fuck you was high-praise indeed, especially coming from a woman as commanding as her.

"Sit on him, that's it," she said, watching close.

I stared down my body, moving my hands to my petals and parting my pussy as I planted it down onto Tom's hungry mouth.

I groaned with relish and stared across at The BJ Fairy. For the moment she was focusing on me more than my husband. His cock lay back against his stomach, twitching intermittently. She watched his busy tongue slip over me.

"Put him inside you," I said. "I want to see it."

She bent over and gave him one last suck, then she held his cock upright and brought her pussy to it slowly.

"That's it," I said, studying close and waiting for the moment of contact.

I watched his pumped-up cock touch her petals and then I felt the sexy biting of his jaw on the inside of my leg as her pussy sheathed him slowly.

Her mouth opened in a silent moan. I knew exactly what she was experiencing. My husband's cock was big, but once you overcame the initial shock of it you started to experience a euphoric fullness.

"God, that's good," she said.

She sank all the way down on him until she'd swallowed every inch. She started to ride him slowly, rocking backwards and forwards as though she was stirring her insides with his length.

As she moved so too did Tom. His mouth slipped along my crease and his tongue poked freely. Sometimes I'd get a little more adventurous and move forward on him. He'd tease around my ass a little ways. It was the best kind of tickling that I'd ever experienced. The sensation was intriguing.

"What's he doing?" she asked, noting the sudden change in my expression.

My shoulders rocked and I pulled them together. "He's licking my ass."

"Naughty boy," she said, and she dragged her nails down over Tom's abs.

He sucked a breath, then darted his tongue up against my ass in response. I pressed down on the muscle as he made a point of it, then he waggled it inside my ass with gusto.

"That's so fucking good," I groaned.

"Isn't it just," she said. "Your husband is *ravenous*."

"Aren't we all?"

I looked across her and leaned forwards again until we formed an Eiffel Tower of sin over my husband. She sat on his cock and I sat on his face as we kissed. Each end of him pleased up effortlessly.

Our mistress knew just what to do to get off. She continued to ride him like a cowgirl and I watched her move through the stages of climax. At first she closed her eyes to concentrate on his cock probing deep, then she held her breath before taking huge gasps of air whenever she needed to fuel the mounting lust inside her.

"That's an amazing cock," she whispered. "You're gonna make me come."

Her jaw shuddered and then the climax gripped her body. She started to wriggle and writhe, crying louder until the entire room was filled with her impassioned wails.

"Come on his cock," I urged, snarling in her direction as I shared her carnal urges.

She started to bounce on him now and I watched his cock emerge from her, covered in a film of her white cream.

"Ride him," I goaded. "I want to see him shoot in that pretty pussy."

She let out a wail of pleasure at my words. My husband tightened up too, as though the muscles of her pussy were gripping around him.

"Ride that fucking cock," I growled.

I started to contract too, my pussy throbbing on the moaning maw of my husband who continued to feast from below. I rode my lips across him, my body tightening as the ripples of climax fluttered through me. It was as though her orgasm was infectious.

"Yes!" I groaned, and the pair of us climaxed on him.

"Good boy, Tom," she said, dropping down on him again and resting for a moment.

She breathed deep and looked across at me as I shuddered out my release. I could feel the come ooze from me but Tom was on hand to lap it up.

I kicked a leg off him and dropped my face to his, kissing him lovingly and feeling the silky texture of my cum in his mouth.

"You deserve to come now, honey," I said, holding his face. "I want you to come."

"Come inside me," The Fairy said. "Come inside me and we'll have your wife lick it out of me."

My jaw dropped open at the notion. It was an aspect of a threesome that I'd never before considered, but now that I did I found the idea thrilling. To feast on her pussy and my husband's seed at the same time felt like the height of sin.

"I want that," I said.

"You want it, honey?" Tom said, getting himself all worked up.

The BJ Fairy started to bounce on him again, dragging her tight pussy along the length of his delicious cock. I lay close by, kissing at his moaning face and encouraging him towards climax.

"Give her your cum, honey," I hushed, my lips close to his ear. "Pump that cum inside her."

"I want it, Tom," she groaned, putting on a show for him.

"Fuck, yes," he cried.

She bounced faster, jerking his cock between her tight folds until Tom was gasping for air. I could see the tension in him as every sinew of his body tightened.

"Come in her fucking pussy. Let me taste it. I want to suck it out of her cunt."

The pair of them wailed in delight at my filthy mouth, then I watched as all the tension that Tom was holding was released at once. His body fell back into the mattress and he let out a long whine.

"Pump that fucking cum," I urged.

"He's coming!" The Fairy cried.

He let off inside her, signaling each rope of release with a moan of pleasured delight. I'd never heard him so excited before in all his life. It was such a joy to watch.

"Fill her up," I cried, staring into the eyes of The Fairy who bit her bottom lip as she continued to glide over him. The sensation of each hot lashing flowing into her must have been incredible.

His moans tapered off and she slung her legs over him, settling at the foot of the bed and parting her knees wide.

I stared into her crease as I moved up off the bed quickly. Tom angled for a better position as my face went between her legs. Before I knew it my tongue was meandering up her folds as I tasted the salted-caramel release of my husband.

"Good girl," she said, holding my head on her.

Tom watched close beside, still breathing hard. He toyed with his spent cock and moved to kneel beside The BJ Fairy.

She couldn't resist another taste of him. Her lips wrapped over his dick and she sucked him clean, licking off the errant cum as I tended to the rest of his seed.

I slid down over her petals and licked lovingly, as though I was a cat grooming one of its friends. The taste of my husband lessened with each lick and soon I could taste the coppery sweetness of her pussy instead.

She pulled my husband's cock from her mouth and looked to me. "You beautiful slut," she said.

She leaned forward and kissed me again, sampling the menagerie of juices that mingled between us. It was such a delight.

"I'll leave you my card," she said. She reached behind her and from nowhere she produced a business-card. She tossed it on the bed. 'BJ' was emblazoned in silver writing across its black face and there was an e-mail address below.

"If you ever require my services," she said.

"We'll be in touch," my husband said.

His eyes followed her as she slinked out of the bedroom and disappeared into the night. When she was gone her turned to me, his face still in shock.

"Did that just happen?" he said.

"If I'm not dreaming." I pinched myself to make sure.

"How did she get in?"

"I don't know," I lied. "Aren't you glad she did?"

"Are you kidding? Fuck!"

"It was so hot watching you come inside her."

"It was hot watching you eat it out," he said joyously.

The pair of us sat there like giddy fans, reliving the moment despite the fact they'd only just occurred.

"When I saw her at the foot of the bed I was like: *Is this real? Is that her?*" I laughed.

"Yeah, it could have been one of the other local blowjob robbers," he said wryly.

I gave him a playful slap and then followed it with a kiss. He wrapped his arms tight around me and we fell back into the mattress laughing.

"Let's send her an e-mail," he said, looking at the card.

"Now?"

"Why not?" he laughed.

"We'll do it later for sure," I said. "But let's take a moment to enjoy what just happened."

I hummed contently and put my head on his chest, listening to his fast-beating heart as it slowly came down from its high.

"We'll do that again soon," I promised. "If not for you then for me."

THE END

Air B'n'J : Couples Threesomes 21

When the lockdown lifted I really wanted to get out there and enjoy the world. I'd been cooped up for so long that all I could think about was living life to the fullest once things got back to normal. I vowed to never pass-up an opportunity again. You just never know if it's the last chance you'll get.

It was under this new philosophy that the trip to Portugal had fallen into my lap. I'd entered a prize draw for a travel company on a whim and wound up actually winning! I couldn't believe it when I opened the letter.

It wasn't quite the fifty-thousand-dollar first-prize that I'd hoped for, but unlimited flights to and around Europe was a pretty good second prize. I didn't hesitate to take advantage of it.

I found someone to rent my apartment from me while I was gone and that was that. A month after the envelope landed on my door-mat I was winging my way to Europe.

My first port-of-call was Lisbon. I don't know why but Portugal—and Europe on the whole—had always held an allure to me. The culture seemed completely different from what I was used to in the states and that was something I was looking for more than anything else. I wanted it to *feel* as though I was in another country, and there was no greater proof of that than stepping off the plane and into the unusual-looking airport.

"Taxi?" I asked after getting through customs.

A swathe of men in shirts descended and it was up to me to choose one of them.

"Rui São José[1]?" I said, causing many of the men to nod in agreement. "You know?"

---

1. https://www.tripadvisor.co.uk/ShowTopic-g189158-i203-k8608178-Sao_Jose_Is_it_a_good_neighborhood_in_Lisbon_to_stay-Lisbon_Lisbon_District_Central_Portugal.html

"I know," one of them said, in better English than the other. "Take me."

As I walked away the men dispersed. The idea of traveling alone was terrifying and that experience hadn't exactly allayed my fears.

My friends had recommended hostels to me but I wanted my first night's sleep to be the best it could be. I didn't want to start my adventure all groggy and tired in a room full of people snoring.

As such I'd rented a room in someone's apartment—Mr. and Mrs. Allan to be precise. Their profile on the website said they were an English couple who'd emigrated several years ago. They looked friendly in their pictures, but then I guess they would. Nevertheless I'd taken the gamble.

"Rui São José[2]?" I repeated again to the driver.

"Yes," he said, and then he typed the address into his phone.

"You know?"

"I know," he said again, still typing. He didn't know, but he at least had a means of getting there.

"How much?"

He waved his hands as though the question wasn't important, then he tapped the meter in the middle of his dash.

"Okay," I said, and I sat back as he began the trip.

I watched the quaint town approach in the distance and stared dreamily out of the window, wondering what the trip had in store for me. It felt as though each day would be a series of tests, but I was willing to meet them head-on. I figured there was no better way of having an adventure than to thrust myself into it.

The streets became thinner and the buildings drew closer as we wound our way to the apartment of Mr. and Mrs. Allan.

---

2. https://www.tripadvisor.co.uk/ShowTopic-g189158-i203-k8608178-Sao_Jose_Is_it_a_good_neighborhood_in_Lisbon_to_stay-Lisbon_Lisbon_District_Central_Portugal.html

Rui São José[3] was the kind of street I'd dreamt about when I imagined Portugal. Leafy plants wound out from the open windows of houses that were painted in ochre, terra cotta and olive green. Residents strolled down cobbled streets and people talked and argued with loud, emotive gestures.

"Here," the taxi-driver said.

I looked up at the yellow building that we'd stopped outside of.

"Twenty Euros," he said, pointing to the meter.

I had no idea if that was a good price or not, but right now I didn't really have a choice. I paid up and he helped me with my luggage, even going so far as to show me how the intercom system worked at the apartment-complex door.

"Lucy?" asked a voice on the other side.

"Mr. Allan? I'm ... uhh ... here!"

"I'll be right down."

I turned to the taxi driver who smiled and nodded before getting into his car and making off down the narrow road.

The door of the apartment opened and a cheery-looking forty-something man appeared. He wore a light, linen shirt and khaki shorts with open-toed sandals (thankfully sockless). If I didn't know he had a wife I might have started flirting right then and there, but instead I stood there smiling.

"Come in!" he said, opening an arm and inviting me over the threshold. "I'll get your bags."

"You don't have to do that," I said, holding it tighter.

"Smart. You should never let a stranger carry your bags."

"Oh no, it isn't that," I lied.

"We've just met. You're right to be cautious. I hope you don't mind a set of stairs?"

---

3. https://www.tripadvisor.co.uk/ShowTopic-g189158-i203-k8608178-Sao_Jose_Is_it_a_good_neighborhood_in_Lisbon_to_stay-Lisbon_Lisbon_District_Central_Portugal.html

"No problem."

I followed behind and Mr. Allan continued the conversation, walking up the steps sideways and talking back down them towards me.

"First time in Portugal?"

"First time in Europe!"

"My gosh! Well, on behalf of everyone here: welcome!"

I giggled. "Thanks."

"Good flight? You must be pretty tired?"

"I'm a little pooped, yeah."

"Air-travel will do that to you. My wife and I are eating lunch if you'd like to join us?"

He opened his apartment door and I walked inside. A cool breeze meandered through. The place was open and airy, with a light-brown wooden floor and a menagerie of plants adding to the overall charm.

"It's so lovely!" I beamed, looking around.

"Thank you," he smiled back, and then his wife came through one of the archways in the hall and smiled warmly. She had short black hair and devilish smile on her pretty face. She wore a long, flowing gown over a baggy pair of slacks and a white tank-top. Her tanned skin looked immaculate.

"You must be Lucy," she said.

She approached instantly with wide open arms. She wrapped them around me and I hugged her. I was taken aback but the hug felt good. It was so warm and inviting and Mrs. Allan sure did smell nice. I suddenly felt self-conscious about my own odor.

"Sorry. I'm a little sweaty."

"Don't worry about that," she said. "Perfectly acceptable after a long flight. Will you be joining Paul and me for a spot of lunch?"

"Do you mind if I just shower and take a nap?"

"Of course not," Mrs. Allan said. "You need to refuel the tank for tonight. Your bedroom is just through that door there."

"What's tonight? Is something happening?" I asked.

"Paul and I are going out and we every much insist you join us. We'd love to show you the city."

"I—I—"

"I told you she'd have her own plans," Paul began.

"No," I said, remembering the philosophy. "I'd love to join you."

"Amazing!" Mrs. Allan said. "You won't regret it."

"The shower's through here," Mr. Allan said, and he showed me the door. "Feel free to use all of my wife's mysterious scrubs and lotions."

"It certainly looks like they're working," I said, looking back to Mrs. Allan.

She raised an eyebrow and twisted her mouth in a naughty smirk. "That's incredibly kind of you to say, Lucy."

"We'll be out on the balcony if you need us," Mr. Allan said.

He put an arm around his wife who was still lingering her gaze on me. I don't quite know how she'd done it, but in one look she'd managed to convey her interest and make it abundantly clear that she was sweet on me. It made me nervous, excited and confident all at once.

I dropped my bag in the hallway and wasted no time in enjoying the privacy of their bathroom. It was adoringly lavished with bright tiles and polished stones, with flowering plants on the windowsill and all manner of scrubs and gels in different sealed pots. It was very 'new-age.'

I undressed and took a look at myself in the long mirror that was positioned opposite the shower. I imagined Mr. and Mrs. Allan enjoying their fair share of fun while they watched their reflections. It was handily placed.

The water was cool and refreshing to step under, flowing from above out of a huge, square shower-head. It felt like tropical rain. Before long I was scooping out dollops of scrub to try and rubbing the crystalline concoctions all over my body.

I started to think of Paul and his wife together under the same shower-head, running their hands over each other's bodies and living the Portuguese life.

The more my mind wandered the more my fingers did too and soon I was cruising them along the folded petals of my sex. It had been a long day and this seemed the perfect way to round it out.

I closed my eyes and focused on the sensation of my swelling clit, and then I turned to look through the glass of the cubicle and out to the mirror beyond.

The water flowed over my curves and I took a moment to admire myself, feeling the confidence that Mrs. Allan had given me blossoming anew.

My shoulders tightened and I sucked a breath, holding it and concentrating on the sensation within. My whole body shuddered and my nipples stiffened as I stifled a groan.

I sucked a deep breath and my jaw shuddered. I let out another moan that I couldn't quite control and then suddenly I heard a knock on the door that shocked the climax into life.

"Lucy," said Mrs. Allan. "Are you okay in there?"

"Y—yes!" I tried, covering my mouth with my hand upon realizing how pleasure-laden it sounded.

"You don't need a hand with anything?"

"N—no," I answered quickly, my body erupting in spasms as I did so.

"Okay, sweetie, enjoy."

I started to giggle soon afterwards, feeling embarrassed by the intrusion. The post-climax glow was strong though and I didn't dwell on it for long.

I toweled off and made my way to the bedroom, falling into the soft sheets and slowly surrendering to slumber.

Before I did though I flashed my mind back to what Mrs. Allan had said. '*A hand.*' Do I need a *hand* with anything? I realized not only had she been offering herself to me, but that I had declined it without thinking. I had broken my new code.

The notion of sleep was stronger than my sense of regret and before I knew it was awakening to a more dimly-lit room. It took me a while to gather myself in my new surroundings. I looked to my phone and saw that it was six o'clock.

I leapt from the bed and dressed quickly. As I wandered out into the apartment I heard soft, elegant piano-music drifting through from the balcony.

I made my way towards it and saw my hosts sat at the table, leaning towards each other after what looked like a romantic embrace. Mrs. Allan moved away and Paul noticed my arrival.

"Sorry," I said, realizing I'd intruded.

"No, don't be," Mrs. Allan said, turning down the radio. "Feeling refreshed?"

"Much better, thank-you."

"Will you be joining Julie and I?" Paul asked.

"I'd love to."

"Ready now?"

I looked down at my light, black shorts and tank-top. "As ready as I'm gonna be."

The pair of them laughed and we set off together. We spent the evening feasting on petiscos (the Portuguese version of tapas,) sipping Madeira wines and dancing to the music of little bands in cutesy bars.

After a wild, fun night together the three of us returned to the apartment. I wondered what would be in store for us back there and Julie wasted no time in letting me know her intentions.

"I'd love to stay up but me and my stud here have a date in the bedroom," she said.

Paul smiled sheepishly, as though it was something he didn't want me to hear.

"Knock yourselves out," I said, trying to hide my dismay that I hadn't been invited.

She dragged Paul away and gave me another lingering look, as though she was inviting me with her eyes.

I returned to my bedroom and fell into the sheets. I stared up at the ceiling and looked towards their room, imagining what might be going on inside.

I was hornier than all hell and a night of revelry hadn't helped. I'd really had my hopes set on being ravaged by the pair of them, or at the very least Mrs. Allan—who looked like she could teach me a thing or two.

I heard a deep groaning coming through the apartment and I knew I wouldn't be able to sleep knowing what was occurring a couple of rooms away.

I rose from the bed and walked slowly through the apartment, getting closer and closer to the deep moans of Mr. Allan.

The tiled floor did much to deaden my soft steps and I made it all the way to their doorway without interrupting the mood.

When I arrived I saw Mrs. Allan sat on the end of the bed, crouched over her husband and slurping lovingly on his thick, hard cock. The pair of them were still clothed, clearly too enamored by each other to waste the time in undressing.

Paul spotted me and shifted, putting a hand on the bed and taking his eyes off his wife. "Lucy," he said.

Mrs. Allan didn't move right away. Instead she slipped her lips down over her husband's cock one more time and dragged them slowly off, seeming to relish my audience.

"Glad you could join us," she said, tossing her hair short hair back and giving me those eyes again.

I stood in the doorway, unsure of where to go from here.

"Like to try?" she asked, and she shook her husband's cock and looked up the bed to him. "Would you like that, honey?"

Paul nodded. "If Lucy doesn't mind?"

"Lucy?" Mrs. Allan said.

"I ... I don't mind at all."

I walked into the room, eyeing the sizeable length of Mr. Allan who lay in wait before me. Julie moved her knees from over him to let me get closer. She kept her hand on his cock and moved it gently.

I put a knee onto the mattress and Julie curled my hair behind my ear and looked up at her husband to smile.

"He deserves it, doesn't he?" she said.

"You both do," I said.

I'd never tackled a cock as big as Mr. Allan's before, or one with as much experience. I'd had a few fumblings here-and-there with guys my own age but nothing compared to what was before me now. Not only was I about to go down on a guy over twice my age, but I was to do it all under the watchful eye of his loving wife.

"Please him," Julie said, and she guided me down towards him.

I moved my mouth to the tip of his dick and pressed my lips over him, listening to him groan above me. Julie dropped her face to the mattress so she could watch me swallow him down.

I closed my eyes and concentrated on his arousal as it slid slowly into my mouth. My lips hugged him tight and I could feel each ridge and vein of him. He was pumped-up with arousal and there was no give to his cock at all. It was like sucking on a rolling-pin.

"Good girl," Mrs. Allan said. "Let's spoil him together."

She moved her face down close to mine and started to kiss me. Despite a night out in the town she still smelled sweet, like an aphrodisiac for the nose.

I moved up off her husband's cock and she started to kiss me. The two of us held his cock together as we embraced and Julie started to move my hand with hers until the pair of us was jerking him in unison.

She looked up at Paul who was staring down in a euphoric kind of disbelief.

"What are you girls doing to me," he laughed, then a deep groan escaped him.

"Nothing more than you deserve," his doting wife said.

This time she pounced on him, feeding his dick into her mouth with fresh gusto. She thrashed on it and I leant away, looking over her body and down her back to her ass that lay beneath her baggy, thin pants.

I rubbed down over her shoulders and she started to hum appreciatively, encouraging me further. I continued down her body until I had a fistful of her ass, giving it a squeeze and playful slap as she continued to feast on her husband's cock.

"I want you to sit on him," she said, pulling back off him.

Julie started to tug at Paul's shorts and he arched his ass off the bed to let her drag them down. I stood back and watched him flail up out of his underwear and slap back against his stomach. *God, he looked big.*

"You want me to undress you too, huh?" she said, and she stood up with me and looked back to Paul.

She started to kiss me, putting her hands on my breasts and another on my ass. My tiny shorts offered little support and her hand squeezed and tugged, moving my panties over my pussy as she did so.

I started to kiss her back, exploring her body the same way she was exploring mine. She didn't appear to mind.

"Keep doing that," Paul said, and when I looked to him again I saw him steadily cruising his fist over his huge cock.

I sucked a deep breath and let it out calmly, trying to stop myself from coming right there on the spot. The anticipation of the fun to come was almost too much. My head began to feel light, but the soft kisses and rough touches of Mrs. Allan did much to placate me.

She moved back away from me and lifted her top over her head, showing me the huge, motherly tits that sat beneath, bound in a purple bra.

"Damn," I gasped, my eyes bulging.

"My husband seems to enjoy them," she smirked.

She looked back to him and reached behind her back, unclasping the strap and letting the bra fall off her shoulders.

"Putting me to shame," I said, moving forward to touch them.

She leaned away and watched down her chest as I played with her big tits pushing them together and feeling the weight of them in my hand.

"Nothing to be ashamed about," she said. "Yours look good enough to eat."

I bit my lip at her overt suggestion, then I moved my face into her breasts and latched my lips over her nipple.

"Yes!" she groaned immediately. It was as though she'd been waiting for the touch of my mouth on her tits the entire time.

She held me against her as I feasted, then she turned back to her husband who watched it all from the bed, jerking steadily and keeping himself stiff.

I could feel her nipple engorging in my mouth and my tongue fluttered over as she cooed and giggled above me. She didn't seem to know where to put her hands, running them along my back and then under my body to cup and squeeze my tits.

"Now you," she said.

I took my mouth from her breasts and she started to pull at the bottom of my tank-top, eagerly lifting it up my body with an infectious smile. I felt wanted more than ever in that moment. There was no greater feeling.

I wasn't wearing a bra so Julie had one less item of clothing to worry about. As soon as they bounced free her eyes were sparkling for them.

"Give them to Paul," she said, and she took my hand and guided me back towards him.

He leaned forward and kicked his legs over the side of the bed, sitting on the mattress and stroking his hands up my nubile body.

"That's it," his wife said. She watched close as he moved towards my nipples.

I stared down and breathed deep, trying to control my emotions and temper my excitement. I didn't want to embarrass myself by climaxing too early.

His hands were sliding up and down my slender back and he was squeezing at my ass. He pulled me towards him and then raced his mouth over my teat. I let out a groan and so did his wife. She seemed to share the excitement in the room and draw from it.

"That's good," she said, stroking my back.

She started to rub in between her legs and soon she was taking down her pants. She stepped out of them and then took my hand, placing it between her legs and letting out a moan of delight as I touched the crotch of her lacy panties.

I could feel her hot flesh beneath. I fingered against it and held her husband's head to my tits. His stubble grazed my soft skin as his wife's hands went down inside the back of my shorts.

She pressed her fingers under the thin waist of my panties, getting a handful of my meaty ass before moving further down and fingering at my aching pussy from behind.

I groaned and let them each please me, looking down on my fingers as they busied away between Julie's legs.

She started to kiss my face, probing her fingers deeper until they were easing through the soaked O of my pussy.

I giggled, realizing that this was it. This was the adventure that I'd been searching for and it had all come to me so easily. I'd just had to be open to it.

Julie could wait no longer. She dropped her own panties and stepped out of them and I turned to look at her body. I hoped that I could have one just like it at her age.

"Look at you," I cooed.

She fell back on the bed and opened her legs wide, showing me everything she had to offer. I stared at her mature pussy and watched as her fingers found it, parting the flesh and showing me the glistening wetness inside.

Paul looked to it and was immediately drawn. He moved off my tits and instead crawled towards her open legs, as though he was a loyal dog that had been conditioned to respond to the sight.

I watched him prowl forwards. I started to touch myself as he bit at the inside of her thigh and I moved for a better view when he ventured further up her legs. I could hear from the shrieks of joy that Paul had made contact.

He rushed his t-shirt over his head and got quickly back to it, leaving me as the only one in the room with their modesty still covered.

I downed my shorts and panties in one and reached between Paul's legs to grab his cock. It was still stiff and pointing down at the bed, al big and thick.

I stared over his back at his wife who was groaning steadily, and then I started to jerk Paul in my fist, bouncing my hand back against his stomach and running it along the full length of his prowess.

He sat on all-fours with his ass pointing back to me and I found it more inviting that I perhaps would have in any other moment.

I licked a finger and touched it to his knot, hearing him groan against Julie's thigh. It was all the encouragement I needed.

I spat on my finger-tips and pushed them over his ass as I jerked him. Paul became more and more erratic but he channeled his energy into his wife, slurping and licking at her pussy with wild abandon.

"He likes that," his wife said, and she seemed to have a pretty good idea where my finger was.

One hand pumped along the thick barrel of his cock while the other was busy drilling his ass. I could feel the tight grip of him on me. My own pussy cried out for attention too.

"Come here," Julie said, as though she could sense my yearning. "Come up here and sit on my face."

I felt my heart quicken at the notion. I crawled over on my knees, passing Paul who looked up briefly from his meal.

"That's it," his wife said, opening her arms to greet my thighs.

I straddled her and felt her wet tongue flick over my petals, parting them and targeting my clit instantly.

The sensation was incredible. I started to rock gently over her face, smothering her with my flesh as she dined-out from below.

Now it was her turn to use the excitement Paul was giving her and pass it on to me—and pass it on she did.

Before long I was writhing mess of ecstasy and my orgasm was approaching fast. I couldn't hold it back any longer, and it was mostly thanks to the expert licks and flails of Julie, who I figured must have done this before.

I fell forward over her and she arched her head back to continue to lick on my clit, then I felt something else from behind.

It grazed inside the cheeks of my ass and I looked back to see Paul pressing his mouth between them.

Soon-enough I was being pleasured by the pair of them, with Julie sucking on my pussy while Paul flicked his pointed tongue all around my asshole.

"Don't stop," I groaned, feeling my body tighten in its familiar fashion.

I shuddered above them, my entire body trembling. The release was winding up like a coiled spring and there was nothing I could do to stop it from bursting free.

All it took was another nudge of Julie's tongue in the right place and another stab from Paul and that was it.

"I'm coming!" I cried, and Paul moved back and gave my ass a hard couple of spanks.

They burst against me and propelled the climax out of me. I was moaning and shrieking, feeling the heat of his spank turn my cheeks hot and red.

My pussy contracted and Mrs. Allan kept her place, sucking and licking on me like I was their very own toy.

"Fuck her, Paul," Julie said, sliding out from under me.

I fell over onto my side and continued to shake. My legs squeezed together and my entire body tingled. My scalp felt filled with static and my head was light for a moment or two.

I awakened back into the room, blinking up and Julie who smiled down.

"Enjoying yourself?" she asked.

I nodded, too breathless to speak, then I noticed that Paul's cock was in her hand and she was jerking him over me.

"Bury it in her tight pussy, Paul," she said.

He moved my legs open and crept between and I looked up at his frame. Despite being over forty Paul was well-kept. He looked commanding and sensual all at once.

He gave me a wink and I started to giggle, but then his big cock was washing up and down the channel of my sex and suddenly everything seemed all too real. I was about to be fucked by someone's husband while their wife was in the room!

"Put it inside her, Paul." Julie said, showing no sign of jealousy.

He steered down towards my tight muscle and then he pressed forwards. My mouth opened to moan and Julie dropped hers to mine, kissing me passionately as her husband drove himself into me.

I opened over him and gripped him close. Julie's tongue was flailing against my own and I was doing everything I could not to cry out in pained pleasure. His cock took me back to being a virgin all over again.

"Yes!" I groaned eventually.

Julie moved the hair off my face and looked down lovingly. "He feels good, doesn't he?"

I nodded and smiled, but then a thrust from Paul made me wince. He felt incredible.

"Give her your cum," Julie said, looking to Paul.

He nodded and started to fuck me, passing his cock through my tight O faster and faster as she whispered words of encouragement beside him.

"Fill her up," she said, looking down on me with a smirk. "Fill up that *young, tight, pussy.*"

Paul let out a bigger groan than before, bucking into me faster and pressing down on top of me. I started to kiss him, yearning for his release as much as his wife now.

"Come inside me," I hushed, holding him close. "Come in me."

"You heard her," Julie said, and I watched as she draped her spit over her finger.

She moved it behind Paul and then a quick moan from him told me everything I needed to know. He kissed me again as she fingered his ass from behind. I felt my pussy begin to tighten again as though it was threatening climax, but the strength of his cock and his thrusts was too much to squeeze out of me.

Instead he burst through me over and over, hitting a spot so deep that I feared it may never be pleasured again.

My words bounced from my mouth as he ravaged me. "Come inside me."

His wife looked back to her hand and then down at me. "Come in her while I finger-fuck your asshole, honey."

Paul groaned and then his whole body tightened. His thrusts became more erratic and his cock seemed to swell within me.

"Give me that fucking cum!" I wailed.

Suddenly he throbbed inside me and then I felt the warm cascade of his opening release.

"Yes!" his wife cried, feeling his asshole wink on her finger. "Fill her up, honey. She's earned it."

"Every drop," I whispered, holding him close and looking over into his wife's eyes.

Julie nodded knowingly as Paul gave me everything he had to offer. His cock continued to pulse in my core and I could feel the slippery warmth coating my insides.

"Mmm," I cooed, closing my eyes to the sensation.

Eventually he pulled out, looking down at his cock as it emerged, all strewn in his cum.

"I'll handle that," Julie said.

She stooped towards it and gave it a lick, delivering a sensual after-care to his spent cock. I watched as her tongue cleansed him of his cum, not resting until there wasn't a drop left.

Afterwards she looked up the bed towards me and moved upwards. I looked at her lips and met them as they approached, kissing her and feeling the impossibly sexy texture of her husband's cum amidst the embrace.

He rolled off to the side, breathing heavily and watching the two of us pass his seed between our lips in a sticky kiss.

Eventually Julia moved off me and smiled warmly.

"So how was your first night in Portugal?" she asked.

All I could do was giggle. If this was the start of my trip, I was in for a wild ride!

THE END

Club Sex : Couples Threesomes 22

When my boyfriend Mark suggested we try out 'Club Sex' I was immediately curious. He and I had a fairly open relationship, but we didn't usually dabble in anything as sinful as the things that went on inside Club Sex.

I'd heard things said from friends and even knew one-or-two people that had frequented the place on the odd occasion, but as yet Mark and I had never dared to explore it.

We were adventurous, don't get me wrong, but we perhaps weren't *that* adventurous. Or we weren't sure we were anyway!

The second he broached the idea I'd jumped at the chance. He'd thought me a little keen but I knew he wouldn't be asking if he didn't want to do it himself. I always aimed to please him like that. I got a kick out of watching him enjoy himself, and I think he got the same kick out me enjoying myself too.

We'd met each other online several years ago. I should have known I was in for a wild ride when he'd fucked me in the ass on the first date, and he should have known he was in for a wild ride when I'd begged for him to shoot his load in there too. We were made for each other.

Club Sex was a fairly non-descript building on the outskirts of town. From the outside you wouldn't even know it was open. I guess places like that didn't really shout about what they were offering inside.

Mark and I stared up at the dimly-lit, four-storey building late on a Friday night. He reached his hand to mine and gave it a squeeze, looking to a door on the ground-floor.

"Ready?" he asked.

I took an excited breath and looked around. "I'm ready to get off these streets at least."

Club Sex was in a derelict part of town, hidden away in the back-roads of disused factory complexes. God knows what it used to be used as. Now it was a place that deviants of all ages flocked to.

Mark led me up to the gate and I clicked across the street in my high-heels and tight, white dress. He was dressed in a shirt and a hugging pair of suit-pants. He wore his best shoes too. He said we should make the effort and I agreed. There's something even sexier about fucking in nice clothes.

He rapped the door that rattled in place and for all the world it felt like there'd be no answer. No light came from the windows above. Only a tiny sticker that read 'Club Sex' above the door gave anything away.

"You think they're home?" I asked, squeezing his hand and feeling a chill.

Suddenly a slot in the door slid open and a pair of eyes stared out. A female voice spoke.

"How can I help you?" it said.

"We're here for Club Sex," my boyfriend said. "My girlfriend and me."

He pulled me closer to him and the eyes shot in my direction. They narrowed in a smile.

"I'm sure they'll enjoy you," she said. "Money first."

"How much is it?"

"Fifty bucks for an hour. Since you're a couple we'll do a buy-one-get-one-free."

"Perfect," Mark said. He had a way of being comfortable in even the strangest of situations.

He peeled a fifty from his wallet and passed it through the slot. The lady took it and then the bolt unlocked at the bottom of the door.

It whined open and inside stood two heavy-set men in suits with folded arms. They wore an ear-piece and made no secret of giving me the once over.

"You want to pat her down?" Mark asked.

One of the guys smiled and then a tall lady emerged from behind them. "I want to," she said. "I have to, in fact."

Mark got checked over by one of the guys while I had the rough fondling of the tall, female security guard to enjoy.

"That fifty is already paying dividends," I joked.

The security guard gave me a smirk and then they parted to let us upstairs.

"Couples are on the second floor," one of them said. "Find yourselves a room and enjoy. Any trouble, just ring the bell near the door and one of us will be there before you know it."

"Shall we?" Mark said, and he offered me up the stairs.

He'd spoken in the past that he always liked me going first, especially up the stairs. It gave him ample opportunity to run his eyes over my ass. I strode forward smiling, knowing that my skirt was probably short enough that he'd get more than an eyeful.

Mark followed behind and as we rose through the building we could hear the groans and moans of the rooms around us. It could have passed for a haunted house had we not have known what was truly going on.

I waited outside the second-floor doorway, just off the landing. Mark walked through it and it led to a corridor with rooms on either side. We walked along and Mark tried the door of a room in the middle. It opened slowly and he peered carefully inside.

"Is it empty?" I asked.

I heard the noise of hand on flesh and then a groan of satisfaction rang out afterwards.

"Come on," he said, beckoning me inside.

I walked slowly down the hall, past each door of sin that told its own story. Our room was larger than I was expecting. The windows had been boarded out. The walls were thin and made of wood. They moved to the touch. A light hung dimly from above.

"Are they …" I asked, pointing.

Mark looked to the circular holes that sat on both walls. There were three on each side of varying sizes. The smallest hole sat in the middle, with the two larger ones on the outside.

"Glory-holes," Mark said, turning to me and bobbing his eyebrows. "Let's have some fun."

He walked to me and took a grip of my ass, pulling me against him and letting me know that he was already well on his way to arousal.

"Someone's pleased to be here," I smirked.

"It's not just me," he said, and as if to confirm the statement a moan rang out from a room a few doors down.

He kissed me and his hand came under my skirt to grip my bare ass. I wore a small g-string that barely covered my pussy.

My hands ran over his body and I gripped his toned ass. He was so well put together that I wondered how I'd ever snared him in the first place. I think our common bond of debauchery was enough to keep us together.

Mark pushed my dress up over my butt and then took two handfuls of it. I fumbled at the buttons of his shirt to get them open, then I felt his third hand arrive between my legs and tickle at my pussy. *Wait a second.*

I looked back behind us to see the long, slender arm of a stranger sliding through one of the larger holes. Their fingers slid back and forth over the crotch of my panties and I could feel the wetness of my pussy breaking against the fabric.

"That feel good?" a sultry, female voice asked.

"Too good," I confessed, then I looked to Mark and bulged my eyes.

"Surprise," he whispered.

He kissed me again and steered me closer to the glory-hole. Our female accomplice reached her hand through my legs and I looked down my body to see her squeezing at Mark's packet. He leaned back and looked down.

"Oh, fuck," he groaned, throwing his head back.

I studied his face, relishing the excitement that the encounter was giving him.

"Take him out for me," I begged, looking down.

The woman was experienced. Her arm had the slightest look of age to it, freckled on the wrists and hand. With just her fingers she managed to unfasten my boyfriend's belt, then she slid down the zipper and soon she was tugging at the waist of his boxer-shorts.

"Give me that cock," she urged.

I walked away from the wall and turned to watch as Mark helped our mistress take his cock out of his pants. It sprang free, as hard as ever and I stared in amazement as she took a grip of him and started to jerk him in front of me. I'd never let a woman do that to him before.

"That's it," she snarled, beating her fist over his cock.

For a second I didn't know what to do with myself, but Mark put his hand behind my back and guided me over to the wall.

I crouched at his feet and looked through the hole to see a surprisingly attractive woman on the other side.

"Hey there," she said, smiling as the continued to pump her fist over his dick.

She looked to be in her late forties, possibly even early fifties. She had long, blonde hair and a devilish grin. Her tits were pushed up in her tight dress and her body looked well-toned, as if she worked-out. I bit my lip as I watched her work, looking at her hand jutting through the portal and staring as it gripped Mark's cock tight.

"Put it in your mouth, honey," our stranger said.

She steered his cock towards me and stared eagerly through as I curled my hair behind my ear and leaned forward for his big, meaty dick.

She squeezed the base and I watched the veins flare up from the pressure. When I slid my lips over the tip I could feel how stiff he was. My mouth moved over him and I pinched my lips around him, flicking my tongue out of sight as I listened to our helper begin to groan.

I popped my mouth back and stood up a short ways, looking through the gap and seeing that our guest was panty-less. Her fingers were toying with her kempt pussy and she seemed to be getting just as much satisfaction as my boyfriend.

I stood up close to him and whispered into his ear. "Should we invite her round?"

He looked at me in disbelief, but the grin that blossomed on his face was answer enough.

"Wanna come join us?" I asked.

"It'd be my pleasure, honey," she replied.

My heart beat fast as I listened to her leave the adjacent room. I could hear her walking down the hallway and then there was a knock at our door.

Mark opened it wide and our guest walked in. Striding with confidence and moving straight towards me.

"I'm Megan," I said, but instead of replying she put her lips straight on mine and gave me a long, deep kiss.

My boyfriend closed the door as we continued to make-out and I felt her hands begin to explore me. She went straight to my exposed ass and started to squeeze, sucking a breath and then leaning her head away from me.

"First time?" she asked. She looked back to Mark.

"It is," he said. "But I'm starting to think we might be coming back."

"You should," she said. "You can have a lot of fun here. I'm Annabel."

"Nice to meet you, Annabel," Mark said smoothly.

"I haven't forgotten about you," she said. "Come here, stud."

Mark walked forwards and Annabel crouched beside the wall opposite to the room she was in. She pulled me down with her and I knelt at her side in the middle of the room. Mark came close, his big cock swinging on his hips.

"Can you girls share?"

"I suppose so. As much as I'd like it all to myself," Annabel joked.

I nudged her playfully, feeling instantly at ease in her care-free company.

"Put it on my tongue," she said, curling her finger. She stuck her tongue out from her mouth and rested it there in wait. She seemed the perfect slut.

Mark did as requested, setting his cock down against her. She moved her head forward as soon as he made contact and then she started rocking over him. Her hand started to squeeze his balls and then she pulled her mouth off him with a pop, gripping his cock at the base and pointing it towards me.

I raced my mouth over it feeling my boyfriend's arousal rush into my throat.

"She's good," Annabel swooned, moving my hair back and looking up to my boyfriend. "Does that feel good?"

"So fucking good," he groaned, moving his hips slowly and fucking my mouth.

I clacked my throat on him and then pulled back, my face red from my efforts. Spit drooled from my mouth but Annabel was on hand, quickly moving it back up and rubbing it gently around my mouth before kissing me.

"Well, hello," Mark said suddenly, and I looked up at his face to see him staring at the wall closest to us.

I leaned forward to see and impressive-looking cock jutting through into our stall. Annabel barely even flinched. She pounced on it and soon she was sucking the guy in the other stall like her life depended on it.

I was caught up on the wave of eroticism. I couldn't describe it. The energy in there was so *sexual* that nothing felt off-limits.

I moved my mouth back over my boyfriend and started to jerk him, teasing under Annabel's skirt as I did so and fingering along her folds, just like she had done to me.

She started to groan and the guy in the stall groaned with her. She was really working fast, as though his cum-shot was something that needed to happen quickly. And it did.

Soon she gasped forward off him and I stood up quickly to watch as a jet of hot spunk fired against her chest. She caught it and watched it drool down into her cleavage, encouraging the stranger to give up his release.

"Every drop," she said sweetly. "That's it. Every drop."

I jerked Mark's cock slowly as the pair of us watched her drain him. She squeezed at his balls and raced her mouth over the tip quickly, pulling back just in time to catch the next spurt of cum on her chest. She seemed like a professional.

"Good boy," she said steadily. "Good boy."

The cock disappeared as quickly as it arrived and Annabel looked down at her cum-strewn chest.

"That was fun!" she exclaimed. "One of my quickest."

I felt a strange compulsion to help her clean up. I crouched down to the floor next to her and studied the pearly cum that draped over her chest.

"Want a closer look?" she asked, leaning away and showing off her chest.

I pulled at the top of her dress and her tits sprang free, accompanied by a shocked giggle.

"You *do* want a closer look," she said.

I licked at the cum, finding it sweet and bitter all at once.

"You sure this is your first time?" Annabel asked.

"I think so," Mark said, feigning suspicion as I lapped up the cum that had spilled all over her tits.

Annabel's nipples stiffened and I moved my tongue to those, circling around them and feeling the perky teat against my tongue.

"My God, Megan," she groaned.

Mark walked forward and soon Annabel was sucking on him again, jerking his cock in her mouth as I toyed with her big tits.

"Let's get you inside her," Annabel said now and she tugged Mark's pants further down his body.

Mark took his cue to undress, racing off his shirt and stepping out of his fancy shoes. I kept my dress on but Annabel helped with my panties. She moved them down over my ass and then swooned as she stared at my kempt pussy.

"Looks delicious. May I?"

"Please do," Mark answered.

I put my foot into the big glory-hole, using it as leverage as I opened my legs for Annabel who crouched beneath us.

She tongued up into me and I let out a moan of approval, leaning my head back and realizing that it was the first time I'd ever let a woman do that. I don't know why I hadn't done it sooner.

Annabel moved just right, tonguing gently at first then rougher when she felt it necessary. I could feel my clit stiffen and swell immediately and my sex started to ache out its juices slowly, preparing itself for Mark.

He arrived behind me, hugging me from behind and squeezing at my tits. He tugged the bust of the dress down until he could get at them and Annabel continued to slide her tongue along my pussy as Mark's cock peered through my legs too.

I could hear from his breaths that was treating him as well, kissing at the tip of his cock and then returning to me to continue her work on my folds.

She reached beneath and took a hold of Mark, watching closely as she brought his cock to the tight, wet O of my pussy.

"That's it," she said carefully.

I looked down to see her studying it closely, as though she was paying carefully attention to everything in case she needed to recall it later.

Her face was a picture of desire. When Mark thrust forward she burst with joy, staring up at me to watch the resulting reaction on my face.

"That must feel good," she said.

"So good," I trembled. I thought I was going to come instantly. Mark felt harder than I'd ever known him and the added naughtiness of having another woman watching us was just too much to contend with. As if that wasn't enough, another cook peered through the glory-hole and Annabel tended to it quickly.

"My lucky day," she said, and she sprang into action.

Mark held my hips and started to fuck me. I put my hands against the wall to push back, then I felt the hand of a stranger grip my ankle through the large hole that I stowed my foot.

He held it steady, using it for leverage as he worked his cock in and out of Annabel's mouth. She stayed still on her knees, letting the new stranger use her mouth as his fuck-toy.

"I can't believe this," I whispered.

Mark gave my ass a spank and then I felt his finger on my asshole, teasing it with gentle presses that accentuated the sensation of his powerful cock sliding through me.

I could feel each ridge and vein of him as he passed through my core. I was so sensitive to him, I couldn't explain it. It was like the occasion was delivering more excitement than the act.

Annabel was now jerking her new conquest hard and my eyes were focused on his cock, waiting for it to explode just like the last one.

I could hear him breathing on the other side of the wall and then I felt him grip tighter at my ankle. His knuckles turned white and suddenly a giant rope of cum sprang free, shooting right over Annabel and lacing my standing leg. The heat of it felt amazing, but neither Annabel nor Mark noticed.

Instead Annabel was too busy coaxing out the rest. She beat him fiercely and this time some of the cum found its way to her face. It lashed over her and she let out of a sigh of pleasure, as though the sensation was heavenly.

The cock disappeared and Annabel stood up and turned to me.

"Fuck!" I exclaimed. "He made a mess."

"He sure did," Annabel said, holding one of her eyes closed. A rope of cum had pinned it shut.

I used a thumb to ease it aside and then I started to kiss her. I licked the cum from her face and brought it to her mouth like a mothering bird. We spread it back and forth in the embrace as my boyfriend continued to fuck me hard from behind.

"You gonna do the same to her?" Annabel asked, looking to Mark.

"If that's what she wants," Mark said.

"You like it on your face?" Annabel asked.

"I do," I said. "But I also like it inside me."

"Good girl," Annabel said. "I'd love to clean up the mess."

Mark took a harder grip at my hips and started to fuck me so fast that my tits swung beneath me.

"He's raring to go!" she exclaimed. "And what do you like, stud?" She put a hand on Mark's shoulder. "I'll do *anything*."

The way the words left her mouth you could tell that she meant it. I wasn't expecting Mark's answer.

"I want you to tongue my ass," he said. He gave me another spank and I felt the heat rush to the surface of my butt.

"You do?" I asked.

"Yeah," Mark said confidently. "Put your fucking tongue in my ass, Annabel."

"I like a man who knows what he wants," she said, and dutifully she moved behind him.

Mark adjusted his stride and Annabel moved out of sight.

"Tell me what she's doing," I urged.

"I can feel her hands on the inside of my thighs," Mark said. "She's spreading my ass."

I started to breathe quicker, channeling my boyfriend's excited words through my body.

"I can feel her breath on me. I can—oh fuck! Oh, fuck, that's it. That's it."

"Is she licking you?"

"She's licking my fucking ass, honey," Mark cried.

A black cock came through the glory-hole beside us, but Annabel was too preoccupied to service it.

"Go on," Mark hushed.

I reached out a hand and grabbed the thick, black cock, squeezing along its length and listening to the grunts on the opposite side of the wall.

Mark jostled me into position and soon it was close enough to suck. I did just that. My mouth raced over the tip and I tried to mimic the movements I'd seen Annabel doing. She seemed to have a way with these anonymous cocks, although I'm guessing these guys are already pretty turned-on anyway.

I squeezed at his huge balls, feeling Mark surging into me and listening to the groans he made behind me as Annabel continued to slide her tongue around his asshole.

Every now and then I'd feel her soft, slender fingers framing my boyfriend's cock as it sat in my pussy. She'd squeeze at my pussy lips and run her fingers slowly along the folds, teasing at my clit and jostling it free of the hood.

"Oh, fuck!" I mumbled, my mouth full of dick.

I could feel an orgasm approaching. I beat the stranger's cock more fiercely as it started to grip me and my pussy squeezed around Mark's intrusive cock. There was no way he was going to pull out, and that made the whole thing even wilder.

I started to jerk wildly, groaning and moaning and matching the cries of the stranger in the cell opposite. I felt him stiffen and swell and I raced my mouth over the tip of his dick, feeling the heat burst into me suddenly. It was the last temptation I needed.

"I'm coming," I wailed, letting the cum drool from my mouth as another blast struck my face.

My hand jerked out the stranger's release as my whole body shivered with lust. My pussy flexed and massaged Mark inside me and he too became erratic.

"Oh, honey," he hushed, passing his dick through me faster. I think the sight of that huge cock exploding on my face was enough to drive him over the edge.

I beat the last of the drops from the intruding cock and it hung there with a string of white cum dangling from the tip.

"I'm gonna come," Mark said, and suddenly the breaths rushed into him faster and longer.

I raced my mouth over the black cock, cleansing the head of his final release and popping my lips free.

He disappeared just as I felt the swell of Mark inside me and then suddenly the heat came. It rushed into me, lashing my insides with thick, creamy ropes that Annabel helped to coax out. His asshole must have been winking on her tongue.

"Good boy," she encouraged, and I could feel her fingers gently wandering over my pussy lips.

Mark thrust his cock through me, sending the cum deep and coating his dick with it. His breaths slowly tapered off and then he pulled out of me. He was barely gone from me for a second before I felt the lips of Annabel on me, replacing his throbbing cock.

"Oh, God, yes," she groaned, and she lapped at the escaping cum that drooled slowly out of me.

I let her feast on me, keeping my footing in the glory-hole and moaning up into the room. Suddenly I felt another tongue on my asshole and I looked back to Mark. He must have been keen to let me know how good it felt and boy, did it feel good!

He tickled around my knot as Annabel flicked her tongue through my folds, swallowing down my boyfriend's seed as though it truly belonged to her.

When she was done I turned around to take a look at her. The three of us were breathing so heavily. I don't think any of us could believe it. We started to laugh.

"Now *that* was one for the scrap-book," Annabel said. "Want to taste him?"

Before I'd answered she'd walked forward and started to kiss me. Our tongues fought against each other and in the embrace I could feel the slick, saltiness of Mark on her lips.

"You want some too, lover-boy?"

She walked to Mark and kissed him too. I watched his eyes close as he enjoyed her. When she was done she brought his hand to mine and I gripped it tight. She straightened her dress and covered her tits.

"You two be good now," she said, and just like that she left us to it.

I started to laugh, fondling the hair on Mark's chest and holding him gently. He kissed me and it felt oddly romantic. This was *not* a romantic setting! As if to prove that another cock arrived at the wall.

"Come on," Mark said, and the pair of us dressed quickly as the hard cock hung there expectantly.

Mark opened the door to leave. "Another time, buddy," he shouted.

We fled the building laughing, having discovered more about ourselves than most people do in a lifetime. Club Sex would definitely be a place we'd visit again. Who knows, maybe Annabel would be our sexual guide once more ...

THE END

All In : Couples Threesomes 23

The poker game between my husband and his 'associates' had been going on now for hours. I'd stepped out of the room several times for a Martini, and slowly the six players at the table had dwindled.

Now all that was left was my husband, James, and his opponent, Olga Valenko: the sexiest, most dangerous woman in the entire world. The daughter of an oligarch gives a person a certain corrupt start in life. Olga had really dialed things up to eleven from there.

I sipped a drink from the sidelines, watching as James carefully massaged his chips as he kept his focus on the raven-haired vixen. If the rumors about Olga were true then it might not just be James she had eyes for.

As if she could hear my thoughts she took a glance at me as I stared at the pair of them, lingering a look on me just long enough to make me feel intrigued.

"Your wife?" she asked as James glanced under the corners of his cards.

He took a look back to me and winked. "My world."

"How sweet," Olga said, forcing a fake smile.

"Fifty thousand," James said, pushing his chips forward.

"A sizable amount pre-flop. You must have a good hand."

James said nothing, staring across at Olga with the confidence that had allured me in the first place.

"All in," Olga said. James barely flinched.

"All in," James replied.

There were short gasps around the dimly lit room. One man rolled his moustache between his fingers.

"You don't even come close to matching me," Olga said, staring down at her sizable stack of chips.

"So you get some back when you lose," said James.

A chuckle came from the bar.

"Your wife," Olga said simply. "You and your wife."

"What about us?"

"If you lose this hand, I get the pair of you to myself."

James looked back at me and I gave him a subtle nod. Some of the spectators laughed in disbelief.

"Have it your way, Mrs. Valenko."

"It's *Ms.* Valenko."

James nodded an apology and downed his whiskey. "Shall we?"

Olga turned over her cards to reveal a club-suited ace and king. James did the same, revealing a pair of aces. The audience, rightfully, gasped. All I could do was smirk.

The dealer turned three cards in succession, one of which was a king. Olga took in a deep breath and her brown eyes sparkled brighter than the diamond-studded necklace that dipped into her plunging cleavage.

The dealer then turned over the ten of clubs, giving Olga a chance at drawing a flush that would beat James's pair.

"It's all come down to this," James said coolly.

The dealer dropped the last card down and the place erupted. A handsome, red king stared up from the table and Olga clapped her hands.

"Well done," James announced, seemingly unfazed.

I never fully understood his job. I gathered it to be some form of espionage, but I couldn't complain. It had taken me all around the world, dining in some of the fanciest restaurants and mingling with royalty and celebrities. Every so often James would disappear for a day or two, but he'd always come back to me. Sometimes he'd let me in on one-or-two things.

What was transpiring now would only go on one way: James's. Whatever was to follow, it would all be part of his plan. I'd seen it a thousand times before. If he was at a disadvantage, it was because he wanted to be.

"I want the winnings deposited directly into my father's account," Olga said to the game's manager who stood close by.

"So that was a loan from Daddy?" James asked.

"A gift," Olga clarified.

"That's some gift."

"I expect you at my suite at nine," Olga said. "Wear something nice so I can enjoy it before I tear it off."

Olga stood up from the table and her bodyguard escorted her from the room. Her sparkling dress hugged tight to her shapely figure. She was big in all the right places.

James pushed the chair back and walked calmly towards me. "It'll be fun," he whispered, kissing me on the forehead.

"Oh, I know, James," I smirked. "It always is."

***

Olga's quarters were less of a suite and more of a complex. They stood apart from the main hotel, secluded in their own grounds with a pair of body-guards at the front-gate and several more patrolling the perimeter. James walked forwards and lifted his arms in a t-shape. A bodyguard approached and frisked him vigorously.

"I'll warn you to be a little more gentle with my wife," he said, his jaw tight.

I lifted my arms demurely, but there was scarcely a place to check. My dress covered my chest, but only just. As the second body-guard approached me his eyes darted down to the line of cleavage.

"It's a formality, dear," James said. "Try to enjoy it."

I couldn't help but smile. He always had a way of putting me at ease. We locked eyes and I enjoyed that strong, handsome face of his as the body-guard shook me roughly.

"Ms. Valenko is outside on the veranda," 'Henchman A' said.

"Shall we, dearest," James said, offering a hand.

I straightened his bow-tie and then put my palm in his. He led me along the decking and around the outside of the lavish building.

The sea rolled in the darkness beyond, lapping gently against the beach. It was a cool night, which was rare, but welcome. It had the adverse affect of stiffening my nipples so that they punched right through the white dress that I'd picked out for James. I knew he liked this one.

"What a lovely evening," said Olga as we approached the table.

There was a spread of sashimi and champagne already laid out. It looked like an oil-painting. The light from the veranda's chandelier illuminated everything beautifully, especially our host.

Her skin glowed from her moisturizer, but she looked no less dangerous. There was just something in her eyes. It looked as though she could kill you at any moment and not even flinch, but that didn't make her any less beautiful. She was called the Widow-maker for good reason.

A waiter that I hadn't noticed before pulled out a chair and Olga offered it to me.

"Looking ravishing this evening, Mrs. Bourne," she said.

"I thought I would make the effort, as requested."

"When I say ravishing, I mean it. I'd every much like to ravish you, Mrs. Bourne."

"That's quite the compliment."

The waiter showed me the bottle of Champagne: a 1995 bottle of Krug. I nodded and tried to hide my excitement.

"Odd pairing, don't you think?" James said. "Sashimi and Champagne?"

"I'm a big fan of a mixing of cultures, James. Japan meets France." She gestured to herself and then us. "Russia, meets England. It makes for the most *interesting* of flavors."

"Well, I've certainly got the stomach for it," James said, looking between Olga and me. It was no secret that part of James's job was seduction. In me he'd found a woman who not only didn't mind it, but sometimes actively encouraged it. Perhaps that was why we got along so well.

"You've got more than just the stomach for it, James," she said wryly.

I took a sip of the champagne. It was *heaven*.

"Do sit down," Olga said. "I was thinking we could eat first and then work up the appetite for it afterwards."

I didn't pretend to follow the conversation. Every so often Olga would address me to tell me how nice I looked or—on one occasion—to tell me how inviting my nipples looked as they punched through my dress.

Between that I watched as James steadily extracted his information, guiding our guest with subtle compliments and linguistic encouragements, all expertly crafted and delivered. In just half an hour James knew where one of her off-shore accounts were, as well as the surname of one of her father's mystery business-partners. All of which had been relayed to the command-centre via the microphone in his Rolex. I hoped it would be muted later that evening ...

"So tell me about yourself, Mrs. Bourne," Olga said now, turning her attentions to me. The champagne had had its desired effect on her. She seemed looser and more approachable.

"I'm a good-time gal," I joked. James had often stressed the importance of playing up to my blonde hair and big tits. 'A girl can go far with that figure,' he'd say, 'but she can go even further with a mind like yours.'

"Along for the ride," Olga said, fingering the rim of her champagne glass. "I can respect that."

"If you can't be here for a long-time, you may as well be here for a good-time."

Olga raised her glass. "I can drink to that." Her accent came thicker once the alcohol had lubricated it.

"I trust you didn't just bring us here for dinner and a drink," James said.

"You've done your research then," said Olga. "I'm sure they briefed you on that ugly nickname they have for me."

"Well I think it's exciting," I said. "The Widow-maker. Kind of sexy, isn't it?" I feigned a giggle.

"Sexy?" Olga looked offended.

"Yes!" I cried. "It's so seductive. And so perfect for a woman like yourself."

"And what is that supposed to mean, dear."

"Look at you," I said. James watched on calmly. "You've got a body to die for."

Olga blushed, disarmed.

"I think that's what the nickname means. Any man would kill for it. Or woman," I continued.

Olga's eyes shot to mine. I had her. Olga wasn't the only woman well-versed in seduction. I had a hunch that she'd be on the back-foot if ever a woman made advances on *her*. James looked positively impressed.

"Should we take this inside," he said. "Or perhaps I should leave you to it?"

"I won the both of you," Olga said. "I intend to claim my prize."

She gave a gesture and then moved from the table, offering us through the wide-open set of foldable glass-doors.

The room inside was resplendent with beauty. The interior designer had had a field-day. No expense was spared.

Olga dismissed the body-guards inside who walked away dutifully, no doubt to patrol the perimeter while their mistress had her fun.

"Close the doors on your way out, boys," she said. "I want to test if they're as sound-proof as the hotel-manager claimed."

I bit my lip and looked to James. There was something very big and stiff in his pants, although I couldn't yet rule out the possibility that it was a new gadget that he hadn't told me about.

She stared across the room at us, stood on the other side of the low, marble coffee-table that sat on the Alpaca rug.

"Time to do what we're here for," she said.

James and I watched as she moved a hand behind her dress and unzipped it at the back. She pulled it forward and let it fall down with gravity slowly. Her cherubic, firm tits became visible and both James and I couldn't help but admire them. You can be an international murderess, but a good body is a good body, and the Widow-maker had just that.

"She's so pretty, James." I swooned.

It was the truth, of course, but I wanted to butter her up some more too.

"You're not joining me?" she asked, cocking her head in my direction.

I looked to James who moved behind me, sliding the zipper down my back and whispering in my ear: "I love you."

I felt my heart swell, taking some of the blood from my pussy which was now salivating along with my mouth.

"Undress her for me, James," Olga said.

"For *us*," James added.

"Of course," Olga smiled.

James pushed the shoulder straps off me and my big tits bounced free, visibly jutting forwards now that their shackles were released.

"Such full breasts," Olga said, staring.

James peeled the dress down off my chest until my stiff nipples hit the cool breeze of the air-conditioning. Olga advanced across the room, her black dress only half-way down.

"I've been wanting to get my mouth around those all night," she said.

She launched herself on me, bending her knees and suckling on my stiff teat. I shrieked gleefully as I felt her devilish tongue swirl around the stud, coaxing out yet more juices that flooded my pussy.

"She's an animal, James!"

"She's a predator," he replied, stroking his hand along her bare back.

James pushed the dress down over her ass and I could see the whale-tail of her tiny panties. The strip of fabric disappeared into the plunging cleavage of her big, round cheeks.

James moved behind her and looked over her back at me. Suddenly he underarm-slapped her ass and took a squeeze. Olga breathed deep, clearly enjoying the stinging sensation that my husband's big palm had delivered.

She pulled her mouth off me and looked up into my eyes. Her mouth came close and we started to kiss, just as James was beginning to slide her panties down off her ass.

As we kissed I felt her jaw tighten and soon she lost her focus. Her lips drifted away from mine and I saw her anguished, furrowed brow as her face contorted in ecstasy.

I looked over her back again to see James's face buried between her ass, licking at God-knows-what. Whether it was her pussy or her asshole, Olga was clearly enjoying herself.

"Does that feel good?" I asked, putting a hand around her slender neck.

"Yes," she shuddered.

I squeezed at her throat.

"His tongue feels so good around my ass," she groaned.

"Naughty James," I teased.

His eyes opened and he gave me a wink as he continued to tickle her knot. I squeezed harder at her throat and relished the look of her face as it turned redder.

She strained a groan and then pushed my hand away forcefully, moving forwards off of James's face and putting her body against mine.

Her hand rushed up under my dress and she pressed quickly against the wet crotch of my panties. Her fingers pushed against my clit and she started to kiss me.

I moaned against her, realizing now that it was the first time a woman had been this intimate with me.

Olga pushed my dress further down until my white, lacy panties were visible. As my clothes fell to the floor Olga descended with them, kissing first at my chest and breast and then further down my stomach until she was crouched in front of me.

"I want to taste her, James," Olga said. "I want to know what it's like to be you."

"I'm sure my wife is happy to oblige you that."

I bit my lip and stared wide-eyed to James. As I did so Olga slid her long nails down inside the waist of my panties and then tugged them down off my pussy.

The fabric broke from my wetness and revealed the landing-strip of fur that lay kempt beneath. Olga wasted no time. Before my panties were at my knees she'd pressed her face into my crotch. Her tongue washed wildly over me and my shoulders bunched together.

I looked down over my tits to her. One of the most dangerous women in the entire world was now eating feverishly at my pussy. Being the wife of an international spy certainly had its fair share of advantages.

Her eyes stayed shut and she lavished me with licks and kisses, as though the pre-meal hadn't been enough.

"Beautiful," she cooed, pulling back off me and staring at my wet snatch. She looked back to my husband.

"Looking decidedly *clothed* there, Mr. Bourne," she said.

"I trust you two ladies can help me with that?"

Olga made a show of wiping at her mouth. She stood up and turned to James. Something about those high-heels and garter-belt really made her look a snack. That big ass of hers looked good enough to eat. James already had.

"Let's help your husband, dear," Olga said, advancing on James.

James deftly pressed a button on his watch. Olga arrived in front of him kissed him deep. James put a hand on her ass and I watched her enjoy him. I knew how good that mouth of his felt when it was on you.

I walked behind Olga and sandwiched her between the pair of us briefly. My hips pressed forward against her ass and I kissed at her soft shoulders and neck.

She groaned appreciatively and then fumbled at James's bow-tie, unfastening it so that it hung around his neck.

She was quickly on his buttons, unfastening each one until enough of his muscled chest was exposed. She rubbed her hands over him before she finished tackling his shirt.

"I want this man," she said. "I want this man for myself."

"I'm afraid for tonight you'll have to share," James said, winking at me.

My finger slid underneath Olga and I teased them over her pussy, stroking along the folds and feeling the wetness of her tight O break over my finger. She was just as sodden as I was.

"Oh, yes, Mrs. Bourne," she groaned, throwing back her hair.

I plunged a finger deep and coated it in her juices, then I pulled it free and offered it to Olga. Olga took a grip of my wrist and stared down at the wet digit, then she moved my hand forward and offered it to James.

"Taste me," she insisted. "I want to know if a man with a palate as fine as yours appreciates me."

"If it's anything like your asshole I'm sure it will be divine," James smiled.

Olga pushed my hand closer to James's mouth. He gripped my wrist too and then he locked eyes on Olga as he opened his mouth over my fingers.

He rolled his tongue around them, cleaning them of her wetness. Olga sucked a breath deep. She seemed to enjoy it *very* much.

"Well?" she asked.

"As sweet as the champagne," James said.

She let out a soft laugh before looking to me. "Take out your husband's cock."

"Nice and hard for me?" I asked him.

"I don't think there's a chance of anything else whilst I have you two in front of me."

Olga moved away and sat down on the plush, gray sofa. She split her legs wide, unashamed by her nudity. Her long fingers tickled at her clit as she watched expectantly.

James untucked his shirt and pulled back his dinner-jacket as I started to unfasten his belt.

"I never thought I'd see the day," Olga said, continuing to slide her finger over her folds. "Mr. Bourne, right here in front of me, ready to show me his cock."

"I hope it brings you a lifetime of happy memories," James smirked.

I sunk my hand down into his briefs and felt that slab of hard meat. I pulled him out and gushed with pride, moving aside to let Olga enjoy him too.

"My, my," she said slowly. She looked entranced by it. "Such a beautiful cock."

"Isn't it just," I agreed.

I started to slide my hands slowly along its length, watching his flesh move over the barrel. Olga leaned forward on her seat.

"Bring him to me," she said.

I dropped James's pants and helped his shoes and socks off his feet whilst he removed his shirt. He looked a picture. If I had to design the perfect man, it would have been him. He was so muscled and well put together, it was as if someone had crafted him as part of an experiment.

His cock stayed rock-hard and I led him forward by it, pulling gently and guiding James towards our one-time mistress.

"Watch me suck him," Olga said, staring up at me.

"It would be my pleasure," I told her.

Her mouth opened wide and she shut her eyes, plunging her lips over him and then closing them tight, halfway down his shaft.

James closed his eyes and sighed. I'm sure a thousand women had sucked his cock in his time, but it looked like he never grew weary of it. He looked to me and then beckoned me on to him with a finger.

I moved to him and we started to kiss while the Widow-maker took charge of his cock. I could hear her feasting noisily on him, sloshing his cock in her spit-soaked mouth. The next time I looked to James's big dick it was covered in a film of her saliva. The light from the chandelier danced off it and the head of it shone like a beacon.

"Put him inside me," Olga said, looking to me.

She turned around and crawled up the sofa, pointing her big ass back towards James and inviting him between her cheeks.

"Enjoy her for me, honey," I told him, taking his cock and jerking him forwards.

Olga stared ahead and waited. When the slick tip of his cock touched her pussy-lips she hissed a breath and dropped back, quickly enveloping him between her soaked petals.

"That's it," I said slowly, watching her sheath him.

I started to play with my pussy as she swallowed the rest of James's inches inside her. She took him all with a hearty groan. I knew the noise well. I'd made it many-a-time when I'd had the pleasure of taking that magnificent cock inside me. It was molded in just the right way to tickle at my insides.

"Oh, James," Olga cried, sounding less and less like a super-villain every second and more like a mewling harlot.

She bounced back on James's cock and he stood there and took it, looking down on her delicious ass and watching as she jerked him between her pussy.

"Feel good, honey?" I asked.

"She's tight for a Russian," James said sagely.

Olga looked back at him and smirked before addressing me. "Don't neglect yourself, dear."

I perched up on the sofa beside the pair of them and started to play, opening my legs wide and showing my body to Olga who made no secret of drinking me in. It was hot to have those dangerous, dark eyes all over me.

"Play for me, Mrs. Bourne," she said. "Play for me while my tight pussy makes your husband come."

I gasped in faux-shock. "You want his cum, do you?"

"More than anything else," Olga said.

James shot me a glance, clearly concerned that she might have ideas.

"But I want to see it," I fawned. "Trust me; you'll want to see it too. Watching my husband pull out his load is a sight to behold. I've never seen so much."

"Is that so?"

"There'd be enough for the both of us," I told her.

"Now you have my interest," Olga said. "What do you say, James?"

"To what?" He gave her ass a slap and bucked into her faster.

"What do you say I pull out your cum all over me?"

"I can't think of many better ideas," James said, breathlessly pumping his stiffness into Olga.

She squirmed back on him and started to breath faster, arching her back as though she was howling to the heavens.

My fingers spun faster on my pussy and I felt my clit stiffen as I watched. I could see from Olga's expression that she was close. From my own experience I could never last more than a few minutes on that gorgeous dick of his without climaxing.

"Oh, James," she cried, and her head dropped. She let him take control.

He put both hands on her ass and really started to pump himself into her. The sound of his hips clapping against her big ass rang out through the room, coupled by the moans of both Olga and me.

"That's it, girls," James said, as commanding as always. "I want you both to come for me."

"It would be an honor," Olga whispered.

Her ass tightened and the throes gripped her. She tossed her black hair wildly and continued to groan skywards. Just watching how freely she enjoyed herself was having an effect on me too.

I started to groan along with her, joining her chorus of debauched cries, much to the delight of James. He looked between us, marveling at the show we both put on for him, then he stared down at his swollen cock as it darted back and forth through her delicious pussy.

Finally she fell forwards off his length, trembling uncontrollably. Her muscles twitched and her body convulsed as she groaned, lost in her own climax.

Mine was ravaging me too, but I knew that the main event was yet to come.

"And I thought you had the stamina …" James said, shaking his head.

Olga turned over and narrowed her eyes. "Let us see your stamina," she said. "Give me your cock."

I was still moaning as the ecstasy tore through me. I watched as my husband walked onto her. Olga gripped her hand around the barrel of flesh, smoothing her pussy juices along it. She spat at the tip and then started to jerk quickly.

"Let's see his stamina, shall we Mrs. Bourne?"

"Yes!" I cried, writhing beside her.

My legs tightened and I watched as Olga set off at a terrific pace. Her hand flurried down over his length, pumping back and forth with vigor until the whole thing was a blur.

James's lip curled and his head fell back. He put his hands behind his back and I watched his knuckles turn white as one hand gripped the wrist of the other.

"Come all over her, James," I cried.

I was coming out of the other end of my climax and I didn't want to miss this. Olga had no idea what she was in for. Her face was dangerously close to his primed cock.

"Do what she says, James," Olga snarled, then she spat onto his cock and continued her vicious pace.

James pecs bounced as he flexed, then suddenly he took several quick breaths and opened his eyes wide to stare down.

"Yes!" I cried in anticipation. "Yes, James!"

"You asked for it," James strained.

His knees bent slightly and his stomach bounced in and out, then suddenly he froze.

"Here it comes," he warned.

"Pump out his cum, Ms. Valenko," I cried.

Her face was a picture of excitement. She wanted it bad, and she was going to get it. Suddenly the first arcing rope splashed forward across her face, leaping across the short-divide and scattering all the way from her forehead to her chin.

"Oh!" she cried, narrowing her eyes for the next blast.

"Give it her James," I cried, and give it her he did.

One rope, two ropes, three ropes and more burst free from his cock, splashing over the gleeful face of Olga Valenko until she was barely recognizable. She had front-row seats to the eighth wonder of the world, and she wasn't about to leave the show early.

"Every drop," she gasped, and I watched the cum web over her mouth and then fall inside.

She rolled her tongue over it in her mouth and then drank it down, as though it was some kind of super-serum.

James wasn't yet done. More and more bursts of his hot cum spat out from his cock, propelled by the deep grunts that lurched from his lungs with each contraction.

The cum dripped down off Olga's chin and started to coat her chest, then finally the strength of the bursts subsided.

Olga opened her mouth and caught the last flurry on her tongue, still pumping hard at James's cock as though she was determined to milk him for all he was worth.

"Good boy," she said slowly. "Good boy."

James breathed deep and heavy, staring down at his exorcised cock. Olga finally freed him from her sticky grip. She looked down at her tits and pushed the cum from her eyes.

"I've never seen anything like that before," she laughed.

"I did warn you."

"Come and kiss me," Olga said, looking to me. "Kiss me and kiss your husband's terrific cock for a job well done."

I moved across the sofa to her. My fingers pushed a lock of hair aside and I held her face steady. She was a damn-mess, but it was one of the hottest fucking messed I've ever seen.

Tentatively I touched my lips to hers, feeling the warmth of my husband's love instantly. Olga was less coy. She pushed herself onto me and we passed his seed back and forth. The cum started to cover my face now, spreading between us like a growing lattice-work of vines.

Olga licked it off my face and I returned the compliment, then James introduced his cock between the pair of us and we just kept on going.

Soon we were jerking him between our lips, cleansing and kissing his cock as though it was a God worthy of prayer. It was certainly something to be revered.

Finally Olga broke from the sordid embrace and blinked up at James.

"Thank-you for a lovely, evening," she said.

"The pleasure was all ours," James said.

Olga collapsed back into the sofa, looking more contented than ever. She rubbed the remaining cum into her face as though she liked the feel of it against her skin.

"Goodnight," she said.

She hummed contently and seemed to fall into a deep, almost immediate sleep. She kept this serene smile on her face as her breathing changed. I could scarcely believe it.

"Well done, lover-boy," I teased, pinching his ass.

"Let's get what we came for and get out of here," he said out the corner of his mouth.

James took something from her handbag and then moved his wrist-watch towards it, pressing another button on its side until the face of it flashed green.

He looked to me and nodded.

"Good night, *Ms.* Valenko," he nodded, gathering his clothes.

We didn't even bother to dress. Instead the pair of us walked out naked and James saluted the body-guards outside on the veranda.

"I'd give her a few hours if I were you," he said.

At first they seemed aghast, but then they spotted me. Their eyes were all over me, but thankfully the dress in my hands covered most of my modesty. The only thing they could truly dine-out on was my ass, and I was happy to let them.

"A job well done," James said, putting an arm around me. "We'll make a spy of you yet."

I put my head against his shoulder and he held me close as we walked off into the cool night air, heading for his classic sports-car and then to God-knows where.

It was the life.

THE END

Making Rent : Couples Threesomes 24

The apartment-complex wasn't the most savory of places, and the well-dressed Mr. & Mrs. Hendricks looked somewhat out-of-place as they walked through the disheveled courtyard.

The empty pool told you everything you needed to know, but if you hadn't quite made up your mind then the empty beer cans and bent spoons were on hand to help you out.

"It's all just such a mess," Mrs. Hendricks said, "but it intrigues me."

"*Intrigues you?*" her husband scoffed.

"Their way of life, David. I find it ... mysterious."

"People do what they need to do to survive."

"I suppose you're right."

"And part of surviving sometimes involves missing rent."

"I do wish you'd let our agents take care of this," his well-to-do wife said. "Then we wouldn't have to get all mixed up down here."

"I thought you'd appreciate the day out."

Mrs. Hendricks let out a laugh as the pair of them rounded the metal staircase and walked sheepishly up it to the second floor. It groaned beneath them.

"Is this the first problem we've had with"—Mrs. Hendricks checked her clipboard—"Tori?"

"Second," her husband replied. "There was a slight issue after she installed a stripper's pole in our living-room."

Mrs. Hendricks gasped. "You didn't tell me about that."

"I thought it best to keep quiet."

"So she's a stripper?"

"She certainly looks like she could be, Marie" Mr. Hendricks said.

"Honey!"

The pair of them walked to the door of the condo. They'd bought it as an investment several years ago, but so far it was proving more costly than lucrative.

"I hope she has some clothes on," Mrs. Hendricks said out the corner of her mouth.

"Just because she's a stripper, it doesn't mean—"

The door of the condo opened and the leggy frame of an attractive brunette appeared. Her hair was down, flowing and lustrous, and her silk-looking dressing-gown was open far enough to draw the eye. Her glamorous appearance didn't seem to fit with the look of the place.

"Mr. Hendricks," she beamed, rolling her tongue along her pristine, white teeth.

Mrs. Hendricks looked to her husband who wore a dreamy smile. She nudged him gently with her elbow.

"And Mrs. Hendricks," Tori said, trying to keep the same affectionate tone. "To what do I owe the pleasure?"

"Well ..." Mr. Hendricks began.

"I'm afraid it's the rent," his wife interjected. "You're late. Quite late."

"Oh," Tori said. "How late?"

Mrs. Hendricks looked down at her clipboard, even though she knew the answer. "Uhm, four months."

"Gosh," Tori said, covering a hand to her mouth and looking forlornly at Mr. Hendricks. "I didn't know you needed that every month."

Mrs. Hendricks stood speechless.

"Come in," Tori said. "I'm sure we can figure something out."

"There's really nothing to figure out," Mrs. Hendricks said, but Tori had already retreated back into her apartment.

Mr. Hendricks breathed a sigh and then nodded to his wife to cross the threshold. She strode forwards and he followed dutifully, looking at her tight dress as it stretched across her big ass. Mrs. Hendricks was no spring chicken—being almost twice Tori's age—but she definitely hadn't lost it. Her husband knew all too well that she could be a little fire-cracker herself if she wanted to.

"So you're a stripper," Mrs. Hendricks said, jumping in with both feet.

Tori looked to Mr. Hendricks as though he'd betrayed her trust. "I am, yes."

"And that's not paying very well?" Marie continued to probe.

"I do okay," Tori said.

"And yet here we are," Mrs. Hendricks said.

Her husband pulled out the collar of his shirt and cleared his throat.

"I just don't have the money right now," Tori said. "But I've made some good investments and I've got some returns coming my way soon, I promise."

"Promises don't count for rent," Mrs. Hendricks said.

"What does?"

"Money, mainly," Mr. Hendricks said.

Tori sauntered over to the smooth, shining pole in the middle of her lounge. It shot up from the floor and hit the ceiling. She took a grip of it and swung around it, tossing her hair. She faced away from the pair of them and arched back until she was looking at the pair of them upside-down. "You don't take any other form of payment?"

Mr. Hendricks stared to her open, inviting cleavage, his eyes wide. Mrs. Hendricks looked from her husband to Tori and back again.

"What did you have in mind?" Mrs. Hendricks asked, curious.

Tori stood up and leant against the pole, looking back to the pair of them. "I wouldn't like to say ... "

"If you don't say then how can we negotiate?" Mrs. Hendricks said. "Just remember that this condo is owned by my husband *and me*."

Tori narrowed her eyes and stared a sultry stare at Mrs. Hendricks. She was well versed in the ways of subtext.

"Something for both of you?" Tori said.

Now it was Mr. Hendricks' turn to double-take at his wife.

"That might work," Mrs. Hendricks said. "Depending on what was on offer of course."

"How should I know what to offer?" Tori asked.

Mrs. Hendricks made a show of drinking her tenant in. She ran her brown eyes up over Tori's little feet and up her long, smooth legs, settling finally on her dazzling, blue eyes.

"If it was me making an offer," Mrs. Hendricks said, "then I'd bear in mind that I owed four month's rent. I would want to make a fitting offer."

Tori bit her lip.

"But that's just me," Mrs. Hendricks said, knowing that she'd planted the seed.

Mr. Hendricks grabbed his wife by the elbow and turned away from Tori for a moment. He spoke in a hushed growl. "Honey. What are you doing?"

"Having some fun," his wife replied. "We're not getting the rent, so we might as well get *something*."

"What did you have in mind?" Mr. Hendricks hushed back.

"You can fuck me," came Tori's voice, having overheard the exchange.

The pair of them turned to her. She was stood with her legs astride, looking as confident as ever. With a body like that it was easy to be.

"I'm sorry?" Mr. Hendricks began.

"I think what my husband meant to say was: 'That sounds good.'"

Tori smirked and Mr. Hendricks shot a look of shock to his wife. "Marie!"

Mrs. Hendricks shrugged. "I should very much like to watch," she said. "Perhaps there's a thing or two I can learn."

"Marie!" Mr. Hendricks cried again.

"Come on, honey. You're about to fuck a damn *model*. Most guys would be chomping at the bit. This whole 'pretend to be appalled' thing isn't washing."

"A model?" Tori said, looking hopefully at Mrs. Hendricks.

"You need to look in the mirror more," she replied.

Her husband watched as his Mrs. Hendricks sauntered over to her younger tenant. The two couldn't have been more at odds. Tori stood almost a foot taller. She was younger, more attractive and decidedly less clothed.

Mrs. Hendricks looked over her spectacles, studying Tori as though she were up for purchase. "I think my husband would enjoy himself," she said.

"I'd make sure he did," replied Tori. She looked to David now. "He can do *whatever* he wants to me."

Mr. Hendricks dropped his shtick. He stared at Tori as he smoldered in his sharp suit. Even at forty-five he was suave and handsome. He'd felt ill-at-ease outside, but a woman's body was something Mr. Hendricks was well versed in. He'd had his fair share before Marie.

"You remind me of a guy I dance for," Tori said.

"Oh yeah?"

"Almost. You have a nicer smile."

Mr. Hendricks beamed as if to show it off.

"Don't get too cocky, dear," Mrs. Hendricks said.

"So how do we do this?" Tori said.

"Fairly simply," said Mrs. Hendricks. "You get on your hands and knees, crawl over there and start sucking my husband's cock."

Mr. Hendricks shot his wife an impressed look. She was clearly in the mood.

"And the rent issue just goes away?" Tori asked.

"After he comes," Mrs. Hendricks said.

"In my mouth? On my face?" Tori asked, nonchalant.

"Inside you," Mrs. Hendricks said. "And I'm going to tongue it out."

Tori laughed in shock. Finally Mrs. Hendricks had said something that had shocked her.

"I've never done that before," Tori said.

"It's quite the experience," Mrs. Hendricks said sagely, and Tori looked at her in a new light, realizing that the tidy, light-blue suit-jacket and pencil skirt were merely a façade. Mrs. Hendricks could be as dirty as they come and it seemed she had something to prove.

Tori stared, amazed and silent.

"On your knees," Mrs. Hendricks ordered.

Tori bit her lip again and quickly dropped to the floor, steeling her eyes on Mr. Hendricks' crotch and stalking slowly towards him.

Mrs. Hendricks watched proudly. The silken gown rode up over Tori's ass and the mature landlady eyed at her pale, juicy flesh. Her ass bounced and flexed with each stride forward.

She moved slowly, watching as Mr. Hendricks' crotch started to swell. She gave him ample time to get hard, but he didn't need it. The second his wife had even started to hint at what was to come, David's cock had started to twitch.

"Ready for her, honey?" Mrs. Hendricks asked.

"Oh, I'm ready, Marie," David said.

"He looks ready," Tori laughed.

"Take him out of his pants," Mrs. Hendricks said coolly, and she walked across to get a better view.

Mr. Hendricks kept his hands by his side and stared down as Tori tackled his belt. She slipped it through his pant-loops and went straight for the button, opening it quickly and pulling down his zipper.

"She's ravenous," Mrs. Hendricks said, watching close.

The couple stared down as Tori fished excitedly inside her landlord's pants, producing something that Mrs. Hendricks had seen countless times, but that still made her wet with excitement.

"My, oh my," Tori said, holding the thick appendage.

Mr. Hendricks was well put together. His thick, mature cock looked a pretty picture in Tori's slender, younger hand. She stared down her nose at the target as her landlady-come-mistress sucked a deep breath.

Mrs. Hendricks felt her nipples stiffen with excitement. She moved her hand beneath her suit-jacket and squeezed at her breast, watching as another woman tackled her husband's cock.

"Get him in your mouth you naughty slut," Mrs. Hendricks ordered, and the insult struck Tori like riding-crop to the ass.

She sucked a quick breath and pounced on him. Tori relished the attention. That was why she had become a stripper; on stage in front of all those guys who wanted but couldn't touch ... and now here she was, touching someone else at his wife's request. It was a sordid affair.

Mr. Hendricks threw his head back and groaned, looking down in disbelief as the full lips of Tori slid down over his thick pole, drinking in every inch.

She pressed herself deep down on him, forcing him right to the back of her throat and beyond. Ordinarily such party-tricks were kept in the locker, but this felt to her like a special occasion.

More than anything she found herself wanting to impress the more experienced onlooker.

"Good," Mrs. Hendricks nodded.

"Are you seeing this?" Mr. Hendricks said, looking down in awe as Tori's lips inched down to the hilt of his sizeable cock.

"I don't have plans to look anywhere else," Mrs. Hendricks said, and as if to make the point she dropped to her knees to join her tenant.

Tori looked out of the corner of her eye to Mrs. Hendricks and then she slowly peeled back her lips, revealing the stiff, wet cock like the dirtiest magic-trick.

She slid all the way back off him and then giggled, wiping some drool off her chin before pointing the cock in Mrs. Hendricks direction.

"While you're down here?" Tori shrugged.

Mrs. Hendricks curled a lock of hair behind her ear and leaned forward. It was a strange sight to behold. The well-to-do, smartly-dressed lady was gradually swallowing the second-hand cock of her husband as their new plaything watched on.

"Good," Tori said slowly. "That's hot."

Tori leaned underneath and started to suck on the hanging balls of Mr. Hendricks. A heady groan left him now and his knees became weak. He'd never had two women before.

"You're spoiling me, girls," David said, looking down on the both of them.

His wife pulled back and blinked up at him, leaving Tori to roll his balls through her lips. "She's not finished yet."

Tori gnawed her way up along the shaft of her new lover, bouncing the tip of his cock on her tongue playfully before rising on her knees and sinking him back into her throat.

Mr. Hendricks groaned louder now, pulling back his suit-jacket and tossing it aside. He was in the mood.

Mrs. Hendricks opened Tori's gown and pulled it back off her shoulders to reveal the lingerie beneath. In an effort to save money, Tori had made sure all of her underwear was 'fit-for-work.'

"Look at her, honey," Mrs. Hendricks said, and she reached her hands down from Tori's shoulders and squeezed at her full breasts.

Tori moaned and David felt the vibrations of it along his shaft. She stroked her tongue on the underside of him as she slowly released his cock again, then she took it in her fist and gasped.

"I want it," she said, pumping along it. She looked up to Mr. Hendricks and then back to his wife. "I want it inside me."

"Have it," her mistress said, and she took off her own suit-jacket now to show-off her sizable charms.

"I want you too," Tori said, standing up and breaking rank.

Mrs. Hendricks breathed calmly and looked to Tori's attractive face. Her eyes slipped down to glance at Tori's full lips that second earlier had been wrapped around her husband's girth.

"Have me," Mrs. Hendricks said, shrugging.

Tori put her hand behind her landlady's head and pulled her in. The pair started to kiss and Mr. Hendricks watched on, steadily jerking his hard cock and wondering just where things were going to wind up.

Their kiss blossomed and turned even more passionate and soon Tori was fingering at the buttons of Mrs. Hendricks' freshly-ironed shirt.

"Show me those big, mature tits," Tori said, snarling like an animal.

Mrs. Hendricks finished opening the shirt, then she pulled it back off her shoulders and pushed her chest forwards.

Tori instantly sank her face into the full cleavage, kissing and biting on the soft flesh. Not to waste time, Mrs. Hendricks quickly unfastened the clasp at her back.

"Good girls," Mr. Hendricks said. "Good girls."

He jerked his cock and watched as his wife's bra slipped off her. Tori kissed her way quickly to her nipples and soon she was sucking hard over the node.

Mrs. Hendricks let out a giddy cry and held the younger slut against her, letting her feast for the moment.

Mr. Hendricks—feeling somewhat left out—moved behind his tenant. His hands gripped at Tori's tits as she sucked on his wife and then he unclasped her bra too.

Tori whipped it from her shoulders and turned around, wondering just what to do with herself.

She started to kiss Mr. Hendricks now, pushing her body against him and feeling the hard slab of flesh settle against her thigh.

Mrs. Hendricks was quickly on hand. As her husband's eyes stayed closed in the embrace, Mrs. Hendricks started to pull down Tori's tiny panties.

Tori continued to wrestle with Mr. Hendricks' tongue, stepping out of her panties with no sign of bashfulness. She knew just how good she looked naked.

When Mr. Hendricks finally pulled away from her he was surprised to be staring down at the thin landing-strip of hair that sat above her pussy.

"Looks good, doesn't she?" Mrs. Hendricks said, eyeing her from the back.

"Let me check," Mr. Hendricks joked, and he moved away to walk a full-circle around her. As he did so he stepped somewhat clumsily form his pants and kicked off his shoes.

"Does she meet your standards?" Mrs. Hendricks asked, tongue-in-cheek.

"She no Mrs. Hendricks," David said, "but she'll do."

Tori giggled and turned back to face them as the pair shared a brief, romantic kiss. "Cute," she said.

"Fuck her honey," Mrs. Hendricks said, decidedly less cute.

Tori clapped and dropped her ass to the rug, opening her legs wide. She pointed her pussy right at the pair and relished the shocked, impressed look that flashed briefly on their faces.

"Good enough to eat," Mrs. Hendricks said wryly.

"Be my guest," Tori offered, sliding a finger along her petals.

Mrs. Hendricks took a look to her husband.

"Go ahead, honey," he said.

Mrs. Hendricks unzipped the side of her skirt and let it drop. Tori's eyes widened at the sight of her mistress's high-stockings and lady-like suspenders. She was like a mature centre-fold—a far cry from the stiff suit that had walked in.

"Come here, you," Tori said, curling a finger in Mr. Hendricks' direction. "I want you back in my mouth.

He hurried his shirt off and walked to her in only his socks, dropping to his knees and angling his dick quickly towards her waiting, open mouth.

Mr. Hendricks slotted himself home and felt that now-familiar, warm embrace. He looked down as his wife got in position between Tori's legs, bending forward and pointing her ass back towards the apartment door. It cut a fantastic shape from his vantage point.

"We've not done something like this for a while," Mr. Hendricks said suggestively, looking down at his wife as she stared at her target.

"No we haven't," Marie said, and Tori could feel her breath on her sex.

She hummed contently, groaning louder when she felt the mature, experienced lips envelop her dampening pussy.

She drove deep over Mr. Hendricks' cock, putting him back in her throat and dining-out on the sudden lack of oxygen.

Mr. Hendricks took a grip of her neck and squeezed at the sides, pinching hard and giving Tori a giddy, heady sensation.

Her scalp prickled and her whole body tingled with ecstasy as Mrs. Hendricks' tongue wound up towards her stiffening clitoris. She searched it out with ease and flicked over the bean, listening as Tori groaned loud.

She unsheathed the cock from her gullet and suddenly the condo became a chorus of groans as Tori instantly started to come.

Mrs. Hendricks ate faster, encouraged by her subject's reaction. Mr. Hendricks started to beat his cock over the young beauty, enjoying the show. The orgasm gripped her, possessing her like a demon.

"Yes!" she grunted, writhing on the rug. "Oh, fuck, yes!"

Mrs. Hendricks was like an animal too. She fought hard to keep herself clamped over Tori's drooling pussy, riding her crotch like it was an unruly feedbag. Her tongue lashed down the crease and she tasted the sweet juices as they slowly slid from Tori's pussy.

"Oh, fuck!" Tori groaned, enjoying the climax to the fullest.

She writhed wildly and then appeared to come back to earth, opening her eyes and catching sight of Mr. Hendricks' hard cock.

She launched on it and started to suck feverishly, gripping the shaft and jerking him. Her mouth tongued and kissed at the bulbous, sensitive head whilst her hand worked fiercely below.

Mrs. Hendricks vacated Tori's sex and wiped at her mouth, watching the ravenous fashion with which she tackled her husband.

"Steady now," she warned. "Remember where I want his cum."

Tori pulled back, tempering her excitement. "Then do it," she said. "Fucking cum in my pussy."

She said the words with such certainty that Mrs. Hendricks started to wonder who wanted it more.

"Fuck her, honey," Mrs. Hendricks said. "Fuck her and shoot a load in that tight body."

He needed no second instruction. He worked his way from his spot at her side and moved in between her legs.

Tori looked down and watched as Mrs. Hendricks was replaced by Mr. Hendricks. He angled his cock towards the wet, soaked groove and pressed against her, dipping his cock into the mix of his wife's saliva and Tori's cum.

"Yes!" Tori groaned, feeling the thick girth stretch her.

The muscle of her pussy sprang open over the intruder and then she took the next few inches quickly. Mr. Hendricks was immediately enamored by the warm, wet embrace as her pussy pinched around him.

"Put yourself on my face," Tori said, looking to Mrs. Hendricks. "Ride my mouth."

Mrs. Hendricks bit her lip. "You sure know how to excite a lady," she said.

Tori closed her eyes and her stomach tightened as Mr. Hendricks drove the last of his inches into her. She could feel the tip of him tease at her cervix, opening her eyes just wide enough to see her approaching mistress. Mrs. Hendricks had slipped her panties down and was wearing only her stockings and suspenders now.

"Yes!" Tori whimpered. "Sit on my fucking face."

Mrs. Hendricks straddled the whining damsel and Tori stared up as the round butt of Mrs. Hendricks dropped over her. Those delicious curves framed the equally delicious, mature pussy and Tori watched as it approached from above.

It came so near that she could no longer focus on it, then she felt the soft flesh smudge against her waiting lips.

Tori groaned and so too did Mrs. Hendricks. Her tongue lashed up into the core of her mistress and Mrs. Hendricks let out a moan, leaning back and staring into the eyes of her husband.

Their gaze met lovingly, but there was nothing romantic about what was happening beneath. Tori's tight pussy was gripping the adulterer close and at her other end her busy tongue was ravaging the shaven folds of Mrs. Hendricks.

"Fucking use me!" Tori cried from beneath, briefly finding air.

Mrs. Hendricks started to grind over her face, rubbing her wet pussy over her nose and treating herself to Tori's pointed tongue. It probed deep and fed on the sweet juices that began to roll free.

"How are you doing there, honey?" Mrs. Hendricks asked.

"I'm not gonna be much longer," he said, wincing with an ecstatic, breathless look on his face.

"Shoot it," Tori demanded. "Shoot your fucking cum."

Her words echoed up off the wet flesh of Mrs. Hendricks, who continued to ride. She wriggled her hips back and forth and gave her final commands.

"Come in her, honey," she said over and over. "Come in that young, pretty pussy. Fill her right up. Fill her up with that hot cum and let me lick it out of her."

The words were a turn on for all of them. Mr. Hendricks couldn't believe what was being asked of him, but he had no intention of doing anything else. He knew better than to disappoint his wife.

"Shoot it, Mr. Hendricks," Tori begged, opening her legs wide.

Mr. Hendricks doubled his efforts, pounding down on Tori's pussy like he owned it. He put his hands either side of her and held himself above, working hard from the hips and drilling into the wailing damsel.

"Yes, honey," Mrs. Hendricks continued. Her fingers worked busily on her clit as she watched her husband have his fill. "Shoot it. Fucking shoot it."

He gave her the final few pumps. Mrs. Hendricks spotted the familiar, pained expression. She knew what it foretold. He was ready.

"Fucking shoot it," Mrs. Hendricks declared, and right on cue her husband let out a tremendous, aching groan that lurched from the pit of his stomach.

The whole room fell deeply silent. All that could be heard was the fast, excited breaths of Tori as she waited to be filled.

She felt his cock throb, greeting it with a moan before feeling the sudden rushing heat as it blasted into her.

"Yes, yes, yes!" Tori groaned, and Mrs. Hendricks kicked her legs off her to give her some space.

The mistress stroked at her tenant's hair, dropping her face and talking close to her ear. "Take his cum," she said, soothingly. "Take his fucking load."

Mr. Hendricks worked his cock steadily, slowly rocking it in the drenched core of Tori. It turned slippery and sticky, filling to the brim with his seed.

"Every drop," Mrs. Hendricks said. "Every last drop."

She watched her husband fall back to earth. His focus came off the ceiling and he stared down at the ravaged pussy of Tori. Gradually he pulled backwards, revealing his slick, glistening cock and the cum that filmed it.

"Good," Mrs. Hendricks said. "Now it's my turn."

Mr. Hendricks scooted away, but kept himself close. He wanted to see this.

Tori took several deep breaths, staring up at the ceiling. Her face and chest were flush with a red hue. She propped herself up on an elbow and looked down as Mrs. Hendricks got into position.

"Eat him out of me," Tori said.

Mrs. Hendricks felt as though she was the slut now. She stared into soft-pink petals. The cum inside was easy to spot. It was slowly oozing outwards, looking all pearly and white.

"Fuck," Mrs. Hendricks whispered, and she moved her face between Tori's legs.

Tori's eyes closed again as she felt Mrs. Hendricks tongue anew. This time the sensation was different. The cum was like silk, sliding over her primed pussy majestically.

She could hear the lapping, sticky mess as Mrs. Hendricks tongued out her husband's love. Mr. Hendricks watched, awe-struck. His hand tugged slowly as he sat, hypnotized by the sight of it all.

Mrs. Hendricks felt a delightful depravity grip her. She loved the sensation. It was like a drug to her, coming down off her pedestal and relieving herself of the business-woman-like persona.

"You naughty slut," Tori giggled, watching as Mrs. Hendricks continued in earnest.

She lapped, licked and sucked until there was nothing more to be had, cleansing Tori's pussy to the extent where it looked as though nothing had happened. Afterwards Tori curled a finger to Mrs. Hendricks, staring at her lips.

"Come here and kiss me," she said sweetly.

Mr. Hendricks watched on as his wife shared his cum, passing it across on an outstretched tongue that Tori sucked passionately on. The two sent his love back and forth and the volume of it lessened as they did so as each of them swallowed it down.

Mr. Hendricks walked over in one final act, sandwiching his cock between the wrestling lips of his wife and new lover.

They obliged gladly, kissing at either side of him and lapping up the last of his cum until Mr. Hendricks too was cleansed of the evidence.

"Consider your rent paid," Mrs. Hendricks said, rolling her tongue over her teeth.

"I think maybe we can come to a new *arrangement*," Mr. Hendricks said.

"Works for me," replied Tori. "I'd do that for free."

"You really shouldn't be telling us that," Mrs. Hendricks said, offering one last bit of advice. "We just might hold you to it."

THE END

Join The Mailing List[1]

Get **7 FREE EROTICA STORIES** and **WEEKLY DEALS** you join my Mailing List[2] - http://eepurl.com/b0ma0X

---

1. http://eepurl.com/b0ma0X
2. http://eepurl.com/b0ma0X

More Titles From The Publisher[1]

Cuckqueans Erotica Bundle 12-Pack : Books 1 - 12[2]

This collection features books 1 to 12 of the 'Cuckqueans' series.

Stories include : 'Watching My Husband Fuck The Girl Nextdoor,' 'Another Woman in My Bed,' 'Watching My Husband Fuck The Girl From The Pool,' 'Another Woman in Our House,' 'A Slave To His Mistress,' 'Watching My Husband With My Bridesmaid,' 'Eating My Husband's Cum From Her Pussy,' 'Booking A Call-Girl For My Husband,' 'Auctioning Off My Husband's Cock,' 'Sucking My Husband's Cum From Her Pussy,' 'Peeping On My Husband Fucking The Neighbor,' & 'She Ordered Me To Fuck Her Husband - Now I'm The Boss.'

Cuckqueans Erotica Bundle 8-Pack : Books 1 - 8[4]

---

1. https://itunes.apple.com/us/author/tori-westwood/id596852358?mt=11

2. https://itunes.apple.com/us/book/id1451853383

3. https://itunes.apple.com/us/book/id1451853383

4. https://itunes.apple.com/us/book/id1439736072

This collection features books 1 to 8 of the 'Cuckqueans' series.

Stories include : 'Watching My Husband Fuck The Girl Nextdoor,' 'Another Woman in My Bed,' 'Watching My Husband Fuck The Girl From The Pool,' 'Another Woman in Our House,' 'A Slave To His Mistress,' 'Watching My Husband With My Bridesmaid,' 'Eating My Husband's Cum From Her Pussy,' & 'Booking A Call-Girl For My Husband.'

Cuckqueans Erotica Bundle 4-Pack : Books 1 - 4[6]

---

5. https://itunes.apple.com/us/book/id1439736072

6. https://itunes.apple.com/us/book/id1421999670

7. https://itunes.apple.com/us/book/id1421999670

This collection features books 1 to 4 of the 'Cuckqueans' series, where women yearn to treat their husbands to another female beauty while they watch on. The mistresses in this bundle will allow the cuckqueans to join in, but it's strictly on their terms! One thing they all get to do is clean-up the mess afterwards!

Cuckqueans Erotica Bundle 4-Pack : Books 5 - 8[8]

Stories include : 'A Slave To His Mistress,' 'Watching My Husband With My Bridesmaid,' 'Eating My Husband's Cum From Her Pussy,' & 'Booking A Call-Girl For My Husband.'

Cuckqueans Erotica Bundle 4-Pack : Books 9 - 12[10]

---

8. https://itunes.apple.com/us/book/id1440172795

9. https://itunes.apple.com/us/book/id1440172795

10. https://itunes.apple.com/us/book/id1451458378

Stories include : 'Auctioning Off My Husband's Cock,' 'Sucking My Husband's Cum From Her Pussy,' 'Peeping On My Husband Fucking The Neighbor,' & 'She Ordered Me To Fuck Her Husband - Now I'm The Boss.'

Sinful MILFs Mega-Bundle : Books 1 - 12[12]

'*Sinful MILFs Mega-Bundle*' features books 1 – 12 of the Sinful MILFs series. features 12 naughty stories of confident women claiming innocent men in hot erotica encounters. The ladies have targeted their prey and they're going for the kill! Read as they

---

11. https://itunes.apple.com/us/book/id1451458378

12. https://itunes.apple.com/us/book/id1291770936

13. https://itunes.apple.com/us/book/id1291770936

tackle men like pros, getting exactly what they want and sometimes a little more! Strictly Adults Only!

Stories Include : 'I Claimed Him After Ballet Class,' 'He Finished Inside Me in the Gym,' 'Virgin In My Car,' 'Claimed Through the Gl*ry H*le,' 'His Graduation Surprise,' 'Hot Spring Sex,' 'He Came Inside Me,' 'Taking Him in His Cell,' 'I Need His Hot Love,' 'My Virgin Stablehand,' 'Claiming My Male Secretary,' and 'I Claimed Him by the Pool.'

Sinful MILFs Mega-Bundle : Books 13 - 24[14]

[15]

'*Sinful MILFs Mega-Bundle*' features books 13 – 24 of the Sinful MILFs series.

Stories include: 'Full of Him in the Art Gallery,' 'Claiming Him in His Bedroom,' 'I Put Him in My Mouth by Accident,' 'Decorating Fun With My Stud,' 'Taking Him & His Girlfriend,' 'Any Length Will Do - Even His,' 'Taking Him Through The Window,' 'Making Him Take Me Rough,' 'First Time Anal With My Lodger,' 'Drilled By Him At The Dentist,' 'His Beautiful Thickness' and 'Anal For His Birthday.'

Sinful MILFs Mega-Bundle : Books 1 - 24[16]

---

14. https://itunes.apple.com/us/book/id1380246381

15. https://itunes.apple.com/us/book/id1380246381

16. https://itunes.apple.com/us/book/id1381578959

17

'Sinful MILFs Mega-Bundle' features books 1 – 24 of the Sinful MILFs series. Read how sultry women take their virginal counterparts in desperate fashion, dominating them with their sexual experience.

Real MILFs 12 Pack : Books 1 - 12[18]

19

'Real Milfs 12 Pack Bundle' features 12 naughty stories of mature, confident women deflowering their innocent virgin men in hot erotica encounters. The cougars have targeted their prey and they're going for the kill! Read as they tackle stiff members like pros,

---

17. https://itunes.apple.com/us/book/id1381578959

18. https://itunes.apple.com/us/book/id1225639080

19. https://itunes.apple.com/us/book/id1225639080

getting exactly what they want and sometimes a little more! Strictly Adults Only!

Stories Include : *'MILF's Pride,' 'MILF Took Me In The Butt,' 'Taking His Seed,' 'Home Schooled In Sex,' 'MILF's Masquerade,' 'MILF's Motel Fun,' 'Take Off My Panties,' 'MILF Nursed Him,' 'Milf Milked,' 'Desperate to Claim Him,' 'Me And My Friend Claim Him'* and *'I Had To Take Him Inside Me.'*

About the Author

Connie Cuckquean writes that sinful erotica that you crave, about housewives letting their husbands have everything they desire while they watch!

License Notes

This eBook is licensed for your personal enjoyment only. This eBook may not be re-sold or given away to other people. If you would like to share this book with another person, please purchase an additional copy for each recipient. If you're reading this book and did not purchase it, or it was not purchased for your use only, then please purchase your own copy. Thank you for respecting the hard work of this author.

Lightning Source UK Ltd.
Milton Keynes UK
UKHW010721070223
416609UK00002B/763